Praise for t̶h̶...
a new thrill-master,
WILL STAEGER'S
PAINKILLER

"Palpable excitement. Relentless action.
A terrific character. A perfect summer read."
David Morrell, bestselling author of *Creepers*

"Cross Hiaasen with Clancy and you'll get
Will Staeger's *Painkiller,*
a thrilling jaunt through the backwater islands of the
Caribbean and the back rooms of Washington . . .
Flush with humor, insight, and political intrigue,
here is a debut not to be missed."
James Rollins, bestselling author of *Map of Bones*

"Spectacular . . .
A wild mix of black comedy and technothriller."
Connecticut Post

"A terrific debut . . .
Cooper is a hero for our cynical age,
and Staeger gets it all dead right.
Say hello to a major new talent."
James Siegel, bestselling author of *Derailed*

Books by Will Staeger

PAINKILLER

Coming Soon in Hardcover

PUBLIC ENEMY

WILL STAEGER

painkiller

HarperTorch

An Imprint of HarperCollins Publishers

HARPERTORCH
An Imprint of HarperCollins*Publishers*
10 East 53rd Street
New York, New York 10022-5299

Copyright © 2005 by William H. Staeger Jr.
Excerpt from *Public Enemy* copyright © 2006 by William H. Staeger Jr.
ISBN-13: 978-0-06-076588-0
ISBN-10: 0-06-076588-7

First HarperTorch paperback printing: May 2006
First William Morrow hardcover printing: July 2005

HarperCollins®, HarperTorch™, and ♥™ are trademarks of Harper-Collins Publishers Inc.

Printed in the United States of America

Visit HarperTorch on the World Wide Web at www.harpercollins.com

10 9 8 7 6 5 4 3 2 1

FOR NADINE

(the list of reasons runs longer than this book)

painkiller

He couldn't remember coming here; he didn't
know where he was. Jagged leaves, black in the wet night,
whipped his cheeks as he ran. Sores bled beneath a torn jersey. A gust of wind knocked him off balance, and he slipped,
fell, and rose again. Hurling his diseased body through the
jungle, he couldn't find sufficient oxygen to fill his lungs; few
of his muscles obeyed the orders from his brain. None of this
mattered.

All that mattered was the pain—and the need to escape it.

Rifle shots cracked, the equivalent of snapping twigs in
the roar of the hurricane. Figures emerged from the jungle
behind him—rain-soaked wraiths shouldering heavy firepower. Voices barked, and with sudden brilliance a flare
arced into the sky. Its parachute caught and held, bathing the
fleeing man in daylight.

He may have registered a thought—memories of home,
of yesterday, of five years ago. Of Simone. In that instant, it
might all have come back to him; it might not. In the next, he
fell, dropping eighty feet in the darkness. His legs churned

on, pumping, until the rocks at the base of the cliff drove them into his pelvis.

Flashlight beams pierced the sky—rotating, descending, settling on his broken remains. It was only a matter of seconds before he was moving again. Propping his upper body on shattered elbows, he lunged forward, fighting the surf as it pummeled him. He climbed across one boulder, then the next, until, sluglike, he pulled himself onto the wooden planks of a dock. Clawing at the rain, his bloody fingers stretched, reaching for the vision that appeared to him at dock's end. Moored against the farthest piling was a rowboat—an eight-foot dinghy, slapping and banging itself to pieces, restrained only by a fraying rope that wouldn't survive the hour.

A star-shaped muzzle blast burst from the lip of the cliff. Another pulsed beside it, and in seconds the brittle pier was chewed to pieces by a fusillade of armor-piercing shells. He was nearing the end of the dock when one last bullet struck him in the back, and the pain that had propelled him ebbed. His struggle slowed, then ceased.

The hail of gunfire subsided; the airborne flare splashed into the sea. The flashlight beams pulled skyward and vanished. Finally, as the torrent raged around him, the man slumped, incapable of completing his escape.

2

Six o'clock in the morning and already the phone was ringing. There was no answering machine, and anybody with the number knew the rule: emergency use only. This meant the caller would persist, so if Ronnie didn't get up and answer it, the phone might ring all day. Pulling his spindly legs off the cot, he organized his hair with a zigzag jerk of the hand, established a ponytail with the aid of a rubber band he kept around his wrist, and pulled on a military green baseball cap that said CONCH BAY, BVI.

A thick rain pelted the metal rooftops of the beach club, where gray daylight had begun to offer the palm trees some definition. In thirty, maybe forty minutes, the sky would be blue, the sand dry—the island drying out like a wet paper bag in a hot oven—but as Ronnie emerged from his trailer, the rain had yet to abate, and it dumped on him. He ducked into a cubbyhole behind the open-air kitchen, where the phone continued its insistent ringing until he answered it.

"Conch Bay," he said. In Ronnie's Liverpool brogue, the words came out *Kunk Bye.*

The voice on the other end of the line spat out a request. In hearing the caller's aim, Ronnie took a look behind the garden, where he could see, even in the dim morning light, the stark outline of bungalow nine. Nine was built of cinder blocks and painted a luminescent hue of yellow; windows and doors screened, it appeared older, shorter, and more eroded than its brethren, squat and fierce in the face of their more recent construction. It shared with the others the architectural feature of a boxy porch standing six steps above the garden—high enough for a view of the lagoon.

Completing his second stroll through the rain, Ronnie ascended the stairs and banged on the door.

"Cooper!" he said, and took a step back.

It took a while, but when it did, the reply came in a baritone, the voice sludge-thick with hangover phlegm.

"Keep out."

Ronnie grinned. "Brought you a gift, Guv. Mutual friend of ours. You wanna guess who it is? You get it right, she says she'll come in."

Another silence.

Then the voice said, "The new one. Dottie."

"Nah," Ronnie said, talking fast, "just pulling your leg, old man." He took another backward step. "You got a phone call. It's Cap'n Roy. Says he's got a problem—'emergency situation,' he says. Gotta run now—"

Ronnie made his move, ducking and spinning, arms flailing for protection, but Cooper covered the distance from bed to door in one long step. Fully naked, pivoting at the hip, the permanent resident of bungalow nine got his full weight behind the Ken Griffey Jr. Autograph-Special Louisville Slugger and smashed the front door's jalousie panes to splinters, the bat bursting through the window's mesh screen and sending shards of glass flying across the porch.

"Run, boy," Cooper said, and watched through the fresh hole in the door as Ronnie shot down the stairwell and darted off through the garden. He noted with satisfaction there appeared to be blood on one of the boy's shoulders.

Cooper dropped the Louisville Slugger and listened, eyes closed, to the *chock-chock* of the bat as it settled on the concrete floor of the bungalow. He rolled his shoulders, cracked his knuckles, and pulled in a deep, slow breath, inhaling the pungent scent of the rain.

Blinking against the morning headache, he dug a pair of shorts from a mound of clothes, looked at his Tevas, decided, defiantly, to go without—Cooper thinking he'd show the little pissant that the broken glass lying around the porch didn't faze him. Hell—the first week he spent here, he'd watched the gardener they had that year, a local kid maybe fifteen years old, working all day in bare feet. Walking along those gravel paths with the sharp stones, and the kid hadn't even brought a pair of shoes with him. Cooper thinking at the time that he, given enough practice, could probably do the same thing. And thinking now, a few years in—a few years of walking shoeless over those same stones—he'd developed calluses thick enough to dance the jig in a shark's mouth, were the mood to strike.

Anybody visiting the Conch Bay Beach Club didn't need an owner's manual. Rent a mooring in the bay, consume a savory meal beneath the palm trees, throw back some rum punch at the bar. Bake your skin, snorkel amid rainbows of sea life, sleep with sand in your sheets, wake up to the cries of goats and roosters. No roads, no cars, two minutes of hot water in the shower, and no lights after midnight. It was these and other factors—the fish, the sea, the beach, the rum, the women, casinos, conch fritters, palm trees, blue sky, rain, trade winds, hurricanes, the oppressive heat, lethargic pace, and near-total lack of local white people—that had caused Cooper to adopt Conch Bay as his permanent residence. He'd decided on a bungalow set back from the beach, a swath of fat-leaved foliage dividing it from the portions of the resort equipped with such amenities as air-conditioning, indoor showers, and newlyweds.

He came down the stairs in nothing but the shorts, baggy blue swim trunks sagging to the knee. He didn't duck or hurry. The rain felt good; it was already eighty, eighty-five out. Cooper stood about six three, and there wasn't so much a tan as a dark weathering to him—his skin looked like the peeling hull of an old boat. Scar tissue creased his cheekbones, his nose had been flattened by a couple dozen breaks, and he had the eyes of somebody who'd checked out a few decades back.

The kitchen was dark and empty, its big, stainless steel fridge lurking beside a monster oven. Most hours there was a trio of heavyset West Indian women sweating it out in there, making conch fritters, swordfish sandwiches, or jerk chicken.

Cooper picked up the phone. "Yeah?"

"Eh, Cooper, dat you, mon?"

The words came out fast, like the lyrics to a reggae track. Cooper knew the lyricist all too well—Captain Roy Gillespie, of the Royal Virgin Islands Police Force. Known locally as Cap'n Roy.

"It's six o'clock in the goddamn morning," Cooper said.

"And you telling me."

"Boy says you got something can't wait. If in fact that's the case, Roy, I'd recommend you go ahead and tell me what it is."

Cooper refused to call Roy by his nickname.

"There something here I thinking you maybe wanna see, mon. We down the Marine Base way. Come by 'bout an hour. I know dat boat get you here quick."

"Yeah?"

"Yeah, mon. The Police Force," Roy said, "we be obliged to you, you make the trip." Roy fell silent, waiting for a response.

After two or three seconds, Cooper grunted and hung up on him.

The island of Tortola got up early, its native population of roosters braying out wake-up calls from about four o'clock onward. Narrow Mitsubishi pickups began to speed along the roads as early as five, overloaded with locals making their way to work, everybody carpooling: load up, drop off, repeat. There existed no need for public transit in the British Virgins, since all transit was public.

Tortola's two hills rose abruptly from the sea, one on each side of Road Town. Most visitors came to the BVIs by plane through Beef Island's Terrance B. Lettsome International—twenty minutes east of Road Town by way of a treacherously steep road and locally famous bridge, it possessed one runway, a recently remodeled terminal, and maybe twenty-five cabbies loitering beside a convoy of Mitsubishi minivan taxis. Come by boat, though, and you'd do it through Road Harbor, a quaint blend of colorful oceanfront shops, industrial piers, a single, oddly massive cruise ship berth, and a brand-new ferry terminal beside the old marina.

Cooper passed the vacant cruise ship berth and eased up on the throttle, obeying the harbor's five-knot speed limit.

As he quieted the engines, the sounds of the marina floated to him—the *ping* of cable against mast, the slap of waves against hull. Cooper's hull was a forty-one-foot Apache with twin 572-CID 850-horsepower blowers and MerCruiser drives, a championship racing boat he'd obtained at a price significantly below its market value a few years back. He moved out to the bow, flipping a pair of bumpers over the gunwale, returned to the pilot's seat, kicked the Apache into reverse, gunned the throttle, and killed the engines. Gliding in like an old man of the sea. The boat touched delicately against the Marine Base dock, easing to a halt without so much as a squeeze of its bumpers.

A lanky West Indian in a grubby white T-shirt was already there on the dock, busy dealing with the contents of an orange bucket. The man automatically took the bowline when Cooper tossed it to him; Cooper handled the stern line himself, hopping off and nodding his thanks. The man grinned, nodded back, and returned to his bucket.

Another, shorter man approached the dock. The singular feature of this man was his rigid posture—back held ramrod straight, his chest and shoulders thrust stiffly up and out. Cooper had always thought Cap'n Roy looked like a guy with a stick up his ass, but what the hell, it worked for him, coming down the dock now in his uniform, the pressed white polo shirt bright against his blue-black skin, the gray slacks with the sharp crease, the shiny black cap with a checkered band, even the patent leather shoes. Roy offered an enthusiastic handshake as they came together; at five nine in his shoes, he had to look way up at Cooper, whose tall, slouching profile cut an S-hook against Roy's stick.

"Lemme-be-de-first wida warm welcome for the spy-a-de-island," Roy said. He kept his left hand busy, using it to slap Cooper on the shoulder while conducting the business of the handshake with his right.

"Roy."

"Yeah, mon, we got us some trouble. Lucky findin' it when we did, know what I mean, mon? It still a while now till the *Turquoise Queen* show, all them tourists taking a look."

Roy walked across the dock, reached down, unlashed a line, and tossed it into a hard-bottom inflatable dinghy. He motioned for Cooper to step into the boat. When Cooper did, Roy gassed the fifty-horse Evinrude and nosed the little craft out from the dock, heading deeper into the harbor, around the yacht slips.

"Shortcut," Cap'n Roy said with a wink.

He took them through the outlet stream, tilting the engine to power through the shallow water without grinding the propeller on the rocks. When they came around the breakwater, Cooper saw five, no, six locals, four of them in standard Royal Virgin Island Police Force dress, same as Roy, and two of them wearing what Cooper knew to be the Marine Base uniform: royal blue polo shirt and khaki shorts. The cops were gathered around a heap of soiled rags lumped together on the rocks, the cops keeping active—one taking notes, one with a camera, another shielding his eyes against the sun with his hand, keeping watch. To Cooper, the swirl of activity displayed all too familiar a rhythm.

Cap'n Roy beached the boat on the rocks, shutting down the Evinrude and kicking it out of the water.

"Need to do it on foot from here," he said.

The outlet continued, two or three inches deep, through a bed of rocks, snaking around the breakwater and out into the ocean. Behind them, between the breakwater and the harbor, lay open, overgrown brush, with industrial leftovers peeking through tall grass—the rotting hull of a boat, the rusted body of an original VW Beetle. Walking over the sharp rocks, wearing a yellow T-shirt that said LIVE SLOW across the back, Cooper was thinking that under ordinary circumstances, he'd consider pulling off his Tevas and crossing the bed of rocks barefoot, just to show these soft-skinned white-collar cops what he was all about. Out of respect for what he figured awaited him at the end of the outlet, though, he shrugged off the impulse. While he walked, Cooper contemplated a few different ways to reject the favor Roy was about to ask of him. The man was a sneaky bastard; Roy would figure a way to guilt, or possibly even blackmail him into it if he weren't careful.

Cap'n Roy led him to where his fellow cops were gathered on the beach. They faced the channel now, the breakwater behind them, and at this range, Cooper didn't need the guided tour to understand that the pile of rags was not, in fact, a pile of rags.

Wrapped in shredded clothes, frail and emaciated, with bloated, wrinkled skin that might once have been dark but had by now deteriorated to a bleached jaundice, the semi-exposed torso of a man lay sprawled beneath a scrap of wood. The upper body was covered with what appeared to be sores, though it was difficult to tell—with the body soaking in the sea, the sores were pale and indistinct, little more than jagged, whitish mushrooms on the skin. Both legs were broken below the knee in compound fractures. Cooper tried to remember the name of the bigger bone below the knee—probably either the tibia or fibula—but whichever it was, the bone protruded grotesquely from the skin, the torn flesh whitish and waterlogged like the sores on the torso.

Once Cap'n Roy observed that Cooper had enjoyed a

thorough study of the scene, he straightened whatever bend remained in his spine and motioned to a thick cop wearing the Marine Base gear.

"Riley here," he said, "he come across the body first thing this morning."

Cooper knew Riley a little. Heavy in the face and legs with a flat stomach, he looked like a running back, his skin the color of caramel, a shade or three lighter than the rest of the gang.

"Round about the break of dawn," Riley said, taking his cue, "out checkin' the moorings, I come 'round the point and think maybe the first thing to do be to clean up the mess, seein' these rags here, thinkin' they was rubbish. Then I heard the flies, shooed away the birds, and seen what you now seein', mon."

Riley bent down and picked up a plank, which made Cooper notice the other pieces of wood, nailed together in groups, strewn across the rocks. Down by the water was a bigger grouping, big enough for Cooper to surmise the obvious—the body had come in on a boat. A small one, from the look of it.

"Not much left, but I figure maybe he a tourist," Riley said. "Hurricane take down his big boat, lifeboat don't make it all the way in."

Cap'n Roy interrupted stiffly, "Ain't a tourist though."

Cooper said, "Islander?"

"He ain't from 'round here."

Cooper thought Roy's answer was a little quick.

"Tell you what," Cooper said. "Why don't you sit on it. Wait it out a day or two. Maybe some poor St. Johnnie sends Riley here an e-mail, telling him our boy here didn't come home from work. Ask around, find out if he was dealing. Couple weeks and you'll have it all wrapped up."

"No, mon," Roy said. He shook his head. "That e-mail ain't gonna be comin'."

Cooper looked around at Roy's posse, the cops slouching, mute, exhibiting an array of poses. "How about you take me back to the Marine Base," he said, "so I can get home."

Cap'n Roy gave him a sideways look and made a *cluck-cluck* sound with his tongue. "You know, strange murder case turning up in the police beat," he said, "that'd be somethin' people maybe want to keep an eye on. Case go unsolved—that call not comin' in from your St. Johnnie—then the whole thing might just start lookin' pretty bad on the head policeman. Look especially bad, that policeman up for chief minister next month."

Cooper caught Riley checking him for a reaction.

"People say you know the kind of people I make a point not to know," Cap'n Roy said, getting to it now. "Kind of people could take a body that wash up on the beach, take that body, and put it away. Nobody know a thing about it."

Cooper said, "Those sound like some kind of people."

Cap'n Roy grinned. "People say something else too. They say somebody need help, got himself in a bind he can't fix, he can call on that Cooper, that spy on the island, mon, and he help you out."

"Last year," Cooper said, "that kid, the one got shot up on Blackburn Road—what was his name?"

"Entwine," Roy said.

"You didn't call me when Entwine died."

The mobile phone on Cap'n Roy's waist chortled and Roy made a motion with his hand, Cooper interpreting the gesture to mean that Roy had been expecting an important call, and would Cooper excuse him for a moment. After a few words into the phone, Roy reclipped the phone to his belt. He waved over the RVIPF cops, the men wearing the standard uniforms.

"Got a little crisis, mon," he said, back with Cooper now. "Riley and Tim, they give you anything you need."

Then Cap'n Roy reached out to shake Cooper's hand.

Cooper looked at the hand. It was a clean hand, recently manicured. It looked like a hand that had never been dirty. It looked like a hand that had never done a single day's hard work. Cooper thought that with a hand like that, someday Roy would probably be running more than just Road Town. He knew that Roy and his merry band of performers knew something about the body they weren't telling him, which, to say the least, did not bode well. Still, he thought that if Roy happened to expand his kingdom, outstripping that self-imposed nickname of his, it'd be nice to have the man on his list.

"I might call you sometime," Cooper said. Cap'n Roy kept his hand out. "I might have a question. I might need some help, or a favor. I take that body, and you'll take the call."

Roy thought about this for a moment. Then he said, "Yeah, mon."

Cooper shook his hand, and with that, Cap'n Roy marched off around the breakwater and disappeared into the field of thick brown grass. The RVIPF men followed, leaving Cooper alone with Riley and Tim. He saw that Riley was smiling at him.

Cooper didn't smile back.

"I assume you guys brought a bag," he said.

3

A cadaverous man slathered Grecian Formula on his hair and admired his reflection. Eugene Little used watered-down Grecian Formula to maintain the natural color of his hair, primarily because he'd read in *People* that Ronald Reagan had used the same recipe during his White House days.

Eugene had made himself efficient in the morning. He bathed at night, eliminating the need for a morning shower; he'd roll out of the sack, gargle some Listerine, work the tincture of Grecian Formula into his hair, stir a cup of instant coffee—Folgers or Yuban, whichever he'd found a coupon for—step out the kitchen door in his bathrobe, grab his copy of the *Virgin Islands Daily News,* open his mailbox, dig out the periodicals he cherished—*National Review, Newsweek, U.S. News & World Report*—come back in, get dressed, and get out the door.

This morning Eugene chose permanent-press trousers and a plaid shirt, the short sleeves showing off his pale, skinny biceps and matted forearm hair. He polished off the coffee, tucked the periodicals beneath an elbow, and skittered down the sidewalk. It hadn't been fifteen minutes, alarm to exit. Eugene's bachelor pad occupied a dirty corner of Charlotte Amalie, the only city in the U.S. Virgin Islands. The thing about a squalid neighborhood like Eugene's was that the 7-Eleven was always open, so Eugene could swing by, pick up a plain doughnut and second cup of coffee, and still get to work before eight.

One mile down the road, 7-Eleven coffee in hand, Eugene shuffled up the stairs of a single-story building that looked like any other house on the street, but wasn't, as evidenced by the words engraved on a plaque beside the front door: CHARLOTTE AMALIE MORGUE. Making his way down to the basement, Eugene turned on a bank of fluorescents and checked his in-box, which, as expected, contained nothing. This, along with the neutral scents in the room, meant there was no stiff awaiting his inspection. When they'd left one for him, he could always smell it.

He sat at his desk and whipped out the magazines, deciding to start with *National Review*. He'd broken off a piece of his doughnut and was pulling the lid off the coffee when the phone rang.

He snatched it from its cradle.

"Lab."

"Eugene!" came the voice from the other end of the line. "Just the man I was looking for."

A globule of spittle formed on Eugene's lower lip and a snappy facial tic tugged at his left eye. "Cooper?" he said. "It is Cooper, isn't it? Well, you can just fuck off."

Standing on the Marine Base dock with his sat phone tucked against an ear, Cooper watched Riley and Tim carry what looked like a flattened inner tube down to the dock. The kid walked backward, checking his footing by looking over his shoulder, and Riley brought up the rear. Watching them do it, Cooper observed that the corpse filled the blue vinyl bag no better than a couple of bait fish.

"That isn't a polite way to start a conversation," he told Eugene, "so let's start over. There's something I'd like you to do for me."

"What kind of something?" Eugene said.

"I need to dispose of a body."

"Dispose?"

"That's right."

"Where are you calling from? Are you here in my jurisdiction?"

"No."

"Well then, it's out of the question. I don't operate as some sort of freelance coroner."

Riley and Tim dropped the bag into the Apache's stern. Puny as it was, the body made a solid thud on impact.

"I see," Cooper said.

"Is there no official inquiry?"

"No."

"That's irregular."

"Yes."

"Jesus, you fucking spook," Little said, "what are you asking? What do you expect me to do?"

"That's better, Eugene," Cooper said.

"What do you mean, 'That's better'? I'm not doing you any favors. I've got a reputation to uphold, a law enforcement code to observe. What is it, anyway? Somebody OD out at that godforsaken beach club of yours? Christ—you probably shot the poor bastard. Whatever it is, I refuse to be a party to any foul play."

"Eugene," Cooper said, "I've got a body here. I need you to dispose of it. I need it done, no questions asked. I'm about forty-five minutes away. I was thinking maybe you could send a car to the marina. You know something? You might like this one. Something odd about the circumstances—burn marks like you've never seen."

"You—you actually expect me to just send a car out?" Eugene paused, and Cooper could hear the sounds of him fidgeting at his desk. "What do you mean by odd?"

"You'll see."

The fidgeting stopped. "I'm incinerating it, burning the body," Eugene said, "that's something I'll need to do on my own time. Outside of my normal duties."

"Like some sort of freelance coroner?"

"Spare me—I know how you work. Let me guess. I don't do you this little favor, you make a few calls, and pretty soon somebody's looking into things. Things I don't want anybody looking into. That about how it goes?"

"Not bad," Cooper said. "How much?"

"How much? Well, considering the irregularity—"

"Five hundred."

"Five? Fine."

"Have a cab waiting for me at the fishing terminal."

Cooper flipped the phone into the boat. It landed on the cushion of the driver's seat. From the dock, Riley brushed off his hands with two neat claps, grinned, and said, "All right then, mon. Live slow and nice."

Cooper raised a hand without waving and climbed into his boat.

It intrigued him that the cabby didn't even flinch as Cooper climbed into the taxi, body bag slung over his shoulder, and said, "The morgue." There was only a friendly nod and a flip of the gearshift.

One night, bored under the safety lights at the beach club,

Cooper had taken a hard look at a list of employees on the government payroll of the United States Virgin Islands. Abusing the privilege of his rather lofty security clearance, he'd snatched from Charlotte Amalie City Hall a list of active USVI government staff, and, reading the list on the beach, noticed an American expatriate employed as the medical examiner. Knowing the population of the U.S. Virgin Islands was eighty-seven percent local and thirteen percent expatriate, Cooper also knew a fairly low percentage of the expats ever wound up on the government payroll. He figured there must have been one hell of a story behind this Eugene Little.

Cooper got his hands on Little's job application and medical credentials. A couple days later, with nothing much to do, he made some phone calls to the mainland, found that nobody named Eugene Little had graduated from the schools claimed in the credentials, and, working off a gritty photocopy of Little's driver's license, he checked the handful of federal databases to which he had access. Using his PowerBook's moody wireless modem, Cooper took his time searching and ultimately found a bonanza of dirt on the expat coroner.

Eugene had been born with the name Roger Ignatius Holmby, and under that identity was wanted on ten counts ranging from medical fraud to manslaughter, with warrants outstanding for failure to show for multiple arraignments. Holmby, a former plastic surgeon, had killed two patients and left at least fifteen with some form of permanent disability. Once charged, he'd skipped out on a half-million-dollar bond. Cooper thinking that there was probably an army of bounty hunters going after ten percent of that.

After a while Cooper paid the man a visit, taking his

Apache over to St. Thomas. He caught him around noon, asked if Little was free for lunch, Cooper buying—courtesy of his fairly bottomless Agency expense account. They grabbed a couple of sandwiches at the deli across the street from the morgue and had a nice talk, Cooper telling him, "Your secret's safe with me, Ignatius. You don't have a worry in the world." Watching those nervous twitches, the facial tic going nuts, Cooper laid out what he'd found on him, and told the man he might get a call someday, and that when he did, he should take the call.

You don't just walk in through the front door carrying a stiff," Eugene said, hurriedly escorting Cooper to the examination table.

Cooper dumped the body bag on the steel table and went for his wallet. There were three hundreds and five fifties inside; he came out with two of the hundreds and put the wallet back in his pocket.

"Two hundred bucks is all I have on me," he said, extending his hand. Eugene grabbed the money. "I don't want to see this on the local news, so do it right and do it now. You'll get the rest when I hear nothing about this for three weeks."

"Bastard," Eugene said, backing off a step, keeping a cushion between himself and Cooper. "Coming in here trying to palm your murder off—hey, look at that."

He moved in closer, getting a tight look at Cooper's face.

"Smell bothering you? Not so tough after all, eh?"

Eugene looked at the body bag.

"Why don't we take a look? See what we've got here. Check out this odd set of circumstances. Think you can take it, big man?"

Eugene emitted a piercing giggle, his face mere inches from Cooper's. His breath reeked of stale coffee and vomit. Cooper thought for a moment, and decided that since he'd hooked Eugene's curiosity, he may as well put the coroner to work.

Attempting to hold his breath as a shield against the combined stench of Eugene's breath, Roy's body from the beach, and the overwhelming reek of formaldehyde, he said, "Let's have a look."

At Eugene's urging, Cooper helped him remove the body from the bag. The coroner flipped on an examination light and pointed it at the body's torso. In the bright light, the sores appeared worse to Cooper than they had on the beach. Some of them were six, eight inches in diameter, ragged tufts of raw flesh with bubbly blisters around the rim. The victim's body looked as though it had been stabbed repeatedly by the hot end of a six-foot cigar.

Cooper watched as Eugene did the exam, noticing that Eugene would surreptitiously peer over at him from time to time, maybe waiting for Cooper to say something, maybe trying to figure something out about him. Eugene, my man, Cooper thought, you are one odd duck.

Eugene pulled off what was left of the soiled blue shirt covering the body and set it aside, leaving the rest of the man's upper body exposed—its waterlogged skin, the sores, blisters, and what looked like a series of exit wounds: jagged rips in the man's flesh, clearly torn by bullets. On both legs the jeans, shredded to the knee, looked as though they had caught on something; below the jeans were the compound fractures, one on each shin. Cooper could see that both ankles were severely swollen and probably broken.

The stench of rotting flesh became overwhelming as Eugene, seemingly oblivious, gave the corpse a complete once-over, lifting hands, feet, head, arms and legs, examining the skin, the sores, the fingernails, teeth, eyes, soles of the feet, the numerous bullet wounds. He made muffled grunts as he worked. Cooper stood two or three feet back, giving Eugene a zone in which to roam around the body.

At length Eugene backed off, opened a drawer, came out with an aerosol can, shot it in bursts around the room, put it back, opened another drawer and came out with a Polaroid camera. One body part at a time, he popped a series of pictures—each time pulling out the picture, waving it once or twice, setting it on the countertop, then moving in for another. He had a speed that came only with practice, Eugene working the camera with his right hand, prepping whatever section of the body he was photographing with the other, Cooper thinking this felonious, malpracticing quack had gone ahead and found his groove down here in the islands.

Not unlike himself.

Eugene stepped back and took some wider shots—head and shoulders, the full upper body. When he was through, he set the camera on the countertop next to the rows of pictures. He nodded at Cooper and motioned toward the body with a gloved hand.

"Give me some help," he said.

Cooper at the feet, Eugene at the head, they turned the body over. A new wave of foul air wafted up at them. It smelled so bad Cooper could feel it in his brain. Again Eugene didn't seem to notice.

The victim's back had fewer sores than the front, and the marks were smaller. The skin was smoother and darker, Cooper suspecting this to be the natural color of the man in life. On the victim's back, Cooper saw the cleaner, almost precisely round entry points of the series of bullets that had caught him. He didn't like the feeling it gave him.

When Eugene got to the neck, he started pushing and stretching at the skin. He looked up and jutted his chin at Cooper.

"See this?" he said. "Identifying mark." He left the table and went over to the counter for the camera.

Cooper moved closer and saw what Eugene was talking about. At the base of the neck, barely visible against the skin, was a green symbol, dark enough to all but blend in. Maybe an inch in height, the symbol was composed of a circular top that at its base tapered off into a single vertical line with a horizontal bar below.

It looked like a tattoo.

It also looked religious, half upside-down cross, half right-side-up racquet. A word occurred to him, Cooper not sure if it was right. *Ankh.* He thought ankhs, if that was the word, were Egyptian, which wouldn't make much sense in the Caribbean—but then again, not much did anyway. Eugene came back and started snapping pictures again, grunting while he did it. Finally Eugene set the camera on the counter and jammed his fists against his hips.

"What you've got here is some kind of menial laborer. A young one—I'd estimate him to be nineteen, maybe twenty." He came over to the body, held up one of the hands. "Subject displays deeply calloused hands, fingernails embedded with grime, dozens of scars on the fingers and back of the hand." With gloved fingers, Eugene pulled open the lips. "Both the fingernails and gums show definitive signs of chronic malnutrition. Sores in and around the mouth indicate a lack of citric acid in the diet. Scurvy."

He let go. "Musculature is sinewy, with a great deal of long-term ligament and tendon damage. Less than five percent body fat."

Cooper shrugged off a twitch in his shoulders. Eugene

worked his way around the body and lifted the torso. "Seven gunshot wounds, bullets entering and exiting quite cleanly. He was shot in the back. The bullets did a great deal of damage—not your ordinary bullets. Burns on the chest and abdomen," Eugene said, lifting the body now, exposing the chest, "are, as you say, odd, not like any I've seen. If I were doing a *legitimate* autopsy, I would take tissue samples, see what kind of residue is there, get some indication as to what burned him." He extended one of the body's arms. "There are also tracks on both triceps. Could be heroin, which, *normally,* is simple to test for. The back of the upper arm is a difficult place to self-inject, by the way."

He let go of the upper body and moved around to the legs, Cooper watching him as he went. "Compound fractures of the lower legs indicate the victim fell from a great height, difficult to tell exactly how high without analyzing the bones. Ankles are also broken, with extreme ligament damage."

Eugene pulled up abruptly.

"Listen here," he said. "I'll need the rest of that money now."

Cooper's thoughts, mired as they were in tattoos and ankhs, were making him uncomfortable. He was thinking that he'd seen a symbol like the ankh-tattoo on the victim's neck somewhere before, and not just in a history textbook, or museum. Eugene wasn't helping his malaise, Cooper watching the friendly neighborhood medical examiner shuffle around the body, ratlike, Eugene blinking like a pervert, sniffling between sentences while he sought a second handout.

Goddamn that Roy.

Cooper pulled out his wallet. "Here's what we're going to do, Ignatius. Run those tests you're talking about. All of them—including ballistics, assuming you can find any bullets. Tell me what comes back. You do that, I'll give you another hundred now as a down payment on a two-hundred-dollar bonus. Payable when I see the results. You still get the rest only if nothing hits the papers."

Eugene glared at him, sniffling. "To do the rest, the full autopsy, I'll have to do that after hours, you understand? The tests on the bones, the burns, tissue samples, the soil samples from underneath the nails"—the tic snapped at him again—"I'll tell you, Cooper, I get charged lab fees for that, we don't do it all here. And there are going to be questions. Especially if I send anything to ballistics."

Cooper stuffed his last hundred-dollar bill and two of the fifties in Eugene's pocket. Up close, he could hear a wheezing sound. It came from Eugene's nose.

"There's your whole bonus," he said. "That puts us back at three hundred more when I see the test results, and when I'm satisfied you haven't squealed. That'll make seven bills total—negotiation over."

He walked over to the counter, looked around until he found the Polaroid of the tattoo—the ankh, if that's what it was—and took it. Even in the harsh, bright light of the flash captured on film, the symbol was hard to see against the victim's dark skin. Cooper grabbed another few pictures that interested him before heading for the stairs, and the fresh air that waited beyond. On his way across the room he turned and took in Eugene, who stood watching him from beside the body.

"Live slow, Ignatius," he said, then walked out of the morgue.

4

Cooper was down deep. He'd been under for two minutes, holding his breath, and could handle another three if he felt like pushing it, just the way he'd seen in a *National Geographic* documentary about the South Pacific. It was there where it seemed armies of twelve-year-old boys swam as far down as ninety feet and stayed under for upward of seven minutes. They went down there to haul in illegal, mile-long nets laid by rogue fishermen selling their catch to multinational fish-packing firms. Cooper thinking, as he had watched the show, that child labor laws didn't have much bearing on the people of the remote South Pacific, but man, those kids could swim.

One lazy afternoon around twelve years back, thinking of the show, he decided to see how long *he* could hold his breath beneath the waves. He parked his boat over a wreck that was famous with the SCUBA set and dove, wearing nothing more than swim trunks, goggles, and his dive watch. No tanks, no fins. He made himself stay down for sixty seconds, then ninety, then two minutes, diving so deep that after a few hours of it—constantly popping his ears to equalize the pressure—Cooper felt as if his head would implode. That first night he came back to the Conch Bay Beach Club with a migraine that lasted a week, but he went right back out when he felt good enough to do it again.

Couple months later and he was staying down like those South Pacific natives, feeling like the Man from Atlantis— scare the shit out of the occasional honeymooners, their eyes bugging out of their masks, mouthpieces blasting off in a cloud of bubbles as they bolted for the surface. Cooper the moray eel, popping out of a shadowy pocket ninety feet down.

Today he had the Apache anchored a quarter mile off the northeast corner of St. John while he tooled around a wreck somewhere just over a hundred feet below the surface. The broken deck of the ship was rife with sea life—coral, anemones, sea urchins, French grunts, some angelfish. Hovering over the stern of the old wreck, he watched a group of parrot fish, some as long as three feet, poking through the coral, rooting out algae. If he kept himself still, he could hear them sucking down their meal. He didn't like keeping still, though, because today, as had been the case for the past week, he found that if he kept himself still, he started seeing and hearing things. Intrusions.

The tranquility he normally found on these dives had been violated this afternoon by a kind of jumpy fear, Cooper constantly looking to see whether Roy's body from the beach would swim out at him from around the next outcropping of coral. He couldn't shake the feeling—it was as though a kind of delusionary sixth sense was telling him the oddly burned and busted body was following him around.

Following another shot of air, he came around the side of the wreck, getting a wide view of it in the clear water. Figuring the boat for a British vessel circa 1880, maybe a little earlier, he could see it had broken into three pieces, but the two masts remained intact. Cooper spotted the pug nose of the resident barracuda, the fish six, seven feet long, big enough to take him if the mood struck. The fish eyed him blankly before retreating, but then Cooper thought he saw another shape in the murky shadows of the cabin.

It was Roy's body from the beach, calling out to him with a raspy screech.

You're all I got, the bloated face said, *you washed-up old fuck!*

Topside, Cooper pulled the anchor on the Apache, stripped off the swim trunks, popped a half-dozen Advil to battle the emerging pressure headache, and rode back to Conch Bay. As always, he made the ten-minute trip nude, blow-drying his sun-wrinkled hide in the forty-knot wind that whipped across the deck of the Apache.

The sun was fat and orange on the horizon when he eased up, drifting to a stop, and tied his bow line to a white buoy about forty yards from the Conch Bay pier. Ignoring the loud gaggle of tourists dining at the beachfront restaurant, Cooper proceeded to piss from the side of the boat for something like three minutes before yanking on a fresh pair of shorts. He splashed the Apache's dinghy into the bay, zipped into the dock, and waited stubbornly in his seat until Ronnie came out from the restaurant and wordlessly assumed the task of tying off the dinghy.

At the bar, he waded through the fat, sunburned people waiting to order a drink, walked behind the counter, and poured himself a very tall Maker's Mark on the rocks. The kid tending bar continued with the cocktails he'd already been mixing. Cooper gulped the bourbon like it was Gatorade, the chilled drink tasting smooth and spicy going down. It worked like a kind of VapoRub against his headache but did nothing to exorcise his new friend the ghost. After consuming a refill, in fact, Cooper watched as Roy's body from the beach strolled up and took one of the stools at the bar, eyeing him with the same, flat look he'd seen in the eyes of the barracuda.

Oh yeah, the ghost screeched from his stool, *the truth shall set you free, mon.*

Cooper poured another bourbon for the road, told the bartender to have Ronnie bring him a ham sandwich, and walked barefoot down the gravel path to his bungalow.

Inside, he lifted from the counter of his kitchenette the Polaroid snapshots from Eugene's photo gallery and found the picture of the tattoo. He stared at it for a while, holding it at different angles beneath the yellowing incandescent bulb hanging over his kitchen table. The picture didn't tell him anything except that he could see now it wasn't nearly as put together, or neatly inked enough, to be an ankh. Cooper wasn't even sure how he remembered what an ankh was, but he knew now he wasn't looking at one. The tattoo was rougher—uglier. A crude, waved pattern rimmed the entire symbol, and a black orb—Cooper thinking it was probably a moon, or star—resided an inch or two from the top of the symbol's main circular head. Whatever the hell an ankh was, he thought, it probably didn't come with a moon.

His bungalow had only the one main room, which came loaded with the kitchenette, plus a bathroom that reached partially out back by way of its outdoor shower. Adjoining the kitchenette was a twin-size bed with no headboard, the bed somewhere around six inches too short for him, a problem he'd never felt urgently inclined to fix. Lurking between the bed and the door sat the room's only other furniture: a squat, upholstered chair and matching ottoman.

Cooper kept his PowerBook on the ottoman. Beside it, a

tangle of wires and devices lay on the floor, some connected, most not. He took the picture and fed it into a scanner he kept plugged into the side of the laptop; when he had the image up on the monitor, he worked it over with his mouse pad, isolating the symbol from the splotchy underlying skin.

He submitted the image as a search key within a classified online database to which he enjoyed unfettered access. The search engine took forty seconds to complete its hunt and delivered three hits. For each, the database software delivered a photo of the symbol it had found along with a body of text explaining its significance.

The first match was in fact an ankh, explained as the ancient Egyptian symbol for life. The passage mentioned alternate names: Ansate cross, Cross of life. Pulling down some of the Maker's Mark, Cooper noted that the ankh's horizontal bar was much higher than the tattoo's. The second and third matches, similar but still not identical to the tattoo, each contained the same description: "A symbol commonly used by practitioners of religious ceremonies involving ancestor worship and communication with animistic deities, e.g., voodoo." A more general explanation of voodoo followed, which Cooper had no need for. Live in the Caribbean long enough, and you saw your share of it. You also learned pretty quick that nonpracticing West Indians were generally superstitious enough to steer well clear of black magic and its practitioners. Hell, he thought, maybe Roy had made a savvy move after all: run across a voodoo tattoo on a body washed up on the beach and I'd dump it off on somebody like me too.

Roy passing the buck, though, didn't do anything for the body on the beach, or its ghost either. Fucking kid dies a horrible death, and some two-bit local chief of police arranges to send him straight to the crematorium—no murder case, no investigation, nobody meting out justice—hell, nobody giving a flying leap.

Eh, Cooper, dat you, mon? It's me, your old buddy Cap'n Roy. We down the Marine Base way. Come by 'bout an hour and help me fuck over this poor bastard now that he done died.

You're all I got, you washed-up old fuck.

Cooper jumped as three loud bangs sounded through his bungalow. The bangs were followed by a dull thump, then footsteps retreating down the stairs.

Deciding, after due consideration, he was in no mood to chase Ronnie through the garden with the Louisville Slugger, he rose, opened the door, retrieved the wax-paper-encased ham sandwich from the floor of his porch, and more or less inhaled it while standing in the doorway.

If he had to, he could do some digging. Nose around some of Puerto Rico's *botánicas,* find somebody specializing in voodoo tatts—somebody who could tell him where somebody wearing this one might have hung out. He had a few people on his list who lived in that world; in fact there was a certain San Juan detective who might just do, a guy at least two or three notches further along than Roy on the corruption scale. Then again, Cooper didn't like Puerto Rico all that much. And he liked the other voodoo hotbeds, Haiti and Jamaica, even less—life at Conch Bay suited him just fine.

He closed the PowerBook, polished off the bourbon, and took a lukewarm shower under the stars on the back porch. The sex-starved housewives down at the bar always preferred it if you started the conversation smelling like a rose.

Ordinarily, he would see the same three dreams: a trilogy. One would always follow the next, so that over the course of every few nights, he would get the whole story. Deviation did not occur.

On the nights they came, he would fall asleep for two or three minutes, only to wake up shivering in a cold sweat. Getting the feeling that if he moved an inch, the draft of cold air against his skin would induce frostbite. Get out of bed, change his shirt, use a different pillow, then soak them both again over the course of another ten, fifteen rotations. He endured a sense of sheer exhaustion—it seemed the most difficult, irrational task to turn on a light or read a book . . . and always there was the determination to get back to sleep. In the routine, he found comfort. He knew what to expect; he knew what was coming.

Tonight's dream began on schedule, episode one of the trilogy, the story beginning again after the sixteen thousandth playback of episode three. He'd seen the latest incarnation of the concluding installment maybe two nights before Roy had called him about the body on the beach.

There was darkness—black night, lasting for days on end. And there were scents—dank, musky, rich odors, the scents of mold, soil, mildew, rot, and the coagulating secretions of his own body. He heard the sound of a deadbolt opening, deafening after weeks of silence. He reached out, tried to grasp the massive door handle to hold the door closed, but they came in anyway and grabbed him. They moved him along; he was walking, but not easily, an utter lack of strength in his legs. There was light, but it was dim, like the vanishing light of the moon's crescent in the last moments before a lunar eclipse—*lunar eclipse,* Cooper thought, as he remembered always thinking. Of course, he was wearing the blindfold. Light was seeping in around its edges.

He found himself in a chair with no seat, tied to the frame, bound, ass poking through the seat hole, the rest of him dangling, vulnerable. In burning streaks against his naked ass, they whipped him. They whipped him as they always did. He heard the things they said as the stripes of agony writhed up through him—*This is for the manhood of your country . . . We'll take America's cock*—the commentary delivered in the comical accent, Cooper thinking every time of Speedy Gonzales. He felt pain in its purest form as the whip strafed him, every strike sending a rush of red through his head. The red bled into his vision, it bled everywhere, until there was no distinction between senses, the pain reaching first to extreme peaks, then descending gradually into comfort as he fell into a comatose state, in there dancing with death.

Another dark time came. Days, weeks, longer, shorter, sleeping and waking blurred. A circuit of horrors: solitude, darkness, light, torture, solitude. And occasionally a serving of food, slipped through a rectangular hole in the door before the opening was slammed shut again. This, he knew, was where he would awaken, lift the blindfold, and, before eating his single, rock-hard tortilla, vow quietly to himself that the next time they came for the whipping, he would kill them all.

And so he lifted the blindfold, a single line of light at the base of the door illuminating the tortilla lying on the floor. To Cooper, it seemed too bright. He didn't remember it this way. He tried to speak, to utter his vow, but nothing came from his lips. They failed to move. He couldn't speak.

The light beneath the door brightened, bathing him in its soft glow. He felt a sudden pang of fear. Unsure how to proceed, he crawled painfully to the tortilla, snatched it, began eating. Chunks fell from his mouth as he ate. In desperate need of the calories, he reached for the pieces he had missed—

And saw the burns on his torso. Whitish, waterlogged sores, covering him—stark, swollen mushrooms embedded in his raven skin. His sinewy legs were fractured below the knee, the ankles snapped grotesquely—

Cooper opened his eyes.

The ceiling fan in his bungalow spun lazily. A drizzle tapped the metal roof; he heard a gull caw from the garden. He could still taste the woman he'd brought back from the bar—fruity cocktails, cocoa butter, salt from the sea, the poisonous tang of cigarette smoke on her breath. She'd been twenty, thirty pounds overweight, and Cooper hadn't minded at all.

Maybe that ghost had been talking to Roy, Cooper thought, and that's why Roy had called. *Eh, Cooper, dat you, mon? There something here I thinking you maybe wanna see.* Leaving out the other part: *This dead bastard, he been talkin' to me, found him on the beach and can't get him out of my head. I thinking maybe we pass him onto you, mon.*

Rising to find a pair of shorts, he reflected that it may have taken the entire eighteen years of his stay, but now he could chalk it up as official: he was a superstitious West Indian just like the rest, a belonger now, somebody who knew enough about the way things happened 'round here to understand you were better off following the signs if you could read 'em.

To know that he was better off listening when some poor dead bastard happened to be talkin' to him.

There something here, that screeching ghost of a poor dead bastard telling him again, *I thinking you maybe wanna see, mon.*

5

Traveling light, only a single bag strapped over her shoulder, Julie Laramie came through the sliding glass doors of the United baggage claim at O'Hare trying not to appear as though she were looking for somebody. She wondered how she would look to him; whether she'd look the same, or older, or possibly better. This morning she'd pretended she wasn't carefully picking out the jeans, the thin V-neck cashmere sweater, the leather jacket to wear over the sweater, the Doc Martens—she liked the boots because they matched the leather jacket and made her legs look thinner than they were. Laramie decided he would think she looked better. Why wouldn't he? She did.

Coming out onto the sidewalk, it occurred to her that what she was doing was ridiculous. She could have called anybody—pick any historian out of the phone book, or maybe just walk across the street to the nearest Beltway think tank, in order to get her questions answered. But as she'd told herself before dialing up Eddie Rothgeb, she wasn't permitted to show classified documents to such people. Of course she wasn't permitted to show them to Eddie Rothgeb either, but to Laramie, Eddie would always qualify as the exception, since she wouldn't even have her job if it hadn't been for him. Still, coming here involved other perils, and perhaps she should have considered them.

The maroon BMW jerked to a stop on the other side of the island. He had told her about the car when she called, a maroon 525i—said he'd gone all out. Laramie had laughed over the phone and said something like "pretty sporty," but she knew it wasn't a move toward sporty at all. It was a move to a four-door sedan, in as conservative a color as he could find. She hadn't talked to him in maybe a year, and wasn't supposed to care, but it still made her mad that he'd bought it.

Rothgeb got out of the car and stood across the hood from her, and Laramie thought that he, at least, looked exactly the same. It wasn't what she expected—or maybe she'd expected it but hadn't prepared herself for it. Why would he look any older or any worse? Did three years change any man? Round, wire-rim glasses, beard trimmed short, blue Oxford button-down, red crew neck sweater over the shirt. Worn jeans, ratty Converse high-tops. The ageless professor slumming on a Saturday, exuding wisdom beyond his years. His eyes were the same too—she could see the blue in them twenty yards off. He waited beside the fender until she stepped over the curb and stopped a few feet in front of him.

"Laramie," he said.

Just like the first time, when she'd come into his gray cubicle during office hours and he'd known her name on sight. He came around to open the door for her, something she remembered he always remembered to do.

"Climb in," he said, and she tossed her bag into the backseat and watched him come around. When he got in, he fastened his seat belt, started the car, and looked over at her. Laramie was thinking that she hated the way he buckled his seat belt when he said, "Remember a place called Sandbags?"

"Sure," she said.

"I figured we'd start off with a little food."

He worked the car out from behind a shuttle bus, using the left-hand blinker as he went. He always signaled when he changed lanes.

"Why not," Laramie said.

Northwestern University Associate Professor Edwin Rothgeb kept the same little gray room he'd claimed as an office a dozen years ago, and maintained the same office hours he'd kept for a decade running—Monday, Wednesday, and Friday, 8 to 10:30 A.M. Something Rothgeb liked to do, though, when it came to more substantive off-line discussions, was to set a meeting on a Saturday, early, when there wasn't a student or faculty member in sight. For these sessions he held court in one of the big old classrooms in Scott Hall, where nobody would bother him.

Everything had been fine as they caught up on the drive over, Laramie asking Rothgeb about this year's freshman class and telling him about the rigors of her Agency training program at Camp Peary. They'd kept the conversation going for the walk across the quad; Rothgeb unlocked the faculty entrance and let them into the big lecture hall, and they sat at the table in front of the blackboard and spread out the sandwiches.

Then Laramie asked him how things were going with Heather.

Rothgeb smiled, said that things were fine, took a bite of his Genoa salami sandwich, and didn't say another word for the rest of the meal. Laramie ate her turkey sub and sipped on a Diet Snapple iced tea, trying in vain to think of something to say. At length, Rothgeb took his last bite, wiped his mouth with one of the brown paper napkins, and smiled the same way he had smiled when she'd asked him about Heather.

"I'm full," he said, and adjusted his glasses. "Let's have a look."

Laramie reached into her bag and came out with two overstuffed manila file folders. When she handed them over, Rothgeb rolled up his wax paper wrapper, cleared everything but his root beer off to one side of the table, and, wordlessly, began reading.

Laramie stood.

"Better let you concentrate," she said, and slipped out the door.

Remembering it was down by the other stairwell,
Laramie found the bathroom. It smelled of ammonia, as though the janitor had scrubbed it the night before. When she emerged from the stall, she thought about the heavy reading Eddie had in store and decided she may as well head upstairs—have a look around.

When she got to the third floor she saw what she knew she'd see: the same bulletin board, the doors, closed this morning, the classrooms closed off behind them. She wandered down the hallway lit only by the natural morning light, the floor both shiny and dull, and came to a door. She stopped in front of it and stood there like a child. After a while she reached out, ran her hand across the strip of wood with his name on it. She felt the letters.

Ed Rothgeb.

Once, she'd gone in there, ostensibly to review some assigned reading, and hadn't come out for a long while. She'd been in there for a long while many times before, mentor-pupil conversations stretching from minutes to hours, but not so long as during the time that came to mind. Laramie couldn't remember now what it was that had turned the conversations from academic to personal, but she did remember the feeling those meetings gave her. Thinking the whole time that it probably wasn't a good idea telling a professor the kind of things she was telling him, but since he always followed with another question, she would keep talking. And she watched his eyes watching her, those piercing blue eyes, the smartest eyes she'd ever seen, cautious behind the wire-rim eyeglasses, but *piercing*.

At some point he started telling her stories of his own, none of which she heard, all of it merging into one big stream of words, Laramie thinking then that if she could just keep him talking she could hear his voice some more and keep watching his mouth as it spoke. Then that Saturday meeting happened, a morning meeting that became an afternoon meeting. She remembered the way he leaned across the desk to touch her cheeks, to feel the heat in them, and Laramie closed her eyes and imagined his voice and his eyes and his mind wrapping entirely around her, and then she heard a stapler and a pair of books tumble to the floor and she felt his gentle lips on hers, and she opened her eyes and saw them, those piercing blue eyes, looking right back into hers, and the man she had thought about, four feet away but untouchable, touched her, and so she touched him. It took a while to build, Rothgeb being respectful, but when it happened that afternoon it happened on his desk, Laramie supposing because they had both thought of it happening that way.

Eddie Rothgeb was everything Laramie thought she had ever wanted in a man, and she told him so. He had helped her find her calling, helped her out of her shell, given her a sense of comfort and confidence she hadn't found at home. To Laramie he was everything except courageous, the sensuous Eddie Rothgeb already locked inside his four-door-sedan marriage, Laramie too young and stupid to think about it that way with the temptation of the man before her in his office, feeling like he belonged to her.

Laramie let her fingers drop from his nameplate. She reached down, knowing what would happen but still unable to resist trying. She turned the doorknob.

It was locked.

She thought, Of course it is.

Laramie went back downstairs.

You've got something here," he said, "or at least it's likely you do. And you've conducted an astute analysis. But you didn't come here to ask me if I think you've got something, or whether I think you're good at what you do."

Laramie watched him from one of the wooden chairs a couple rows back, the only student attending his lecture. She felt more comfortable now that they were talking about her documents instead of Heather Rothgeb.

"No," she said. "I didn't."

"You came to ask whether you should tell them you've got something here."

"Yes."

Rothgeb unclasped his hands, removed his eyeglasses, set the glasses on the table, leaned back in the chair, rubbed his face with both hands, and finished the act exactly the way she knew he would—by stroking his neat little beard with his right hand, sliding his thumb along one jawline and his index finger along the other. He retrieved the glasses from the table, placed them back on his face, and reclasped his hands.

"Actually," he said, "I don't think you came to ask that question at all."

Laramie didn't say anything.

"I know you, Laramie, so I'm aware that you've already made your decision. But let's run through it anyway.

"You've shown me satellite photographs of a significant military operation, which appears to be either an ordinary war game, or, as seems more likely from its size, genuine preparations for an imminent invasion. These activities were unpublicized, and successfully executed either during total cloud cover or on a schedule designed to avoid what are supposed to be classified spy satellite schedules—at least they were successfully executed in secret until you decided to look a little closer. Image selections from alternate source satellites yielded a more complete view of the operation. In short, from all appearances, it's a reasonable bet that an invasion is about to take place, possibly within months."

Laramie listened, a student hearing her paper read before the class.

"As an analyst who's done her homework on the region to which she's assigned, you've added some educated suppositions. According to you, the ideological leanings of eight of the eleven members of China's Standing Committee of the State Council—including the premier—make it likely, almost beyond a reasonable doubt, that the council as a whole would not, in today's environment, plan or approve such an invasion. You postulate that the fundamentalist vice premier overseeing China's military, General Deng Jiang, possibly in alliance with the intelligence chair, is planning either to win over the council and gain his comrades' approval, or to conduct the invasion, as I believe you put it, 'with or without the council's authorization.' Due to the supporting evidence of a regional military draft, you conclude that General Deng, at least, is confident the invasion will actually take place, and we should take measures under the assumption that it will."

Laramie nodded one short nod.

"The question," Rothgeb said, "is whether you should tell your deputy director, or whoever it is you report to these days, what he wants to hear, or whether you should tell him what you believe he needs to be told."

Laramie shrugged. "Correct as usual, your majesty."

"Well, obviously," he said, "you should tell him what he wants to hear."

"Come on."

"Now don't get all hot under the collar."

"Did you or did you not just look at those files? The pictures, my notes—"

"I saw the photographs, I read your notes, and your analysis is excellent. Your report does not, however, conform to Agency protocol and is based almost entirely on speculation."

"Speculation?"

"This could be something," Rothgeb said, "or it could not be something. It probably is. But unless you've been looking at these satellite shots from under a rock, you know as well as I do the political climate in the nation's capital in which you are—for the moment at least—gainfully employed."

"Of course I'm aware—"

"Since the administration is in the process of publicly sanitizing our country's relationship with the leaders of a nation you've now exposed as proactively hostile to our foreign policy on the issue of Taiwan, I shouldn't need to tell you, Laramie, that you're sitting on something that might just burn your ass." Rothgeb drew out the last phrase, enjoying one of his brief forays into off-color language.

Laramie found that virtually everything Eddie Rothgeb said or did annoyed her.

"This is information the administration should have," she said, "in order to determine appropriate foreign policy. Including which relationships the administration should be sanitizing."

Rothgeb chuckled.

"You came out to see me today," he said, "because you know what's going to happen if you submit a version of the report that includes your speculative conclusions. You do it, and you know full well they'll say you've submitted an inflammatory document displaying little more than bad political judgment. They'll instruct you to revise your report."

Laramie could feel it coming, the punch line of the professor's lecture.

"However," he said, "if you tell them what they want to hear, you'll continue to remain a trusted aide to whoever it is that receives your report. With a little guidance and luck, such political savvy will lead you to a long and fruitful career at CIA." He scratched a temple. "It's a significant issue these days if you include editorial commentary in an official memorandum. You could still make your point without the editorial—say what you see and let them figure out what it means. Which they will."

After a moment of nothing but the sickly buzz of the classroom's fluorescent lighting, Laramie said, "That's your advice?"

"I'd say it's my definition of politics," he said, "more so than my advice."

Laramie felt a sensation of emptiness. It was not unfamiliar.

"You want to tell me," Rothgeb said, "what it is you're not telling me?"

Laramie would have smiled had she not been trying to remember whether Rothgeb had always irked her to this degree. She shrugged instead, and looked away.

"When did you submit it?" Rothgeb asked.

"Yesterday," she said. "I submitted the report yesterday."

Chuckling again, Rothgeb took the sandwich wrappers and the brown paper bags and put them into a wastepaper basket under the table. "In your bullheaded way," he said, "you've done exactly what they hired you to do. Your boss, and his boss, and his boss will now know about the issue you've unearthed. After lambasting you, my guess is your superiors will either seek a second opinion on your intel, or, more likely, sit on it until the intel becomes more relevant to their own career advancement."

"They can't sit on this."

"Oh, but they can, and will."

"How?"

"That," he said, "is how they've come to hold positions of influence in our nation's capital. Or near to it, at any rate."

"Isn't your outlook a bit bleak?"

Rothgeb sighed. "You aren't thinking practically. If you feel your discovery warrants action and you don't get any from your superiors, you'll simply need to get their career advancement lined up with your agenda. Or," he said, "as typically works better in Washington, the converse."

Laramie leaned forward in her seat. "You buried the lead. You're recommending that I get them fired if they don't act?"

"Correct."

"That's ambitious." She shrugged. "Obvious point here, professor, but last time I checked, *I* work for *them*."

"Laramie, you don't need to be an intelligence analyst to understand to whom your bosses report. In fact, I believe we routinely cover that topic in the standard freshman political science course."

In those classes, Laramie would always stay right with him, maybe keep a step ahead of his lecture outline. It took concentration, but she figured she ought to be able to handle him even better today.

"You're saying they work for the president," she said. "CIA being a part of the executive branch—"

"Nope," he said. "Follow the money."

"Oh. Congress. The Select Committee on Intelligence, for instance."

"Correct."

He stayed rooted in his seat at the table. Laramie knew Eddie was playing his fishing game; if you were too dense to tell him what he was about to teach you, he wanted to make you ask for the punch line. Out of practice and out of the mood, she declined the challenge, taking the bait like a freshman.

"I guess I'm still not following you," she said.

"As you know, in addition to authorizing the salaries of your superiors, the congressional committees that hold intelligence oversight responsibilities also hold regular hearings in which your superiors report to them on various issues of significance."

"Of course."

"And believe it or not, there may well be a representative on such a committee who would share your opinion of the classified SATINT you're currently parading around college campuses."

He stood, reached down, and pushed Laramie's manila folders across the table.

"You can spare me the next question," he said. "The answer is, yes, I can probably get you a personal e-mail address or two belonging to members of such committees."

Laramie remained in her seat for a minute, thinking through what he was recommending. It was not a low-risk scenario.

She stood, came over to the table, and returned the folders to her bag. They walked out of the room together; when they came into the hall, Laramie turned and faced him. A few long seconds passed, Laramie looking up into those piercing eyes, Rothgeb looking a little uncomfortable. Laramie didn't make any move to turn away.

"I don't like your car," she said. "It isn't sporty at all."

He didn't smile, but she could see the warmth in there behind the cool blue surface of his eyes.

"I already knew you didn't like it," he said.

6

Cooper didn't like to moor his boat in San Juan harbor, so despite his hatred of the airline he caught the early American Eagle flight into San Juan's Luis Muñoz Marin International, easily the worst airport in the Western Hemisphere but still better than the harbor. He chose a red convertible Mustang at the rental counter and took the shuttle to the lot, a process that only took ninety minutes from counter to street.

That put him around nine-thirty as he pulled into a convenient red zone in front of the San Juan Police Department. Once inside, he waved at the desk sergeant, who didn't know him, and walked into the squad room. He approached the desk of Detective Manolo Pérez, who was sitting there sipping a Burger King coffee.

Pérez, who went by Manny even to his enemies, looked up, nearly jumped, and said, "Jesus. Cooper."

Cooper was wearing a banana yellow Tommy Bahama short-sleeve shirt featuring green illustrations of parrots. "The hell are you, Manny?" he said.

"They let you just waltz right in?" Manny was acting casual now, going back to his coffee while he spoke.

"Been told I look like a cop," Cooper said. "Lucky me."

He noticed Manny wasn't reading anything or doing any paperwork. On the desk he saw a blotter, calendar, and phone—no notes, no forms, no files. Manny was doing nothing but sipping the coffee, probably chasing a BK breakfast sandwich with it. As if this weren't his real office. Which it wasn't.

"Looks like you're working that big homicide case," Cooper said. "Reviewing the file, following up on some leads to start the day. Hell, maybe you'll even give it some more thought while you're having some plantain chips and a couple of Miller Genuine Drafts on your three-hour lunch. You'll be taking that lunch in what, about an hour?"

Eyes shifty, taking in the squad room, Manny said, "Nice to see you've maintained your sense of decorum." Then he leaned forward and lowered his voice. "Fucking *gringo,* you don't just come in here and say all that in the middle of the floor."

Cooper deposited himself in the chair alongside Manny's desk. The detective wore a pale brown long-sleeve shirt that looked to be made of silk, the collar unbuttoned, Manny showing off his brown skin and scant few curls of chest hair. He had a big head of wavy black hair and a neat black beard that hid a developing double chin. A thin gold chain snaked around the base of his neck.

Cooper set the snapshot of the tattoo on the empty desk and pushed it over.

"Nineteen-year-old kid washed up on the beach in Road Town," he said. "Had that tattooed on his neck."

"And I care about this why?"

Cooper looked at him. He gave Manny some time, knowing that the detective would give some thought, there with the coffee, to some of the other things Cooper could be saying in the middle of the floor. A few things Manny wouldn't want his fellow cops hearing.

"He was shot in the back," Cooper said after a while. "Had both legs broken, like maybe he jumped off the tenth floor of a building trying to get away. Could have been using, but was probably getting shot up by somebody, I'm guessing heroin. Mark on his neck is a voodoo sign."

Almost involuntarily, Manny peered at the picture. "Hard to tell," he said.

"Not for you."

Manny shook his head. "Might have seen something like it along the way, but the people you're thinking of don't use it."

"Maybe not," Cooper said, "but they might know who does."

Manny shrugged.

Cooper said, "You know, this kid could have been a mule. Or hell, maybe he saw something he wasn't supposed to see. Any way you look at it, somebody wanted him pretty dead. Means to me somebody had something to hide. Probably something worth hiding."

Manny looked at the picture again.

"There's a cop I know here in San Juan," Cooper said, "possessed of a keen olfactory nerve. Where others blindly pursue justice, or arrests, he also knows when a case presents an opportunity to pad his numbered account in the Caymans."

Manny leaned back in his chair and pushed the coffee to the other side of the desk.

"You show me that picture," he said, "you don't even need to tell me the story. The smell of money ain't what's coming

off that one. You know what that picture smells like? An outhouse, *ese*. Smells like you're knee-deep in shit."

He stood up.

"Fuck you, Cooper. I'll give you a couple hours, but that's
it. I got that lunch to get to."

Cooper entertained himself by waiting to see
whether Manny would offer to buy the tickets. He didn't, so
Cooper paid the twenty-four bucks. He saw on his stub that
the first fight began at noon.

The sunglassed Manny eyed his ticket when Cooper gave
it to him.

"Shitty seats," he said. "Listen, *ese,* I'll meet you inside—
and I may need to spread some goodwill. Know what I'm
saying?"

"Bill me," Cooper said. He handed his ticket to a stout old
man in a red vest and pushed through the turnstile.

The cool blast of the *gallera*'s air-conditioning system
dried his sweaty skin. He flagged down a girl in a halter top
and short-shorts slinging a concessions tray, bought a beer
from her, pulled down a few ounces of it, and thought that if
he had to wait for Manny to find whoever it was the cop was
looking for, he may as well figure out how to make some
money on the noon fight in the meantime. He crossed the
lobby to the credit window, laid down a MasterCard displaying a name that wasn't his, and bought a five-thousand-dollar
credit line. The teller, who, like ninety percent of the people
in here, was middle-aged, male, and overweight, pushed a
bright blue plastic card across the counter. Cooper slipped it
into his breast pocket, the card sticking out by an inch or two,
enough to show the officials how much he was good for.

He found the hall that led to the ring; it was lit like a Best Buy. A velvet rope kept you a couple feet back from the glass, but even standing on the other side of the rope you could poke your head in, almost against the window, and get a good look at the birds. The walls in the narrow hall were composed of cages, each about two feet square, stacked in three rows, so that the top row of roosters stared back at you from eye level.

Cooper found one of the noon combatants and scoped the gamecock out, leaning in until his face was an inch from the glass. The rooster stood his ground. Cooper thought the foot-tall bird looked like somebody had just given him a haircut and removed his pants—the feathers on his wings and neck were slicked back, his legs and tail plucked, the skin red, swollen, greased. There was a splash of gold in the feathers of the rooster's neck, Cooper thinking this was one proud-looking bird, his handlers unable to make a fool of him despite the plucking. He found the second fighter, a smaller, fatter, relatively unkempt bird, his feathers a mottled black and white. This one bobbed hyperactively around his cage.

Cooper decided to go with the black-and-white scrapper—unless the fix is in, he thought, I'm walking out of here a few grand to the good.

The handlers pulled the two birds out of their cages, taking them into the back room. Peering through the empty cage of the black-and-white bird, Cooper caught a glimpse of Manny talking with somebody against a concrete wall. The guy was tall, taller than Manny by a foot, and dark—made Manny look like a *gringo* himself. Cooper watched as the black-and-white rooster's handlers gathered behind the cages and took his bird away, the crazed animal pecking and scratching the whole way. When the entourage had passed, Manny and his buddy were no longer there.

Cooper took his seat while the birds were positioned beneath Plexiglas boxes on the artificial turf of the cockpit. The roosters were going crazy, trying to get at each other with the sharp wooden *espuelas* their handlers had strapped to each leg. Cooper had heard that gamecocks were fed a pregame meal of brandy and coffee, Cooper thinking he'd be whacking away at the box too—pants off, legs greased, drunk and java-juiced, about to get gouged to death if you didn't strike first. Bring it on.

Manny took his seat beside Cooper about three minutes into the fight. Even at noon, the arena was packed, circular rows of middle-aged men rising steeply up from the cockpit, the shouting rising to a fever pitch as the birds beat the shit out of each other.

"Vámonos, ese," Manny said. "Got what we were looking for. Maybe you should have stayed in the car—when I show you what it cost us, you going to wish you kept your twelve bucks."

"Who said I was paying?"

Manny ignored him. "The guy runs everything into PR out of Haiti's name is Ocholito," he said. "He tell you what you want to know. Or maybe he tell you there nothing to find. Either way, nobody going to know nothing if Ocholito don't."

The golden bird knocked Cooper's scrapper to the turf and pounced. The official let this play out for ten or fifteen seconds before separating them. The handlers descended on the ring and repositioned the birds. They squawked and flapped their wings.

A cacophony of shouted bets shot forth, people raising

hands, calling out odds. Cooper started pointing his fingers and snapping out *"Sí!"* Putting three, four grand on the line, getting fifteen, twenty-to-one odds.

Manny said, "You betting on the wrong bird, *puto*!"

They released the birds and let them fight. Cooper's was down again in seconds, his opponent tearing chunks of meat from his legs with the *espuelas*.

"Why would it cost me to see Ocholito?" Cooper said.

"Ocho prefer not to be found," Manny said, "so he shacks up somewhere new every couple months. Some new *mamacita* always waiting in line. You need to know which woman, you want to talk to him."

The scrapper lifted himself off the turf and engaged in another twenty seconds of warfare until his adversary practically beheaded him with a swipe of the *espuela* and he toppled, dead.

Cooper shrugged and rose.

"The fix was in," he said.

7

Cooper beheld a cannabis leaf. Made of wood and painted the colors of the Jamaican flag, it overhung the entrance to a store advertising 99¢ palm readings. Above the cannabis leaf stood a second-floor apartment.

Manny came around the car but hung back at the curb.

"Don't know her by name," he said, "but she'd recognize me quick. Send Ocholito packing before we say *bueno' día'*. You should go in alone."

"*Gringo* like me?" Cooper said. "Probably make me for a cop while I'm standing out here."

"Don't sell yourself short, *ese*. Maybe you her kind of man. You know something? Ocholito likes 'em big. Whole lotta woman." He grinned. "So do I. Anyway, *gringo* bastard like you visiting a Cataño fortune-teller—at least you a stranger. Probably confuse her. Strike up a conversation while she trying to figure it out, maybe you can get her to spill the beans. Tell you where Ocholito be spending his days."

Cooper looked at the upstairs apartment. "Probably sleeping off a night of ganja-aided love, be my guess," he said.

"I'll stroll around back—his *mamacita* slip him the signal, I'll be waiting with open arms." Manny laughed. "Or maybe legs."

"Come again?"

"You'll see."

Cooper left it at that and went in. His entrance triggered a string of bells dangling from the door, and he found himself overtaken by a fog of foul-smelling incense. He looked for and found the source: a plume rose from a smudge stick beneath the shop's front window. The window may as well have been made of drywall, slathered as it was with black paint; an assortment of goods hung from its frame, Cooper making out dried plants, spice bags, bongs, a pair of what might have been charred whole chickens. A rack offered decks of Tarot cards and bones of varying sizes; lining the wall at the back of the room was an embedded countertop with a gap in the middle.

Cooper waited without speaking, and was beginning to think customers were of little concern to the palm readers of Cataño when a bloated hand split a pair of bead-strings behind the countertop and was followed into the room by an enormous woman in a knit halter top. The knots in the fabric of the halter top were stretched so thin that the fabric exposed more of her breasts than it covered. Beneath the counter Cooper could see the woman's black leather miniskirt, a selection that would have been daring on an anorexic runway model. She had fair skin and plenty of it; ogling the sand-dollar-sized nipples poking through the halter, Cooper pegged the fortune-teller's tonnage somewhere between two-ninety and three-ought-five.

She eyed him up and down, Cooper thinking she was debating whether to eat him.

"¿*En qué puedo ayudarle?*" she said.

"*Bueno' día',*" Cooper said. He stayed on with the Spanish. "I'm sorry to say I've become lonely—having bad luck with the ladies. I was hoping you could tell me what I'm doing wrong. Maybe see if romance is in store, or what I need to do to get it."

"Fifty dollars in advance," she said, "cash only."

"What happened to the ninety-nine cents?"

"Different topic."

Cooper found correct change. She snatched the bills, parted the curtain, and gestured for him to enter.

Behind the beads was a single swath of floor space crowded with opened boxes, cleared in the center to make room for the card table that stood there. The table, Cooper saw, actually featured a crystal ball. At the back of the room was a stairwell leading up, and a door, presumably leading out.

They got started side by side at the table, Ocholito's *mamacita* asking for his palm, reading its lines in the dark, her fingers working over his wrist and forearm. Cooper felt the rush of endorphines from her skilled hands, thinking she knew what she was doing—focus on the heavy-handed massage therapy and you'll wonder, a couple days later, what you did with your watch. I leave it out on the beach?

"I can smell her on you," she said throatily. "Either you are modest, or a liar. You've had women recently, or they have had you. I can smell the last one's pussy and there will be others soon."

Cooper leaned in and sniffed his forearm.

She let her fingers wander above his elbow and probe the

inside of his biceps. She leaned against him, close enough to bite a chunk off his nose, a wide breast pillowing against his shoulder. Her bulbous lips drifted past his face and brushed his earlobe. "Maybe you come looking for love," she croaked in an addled whisper.

Cooper shivered. "Could be."

"You couldn't handle me in your wildest dreams, *gringo*." She dropped her eyes to his palm. "Still, lucky boy, I see somebody be coming for you."

"That so?"

"Somebody who give you what you need." Her massage spread to his shoulder, then the back of his neck. She had strong fingers, the big woman's one-handed technique giving him a hard-on, but something about her technique disturbed him.

"What is it I need, exactly," he said, then realized the nature of his discomfort as she dug a clawed hand into the back of his neck and rammed a big-boned knee into his groin. He could feel both his testicles mash against the blow, her knee following through and toppling him backward. He'd have laughed had the blow not stolen his wind; grimacing, he flipped like a falling cat and found his legs before the floor found his ass. He had his gun out before he landed too, his Agency-issue FN Browning, Cooper pointing it at her with the palm she'd been reading. He didn't need it, since the fortune-teller had already wheeled and begun to run, all relative terms considering her carrier-group maneuverability.

"Ocholito, ¡vámonos! ¡Policía!" she spat in the direction of the stairwell.

Cooper took an elbow and pivoted to extend a leg across her intended course; she caught his shin and toppled violently. He came around the table and stood over her, and as she withdrew what looked like a Swiss Army knife from the panties beneath the leather skirt, Cooper slugged her in the jaw. She went limp, a pond of flesh on the floor, and Cooper heard footsteps before observing the odd sight of an extremely short man in a red top hat charging mostly nude down the stairwell and out the door. Daylight burst into the room, blinding him, and as he felt his way out, the thought occurred to him that he had just witnessed the escape of The Cat in the Hat from the upstairs apartment.

Hustling into the alley, he found only a rusted Hyundai propped up on cinder blocks beside a Dumpster. He crouched, advancing gun-first around the Dumpster, then let his gun arm drop.

His back against the wall just past the Dumpster, Manny was lighting a particularly long joint for The Cat in the Hat. The Cat, whom Cooper presumed to be Ocholito, toked a lungful of weed and nodded his approval.

Cooper resheathed his Browning in the small of his back and took his first good look at the little man. Four foot nine at best, he wore a knotty beard that looked as though it would never grow all the way out, and like the taller man Cooper had seen conferring with Manny at the *gallera,* Ocholito was dark enough to make the cop look pale. The red top hat was half as tall as the man himself, and Ocholito wore a robe—satin, red like the hat, and unsecured, his manhood hanging unabashedly exposed to the Puerto Rican sunshine. Cooper now understood why Ocholito preferred, as Manny had put it, a whole lotta woman: in his own way, the four-foot-nine Ocholito was a whole lotta man.

Ocholito passed the doobie, and Manny sucked down a

lungful of his own. Once he'd held it awhile, Manny said, "*Mi amigo* here, he's looking for some answers nobody going to have but you, Ocho."

"Oh yeah, *c'est vrai?*"

Ocholito's voice was deep and oddly rough, like somebody with sand lodged in his larynx.

Cooper pulled the picture of the tattoo, thinking he ought to open a PI firm—we handle your problems when you're already dead, just contact us in our dreams and we're on the case. Hundred percent pro bono. Keeping his distance, he reached out to hand the snapshot to Ocholito.

"A kid who washed up dead in Road Town," he said, "had that tattooed on the back of his neck. Voodoo symbol for death, the way I understand it. Had some tracks on his arms too. What I'd like to know is who uses the tatt—kid was running drugs, got caught stealing, I'd like to know who he was muling for. Somebody wearing that sign, maybe it makes him a banger—Eighty-seventh Street Voodoo Crips, I don't know. Maybe you do."

The Cat in the Hat glared at him, causing Cooper to observe that one of Ocholito's eyelids was permanently wrinkled shut. The little man snatched the picture with manicured fingernails painted a high-gloss black and looked at the snapshot.

"Where your boy die again?"

"Body washed up on Tortola. Where he died? Anybody's guess."

The Cat in the Hat returned the picture and shook his head.

Cooper said, "Doesn't mean anything to you?"

"*Personne,* nobody kill him," Ocholito said in that sandy voice.

Cooper waited for further clarification. Getting none, he said, "Trust me, the boy was killed."

"Nobody kill him 'cause he already dead."

Cooper eyed the snapshot, seeing nothing more than he'd seen any other time he'd looked at it. "You're telling me you can see from a picture of his neck he was already dead when they shot him?"

"That picture you showin' me," Ocholito said, "ain't no tatt."

"No?"

"*Non.* What you got in your hand, that be a picture of a brand." Cooper wasn't sure how he could tell, but he knew what was coming before Ocholito said his next words. "*Et mon ami,*" Ocholito said, "the brand you holdin' be the mark of a zombie."

Manny and Ocholito traded tokes. Cooper examined each man as he smoked, attempting to determine whether this might all have been a practical joke, planned months in advance by Manny, The Cat in the Hat, and Cap'n Roy.

"Assuming," Cooper said, "I buy into that particular side of voodoo myth, I'd still like to know who uses the, uh, brand."

"Nobody here."

"Here, meaning—"

"Only place that shit go down for real, be Haiti, or maybe the DR. *Pas ici.*"

"Zombies," Cooper said, "being in short supply outside of Hispaniola."

"No, there plenty in Louisiana too," Ocholito said and grinned. A gold tooth gleamed when he smiled. "But that about it."

"Who in Haiti would use it?"

"*Je ne sais pas.*"

Cooper stomached his proximity with Ocholito's naked member and stepped closer.

"Horseshit," he said.

Ocholito's expression and stance remained fixed, Cooper reading him immediately as a man who dealt with disrespect in ways that did not reside in the moment. Overendowed and not to be fucked with—outside of his exhibitionism and taste in women, *Le Chat dans le Chapeau,* Cooper thought, has it going on.

"I'll give you some advice, *mon ami,*" Ocholito said. His voice had deepened to where he sounded like a Buddhist monk in song. "Journey you about to go on, maybe things be better, you stay home. You ready to pay the price?"

"Depends."

Ocholito smiled again. "Maybe we bring you into the *voudaison,*" he said, "find you a *loa.* Mine, he give me powers most people only dream about. But the price be steep."

"You asking me to sell my soul? Cosmic debt I've been running up pretty much drained that bank account."

The Cat in the Hat emitted a Buddhist-monk chuckle. "We'll see about that."

Ocholito looked at Manny, giving him some kind of signal; needing no translation and too annoyed to negotiate, Cooper pulled a stack of fifties from his wallet and handed The Cat in the Hat four hundred bucks. Ocholito snagged the money with his high-gloss fingernails, and Cooper stepped off, giving Ocholito back his private space. The little man sucked down the last of the joint, held his breath for thirty seconds, exhaled, and nodded.

"Once you out of the country," he said, "you out of the loop. So I ain't your best source. *Pas encore.* But that picture you showing me be some version of the brand the *bokor,* black-magic witch doctor, burn into the skin of somebody fail to make the sacrifice he been told to make. Basically it be the brand marking somebody that *bokor* done zombified. Anybody spend time in the *voudaison* tell you that—but where, when, who done burned it in, well, *je ne sais pas, mon ami.* Your guess be as good as mine, since them *bokors* be workin' outside of mainstream voodoo."

He flicked the remnants of the joint to the pavement and to Cooper's great relief folded closed the robe and knotted its strap above his equine protuberance.

"Somebody might be more up to speed," Ocholito said, "be a man name of Benoit. Reynold Benoit, M.D. He live mainly in Port-au-Prince; by day, he work in conventional medicine, out of Hôpital H. L. Dantier."

Cooper stored this. "And by night?"

Ocholito grinned, showing off that gold gleam. "That," he said, "be why I'm giving you his name."

Cooper nodded.

"Well, Little-eight," he said, "I'd love to continue our conversation, but Manny's backlog of unsolved cases beckons."

He jerked his chin at Manny, walked around the Dumpster, and cut back through the store, finding no sign of the fortune-teller on his way to the car.

It took him ninety minutes at the blackjack tables of the El San Juan casino to put himself ahead for the day, net of the rigged cockfight and four-hundred-dollar Cat in the Hat peepshow. Around 2 A.M. he found some company in a pair of inebriated sisters from New Jersey who needled him until he agreed to accompany them to the suite somebody had procured for them, where they shared some of Jamaica's finest and a three-for-all in the suite's whirlpool tub.

Once the ladies' presence had depreciated to a two-tiered snore pattern on the overcrowded king-size bed, Cooper pulled a Coke from the minibar, rode a pair of elevators back to his own room, and took his PowerBook out to the balcony. He was thinking he was only willing to go so far to find answers—even when the questions came to him in his dreams, screeched by the dead—and, given this, it occurred to him the Internet was a lot closer, and certainly a more pleasant place to visit, than Port-au-Prince, Haiti, sometime home to Reynold Benoit, M.D.

By way of his access to a set of online databases, he found varying theories on whether the ritual of transforming a living person into a walking corpse actually worked, or was simply the longest-running urban legend on record. If it was only myth, much of the credit for originating the legend went to a pair of books, published a century apart—in 1884, a bestseller documented savage cannibalistic voodoo rituals; recently, a more scholarly book claimed to have identified the ingredients used by witch doctors, or *bokors,* to reduce ordinary men to so-called zombie status. The recipe was composed of human remains, a certain indigenous flower, and varying amounts of venom extracted from the bouga toad and puffer fish. When properly administered— along with the appropriate black-magic spell—the *coup poudre,* as it was called, supposedly sent its victim into a coma, slowing down his metabolism enough to generate the appearance of death. Bury him, wait a few days, dig him up and feed him *conconbre zombi*—another indigenous plant—and the *bokor* had a custom-lobotomized menial laborer whose friends and family thought had died.

A gust of wind whistled through the El San Juan's main tower, the trades picking up and shifting direction by a few degrees as the city's perpetual nighttime cloud cover broke and the moon materialized. Who knows, Cooper thought— maybe the gust of wind was caused by an evil spirit, a *petro-*

loa, checking in on my progress. Or hell—could be it's Le Gran Maître himself, telling me . . . telling me what? Back off? Keep going?

Then again it could have been the weather pattern and that was it.

Either way, he decided he'd go ahead and call it a voodoo moon: a voodoo moon, telling me to get my ass out of San Juan.

He closed out his Internet connection at four-forty-five. American Eagle, he knew, ran the first flight to Terrance Lettsome at five-fifty; if he got the hell off the balcony he could make the flight and be back in the spiritually protected environs of the Conch Bay Beach Club in time to catch the late morning rays. Toss back a sweet cocktail, maybe a piña colada or a painkiller, and see if boredom, sunshine, and syrupy booze could accomplish what gambling, rapture, and herb had not:

Clear this fucking head of mine, he thought, of *petro-loas,* Puerto Rican cops, and *Les Chats dans les Chapeaux.*

8

Forty miles north of Beijing, an unmarked stretch limousine wound its way up a ribbon of highway. At the wheel sat a portly old driver in standard-issue People's Liberation Army fatigues—his knuckles, exposed in two clumps on the steering wheel, as gnarled as the trees flashing past the limo along the road. It was eight in the morning, and already there was a muggy weight to the air.

At the top of the hill the highway transitioned to a dirt road. A guard shack materialized, and a soldier wearing similar fatigues emerged from the booth. He spoke in Mandarin.

"Proceed, old man," the soldier said.

The driver steered into a parking lot, the limo kicking up dust as he parked it behind a row of wooden stables. He locked the parking brake, got out, stood with his back to the car, and fired up a black-market Winston.

He made sure nobody saw him do it.

As the team worked the ball around and dished it ahead of him, General Deng Jiang spurred his horse into a dash. He corralled the pass and came around with a looping swing. *Crack*—mallet on ball. As usual, he scored; Deng did most of the scoring here.

The majority of his teammates were People's Liberation Army deputy ministers, but there were others—an admiral, a few captains, even a pair of bureaucrats who'd kissed sufficient ass to get an invite. Feeling good about himself, Deng ignored the fact that most of these players weren't simply ten or twenty years younger but also ten or twenty grades his junior and working for him—meaning they were out here letting him hog all the glory and win at will. Any other result and the opposing players were destined for a prison camp in Tibet; in any case, few of them had any interest in being here to begin with. Most had never even heard of the sport before Deng's summons delivered them to his private polo field.

During the days that followed his weekly contests, Deng found himself better equipped to travel back down to Beijing and endure the intolerable—base closures, project cancellations, the retirement of loyal, old-guard soldiers. After his private game he could do these things with greater purpose, Deng getting at least a semblance of that old feeling back, the sense that he still commanded the military of the greatest nation in the history of mankind. That he wasn't merely the grim reaper with a budget ax, a treasonous bean counter shaving away a new layer of the people's heritage with every dab of the pen.

The morning's farce concluded and a servant arrived to assist his dismount. Deng looked for and found his driver, seeing the man leaning against the limousine behind the stables. Deng watched as the old man flicked away the cigarette and did his best to look busy, whipping out a rag and polishing one of the limo's fenders. The driver had been loyal to him through twenty years of service, and remained so, even now, in retirement; Deng allowed him the slack he would never grant others under his charge.

The old servant was getting ready to take Deng back to reality. Past the gnarled trees, down the hill, and into the abyss of deteriorating military might. Despite the satisfaction brought on by the game, this was when Deng typically began to feel the slow burn of anger—the quiet rage of a man returning to the coal mines for another miserable day along the journey to death.

Today, however, was not a typical day.

Changing into fatigues in his private dressing room, Deng checked the date on the face of his watch for what might have been the hundredth time. It was true, as he had confirmed it to be true all morning.

Today was, in fact, the day he had been waiting for.

Today, he would catch a glimpse of tomorrow.

The blades of the PLA Z-9 helicopter thopped against the humidity, its landing skids settling on the tarmac of the Shandong PLN base. Deng rode in the rear, reclining on the leather seats of his airborne military limousine. He held on for nearly three minutes before giving the order to open the door—he would make them wait, encourage these men to think about who it was who was about to exit the airship. He peered through the bulletproof window beside his seat; the window afforded him an awesome sight.

Shoulder to shoulder, back to front, stretching the length and width of an entire military airstrip, there stood in formation some twenty-five thousand troops. Behind the first few thousand men were hundreds of vehicles—tanks, trucks, armored cars, jeeps—and, behind these, dozens of additional helicopters, rotors blazing, plus a score of fighter jets.

Standing at the front of the formation, elbow locked in salute with the others, was Rear Admiral Li Zhu. Li's breast and shoulders gleamed with medals; his skin was of a much darker complexion than most of the soldiers behind him, his expressionless face angular and lean—a career soldier who hadn't let himself go. As loyal, Deng thought, as his driver, and entrusted with more secrets than he ought to be. Li was fifteen years his junior and, in Deng's estimation, about half as quick on a horse. The general almost felt guilty about beating Li on the polo grounds, so easily did victory come.

As the rotors of the airborne limousine lost steam, Deng waved one of his elite guards to the door. The guard saluted, slid the door open, and rolled out a modular stairwell. A second sentry accompanied the first out the door and each took his assigned position at the base of the stairwell.

Deng came out, stoic, pausing on the last stair before descending to the tarmac. He knew the medals adorning his uniform to be blinding in the sun, easily dwarfing Li's; it was good to let the soldiers admire them. At length he stepped down to the runway and crossed the twenty meters of asphalt between himself and Admiral Li, who held his salute until Deng, passing, dismissed it with one of his own. Over the rotors, turbines, and diesel engines, it was hard for Deng to make out the words as Li spoke, but it sounded to him as if the admiral said something about how honored he and his men were to receive such a great leader as their comrade general and State Council vice premier here at Shandong's humble naval base.

Deng acknowledged Li's comments with a halfhearted nod and continued walking.

They had a hundred-meter walk to the first in a convoy of jeeps; once they climbed aboard, the procession jerked to life. The head jeep leading the way, it was only a matter of seconds before the convoy vanished into the sea of troops.

Deng called it the War Room. It was one of seven he'd personally designed, ultimately ordering six built as impenetrable underground bunkers beneath China's six largest military installations, and a seventh aboard a People's Liberation Navy nuclear attack submarine. The technical name for these installations was Military Operations Oversight Facility, but the way Deng saw it, he could run a war out of any one of these rooms, so he'd gone ahead and fallen back on the default term.

Given the method by which military powers had come to engage in war, Deng's War Rooms offered the ultimate control seat. He had spared no cost, not in construction budgets or, more important, the spy operations that fed the engineering effort behind the construction. PLA technology, represented best by that which was fed into these War Rooms, had nearly matched that of the American military-industrial complex, mainly due to the fact that Chinese army intelligence had stolen most of the significant technological innovations developed by American military contractors.

From his War Rooms, Deng could watch everything imaginable related to any armed conflict conducted by his troops. Any image that could possibly be generated in the field was projected on massive plasma screens; he could control every aspect of war with the flip of a switch, from ordering blood work on a soldier taken ill in Kazakhstan to the launch of biological warheads in the European theater. All he had to do was whisper a command to the technicians manning the main keyboard.

The land-based War Rooms were built deep underground, shielded behind twenty-foot-thick walls of titanium, concrete, and lead, designed to deflect the electromagnetic pulse of an adjacent fifty-megaton nuclear explosion. The power supply was quadruple-redundant. Any military action China was capable of undertaking, Deng could activate it from his War Room throne, and virtually no one could stop him from doing whatever he chose to do while he was planted there.

Admiral Li led the general out of an elevator and down a bright hallway. At the end of the hall, the admiral ushered him through an immense vault door, where a fresh duo of military police snapped off salutes and the two MPs who had escorted them thus far turned and left.

Inside, it was dark, though not pitch-black. The room possessed a luminescent glow—similar, Deng liked to think, to the glow of a beach under the light of the moon. Deng could hear the familiar orchestral cacophony: the clatter of keyboards, the whirring of computer fans, murmured conversations of a hundred hushed voices. Li led him up a stairwell to a room resembling a film projection booth: the Control Box—Deng's throne, from which he beheld the glory of his creation.

Spread in a crescent before him, built precisely two meters below the level of the Control Box, lay the heart of the War Room—a deep amphitheater sprawling under vaulted ceilings, the room about the size of a polo field. A staff of more than a hundred men scurried back and forth in the air-conditioned darkness; endless rows of workstations, radar and sonar monitors, electronic map displays, telecommunications and video conferencing systems, and the halogen reading lamps positioned throughout the room combined to form the glow Deng had observed upon entering. A pair of technicians manned the Control Box, a room resembling the cockpit of a commercial airliner; an opening at the front of the cockpit, six meters wide by two tall, offered the view to the main floor and could be sealed, Deng knew, by a soundproof, one-way-mirrored glass shield at the touch of a button.

Deng and Li were shown to their seats by one of the technicians and handed a pair of wireless headsets. Deng pulled his over his ears.

Li bowed. "You'll be presented with a time-lapsed but otherwise complete presentation of the invasion simulation exercise." He waved to one of the technicians. "Begin!"

Commencing an instant later, and for the next fifty-one minutes, Deng's senses were assaulted by war. He watched a campaign waged from sea to land, primarily through the images on the multiple high-def plasma screens—views from spy planes; angles from tanks, personnel carriers, helicopters, aircraft, soldiers' helmets; enlarged images of radar screens depicting opposing troops; reports from embedded foreign correspondents assessing the strategy and carnage. Incoming status reports blasted across a loudspeaker system; in addition to the full media coverage, the simulation included the meticulous replication of calculated diplomatic responses from world leaders. Strategic decision making was displayed via security-camera angles eavesdropping on senior staff meetings held at the command bunker.

If he didn't know that the exercise depicted had already taken place, Deng would not have been able to tell the difference; for all intents and purposes, the simulation was nothing short of real war.

At the conclusion of the presentation, Li tugged off his headset.

"You'll find we surpassed your objectives in every aspect of the exercise." He reached across the desk and handed Deng a thick report.

Deng's eyes found the report on the desk, and Li beside him. He stared at Li for longer than he wanted, knowing his eyes were lit with a sort of euphoric lunacy—something he didn't particularly want Li observing. No matter: he had seen a slice of tomorrow, and he liked the way it looked. He broke eye contact and stood.

"It is upon us," he said.

Li rose to proffer a salute, but Deng had already reached the exit hall, so the gesture encountered only empty air.

The general had seen what he'd come to see.

9

Laramie had chosen a black suit, looking the part on a Monday morning she had not been looking forward to. The call came at nine-fifteen; it was Peter M. Gates's secretary, known as Miss Anders, who asked whether she had a moment to come and visit with Mr. Gates.

Gates.

She hadn't expected that.

Gates was something of a legend, a three-term deputy director of central intelligence. He was easily one of the ten most powerful men in Washington—probably top five, as few understood how much influence one possessed as the chief operating officer of the world's largest cloak-and-dagger outfit.

The summons from Gates meant one of two possibilities: either Laramie was being pulled in to join a task force investigating the discovery she had presented in her report; or, as Eddie Rothgeb might have put it, Gates was about to burn her ass.

Coming out of the elevator on the seventh floor, Laramie passed a pair of desks in a yellow hallway with brown carpeting, the waiting room for both the DCI and DDCI. Behind one of the desks sat Miss Anders, an older woman wearing a tall head of dark hair and a candy-apple-red suit jacket. She looked up from her desk, asked Laramie to state her name, and when she did, told Laramie she could go right in.

She came in between the two men who were already in the office with Gates. Laramie knew them and had expected they might be here—Malcolm Rader, her direct boss and China section head; and Stephen Rosen, DDI, head of the directorate of intelligence. It was evident from Rader's and Rosen's expressionless faces that they'd held a full premeeting before she'd arrived. It appears Rothgeb's predictions, she thought, are about to play out like a scene in a movie Eddie is secretly directing.

She approached Gates's massive desk and shook the DDCI's hand as he offered it. Gates was tall, gray, and coiffed, Laramie thinking he should have chosen to work in private industry, since she was sure he'd have made CEO at any company he joined based on appearance alone. Miss Anders stepped in from her cubicle, pulled the door closed, and left.

Gates motioned for them all to take their seats. "Is Rader here taking care of business?" he asked. "Go ahead and tell me if he's causing you any undue stress."

The men in the room chuckled. Laramie offered a tight-lipped smile and a glance at Rader. "No, sir," she said, "Malcolm is great."

Laramie's chair was uncomfortable, an antique with little more than a flat, rubbery pad as a cushion. Sitting there, she got the full impact of the view: Gates behind his burly desk, an American flag on the wall above one shoulder, an acrylic portrait of the president behind the other. There were picture frames on the desk, facing his guests rather than him. Most showed a solemn Gates shaking hands with various important people.

"Sorry we haven't met before now," Gates said. "Where do you hail from, Laramie?"

"Hail? California, sir."

Gates snuck a glance at Rader, giving Laramie the sense that he'd sought a more sophisticated answer—maybe, she thought, he'd been asking about her collegiate alma mater when he'd used the word *hail*.

"Skip the 'sir.' Nor Cal or So Cal? That what they call it?"

"Some do," she said, "and I'd be So Cal. San Fernando, originally."

"And you've been with us how long now?"

"Three and a half years."

"Enjoying it?"

Laramie hesitated. "There've been some surprises," she said, "but I think I've got a pretty good handle on things."

"You enjoy it though?"

She looked at him. "Yes," she said. "I enjoy my work a great deal."

Gates picked up a photocopy of Laramie's report from his desk and said, "Regarding your analysis of the satellite photographs and accompanying intel, we appreciate your speculations, but I'm going to go ahead and say that we have a problem with your interpretation of the facts. We also have a problem with your style."

He looked her in the eye for a few long seconds. Laramie held his gaze.

"Our nation," he said, "is building a harmonious association—both economic and political—with our neighbors in the Far East. As an analyst assigned to that region, you ought to be able to recognize that the administration isn't going to jump to any conclusions that might strain this association. Further, as your manager, I must point out that *you* have jumped to conclusions by writing a report totally contrary to mandatory formatting and semantics guidelines. This is egregious and unacceptable behavior."

Laramie resisted the impulse to speak and instead merely sat in silence, the brown leather folder she'd brought with her squared off neatly in her lap.

"Tell you what," Gates said. "Why don't Rader and Rosen give a listen while you take us through your analysis. Perhaps if you walk us through your suppositions, we'll be able to assist in identifying your mistakes."

This, Laramie thought, would be how Peter M. Gates burns your ass.

She handed out a short stack of photocopies from her folder and came around to the side of Gates's desk, where she could face all three men. Then she pulled in some air and laid it out for them.

"During a routine review of satellite imagery," she said, "I discovered two full-scale invasion-simulation exercises, carried out jointly by the People's Liberation Army and Navy. These took place in Shandong province, where there is little to no Western presence. Further, it was clear from the timing vis-à-vis our satellite routes and schedules that the exercises were held in a manner designed to avoid American scrutiny. Because of the scope and method behind each of the operations, the conclusion—or, perhaps, supposition—I reached is that China is planning to militarily annex Taiwan in short order."

She set a hand on Gates's desk. Gates looked at her hand, so she removed it, and instead thrust it into one of the pockets of her suit pants.

"My review of additional intel—including HUMINT gathered by a highly reliable deep-cover officer—yielded the supporting evidence of a Shandong-specific secret military draft. Based on the minutes from recent meetings—obtained by a second source—I believe both the draft and the exercise to have been kept secret from the ruling State Council. The exercise appears to have been supervised by a senior PLN admiral, and I think it's only logical to conclude that PLA General and Vice Premier Deng Jiang had to be aware of the simulations and chose not to disclose them to his fellow State Council members."

She turned to face Gates.

"I understand, sir, the tone of the discussions between the administration and the PRC are positive. I certainly don't need to tell *you* that the current positive diplomatic environment emerged largely as a result of the public stance taken by China's premier—backed by the full council—that China may consider recognizing Taiwan's independence if the economic discussions with the United States proceed to the premier's liking. I took the position I took precisely because there appears to exist some degree of subversion of the premier's public stance, or at least a potentially incendiary hidden agenda, among what is probably at least three of the eleven members of the council's Standing Committee. General Deng has at least two staunch allies on the council, and they have a history of operating in tandem on issues he's pushing, so I'm making the assumption this is the case now as well."

She hesitated, debating whether it made sense to explain

further, then decided quickly that she'd said too much already. She smiled, nodded, and returned to her seat.

Gates watched her sit and waited patiently until she raised her eyes to look at him. When she did, Gates inclined his chin in the direction of Rosen. Rosen turned to face Laramie.

"Kindly revise your report," he said, "to reflect a less suspicious view of China's position on Taiwanese independence, including the removal of suppositional passages speculating as to the intent of the simulation exercises. The revised report will also need to be properly formatted."

Gates paid homage to Rosen's words with a solemn nod. "Following the revisions Mr. Rosen here has so eloquently spelled out," he said, "I would like you to draft a memo, which I will forward to all stations. One paragraph, please." He looked at her, and kept looking at her, and Laramie was beginning to feel self-conscious enough to consider objecting to his stare when she realized what it was he was waiting for.

She pulled a pen from her folder to take notes.

"The memo," Gates said, "should order an operational emphasis on the reporting of intelligence related to the international or extranational transport of military hardware and/or lethal substances with probable military use."

Gates stood. The others followed suit. Laramie finished her transcription, noting, as she wrote the text, that while it contained approximately zero substance, the memorandum he was requesting nonetheless redeemed her analysis. Eddie Rothgeb hadn't scripted *that* part of today's scene.

"I'll need both by noon on Wednesday," Gates said. "Good day, gentlemen. Laramie."

Laramie slid past Miss Anders, moral victory in arm. *Take*

that, Eddie, she thought. *He may well have burned my ass in front of my superiors, but at least the son of a bitch knows I'm right.* She tucked the folder beneath an arm and strode from the Agency's senior executive suite, merging into the usual foot traffic populating the seventh floor's main hall.

10

Ronnie bent down along the path, dug for a couple stones, and came up throwing.

"Cooper!" he said.

Cooper came sharply out of a deep sleep. He knew immediately who it was, and his first impulse was to ignore the provocation—pretend you're still asleep, out-wait the punk, and eventually he'll give up and leave.

The better idea, he thought, might be to lure him onto the porch. A little bit closer to the Louisville Slugger.

"Why don't you have your friends call on your bloody satellite phone?" Ronnie said. "It's six o'clock in the effin' morning!"

After a moment of nothing but the sound of the waves lapping the beach, Cooper rustled inside the bungalow.

"Sat phone," he said, "doesn't come with a secretary."

"Coffee, tea, or me, you fuck."

"Who is it?"

"Eugene Little, and he's flipped. Can't understand a bloody word he's saying."

Hearing, to his disappointment, Ronnie retreat down the stairs to the garden, Cooper grunted as he pulled himself out of bed.

All right, Eugene," Cooper said.

"Cooper, Jesus, where have you been hiding out!"

"What is it?"

"Highly carcinogenic," Eugene said, "that's what it is. Uranium. What do you think of that? Christ, I'm sure you knew it already. Knowingly subjecting me to the hazard."

Standing at the beach club phone, Cooper yawned.

"Uranium?"

"U-238 and U-235, according to this lab report I'm reading, and lethal levels of this particular substance just happen to be spread all over your corpse. Which means all over my lab, my hands, and Jesus, probably in my system already. I'm telling you, I'm expecting incremental bonus pay. It's always something with you."

"Right," Cooper said, starting to listen. "Get back to the, uh, U-238."

"U-238 and U-235, apparently a mixture commonly found in places like Chernobyl and Three Mile Island. Ring any bells? This pathetic bastard you mutilated was directly exposed to radioactive fuel rods. No surprise to you, I'm sure."

"It's a definite, the exposure came from fuel rods?"

"I sent out tissue samples. Hair follicle sections. Trying to find the cause of those burns. I got a phone call from the technician, and I tell you this guy was going crazy—"

"Like you."

"There's a fucking reason for it, Cooper: they checked for

radioactivity on the tissue sample and it tested off the scales. They did a second analysis—called me for authorization to do it, there are extra charges involved—and later confirmed massive quantities of uranium, they called it 'ninety-nine-point-three percent U-238,' on the torso and neck. 'Characteristic signature of nuclear fuel rods manufactured prior to 1987,'" Eugene said. "I'm reading from the report, obviously."

"That what killed him? Which came first?"

"You mean the uranium or the gunshots? I can't answer that. Incidentally, the ballistics report ID'd the bullets as nine-millimeter armor-piercing shells. American manufacture. I'll tell you, though, there was something odd about the time-of-death results. They were inconsistent—as though broad portions of the victim's body had deteriorated to an advanced state of necrosis well prior to his time of death."

Cooper found he didn't like the sound of *advanced state of necrosis*. He resisted the temptation to ask Eugene if this meant the kid was already a zombie at the time whoever it was who'd killed him administered the fuel-rod burn and fired the armor-piercing shells into his back. Maybe, he thought, I should ask him to check for traces of puffer fish and bouga toad venom. Or maybe not.

"I checked my textbooks, Cooper, and many of the symptoms displayed by your murder victim were consistent with extreme radiation sickness. The kind you get from direct exposure. You get vomiting of blood, rapid deterioration of internal organs, sores—like getting terminal cancer and dying from it in five minutes. It's fucking horrible, is what it is."

Cooper wasn't listening. "Mail me the lab results," he said. "I'll give it a thorough read."

"That's after we talk about the additional hazard pay."

"You're starting to get annoying, Ignatius. Put the results in the mail."

He dropped the phone on its cradle.

There were one hundred and ninety-two employees of the Central Intelligence Agency posted in the Caribbean. Since the agency's primary mission in the West Indies was to gather intelligence on the Castro regime, eighty-four of the one-ninety-two operated under some form of cover within Cuba itself. An additional forty-three worked in the Puerto Rico station, serving the dual purpose of Cuba operational support and Puerto Rico–specific intelligence gathering; a staff of thirty-seven, combined, served in Haiti, the Dominican Republic, Jamaica, the Bahamas, the Turks and Caicos Islands, and the Caymans. A small office in Grenada employed eight, and between the nations of Dominica, Martinique, St. Lucia, Barbados, Aruba, and Trinidad and Tobago, another fifteen held full-time positions with the firm. The U.S. Virgin Islands housed an office of four.

In the British Virgins, where there existed no justification whatsoever for an Agency presence, a single employee was stationed: the CIA's one hundred and ninety-second man. Classified as a case officer within the Directorate of Operations, the man served no strategic purpose, reported to no one, and virtually no one knew what he did, or that he existed at all. He was never subject to performance review, would never be denied his stipulated, periodic raises, and did not require authorization in order to be reimbursed for his expenses. For the sake of convenience, the man had decided to list himself in the internal company directory under an alias that held no secondary meaning other than the fact that he'd taken part of it from the character of the hero, and part of it from the actor playing the hero in *High Noon,* one of the only movies he remembered liking.

The name under which he chose to list himself was *W. Cooper.*

As the sole case officer in his territory, he was also, by default, chief of station. This had little import other than to place him on various distribution lists for memoranda, and to give him the ability, for any reason at all, to order research on virtually any topic from the army of analysts housed in Langley. Cooper took advantage of this from time to time, using the Directorate of Intelligence as a sort of public library. He'd always preferred to read nonfiction anyway.

Following Eugene's call, Cooper got an analyst on the phone in Langley and ordered a research packet on the subject of uranium—specifically, U-238 and U-235. The Agency functioned like a transoceanic vending machine, his request yielding a classified ninety-seven-page presentation, delivered via diplomatic pouch two days following his request.

When it arrived, he read the analyst's report on the beach near the Conch Bay Beach Club bar, accompanied by a steady flow of painkillers, claimed on local menus as an indigenous BVI concoction—rum, cream of coconut, pineapple and orange juices over ice, topped off with a dash of nutmeg. Reclined in a chaise lounge, he alternated reading and sleeping, based on the excitement level of the various sections of the report.

The type of uranium detected on Roy's body from the beach, 99.3 percent U-238 and 0.7 percent U-235, was non-weapons-grade uranium, obtained from naturally occurring ore and, as Eugene had indicated, most commonly used as the fuel source in older nuclear reactors. Reactors built during the past twenty years, the report said, generally utilized U-238/U-235 with the U-235 "enriched" to four or five percent. The analyst authoring the report added that while it was theoretically possible to build a bomb using enough 99.3/0.7 percent U-238/U-235, the weapon would be so crude, unstable, and of such low yield that, even if successfully engineered, it wouldn't release greater quantities of energy than an ordinary space heater.

Atomic or nuclear bombs, Cooper read, utilized more highly enriched uranium—either 90 percent U-235 or plutonium-239, a by-product of processed U-238. The report spelled out some specifics that put Cooper to sleep within minutes:

> Unregistered non-weapons-grade uranium, when detected, is not considered a violation of nuclear nonproliferation policies. Modern thermonuclear warheads obtain their explosive power from entirely different substances, namely a scientifically controlled fission of highly enriched uranium or plutonium, triggered by a contained conventional explosion and boosted by the secondary fusion of deuterium and tritium.

When he woke up, Cooper thought about that. He had always wondered how nuclear bombs were set off. Whether somebody working on a military base in Kansas could somehow make a mistake with a cigarette and wipe out half the country in the process. He called for and downed another painkiller, then read that exposure to non-weapons-grade U-238/U-235 had been documented to cause "extreme radiation sickness associated with direct and/or invasive contact, occurring during industrial accidents at nuclear power plants and, in fewer cases, reactor meltdowns aboard nuclear-powered submarines." The intel on personnel exposed to submarine reactor meltdowns was difficult to come by, the report said, since most such meltdowns resulted in an imploded submarine and an all-hands-lost scenario. Still, the report contained photos of a pair of bodies recovered from just such an incident. The victims pictured displayed burn wounds similar to those on the body from the beach.

Cooper tossed the DI report on the white sand of the Conch Bay beach and sat upright in the chair. He thought about what it might feel like, eating bouga toad and puffer venom, being buried alive, winding up sometime later in a nuclear power plant or submarine and surviving an otherwise fatal meltdown long enough to be shot multiple times in the back while leaping from a tall building and breaking every bone in your legs—while loaded up on heroin. Go for a swim, wash up on a jetty, get pawned off on a spiritually bankrupt alcoholic with a gambling problem, only to be examined by a murderous, fugitive breast-implant surgeon. Cooper figuring by now that Eugene had probably ordered the body incinerated, that poor bastard's journey concluding in a furnace one story beneath the streets of Charlotte Amalie—radiation going up the chimney and into the breeze. At least this time, he thought, no *voudoun bokor*'s going to pull the guy from the grave and put him back on the Haitian black-magic hamster wheel.

He thought that it wasn't too much of a stretch to put himself into this kid's head. His Central American friends might not have fed him any *coup poudre* potions, but he'd known a state of being about as close to hell as he figured life allowed, and didn't find being passed off as dead to the general public an entirely alien concept.

He and I share something, Cooper thought: not a fucking soul seems to have given two shits about either of us.

My problem, he thought, is that I've exiled myself to this island, where I've got nothing better to do, or too much better to do, or too much fucking time on my hands to do all the things that are better to do, since I know I'll get around to doing them all sooner or later. He couldn't think of any other reason a rational human being would do anything more in the case of the twice-dead zombie from Roy's beach—nothing besides tossing the ninety-seven-page DI report in the sack of garbage Ronnie collected daily from the club's wastebaskets, and going for a swim. Problem with doing that, he thought, is that the fucking ghost that Roy pawned off on me will wind up sticking around. He'll keep me from wreck-diving, bodysurfing, tanning, eating, boozing, and toking my way through the pain from this festering wound of mine, a pain I'll never kill—best I can do is medicate it, so the goddamn medication had better work.

And thanks to Roy Gillespie and his voodoo handoff, I'm getting no relief.

"Fuck," he said, pulled off his tank top, kicked away the Tevas, and went for a swim.

11

Knowing not a single decent combination of commercial flights existed for the Tortola-to-Haiti route, Cooper grudgingly pulled into Port-au-Prince aboard his Apache, navigating the squalor of the port at five knots. Sure, he mused, stick to the cruise ship docks, the container port, and it looked like any other Caribbean bay, but shoot for a slot to moor a private boat and you'd discover the truth: pick the wrong spot and the Apache would be hauling coke to Dade County within the hour.

He searched for the U.S. Coast Guard pier, which he knew to be in the general vicinity of the container docks, which themselves hadn't been used in years. The pier wasn't labeled, so it took him almost half an hour to find it. When he did, he coasted in sideways, needing no engine-thrust adjustments following his final throttle kick.

In the main building, he tried out some papers that said he was a Department of Homeland Security liaison working for the DEA. Throw enough agencies into the mix, he found, and you generated enough confusion or fear to get you in just about anywhere. He told the Coast Guard officer he was here to meet with a consular officer at Government House; the officer nodded at the papers and waved him through. Cooper figured he looked to the officer exactly the way the man expected a DEA man would—white polo shirt, worn blue jeans, blank, navy blue baseball cap. Or, he thought, maybe the guy lets anybody in who's stupid enough to come here.

He poked around for Port-au-Prince's version of a cab— an ordinary car, a *publique,* belonging to anyone, with the qualifying feature of a red ribbon dangling from the rearview mirror. Two blocks from the dock, he nabbed a Datsun minivan. He worked at ignoring the miserable conditions along the fifteen-minute ride through the city.

H. L. Dantier General Hospital didn't resemble any hospital Cooper recalled seeing: neither its stucco exterior or red-tile roof appeared to have been washed in the past ten years, and what might once have been called landscaping had evolved to unruly jungle. Cooper had a fleeting thought that Eugene Little would feel right at home here.

On the second floor, a receptionist asked him to be seated in an adjoining waiting room until a woman dressed approximately like a nurse came out to get him. Cooper couldn't place it, but there was something missing from her outfit: maybe it was the belt, or the shoes, but she looked incomplete, like an actress in a play afflicted by a poorly stocked wardrobe department. She brought him to a room that looked similarly incomplete relative to any doctor's offices he remembered visiting. Not that he'd been to any in almost twenty years.

After Cooper waited in the empty office for a little longer than twenty minutes, Dr. Reynold Benoit entered, Cooper thinking maybe he'd come from the restroom, the way the man held a rolled-up newspaper in his fist. Benoit ran about Roy's height; his skin was a rich ebony, and he wore eyeglasses with the wire frame visible only at the top of the lens, the kind Cooper had seen nowhere else except on Robert Redford in *3 Days of the Condor*.

"How you do, *mon ami*," Benoit said in a tinny, high-pitched voice that was alarmingly shrill. "As I told you on the phone, I'm here takin' this meeting, but you coming from Monsieur Petit-huit, or 'Ocholito' as he call himself him now in PR," he said, "that don't mean much. Not to me. Not anymore."

"Our boy Little-eight," Cooper said, "tells me you're an authority on something I'm interested in finding out about. So I don't really care what he means to you. I care more about you."

"One more thing, since we chattin' frank," Benoit said. "Maybe Petit-huit tell you, *peut-être pas,* but what I know don't come free."

Thinking his twice-dead zombie client was beginning to eat into his self-imposed monthly expense account allocation, Cooper handed Benoit an envelope holding three one-hundred-dollar bills. He'd figured on doing it the classy way, hide the money in an envelope—since he was, after all, visiting a hospital—but Benoit took it, tore the envelope open, and shamelessly counted the money a few inches in front of his face. He nodded and shrugged, unimpressed—but, Cooper thought, not quite to where the good doctor would think to kick him out. Perfect: he hadn't spent more than he needed to.

Benoit folded the money into a neat rectangle and slipped it into the breast pocket of his shirt.

"What you want?"

Cooper withdrew Eugene's snapshot of the brand from the pocket of his jeans and flipped it like a Frisbee onto Benoit's desk. Benoit peered at the picture when it landed but didn't reach for it.

"Amazing thing," Cooper said. "Cousin of mine dropped dead at a barbecue a couple years back. Everybody from both sides of the family attended the funeral. Watched his casket drop six feet down. It was a nice service."

Benoit looked at Cooper through the Robert Redford frames.

"Turns out," Cooper said, "couple weeks back, this same cousin of mine washed up on a beach looking like he'd lived a couple hard years since we saw him at the barbecue. Imagine that—somebody getting pulled out of his grave, brought back to life, used as some kind of drugged-up slave, then put out of his misery once he's outlived his usefulness."

Benoit picked up the picture and tossed it to Cooper's side of the desk. "Unless your family known for interracial marriage," he said, "you as full of shit as Petit-huit."

"Maybe so," Cooper said, "but I know from that brand that somebody here in the great land of Hispaniola fed my poor cousin some *coup poudre,* waited, hell, I don't know, maybe a few days, shot him up with *conconbre zombi,* and put him to work. Might have put him to work in a nuclear submarine too, but that's another story."

"Mon ami," Benoit said, "don't take this personally, but you one crazy motherfucker."

Cooper took the picture back.

"You saw the brand?"

Benoit looked at him. Taking his time.

"Oui," he said. *"Je l'ai vu."*

"Who uses it?"

Benoit leaned back in his seat and shrugged. "You know

as much as you tryin' to make me think you know," he said, "then I don't need to be tellin' you the wrong people hear I'm the one spilling the beans, there be more than three hundred dollars to be paid."

"Eternal damnation," Cooper said, "staved off only by the periodic sacrifice of live chickens?"

"Answer to the question you fishin' for is the Bizango sect of the Petro *voudoun*. Our meeting now be overwith."

Benoit stood, extending his hand. Cooper rose and took it but clasped the doctor's palm in a vice grip when the man tried to let go.

"Where do you suppose one could run across a *Bizango bokor*?" he said.

Benoit fought a wince then went with the flow, Cooper admiring the savvy with which Benoit pretended he had wanted all along to continue shaking.

"Valley behind the hills east of Pignon," he said. "Maybe this side of the DR, maybe not. Village called La Vallée des Morts."

Cooper clamped on. "How do I get there?"

"Easy."

"Fire away."

"*W-w-w,*" Benoit said, "dot-Mapquest-dot-com."

Cooper smiled tightly, gave Benoit his hand back, and, working his way out of the H. L. Dantier General Hospital, admired the impressive method by which Benoit had told him to go fuck himself.

He would actually have taken Benoit's dot-com advice had he brought his laptop along for the ride. There had, however, been no reason to bring it, considering he knew all but Port-au-Prince to lack even the hint of a cellular signal, and microwave transmissions compatible with Cooper's wireless modem to be entirely absent, islandwide. He detested logging on to the Internet with standard dial-up connections—waiting endlessly for a mechanical device to respond to commands was contrary to his character—and so he found a library.

Working off a recommendation from the cabbie who retrieved him from the hospital a mere hour after his call, he found a place that resembled an American library in the same way Benoit's hospital matched an American medical center. Even so, Pignon wasn't tough to pinpoint on the maps the place kept in stock: it looked to him to be five or six hours north of Port-au-Prince by way of a highway called Route 3. Cooper saw that with the exception of a single dotted line—the border with the DR—none of the maps provided by the Rastafarian working the back room charted anything for a forty-mile stretch east from Pignon, on either side of the border. The north-central plateau, as the maps told him the place was called, appeared to deserve nothing more than blank paper on the otherwise detailed drawings. There was one notable exception to this: on the smallest map he was given, a lone French word had been scribbled across the plateau.

Translating loosely, Cooper took the word to mean "badlands."

Cooper strolled around the corner from the library, took about ten minutes to find what he was looking for, knocked on a door, slipped the woman who answered a few words in his best Haitian Creole, flashed her 250 bucks in twenties and fifties, and with that amount, procured the rusted, lime green '74 Chevy pickup she and the family kept parked out front. He could hear the whoops and wails of capitalist glee through the missing passenger-side window as he leaned into a throttle lag you could count in geologic time, the dying engine block coughing as it started out but gaining momentum as it went, Cooper mashing the pedal to the floor.

He headed back into the city and found an open-air bazaar that, from all appearances, functioned as the local equivalent of a Wal-Mart. He maxed out a plastic bag with American candy bars, bottled water, local rum, a blanket and pillow, hiking boots, and a half-dozen T-shirts. It cost him eleven-fifty, Cooper figuring he was lucky the first merchant could break his twenty. For pit stop number two he hit the only gas station for miles, topping off the tank; despite encountering something of a language barrier with the station's owner, he also managed to procure a short, battered oil drum he'd spotted beside the station's twin mounds of trash bags. He filled the drum with fuel too, getting about thirty gallons in there, and secured it in the bed, utilizing, as a sort of poor man's bungee cord, an extra plastic bag he'd procured at the bazaar.

Thinking, *Richard Petty I ain't*, Cooper floored it out of the parking lot, keeping at it until the Chevy reached the point at which its pace registered on the speedometer.

12

The Chevy's radio actually worked, Cooper homing in on some spooky-funky Creole tracks with the radio's bent tuner knob until the reception faded about an hour north of the city. Route 3 was the shittiest, most potholed road he'd ever driven. He remembered seeing sinkholes take out quarter-mile stretches of dirt roads in a documentary he'd caught on the Raid Galouises cross-continent racing competition, but outside of that, Route 3 took the crown.

Further, he soon found you couldn't let your attention wane while navigating Route 3.

It happened twice. He saw nothing for eighty or ninety minutes—no man, no beast, no roadkill, just plain zero sign of life along an endless stretch of speed bumps. Then, suddenly, from around a blind turn, came a converted school bus. Bearing down on him like a bat out of hell, the bus hogged the whole fucking road, its driver playing chicken and ready to mow him down until Cooper skidded into the grass and took out a stretch of saplings to avoid the collision. For the second sneak attack, Cooper at least showed the good sense to career off the highway the minute the bus came into sight.

At dusk—losing faith in his ability to avert another transit bumrush—Cooper decided to heave to. He spied a suitable thicket and drove off-road straight into it, burrowing the Chevy into a bank of ferns. He turned off the tired old engine, threw on the emergency brake, got out, urinated, threw back two Snickers and half a bottle of rum, procured the blanket and pillow, lay back on the pickup's red vinyl seat, and zonked—sleeping like a baby despite the incessant whine of mosquitoes nosediving for his flesh.

He awoke a little before dawn, and after a lengthy struggle getting the Chevy back on the road, logged another five hours of uphill bus-dodging. The roadside foliage lightened, thinned, browned, then vanished altogether by the time he turned a corner and came into Pignon, a sudden rush of cheap housing and emaciated humanity on what had become a beige moonscape of multiple-drought-scarred dirt. Cooper made an immediate guess of forty grand—forty thousand starving Haitians in a shantytown assembled for less than one-tenth that many. He'd seen it before, but witnessing the open sewers, bloated stomachs, and families of twenty peering out at his Chevy from a single room was still a shock—and this, just on the main drag. He tried to recall some recent history to assign the blame—Baby Doc Duvalier's brutal regime yanking a few billion on its way out? A bullshit American economic embargo? Didn't matter—not to these people. Cooper thinking now that Eugene Little might have had it wrong: the body from Roy's beach didn't have to be doing any hard labor to show signs of malnutrition and abuse.

The kid just had to live here.

He ditched the pickup in a roadside rut and kept the keys

just in case, though he held little faith the truck would be there when he returned. Hell, he thought, I probably just made a donation—truck'll be somebody's home in a minute or two. Push it around the corner and you've got a roof ten times stronger than any I can see from here.

A rainbow-hued bus—no doubt one of the Route 3 battle group, he thought—roared to a stop a half block up the road, dropped some people, took on more, and sped past him in a burst of dust and foul exhaust. The shantytown express—cheapest way to travel slum-to-slum, Cooper thinking the bus offered something in the order of a sixty percent chance of death by head-on collision per trip.

He knew that people in a place like this would automatically tag him for one of maybe three classes of foreigner—missionary, doctor, or scientist. Anybody they'd seen before who looked like him had probably held such a role in society, so that was what they would assume him to be. Working with this notion in mind, Cooper hoofed it through the most crowded sections of the village, firing questions at anybody who didn't look like they wanted to roll him for his shoes. He asked if anybody knew the way to La Vallée des Morts, where, he lamely attempted to explain, he'd been told a rare rhinoceros iguana had been seen. He'd come to study it—to verify its existence. It didn't matter what he told any of them anyway, Cooper finding the Haitian Creole that had worked for him in Port-au-Prince didn't do squat for him here. He was ready to toss the pointless ruse and start asking about Bizango zombie-branding techniques when he saw the answer to his troubles coming down a hill behind a set of lean-tos.

A beanpole of a kid, exceedingly tall and exceedingly skinny, was trekking down the barren face of the hill—the

boy maybe seven foot one and a buck-fifty tops, Cooper figuring him for seventeen or eighteen years of age—and, out
here, where rain might not have fallen for two years, the kid
had *a half-dozen fish* dangling from a short length of twine
draped over one of his arms. Cooper thinking the minute he
saw the kid that what he ought to have working for him was
the kind of person tourists usually had to beat back with a
stick in the Caribbean: a guide.

And if he were planning on journeying through uncharted
Haitian badlands in search of a Bizango medicine man with
the aid of a guide, then it might not be a bad idea to do it with
a kid who's been out harvesting his limit of carp in the driest
patch of earth in the Western Hemisphere. With people, he
thought, starving right and left—hoping to score a quarter
cup of rice anytime in the coming year—this kid's got a
fucking sashimi dinner lined up for every night this week.

When the foreigner in the flowered shirt, the *blan,*
came up the hill to greet him, Alphonse knew he had been
wise to listen to the priest and prepare for this day. For
weeks now he had exercised vigorously and fished
doggedly—staying at the lake until sunset to harvest more
protein—even bragged to his peers of the dangerous journey
on which he would soon embark. Some of them scoffed,
ridiculing his piety, advising him instead to take the journey
most of the others took: get the hell off this diseased plain
and find something to steal, maybe deal some drugs with the
proceeds and live the good life in Port-au-Prince. Most of
Alphonse's crew had already done exactly that, though he'd
heard things about the good life they were leading in the urban slums. At least half of them were dead.

Alphonse was different. He listened to his elders, gave them respect, and had taken enough strength from their words to avoid the blasphemed fate of his peers. Alphonse was pious and committed, an open vessel through which Le Gran Maître could exercise His will. And now, with the *blan* in the flowered shirt coming up the hill, Alphonse was ready for his trial—he would embrace his journey into manhood and attain spiritual wholeness on the other side. He flung his catch of carp over a shoulder, allowing the fish to dangle behind his back, so he could offer a respectful posture for the stranger's approach.

It would be best not to alienate one of His messengers.

I'm looking for a guide," Cooper said in his half-assed Creole.

Standing on the incline, fifteen or twenty yards up the slope, he noticed that the two-dollar hiking boots he'd bought at the bazaar were already digging into his heels.

"Wi," Alphonse said. "I am your guide."

Cooper nodded. He hadn't expected much resistance. "Heard of a place called La Vallée des Morts? East of here. Could be over the border."

Alphonse stepped forward, and Cooper noted he was barefoot. It didn't look as though the kid was carrying a pair either.

"I've heard *cette* place," Alphonse said, working somewhere between busted English, ghetto French, and Haitian Creole. "My test is to take you there? *Si ça, c'est vrai,* I will that for you do. *M rele* Alphonse."

They shook hands.

"Nice meeting you, Alphonse," Cooper said. He didn't bother giving his own name. "How much?"

Alphonse froze, looking shocked that this messenger

from Le Gran Maître would offer to pay him. He appeared set to announce his refusal to accept compensation for such a journey when Cooper extended his hand and Alphonse saw in the hand a wrinkled mass of American fifty-dollar bills. Cooper readied to catch the kid's eyes in case they fell from their sockets.

"How about two-fifty now," Cooper said, "two-fifty when you get me there, and a bonus when we make it back—another two-fifty."

Succumbing to earthly weakness, Alphonse snatched the bills, feverishly counted them, and shoved the money deep into his pants. Then he stood very tall and smiled a crooked, yellow-toothed grin.

"I am your guide," he said.

"We hurry," Cooper said, "there may yet be a '74 Chevy with an empty navigator's seat you can do your guiding from."

Alphonse smiled, nodded, and followed Cooper down the slope, his faith implicit. He knew that along the way, Le Gran Maître would help him to understand the strange things this *blan* seemed to say.

13

Laramie hit the parking lot in Langley around seven-forty-five and made for the commissary, where the federal government had recently done her the favor of installing a Starbucks kiosk. The boondoggle had been struck, she guessed, over a fine meal between Starbucks CEO Howard Schultz and somebody like the junior senator from Schultz's home state of Washington—or, she thought, maybe Schultz had taken a meal with none other than Peter M. Gates himself. Either way, the kiosk managed to save Laramie fifteen minutes twice per day, the time it had formerly taken her to dart into Langley proper to grab a cup from the nearest off-campus Starbucks.

Now she only had to walk to the elevator.

She bought a grande latte and sweetened it with Equal. It was still a few minutes before eight when she settled at the desk in her office; this left plenty of time to rewrite the report, generate the cryptic memorandum, and deliver both to the DDCI's desk before he returned from his daily power lunch in the car service provided to the Agency's top brass.

No way on earth, Laramie thought, is Pete Gates doing bubkes with my report, revised or otherwise. His begrudged acknowledgment of her analytical accuracy, coming in the form of the requested memo, amounted to zero in terms of action. In retrospect, she decided Eddie Rothgeb had got it right after all—this was simply act two of the script, where the CIA chief, having burned the ass of his junior analyst for doing good work, proceeds to do no more than cover his own with a bullshit memorandum circulated to all stations—solely so that he could claim he acted on the intel were any shit to hit the fan. Otherwise, Laramie thought, all Gates had in mind was the tried-and-true asshole-manager's technique of burying important information the asshole-manager wants to keep handy for when he might someday need to pull the goods from the bottom of the deck. When it could help boost his political climb to—Christ, she thought, you're a three-term deputy director of central intelligence, what do you aspire to?

She polished off the revision, cranked out the memo, and slipped both into a priority classified delivery pouch.

Swallowing the last of her latte, Laramie decided to find out whether she'd been right. Her self-image needed the boost—or at least, she thought, if she did turn out to be right, then somebody needed to be doing something. Unless nobody cared about the independence of Taiwan.

Maybe nobody did—at least not here.

Laramie's badge granted her unrestricted access to routine intelligence from most of the Far East and Pacific Rim: satellite photographs, census figures, even some items from the field. Finding corroborating evidence in support of her theory on the pending invasion of Taiwan would be challenging, even if such evidence existed in the first place, but Laramie at least figured she had a pretty good sense of what to search for. The question was where to look.

Any general savvy enough to come to oversee the entire military of a semi-superpower, she thought, would—in planning to annex its neighbor—also prepare for resistance. International resistance. And if you had to fight more than one opponent, you'd want to have more than one player on your team. She could look for the same thing—unscheduled military exercises, a calling-up of army reserves, the whole clandestine effort of preparing for war without telling any of your international brethren—and it made sense to take her first look in nations ideologically aligned with the extremist members of China's State Council.

She'd start with North Korea.

Over the course of the day, she made sure to log her standard six or seven hours in the SATINT lab, keeping up with her assignments—the routine monitoring of recently generated satellite imagery, provincial immigration figures, CPI and GNP data for the PRC. Around seven, she got into the compare-and-contrast work, and by midnight had scanned her first swath of North Korea, beginning four months prior to the Shandong exercise. She got home early in the morning, having found nothing out of the ordinary.

Laramie followed the same routine for two days running, took one night off, then got back at it. At ten after midnight on her third evening of work, she had just completed a tenth fruitless search of the same patch of Korean land when the phone in her viewing cubicle gurgled. She tapped the speaker button.

"Mm-hm."

"Laramie."

Though Laramie preferred to label the current status of her relationship with Eddie Rothgeb as "professional-discussions-only," she still felt an odd sensation anytime he called her at work. She couldn't figure it out. Either something was telling her to oust him from her professional life too—*Laramie, make a complete break, you idiot*—or, alternately, maybe when they discussed professional topics it stirred memories of—

It's getting late, she thought.

"Hello, Professor."

"You weren't home," Rothgeb said. "I have your list. The e-mail addresses."

Laramie took a moment to realize he was talking about the list of e-mails for the members of the intelligence committees. When she realized it, though, she decided she didn't particularly care. The ass-burning ceremony, as well as her subsequent zero-sum evidence hunt, had reduced her ambition somewhat.

"Just so you know," she said, "things played out about as you predicted. And I'm not finding any—well, corroborating entities, so to speak."

"Meaning you're looking," he said. There was a hesitation. "You know, you need to be—heck, I'm not sure I want to hear about it."

"You don't."

"I'll fax it to your home."

Neither of them said anything. Laramie's eyes darted from region to region on her wide-screen workstation monitor, fingers plugging away at the keyboard. The SATINT photos flicked past like a deck-shuffle on a slot-machine poker game.

The sound of a clearing throat came from the speaker phone. "I'm sure I don't need to tell you," he said, "but when you send anything—"

"I know, Professor," Laramie said.

"You understand what I'm saying?"

Thinking that the tapped phones at CIA made for awkward conversations, but *come on, Professor,* Laramie said, "I know I can't do what you're warning me against doing. I'll have to be inventive. Origination-wise, you might say."

"Right," he said. "I'll fax you the list."

The speaker light went dark on her telephone console.

Laramie pulled up another week of SATINT, waited for the thumbnails to load, and got back to the visual deck-shuffle. Selecting from the thumbnails based on date and region, she enlarged the grids she found interesting or inscrutable, flipping past those she judged to be irrelevant. Laramie the globetrotter, she thought, spanning the world with keyboard and mouse. She zipped down with the Zoom command. Examined an endless succession of trees, houses, lakes, military bases, airports, factories, farms, streets. Mostly she didn't need to push in any closer than a city block; she could see all she needed in images covering a few dozen square miles of real estate. Flipping, clicking, her eyes drooping, Laramie becoming increasingly pessimistic there would be any—

A small break in the clouds looked vaguely familiar.

She zoomed in twenty times, then fifty, then a hundred, recentering the image as she went. At three hundred times the standard viewing magnification she was able to make out through the cloud break—where pockets of mist still made the images on the ground difficult to isolate—a column of tanks and army trucks.

She cautioned herself that this could have been anything. During any given second of the day, for instance, on every day of the year, she knew there to be a U.S. military convoy transporting something somewhere on one American highway or another. Perhaps the same was true for North Korea.

Except, she thought, *this is exactly what I found in Shandong two days before the exercise*. In the same exact sort of weather she had found on this particular day in North Korea.

She checked the log for the photograph she was viewing and saw that she was looking at film from April 3, two months earlier than the Shandong exercise. She bookmarked the photograph and moved ahead a day, then two, then three, checking the same area, about five hundred square miles, Laramie aware that any military organization with even a limited intelligence-gathering wing would know when these satellite passes came and accordingly, if they wanted, could hide what they were doing. That's how she'd caught the PLA simulation in full swing—by snatching some pictures from a private satellite, shot from a lower angle and on a different schedule. And there it had been: a full-scale imitation of a sea-to-land invasion, staged near the city of Qingdao, on the Yellow Sea. The invasion, of course, perfectly mimicking a PLA takeover of Taiwan.

Back on her Korea shots, April 7 now, fifty miles north of where she'd spotted the convoy—*and look at that,* she thought. *The same damn thing as Shandong.* Another military exercise. Ghostly outlines of tanks in the field. Bright spotting—probably mortar fire or antitank guns—blooming in the fog beneath the thinner sections of cloud cover.

Laramie zoomed all the way in and still wasn't able to see much. This was the kind of thing that the North Korea analyst wouldn't ordinarily spot; with the wider angles the section analysts reviewed in the course of their routine coverage, there would be little to see here, even under intense scrutiny, outside of brighter-than-normal clouds in a remote and otherwise irrelevant part of the country.

But know what to look for, and you find it in three nights of lab work.

Who else, she thought, had signed on here? If, she cautioned herself again, it was anything at all. Which it probably wasn't. It was likely she'd stumbled across a pair of military exercises with no real-world meaning, occurring in the same time period only coincidentally. But spend two weeks instead of three nights, and who else would she find—

She looked at the time stamp on her monitor: 2:39 A.M.

Time, she thought, to leave. As long as she was pulling images that fell within the jurisdiction of her clearances, she knew she was on solid ground—under the inspirational leadership of Peter M. Gates, long hours were increasingly common in what she understood to have been, before his reign, a clock-punching culture—but it was always a variation in one's pattern that tripped the alarms, and she didn't exactly pull all-nighters as a matter of course.

She logged off.

Shuffling across the parking lot—which, as always, remained half-full—it occurred to Laramie that perhaps, for once, she might consider following Agency protocol. Perhaps, having found this second military exercise, she should now discuss the discovery with her immediate supervisor and, with his permission, craft a properly formatted summary utterly lacking in editorial comment and leave it at that.

If she did, Eddie Rothgeb would be pleased.

Before she found her pillow, she found Eddie's fax. Handwritten, and scrawled in a rudimentary code on a single sheet with no cover page, the document contained three names—or at least three sets of initials Laramie took to represent names—and matching phone numbers and e-mail addresses. Alongside each set of initials, Rothgeb had scrawled a pair of parentheticals:

A.K. (NC) (S)

Given her sleep deprivation, it took Laramie a few minutes to translate, but it didn't take a rocket scientist to crack the code. (S) indicated a senator; (NC) was the state designation. As was the case with the majority of her Beltway bureaucrat colleagues, Laramie maintained a loose familiarity with the names of the more prominent politicians on the Hill, so it was fairly clear to her the initials A.K. stood for Alan Kircher, the Republican senator from North Carolina.

She took a moment and identified the other names on the list, but for Laramie there was no contest: if she decided to go for broke and try, by means of a Deep Throat e-mail, to compel Pete Gates & Co. to take her findings onward and upward, then Alan Kircher was her man. She'd seen him, seen too much of him, on *Hardball, On the Record, Hannity and Colmes,* and maybe sixteen or seventeen other prime-time cable opinion shows. She did not exactly share his political ideology, presuming he had one outside of his evident pursuit of under-the-table handouts from the military-industrial complex, but if you want somebody who'll take a different view of your findings—different from the administration's party line as strode by Peter M. Gates and his staff—well, she thought, I suppose Eddie knew what he was doing, didn't he, putting him on the list.

It occurred to her, collapsing in bed, that she was being idiotic even *entertaining* the notion of popping the esteemed Senator Kircher a note. Her newfound inclination to follow protocol was the way to go. Even if she and her theories of "rogue factions" were right, what business was it of hers how and which decisions were made by the leaders of the country? Peter M. Gates's appointment had been approved by a majority vote of the U.S. Senate nearly a decade and a half ago, while she, meanwhile, had gleefully secured her

junior analyst position just under four years back by successfully filling out a copy of the CIA summer internship
form posted on the bulletin board outside of Eddie
Rothgeb's office.

Lemme give you some career advice, Pete, she thought:
Why don't you stick your neck out, roll the dice, and risk your
twenty-year career on the speculative whim of a junior analyst armed with an undergraduate political science degree!

She managed to set the alarm for eight-thirty before
plunging into the bliss of unconscious stupor.

14

The '74 Chevy got them up the mountain in eight hours, Cooper getting a workout cranking the wheel, the pickup climbing the roadless slope fifty times faster than Alphonse could have taken them on foot, but still doing no better than an hour or two per mile. Cooper tacked the Chevy back and forth, thinking if he tried for a more direct course straight uphill, the smallest bump would send them into a backward tumble. From time to time Alphonse would point and mutter a few words; Cooper used his gestures like a compass, always heading, as the looping tacks progressed, toward Alphonse's magnetic north. The needle on the truck's temperature gauge pegged the red zone for the last four hours of the ride, but the truck held out.

Out here on this barren hillside, Cooper kept coming back to one question: where had the kid caught the fucking fish?

At dusk Alphonse motioned frantically for him to stop. Cooper didn't particularly need the prompt, as he could see through the windshield, directly before them, that the earth seemed simply to end. He eased the Chevy to the edge, cranked hard right, and gave himself a view out the driver's-side window.

He could see, even in the twilight, a downward grade that looked to him like the view from the top of an Olympic ski jump. A few clicks down the slope he spotted a patch of green—had to be the lake, or the river, he thought, where Alphonse had caught the fish. Long fucking way to walk, he thought, for six skinny fish.

"We walk from here be go," Alphonse said, stating the obvious in his triple-broken dialect. "The village you looking for? *C'est-li là,* down that bottom."

Cooper threw the Chevy in reverse, backed into a thicket of dead brush, killed the engine, got out, pissed over the edge of the slope in a high arcing stream, returned to the pickup, dug into his bag, and came out with a bottle of rum. He noticed Alphonse staring, befuddled, the kid having watched his every move.

"How 'bout a highball, Kareem?" he said, and reached out to offer his guide a sip from the rum bottle. When Alphonse didn't move a muscle, Cooper cracked the seal and took a swallow. "Cab's yours," he said, and opened his bag to offer Alphonse something from the selection of candy bars and bottled water. Hungry enough to overcome his reluctance, Alphonse chose a pair of candy bars. Cooper pulled out a pair of T-shirts to use as a pillow and climbed into the bed of the pickup with a Milky Way, some water, and the rum. When he'd consumed all three, he leaned through the rear window of the cab, where Alphonse, still befuddled, remained.

"Sleep tight," he said. He rolled around until he got comfortable and dozed off, staring at a sky full of constellations bright enough to make the notion of a telescope seem absurd.

They spent a full day on the downgrade, Cooper seeing insufficient plant life to fuel a brush fire until they came to Alphonse's lake, a verdant swatch of plateau spanning, by Cooper's guess, a quarter of a square mile. The green appeared to be fed by a spring—a trickle of water tumbling downhill inside a narrow crevasse—looking to Cooper like a scale model of your average whitewater rapids, the creek about two feet across where it pooled, six or seven inches wide where it ran at speed. Wordlessly, Alphonse strode past the miniature lake and led him downhill. The foliage dried up and vanished again within yards. Cooper knew how it worked: dry as a bone for a few years; then a hurricane swept through, and the floods that followed tore every hint of vegetation from the slope, leaving even less to dry out over the succeeding years of drought.

They followed the creek as it zigzagged downhill, Cooper's toes bruised and blistering inside his Port-au-Prince-issue hiking boots, the descent taking its toll. He checked his watch at two-thirty; it was bright and hot, a classic Caribbean heat but without the breeze, at least 105 degrees and sickly humid. Soon the pain of his blistering toes began to subside, and before he realized what this meant, Cooper looked up from the backs of Alphonse's feet to observe the fact that they'd reached the base of the grade.

Alphonse pointed into the hazy distance, Cooper noticing the kid did not appear remotely fatigued. Following his finger, Cooper could see, maybe two miles off, in a greener section of the plain they'd just reached, a settlement. There was a patchwork of farmlands, a few dozen shanties, the same creek dribbling its way through town; there were no visible roads coming in or out, just the half-green village, a bone-dry forest behind it, and the endless brownish landscape rising in all directions from the valley.

The thing that appealed most to Cooper about this new-found testament to human survival was the hope that he'd be able to round up a watering hole, maybe find some unique local spirits—no doubt primitively distilled, he thought, but still home-brewed and pure.

He found it in the form of an open-air shack on the outskirts of town, literally a lean-to with a counter crafted from a slab of driftwood, Cooper wondering where you found driftwood in the desert. There were a couple of stools standing against the slab, with some tables and chairs filling out the rest of the place. Four locals populated the joint, pretty much just hanging around—two at a table, one at the bar, and the fourth behind the driftwood slab. Maybe serving. All four appeared dressed for farmwork.

He got the evil eye immediately, Cooper feeling like a drifter coming into the saloon in a Clint Eastwood movie, only with bleeding toes and blistered feet. He ignored the looks and took a stool at the bar. Alphonse followed his lead as he shrugged off his backpack and settled on the seat, Cooper trying to remember a good line from an Eastwood film to offer these boys, but it'd been too many years since he'd owned a television. He opted for the mock-idiotic-tourist routine instead, though he considered it might be fair to say he was in fact an idiot for even coming here at all.

Nodding at Alphonse, he said in drawling English, "Anything they got. Whiskey, rum—maybe something they make themselves."

Alphonse, playing the role, jerked his chin at the bartender and banged out a stretch of his patented triple-broken dialect.

The bartender was bigger than the others, his skin a cup of strong coffee, forehead a little taller than you found on other West Indians, so that it gave the impression of a receding hairline. He smoked a cigarette with a long ash that dangled lazily from his lips. Everybody in here, Cooper realized, was smoking. He guessed the latest in filtered low-tar brands weren't readily distributed in La Vallée des Morts. Secondhand smoke, going to kill him.

The bartender pushed off from the post he'd been leaning on. He didn't touch the cigarette in his mouth, leaving the ashes to fall. He pulled an unlabeled bottle of clear liquid from a box.

"Deux?"

Alphonse hesitated but forged forth. *"Wi, deux,"* he said, and the bartender put a pair of paper Dixie cups on the driftwood slab and filled them before returning to his post.

Cooper looked around the place and got the other six eyes staring back at him, big, white orbs, sunk deep into dark, weathered sockets. The two at the table were young and sinewy, maybe even tough; clearly annoyed at the interruption, these boys formed the epicenter of the evil glare. Cooper put them in their early twenties. The guy seated at the bar was older, closer to fifty, with a short, gray beard that resembled lint balls stuck to his chin. Hunched over his drink, he stared back at Cooper with something like fascination.

Cooper figured the appearance in this bar of a pale, well-fed *blan* wasn't much different from a moose or a bear coming off a yacht and sliding up to the bar at the Conch Bay Beach Club. He saw no need to consider the communal evil eye they were giving him anything more threatening than a symptom of shock.

He dug into his backpack and pulled out the props he'd stowed there, the driftwood slab as good a place as any to take them for a test drive.

On a white sheet of paper, he'd sketched a depiction of the brand. He'd folded the rest of the sheet of paper behind the image, so that he had a rectangle about the size of a four-by-six photograph with the sketch residing within the borders. Also in the stack of goodies he pulled from the backpack was the full set of Eugene Little's Polaroids he'd snatched on his way out of the morgue—the shot of the brand on the victim's neck, a profile of the poor kid's face, and a head-and-shoulders portrait too, Eugene's photography pretty good in that it made the body appear half-alive. Sort of like a mug shot of the kid, only with his eyes closed. The face was bloated and pale, and infested with sores, but it still gave the general impression of the boy's appearance: if the chain-smoking bruiser serving the firewater in Dixie cups had known the kid in life, he'd also know him as captured in death by Eugene's specialized form of photography.

Cooper set a ten-dollar bill on the slab beside the first of the props—the sketch. He caught the bartender's eyes before jerking his chin at Alphonse.

"Ask him to come over again."

This time it took nothing in the way of a prompt from Alphonse to get the bartender to approach. Thinking, Ah, the universal language, Cooper said, "Ask him if he's seen this brand before. There a *bokor* in the neighborhood might be using it?"

Alphonse semitranslated. Cooper watched as the bartender's eyes drifted only briefly across Alphonse, the man keeping his focus on the ten-dollar salary he intended to earn. To influence him a bit, Cooper stuck a finger onto the folded paper, pointing at the sketch.

"This, here," he said as Alphonse finished the translation.

The bartender's eyes worked in their sockets, adjusting from money to sketch. They then ran up to Cooper's face, back down, and, with a lightning-quick snatch, the bartender jerked the money off the bar and pocketed it. He looked at Cooper again, this time with a degree of defiance. Then he fingered the sketch and turned it in a short circle before pushing it back across.

"*Non,*" he said. "*Mwen regret sa.*"

Then he went back to his post. His cigarette had burned down and out, so he fired up another with a paper match and sucked at it, once again leaving the cigarette lodged permanently between his lips. Cooper noticed that there were now grubby fingerprints on the paper holding his sketch.

He took out a second ten-dollar bill, popped it straight, and laid it on the bar in the same manner as before. He pulled the sketch from the bar, tried rubbing off the fingerprints, failed, returned the sketch to his pocket, and came out with the head-on mug shot.

He said, "*Ou ne konnen le témoignage des Bizango, eh?*" then put the picture on the slab. "Then how about my cousin here—he ring any bells?"

Alphonse regarded him with the same befuddled expression he'd displayed in the pickup.

The bartender came over and snatched the money, but when he tried to finger the photograph, Cooper pulled the picture back.

"*Touchez-pas,*" he said.

The bartender snorted, looked at the photograph, shook his head, said, "*Non,*" and stood his ground.

Cooper nodded and popped off another ten. Alphonse looked like his head was going to explode if he saw another bill hit the slab.

"Maybe he could tell us," Cooper said, pulling Alphonse back into the exchange, "if there's anyplace to stay around here. Couple of beds, even some soft earth and a roof. Hot meal wouldn't be bad, would it?"

Alphonse nodded in appreciation of what he understood Cooper to have said—the first sign of fatigue Cooper had noticed in the kid, in any form, for the duration of the journey—and gave the bartender some version of what Cooper had told him. The bartender retrieved the third bill and answered the question; Alphonse semitranslated his response, which Cooper had already understood perfectly well.

"Five houses down," Alphonse said, "*il dit* there be an old lady *là-bas,* she give the beds. Pay that lady the money you be paying here, *il dit* could be she cook supper *aussi.*"

Cooper put his props in a pocket, tossed back whatever the bartender had poured into the Dixie cup—it tasted like sake—and winked at Alphonse.

"Come on, Kareem," he said. "Let's go seek some room and board."

The old woman recommended by the bartender offered them a vegetable stew, which, while it tasted like bat guano, Cooper gladly consumed after the exhausting trek down the mountain. Room and board set him back another twenty—probably ten times what he needed to pay, but Cooper thought he'd keep the free-spending tourist charade going. He'd long since learned that playing a role that wasn't too much of a stretch for him—a foolish honkie spending *beaucoup* money—was about as good a way to elicit knee-jerk overreactions from native West Indians as any. Typically it also went a good way toward ensuring his well-honed interpersonal skills were usefully underestimated.

Noshing on the foul-tasting stew, Cooper swallowed hard, regretting that he hadn't procured a bottle of the bartender's mellow Dixie cup brew before leaving the bar. He could have used it to wash down the food.

They slept fully dressed on a bed of something like straw in the woman's backyard, Cooper keeping his Browning tucked under the belt of his khaki shorts. He slept on his side. They had the blankets from Cooper's backpack, but who needed them; it might have dropped to ninety-five for the night, but there still came no breeze. Cooper listened as he slept, something he'd learned to do a long time ago and didn't have much use for any longer, at least outside of the times Ronnie was in the mood for practical jokes. He hoped he wasn't too rusty—get caught in a deep sleep while an angry farmer tried to off him for his wad of ten-dollar bills.

The first bite didn't come until morning, when a small, wiry guy with the same deep eye sockets as the fellas from the bar gang arrived at the old woman's house. When Cooper and Alphonse came out around six-thirty, the guy was already waiting for them, seated on a box the old woman used as a chair. Cooper was ready for the guy to make a move—didn't look like it but he was, following Alphonse out of the shack—but there wasn't anything to be ready for, at least not yet. The wiry guy said a few words to Alphonse that Cooper couldn't hear, and Alphonse told Cooper that someone wanted to see him, and if they went with the guy he'd take them there.

Cooper agreed and brought up the rear as they walked into the heart of the village and on through to the side nearest the dead-brown forest. It was about a ten-minute walk. The guy concluded his assignment by delivering them to a shanty that, while still small, looked more like a house than any of the other dwellings in town. It was the last building this side of town, set back from the other homes with an actual yard. Cooper could see that their old friend the creek cut through the backyard of the place.

The escort opened the door and stood aside to usher them in. Cooper stood for a moment in the doorjamb to let his eyes adjust, the transition a little difficult as he came inside. Once his eyes had made the shift, he could see that the shades inside the house were drawn. Only one or two lights were burning, Cooper thinking the light must be coming from candles until he heard the hum of an engine running somewhere out back, took another look at the lights, and saw that they featured sixty-watt bulbs in sockets with the lamp shades missing.

Whoever it is who's summoned us to his throne, Cooper thought, he's running electricity off a Honda generator and has the shades drawn so he can show off. Imagine that—a guy so rich he can afford to run electric lamps inside during the bright daylight. Cooper wondered where the guy got his fuel.

There were shelves built into each of the walls, loaded with handcrafted talismans and ornaments—basically a bunch of junk, but junk with one recurring feature: carved into or stamped upon each of the items, Cooper could plainly see a depiction of the mark somebody had branded onto the neck of the body Cap'n Roy had been so kind as to palm off on him.

There were some books on the shelves too, titles he couldn't make out, a couch and chairs, orange shag carpet, and in the center of the room, a metal desk of the sort used by Cooper's fifth-grade math teacher. Behind the desk sat a man.

The man was thick, bald, and bearded, his skin a notch or two lighter than that of his fellow citizens. The robe he wore looked African but probably wasn't, his earlobes were adorned with at least a dozen earrings each, and he was busy laying upon Cooper his own version of the village's patent-pending evil eye. At length, the man jerked his chin toward the couch and chairs.

Cooper sat, choosing the couch. As he did he observed that as with Manny's old buddy Ocholito, the man behind the desk had fingernails that were painted in high-gloss black. Alphonse took one of the chairs; Cooper could see the kid was spooked. Their escort closed the front door and stood inside with his back against it.

"We never seen you before," said the man behind the desk. He spoke in unaccented English, his voice deep, making Cooper think of Barry White on some old Motown television special. The accent made it sound like the guy had been born in Ohio, or Pennsylvania.

Cooper said, "Correct."

"We don't get too many strangers 'round here."

Alphonse flicked his eyes at Cooper, then back at the man behind the desk. Cooper thought about what it meant, this being the richest guy in town, the only guy with painted walls and fingernails plus a backyard generator, undoubtedly the only guy speaking fluent English on top of it. Pulling his mug shot photo, Cooper stood, walked over to the desk, dropped the picture on it, and came back to the couch and sat.

"Friend of yours?" Cooper said.

The man's eyes flicked over to the snapshot, lingered, then refocused on Cooper.

"What it is you looking for, you better off looking somewhere else," he said.

Cooper, getting tired of this room and the people in it, met the man's dead-eyed stare with a bankrupt look of his own, thinking, Match this thousand-yard stare, priest-man. Cooper could feel Alphonse's nervous energy beside him.

"Are you familiar with the person in that photograph?"

"I don't know nothing 'bout what you asking."

"You're sure."

"We have nothing for you," the man said, "and you are not welcome to remain here."

Cooper nodded, rose, crossed the room, retrieved the picture from the desk, and returned it to his pocket. Standing beside the desk, he could see a few things that might otherwise have been hidden from view: papers, pens, pencils, a file drawer unit, what looked like a key-locked fire safe, a cellular phone—older, bulkier, but still a cell phone out here, at least seventy-five miles from the nearest tower. Its charger was plugged into an extension cord Cooper figured hooked up to the generator out back.

While he found this stash of goodies mildly interesting, Cooper figured it wouldn't do any good to ask any more questions of the semimute Bizango medicine man. Anyway, he'd stirred up all the trouble he needed to—all he had to do now was hang around and wait for the reaction.

He tapped the desk, said, "All right, Barry. Live slow and easy now," turned, and walked to the front door, where he made sure to brush his shoulder against the wiry escort who had brought them here.

"Guide me out of here, Kareem," he said on his way out the door.

15

Cooper showed the mug shot to every visible man, woman, and child in town. It wasn't a pleasant sight, what people saw in that picture, but Cooper didn't much care. All the better: if somebody knew who the man had been in life, chances were Cooper could catch the look of horror on the face of even the most secretive citizen of the Valley of the Dead, confirming his suspicions while he figured out what to do about Barry the witch doctor with his lightbulbs, cell phone, and generator. Alphonse did whatever translating Cooper needed, Cooper watching the kid grow more uncomfortable with every encounter. If any of the locals they were meeting recognized the person in the picture, they did a good job of hiding it; maybe, Cooper thought, they were just disgusted with him showing the picture around and didn't want him to know whatever it was they knew—if they knew anything at all.

He began to notice the handful of local men following them around, keeping their distance but watching them just the same. Cooper wasn't sure whether they were following for surveillance, intimidation, or robbery purposes, but he assumed it was a little of each. Sure, he'd flashed those big, fat ten-dollar bills around, but Barry the witch doctor was probably practiced at scaring people out of their wits with his evil eye and collection of zombie-branded trinkets. Maybe, Cooper thought, Barry's M.O. included dispatching a team of shadow-men, the very presence of whom implied that zombification couldn't be far off.

They could watch him all they wanted, but if the toughs came too close he'd consider redrawing the radius of personal space they were being granted by way of the FN Browning.

It was late in the day, nearing dusk, when a young woman approached. Cooper put her around sixteen; she was emaciated like most of the town's other citizens, rough and sinewy, but there was something about her—watching her shuffle across the dusty trail in bare feet and a dress that looked like something medieval farmworkers might have worn, Cooper felt a surge of sexual excitement. He experienced the odd sense of suspecting he knew what she tasted like, could imagine with no effort the scent of the body oils in her hair; as his mind was picturing her worn fingernails scratching at his back, he decided to rein it in and veer off the path the pervert in him appeared to want to take.

She was next to him now, head down as though in shame.

"Bonswa," she said.

Cooper skipped Alphonse. *"Bonswa."*

She asked if it were true—that they were the men showing the picture around. Alphonse started to translate, but Cooper waved him off and handed the girl the picture.

"Wi," he said. *"Sekonsa. C'est ça, là."*

Alphonse had a look on his face that made it pretty clear the journey he'd envisioned was more akin to the trek over the mountain. Not this.

The girl stared at the photograph for a long while. She seemed to be examining the picture the way most everyone had, lost in a kind of mild confusion. There was the possibility that many of them had never seen a photograph, but after his glimpse of the cellular phone in the witch doctor's house, Cooper found some difficulty buying that explanation.

"*Wi, c'est li,*" she said, and handed the picture back. Still looking confused.

"Hold on," Cooper said. "That's him? Who?"

Alphonse watched.

"*Li rele Marcel,*" she said.

Cooper became more aware that they were standing out in the open. "Who—who was Marcel?"

"*Mwen fiancé,*" she said.

"You're sure? It must be difficult to tell," he said, Cooper trying to adjust to the local version of Creole, "looking at that picture."

"Hard, yes," she said. "I don't understand. How can you have that picture?"

"It's a photograph," Cooper said, "a picture, taken with a camera—"

"Yes, I understand a picture," she said, shaking her head, frustrated, "I mean where did you make it? It is not possible."

Cooper looked at Alphonse for a moment. The kid was shifting his weight from foot to foot. He stopped when he saw Cooper looking at him.

"Why not?"

"Where," she said. "Where did that picture happen?"

Cooper said, "On a beach. On Tortola. In the British Virgin Islands. A few hours from here by boat."

She started shaking her head.

"*Non?*" Cooper said. "*Poukisa?*"

She looked at him, had to look way up, and Cooper saw a

glint of green in her otherwise brown eyes. "Because he is dead," she said.

Cooper said, "Well, yes," relieved, having felt some trepidation at the prospect of breaking this news to her. But if she were right, and the body from Roy's beach had been her late fiancé, it all got rapidly very complicated.

"Look," he said. "You sure about this? You're sure that's Marcel."

He held out the snapshot, but she didn't take it again, only shook her head in the affirmative and said, "Wouldn't you be?"

Cooper blinked, appreciating the sophistication of the response.

"How did you know he was dead?"

"How? Because I watched his funeral."

Cooper thought about this for a moment and decided to give one more shot at seeing whether the scenario he wasn't too comfortable acknowledging could be eliminated.

"Listen," he said. "Do you understand where Tortola is?"

"No. It is not possible you saw him somewhere else. He has never been anywhere else. He was born here, he lived here, he died here. He never went to this place, this Tortola."

Cooper stood there, out in the middle of main street in the Valley of the Dead, taking a moment to think about this. Alphonse had begun fidgeting again. Cooper reached out and wrapped his fingers gently around the girl's arm, just below the shoulder.

He said, *"Kouman ou rele?"*

She gave him half a smile and said, "Simone."

"You were there when they buried him?"

"Wi," giving him those brown-green eyes.

"Could you take us there?" he said. "Can you show me his grave?"

Painted on a stake, driven into the earth, was a name: MARCEL S.

Just the S.—no last name. Cooper wondered if these people even used last names. If not, perhaps there had been another Marcel in town, or, as in Asia, the citizens of La Vallée des Morts might put the surname first, S. being short for his given name.

Simone was pointing at the stake.

It was one grave among a few dozen. They were in a clearing located about a quarter mile into the petrified forest, here in the graveyard that told him nothing about the body from Roy's beach other than this: if the corpse beneath the stake was actually the kid named Marcel S., then the girl was wrong—it hadn't been Marcel on the rocks in Road Town.

He found the concept that occurred to him next disturbing.

Leaning down, he thanked Simone and told her he was sorry about her loss. He told her he'd be leaving town now. Simone looked at him, her brown-green eyes as confused as when she had first seen the picture.

"Mési," she said, turned, and padded back to town.

Cooper watched until she vanished behind a grouping of trees. Then he counted the rest of the cash in his wallet—just under eight hundred bucks—pulled out ten fifties, and handed the five hundred dollars to Alphonse.

"Your fee," he said.

Alphonse eyed the cash, but remained still. *"Poukisa?"* he said. "Two-fifty when I bring you this place, yes? The rest—not yet, *non?"*

"Time for you to go home." Cooper found the key to the pickup and shoved it and the money into Alphonse's rail-thin abdomen. "Take the truck. It'll make the trip a little easier on the way down. Drive back and forth, all right? Zigzag."

Alphonse stood his ground.

Cooper said, "You understand?"

Alphonse did not say anything.

"I know you're a religious man, and a religious man should never have to participate in what I'm about to do."

Cooper shoved the money against the kid's concave belly. Alphonse took the money and the key, then counted out two hundred and fifty dollars, handed Cooper the remainder— including the key—and straightened his long spine.

"I am your guide," he said.

Cooper took the money and key from Alphonse's palm, thinking that now, not only would he have to do what he'd already planned on doing, but he would also need to keep an eye on Alphonse while he was at it. He would need to pay close attention, considering the witch doctor's gang was following them around—make sure Lew Alcindor here didn't guide his own way into the afterlife before they made their way back up the hill.

"If that's the way it has to be," Cooper said, "then follow me, big guy."

Cooper didn't like the moon being out, but he and Alphonse were almost done, Cooper finishing the last of it. It was a shallow grave, about three feet deep, and they'd had to scrape their way down with whatever sticks and stones they could find. With the moon out, anybody watching could see them doing it, digging up the grave of Marcel S. in the middle of the night, but to Cooper there was no other way, not once Simone had told him her man was buried here.

He scooped some dirt from the edge of the coffin. They'd

cleared the soil from above the thing, a rudimentary box held together by rusted nails, and with four hands pulling at it he figured they could probably pry the top off now. He was trying to ignore the nausea welling up into his throat, nausea or fear, he wasn't sure which, Cooper out here past midnight in a voodoo cemetery in the badlands of Haiti.

"Get in here, Kareem," he said. "Looks like we can pop it off if both of us do it."

Alphonse murmured something before he came over, Cooper not caring what he said. The kid reached for one of the planks and they tugged at the top of the coffin together, grunting and jerking, the nails screeching as they pulled. Cooper's fingers slipped on the board and he sliced his hand open, but when he got back at it the lid popped off, flying back and tossing them into the mound of dirt they had dug. With Alphonse hanging back, Cooper crouched forward, holding his breath against the coming stench, and moved the last loose board out of the way. In the moonlight, he could see inside the coffin as though it were part of a track-lit museum display.

There was nothing in the box.

A couple rocks, sure, some dirt, but nothing else: no body, no bones, no tattered old clothes. Cooper was starting to sort through this unfortunate confirmation of what he'd already feared to be the case when he heard a voice.

It was Alphonse. He was topside, out of the grave now.

"Monsieur!" he said again. *"Il faut* you come look!"

When Cooper poked his head above ground he saw a sight that gave him chills.

A bunch of figures were coming at them out of the darkness—predatory shadows, approaching from every angle in the moonlight.

He counted eight of them. Spaced five or ten yards apart,

they had managed to form a circle around the open grave about forty yards across. Cooper couldn't see any definition to their dark faces even in the pale desert moonlight; they were shadows, ghostly figures standing there at the edge of the graveyard. Wraiths.

Barry must have had one or two of them following when Cooper had taken Alphonse out of town and up the slope of the mountain. He gave Barry and his band of wraiths some credit, not believing the show he'd put on, either seeing or guessing that they'd come back down once it got dark.

Cooper came out of the grave and stood beside Alphonse, planting his feet three feet apart in the soft earth, knees just bent. Relaxed.

Alphonse wasn't so relaxed. He started to edge away from the hole.

"Sit tight," Cooper said.

"They comin' get us," Alphonse said, his beanpole of a body coiled like a spring. *"Il faut partir."*

"Just stay by my side," Cooper said, "right there where you are."

Cooper was trying to determine what it was they were packing and how they planned on killing him when Alphonse bolted. He called after the kid, but it was no use, Alphonse running for the wrong place, straight for one of the gaps between men, Cooper thinking he should have picked out one of them and bowled the man over, but that wasn't what he did.

Two of the figures jumped him, Cooper seeing what they had now—looked like machetes, though the weapons could have been old lawn mower blades for all he could tell.

"Shit," he said, and, having to do it earlier than he'd wanted, he drew his pistol and cracked off two quick shots, thinking he was probably too late, seeing the arc of a machete swinging down on Alphonse before the slugs broke up the party. Kareem's attackers fell, but the kid dropped to his knees, probably cut bad, he thought, but there wasn't time to check. The other six closed in at speed, brandishing the blades, Cooper seeing a couple of shivs, one of them holding what looked to be a spear.

He didn't hesitate, working his pistol like Player One in a voodoo video game, shooting, stepping back and to his right, shooting again, repeating, so that he moved himself in a circle and got at least one bullet moving toward each of the approaching men before they could close the gap on him. The gun was loud in his ears as he completed the circuit: shoot-step, shoot-step; the closer they got, the easier it became, the specters falling like cardboard cutouts at a shooting gallery. Cooper registering while he fired away that this had to be one of the last places a handgun still gave you an advantage, these guys actually out here fighting with knives the way people used to.

He had to duck under the swipe of the last man's blade, but he came up under the swinging arm with a point-blank shot to his assailant's rib cage and, wraith, evil spirit, or otherwise, the shot felled him, and Cooper was done with the targets in his video game.

He went to Alphonse. Some of the would-be killers were making noise, moaning on the ground, but Alphonse wasn't. He lay flat on his back, silent, his face expressionless but alert, Cooper thinking he looked as though he'd expected this precise turn of events to happen. It wasn't pretty: Alphonse's right arm had been sliced clean through, his blood, black in the moonlight, spreading out all over everything, the soil, his clothes, his legs, his feet. The two dead men Cooper had shot lay beside him.

Cooper looked for and found the kid's long arm. The machete had severed it above the elbow; a length of nearly three feet of it was twitching on the ground a foot or two from the body it belonged to.

He found his backpack, grabbed the inventory of T-shirts from its main pouch, tore off two of the backpack's straps, and did his best to tie off Alphonse's upper arm with the makeshift tourniquets. By the time he finished, the shirts he'd wrapped around the stump were soaked through with blood, but there was at least a chance he'd managed to curtail the blood loss. He tore off another strap from the backpack, took off his shirt, did a scaled-down version of the same tie-off on the severed arm itself, set the arm across Alphonse's waist, and leaned down near the kid's face.

"Hang tight, Kareem," Cooper said. "I'll be right back."

He came through the middle of town, passing the driftwood bar and the old woman's lean-to along the way. The lights were burning inside the witch doctor's house when Cooper came up the porch stairs. He tried the knob, which turned, but the door was latched somehow and wouldn't open, so he kicked it in.

Barry the witch doctor and Cooper's escort from the morning were seated on the floor, cross-legged and facing each other about four feet apart. The place was thick with smoke. They shared a pipe—smoking a little herb, eh, Cooper thought. Get ready to smoke this pipe, poppy.

The escort had whipped his head around in surprise upon Cooper's entry; the witch doctor had not.

"*Allez-y!*" Cooper said to the escort. "*Vas!*"

The guy got up and headed for the door, spouting off at the mouth as he did it. Cooper ignored him, knowing he was the kind who would leave. The witch doctor remained on the floor in the lotus position, eyes closed, Cooper thinking he probably still has a lungful of that weed in there.

"You been warned," the witch doctor said, eyes still closed. "Now you going to die."

"Your death squad already struck out, big boy."

The guy opened his eyes and looked up at him. Given the circumstances, Cooper didn't like how leisurely the look was.

"You be dead soon enough," the witch doctor said.

"Here's a message from Marcel S.," Cooper said, and plugged the witch doctor with the first four shells of the fresh clip he'd popped into the Browning on the walk over.

Barry toppled over backward onto the floor. Cooper came over and checked his robes, but there was nothing on him. It made Cooper think a little more about the bastard's last words, the *bokor* sounding all too confident as he'd said them. *You be dead soon enough.*

He came around behind the desk and rifled through everything he could find—the cell phone, the charger, some trinkets, papers, a short stack of money in the metal box under the desk. He took out the money and threw it on the floor. Under the money, there were some other things. Coins, what looked like a car key, a couple of blank business cards with phone numbers written on them. Cooper recognized the main area code for Puerto Rico on one of the cards. The other he didn't know for sure but figured it for Jamaica. He snatched the business cards and kicked the money, scattering it across the floor, and left.

Graveside, he took the loose end of the strap he'd used to tie off Alphonse's arm and knotted it around a pair of belt loops on his shorts. He let go of the severed arm, and it dangled from his waist—the flexed fingers of the kid's lost hand reaching almost to his shoelaces, but not quite. He retrieved the last of his candy supply, feeding Alphonse a few bites before polishing off the rest himself. He gulped a bottle of water and, deciding to do without the rest, left the backpack beside the empty grave. He positioned himself alongside Alphonse's long, limp body, the kid looking like a snake in the dirt, and then, bending at the knees, he reached backward and stretched his arms out behind his legs to loop them underneath Alphonse.

Cooper got the kid a foot off the ground, crouched deeper, leaned forward, and pulled the boy's skinny body up over his ass. He positioned Alphonse's waist so that he could bend the kid's body around the contour of his hips, and with Alphonse bent around him like a noodle-float in a suburban swimming pool, he was able to clasp his hands underneath the noodle, in front of his body—just above his own nuts, as it turned out. Bobbing once to check the seal of his hand clasp, he shook his head, reasonably satisfied that this was the best he was going to do, and stood up straight.

"Not too bad, Kareem," he said. The kid felt light as a feather, though he'd have to see how long that would last.

He set out and felt the grade wearing on his hamstrings before he'd taken a dozen steps. The blisters on his feet squeezed against the boots and his arms ached. He looked up at the hill, which it did not appear to him he had even reached.

"Christ."

It was going to be a long walk up that fucking mountain.

16

In 1974, at the tail end of the Vietnam War, North Vietnamese strategists, fearing a possible last-ditch invasion by the U.S. Navy, ordered a series of mines planted outside a harbor near Haiphong. By the time local intel overrode the paranoia of the strategists and the order came to sweep the mines, local vessels had been safely navigating the harbor for almost two years. All of the local captains knew exactly where the mines were.

Unfortunately, the new rotation of military personnel supervising the minesweeping operation did not. Operating from a combination of the original specifications and hearsay from local fishermen, the man in charge of the mission did his best, but found that once the harbor and its adjoining channel were ostensibly cleared, the count of recovered or detonated mines came up two devices short. After a cursory second sweep, the commander wrote off the discrepancy, stating in his report that the two missing mines must have previously detonated without incident.

In actuality the missing mines had broken from their moorings almost two years before the sweep.

A typhoon in the fall of 1976 had caused the cables anchoring the two mines to scrape against a marine escarpment for sixteen straight hours; both cables were sheared, one near its mine, the other almost where it had been affixed to the ocean floor. The mine with the shorter length of cable floated to the surface and drifted off in the night, washing ashore thirty miles up the coast along with some driftwood and other debris. It was never discovered except as a sort of jungle gym used unwittingly by local kids.

Trailing its longer, and therefore heavier cable, the second mine remained well below the surface and drifted at a much slower cruising speed into the open waters of the Gulf of Tonkin.

Over the course of the next year, out of reach of even the deepest keel by some hundred feet, the mine made its way through the South China Sea, along the Malay Peninsula, and past the Riau Islands near Singapore. Toward the end of 1977, a storm washed the mine up against an oceanic shelf in the Strait of Malacca, where it lurked for fourteen months, too deep to disturb any passing vessels, and too heavy to be moved more than an inch or two at a time by the lackluster current. Another storm, this time a violent one, carried the mine into the Andaman Sea, where it caught a slow but consistent current, riding the floe through the Bay of Bengal in a looping semicircle down past Sri Lanka into the Indian Ocean.

The mine migrated south through the next winter, passing Madagascar and the Cape of Good Hope before working its way up the western coastline of Africa in the spring, again traveling deep enough to avoid surface traffic. In June of

1980, the mine started across the Atlantic near the equator, and by September of 1981, had reached the coast of Brazil.

Prevailing currents brought the mine slowly up the east coast of South America until, in 1983, it lodged in a stubborn bed of seaweed that appeared to have seized the mine permanently in its morass of brown tentacles. Then a hurricane tore the kelp from its bed, bestowing upon the mine another shot at freedom. With a northbound momentum generated by 1984's particularly harsh storm season, the mine rose past Trinidad and Tobago, up the Antilles chain, and was approaching the eastern seaboard of the United States, due north of Puerto Rico near the Tropic of Cancer, by the end of that year—so that, in the early months of Ronald Reagan's fourth year in office, the mine was floating harmlessly in the warm, clear waters of what was widely referred to as the Bermuda Triangle, about forty fathoms beneath the ocean's surface.

This had been an ambitious journey for the mine, and it showed: with an aquatic forest of barnacles, mussels, algae, and other oceanic vegetation, the mine had grown its own ecosystem that went as high up the food chain as the occasional Atlantic salmon and blackfin tuna. By the time the mine had reached the Bermuda Triangle, in fact, there wasn't a single square inch of steel visible on either the floating orb of the mine itself or the one hundred feet of steel cable dangling beneath.

Between 1981 and 1985, the U.S. Navy launched four *Ohio*-class nuclear attack submarines which it overlooked the obligation to declare under the then-current nuclear disarmament treaties—and which the navy also managed to hide from the KGB. For as long as the navy maintained this ruse—which, for three of the four subs, meant all the way to the end of the cold war—America was able to position ballistic missiles in places that members of the Politburo would have found appalling.

A different fate awaited the fourth sub.

On the third Friday of July 1984, Lieutenant Commander Elmore Bradenman, Lenny for short, had the controls of the USS *Chameleon,* the fourth clandestine *Ohio*-class attack sub. The *Chameleon* was running fast and deep, 180 miles southeast of Key West. The crew of the *Chameleon* had been assigned the brief mission of performing some routine coastline surveillance east of Florida, followed by a Caribbean rendezvous with a second boomer, with which they would be conducting various exercises.

The captain was asleep in his quarters, which gave Lenny, the executive officer of the boat, the chance to do two things: enjoy the command of an entire submarine, and get in some reading. Tonight he was working on the first book by a writer everyone was telling him about; thanks to a rumor that Reagan liked it, the book had hit the *New York Times* bestseller list the week before Lenny boarded the *Chameleon* in Norfolk. The book was called *The Hunt for Red October.*

One quality of submarines that their designers and operators could not help was the occasional random destruction of ocean wildlife. An *Ohio*-class nuclear attack submarine was, after all, nearly two football fields long, and therefore much bigger than any sea bass, tuna, or jellyfish it might have happened to plow into as it navigated the deep blue sea. Many a fish had been bruised or knocked unconscious by the blunt nose, or chewed to bits by the screws of such subs, and while the sonar engineers on board were trained to detect even the smallest metallic anomaly in the surrounding waters, they were required, by necessity, to ignore any indication of an approaching halibut, or patch of seaweed. The latter being precisely what the sonar engineer determined the floating mass of vegetation ahead of the *Chameleon* to be as Lenny Bradenman settled in to begin Clancy's debut novel.

Long dormant but still quite live, the explosive charge within the drifting North Vietnamese mine responded to the punch it received from the bow of the *Chameleon* as the submarine powered through the Atlantic at a speed of just under thirty knots. There was a brief delay after the initial impact, so that the more alert personnel aboard the vessel—Lenny among them—had a moment to wonder what had struck the boat before a dull concussion rocked the sub's port flank.

The old mine, even with ten years of fury stored within, had, at first, little impact on the outward appearance of the *Chameleon*: it simply inflicted a puncture wound on the sub's port flank. At the *Chameleon*'s cruising depth, however, there existed approximately nine times the pressure of that found at sea level. This was not a problem for a submarine with its hull fully intact, but as the puncture opened up in the *Chameleon,* the seams of the hull partially caved in around the puncture and water tore into a series of compartments, any one of which could have been sealed off from the rest of the boat if damaged alone. This *Titanic*-like flooding of multiple compartments caused a simultaneous listing of the sub and a failure of the primary electrical system; dead in the water, the *Chameleon* began a slow descent which LCDR Bradenman found himself powerless to stop. Soon the sub, growing heavier from the flooding, declined past seventy, then a hundred fathoms. It was Lenny's ship to the end—the captain never made it out of his cabin.

He attempted every procedure the navy had taught him and some they hadn't, but at a depth of nearly three hundred fathoms, the last remaining significant sealed portions of the boat folded inward like a crushing aluminum can, and the last of the survivors either drowned, or died under the crush of collapsing metal.

Just before he died, Lenny Bradenman, a lifelong skeptic, took note of the *Chameleon*'s current coordinates. When they registered, absurdly, in his mind, Bradenman reached the obvious conclusion.

My God, he thought. *This is what they talk about. This is how it happens.*

We've gone down in the Bermuda Triangle.

The navy's clandestine salvage effort came up empty. Beginning six hours from the time the USS *Chameleon*'s emergency beacon floated to the surface and ending four years later, a fleet of pseudocivilian survey vessels blanketed the region to no avail. In a hundred, a thousand, then one hundred thousand passes over the same expanse of ocean, the team unearthed shipwrecks from as far back as the seventeenth century, but found no signs of a sunken nuclear submarine. At the end of the fourth year of the search, the navy shit-canned the whole deal, the crew's deaths long since passed off as a training accident aboard another, less secret boat.

One of Lenny Bradenman's final acts had been to send a distress signal in Morse code. Lenny intended the message to serve as an alert to the boat his sonar man had spotted some seven miles off, in hopes that the vessel would detect the missive and come to the rescue of any surviving crew. He grabbed the first man he found and ordered him to tap out a message against the wall of the sub; the kid grabbed a wrench and banged out "S.O.S." fifty or sixty times before succumbing to the elements.

The vessel to which Lenny had hoped to convey his S.O.S. had been classified thirty minutes back as a fishing vessel, wood, thirty-five to fifty feet long. This assessment had been both correct and incorrect. From the surface, the boat did in fact appear to be a fishing trawler; that part, Lenny's crew had got right. The interior of the boat, however, was another matter, since the apparent fishing trawler was in fact a spy ship, belonging not to the Soviet Union or Cuba—which, based on the geography, might have been the logical supposition—but instead to the newly broadened military intelligence wing of the People's Liberation Navy of the People's Republic of China.

When the strange report came in from the spy fleet that week—the fleet being a thousand-vessel unit the new head of the PLN intelligence wing, vice admiral and fledgling polo enthusiast Deng Jiang, had ordered built at the start of his tenure—a senior analyst, sifting through the data, thought that he might have stumbled across something. An Atlantic-based spy boat had reported an underwater concussion followed by an S.O.S. signal tapped against a metal hull, and if the report from the trawler were true, the possibility was self-evident:

Somebody had lost a submarine.

Deng quietly monitored the progress of the obvious U.S. Navy salvage effort. Knowing how the Americans operated, he found this to be a textbook case—the navy's failed four-year "civilian" salvage operation answered Deng's initial curiosity as to who had lost the submarine. Continuing reports told him that the search continued for four years, but in due course the Americans ran out of patience and scrapped the salvage mission.

In the meantime, Deng had been given the whole army.

Not a religious man, and therefore resistant to superstition, Deng had never once considered that a supernatural phenomenon might have caused the disappearance of the USS *Chameleon*. A submarine could sink and be salvaged, or sink and be left to decay on the ocean floor, but one could not simply vanish. Deng was also an extraordinarily patient man, who did not believe at all in luck. He believed, instead, that a man controlled his own destiny, and that luck was earned. Thus, when the U.S. Navy quit their recovery efforts, Deng decided to mount a salvage operation of his own.

The *Chameleon* had sunk in the southernmost portion of the North Atlantic, along a ridge beside the Puerto Rico Trench. Aside from a depth of some four and one-half miles, the Puerto Rico Trench boasted two other compelling characteristics: active suboceanic volcanoes and frequent earthquakes, the latter because the trench lay above a series of fault lines.

The portion of the trench into which the *Chameleon* had sunk was possessed of a peculiar geography. At the edge of the trench, there stood a suboceanic mountain range. From base to peak, some of the mountains measured higher than six thousand feet. Nosing through the depths, the *Chameleon* had struck an outcropping of rock near the peak of one of the taller mountains. The underwater ledge did nothing to slow the *Chameleon*'s downward momentum, but did break off from the mountain and begin its own plunge down the slope. Along the way, the huge lump of volcanic rock tore off numerous similar outcroppings, which in turn generated a massive cloud of silt.

This avalanche meant that as the *Chameleon* struck the ocean floor on the shallow northern side of the trench, it was immediately pile-driven into the muddy bottom by some two hundred million tons of volcanic rock, silt, and debris. When the cloud of silt settled, the *Chameleon* and its crew of 154 sailors had been buried, the layers of mud, sand, and rock covering the length of the sub with somewhere between twenty-seven and forty feet of debris. There was no discernible shape on the ocean floor above it, at least none that resembled an American nuclear submarine, and no detectable metal with any proximity to the surface of the silt.

Four years and eight months later, the nineteen hundred and fifty-seventh earthquake to rattle this section of the Puerto Rico Trench since the *Chameleon*'s demise registered a 6.8 on the Richter scale and sluiced a new, smaller trench north of the mountain range. Over the next three weeks, a two-mile-long stretch of the mountain range slipped into this trench. There were avalanches for months, spurred by aftershocks of the quake, all of which represented nothing more than ordinary geologic activity for the region surrounding the Puerto Rico Trench, with one exception: a portion of the *Chameleon*'s bow had been freshly exposed to the sea.

For the U.S. Navy, who had recently abandoned its salvage mission, the geologic activity that freed the *Chameleon* meant nothing. It passed like the sound of a tree in a forest where no ears were present to listen. For others—namely, the supreme commander of the People's Liberation Army of the People's Republic of China—the Puerto Rico Trench's most recent sequence of earthquakes meant something entirely different.

To General Deng, it meant that the mystery as to the whereabouts of the missing submarine had been solved.

17

Laramie stood in the doorway to Malcolm Rader's office.

"There's a caramel macchiato with your name on it in the commissary," she said. "You've got to take a walk to get it, though."

Laramie knew Rader was a sucker for the sissy drinks at the Starbucks kiosk. A career analyst somewhere near the peak of his tenure, Rader had two kids in college and one ready to hit the road, and it was evident he hadn't made it to the gym since the first kid arrived. Disorganized, absent-minded, and overweight, he compensated for these issues with a frenzied, spastic work ethic—Laramie thinking you never quite understood what Rader was saying or doing, but she couldn't remember his taking a vacation since she'd been working here, and he seemed to be aware of everything. She wasn't even sure whether he took meetings out of the office—another floor, or room, maybe, but she'd never seen him anywhere outside the building.

"What are we meeting about," Rader said, "or talking. And walking."

"Korea," Laramie said. "North Korea, to be precise."

There were three mounds of papers on Rader's desk. He shifted his weight in his chair and nearly vanished behind a particularly massive stack.

"What about it," he said. "Them. Whatever."

"It's about North Korea and China, and how they're related." She let her statement hang out there.

"This is more on your Taiwan theory," Rader said.

"The same."

He frowned, eyes slipping to his monitor—the twin temptations of Laramie's intel and the caramel macchiato competing with his inclination to answer e-mails and remain productive.

Finally he stood. "You're buying, correct?"

"Absolutely."

"Fine."

Rader had hired her. He wasn't exactly a mentor, but occasionally she asked his advice, and when she did, he always accommodated her. The man was a decent boss.

But he wasn't listening.

She'd thought about what she'd found through a second sleepless night, and once she developed a theory—involving speculation, but reasonable, fact-based speculation, with sound conclusions—she'd thought carefully about what to do, and say. She decided to start with him.

"Look," she said, leaning over her coffee, "it's too much of a mismatch. The timing. The politics. All of it. What does the State Council of the People's Republic of China care anymore about North Korea? These nations are not allies—

not politically, not militarily. Think about it, Malcolm: there's no reason the majority rule of the State Council would intend to be identified internationally with Korea. North Korea's foreign policy essentially consists of an annual rotating nuclear-proliferation extortion scheme, while China's embracing capitalism—the council is expanding China's business relationship with the West. Opening its borders. Getting gung ho about free trade. Meanwhile North Korea puts its policy-making energy into threatening the U.S. whenever its people run low on rice."

Rader sipped his sissy drink. "Your point?"

"Bear with me. The other side of this? It's almost not possible that these two exercises are not connected. I considered the possibility of coincidence when I made the discovery, but you know as well as I do—better than I do—that the facts I presented to you on the way down here point, odds on, to collusion: I practice to invade *my* neighbor in June during a cloudy day in a place and time that known paths of spy satellites would not cover—and you practice to invade *yours* in April—on a cloudy day, et cetera."

"Laramie, I will grant you that there is a chance—"

"Malcolm, you're the one who taught me how to find these things in the first place!" She stopped—you had to keep a lid on the volume, sitting in a corner of a commissary known to have been snooped on as a matter of routine. "Listen. I have a theory. You and I both understand the political climate in China, and specifically the political leanings of the members of the council. We could present each member's full dossier to prove the point, but by now the ideology of each of these men is virtually common knowledge. You know as well as I do that it's unlikely—impossible, in fact—that the council has approved any invasion plans. General Deng Jiang is doubtless aware of the exercise, probably overseeing it, and that means he's planning for an invasion, whether with the approval of the council, or not. If he needs to win them over, he can do it through extortion and other old-school techniques—he's used these tricks before. He's an extremist who doesn't fit in, but he's in deep with the intelligence chair and has the goods on everybody from his days overseeing military intel. Okay?"

"With you so far. It's my territory."

"I've learned from the best. But with a second nation's military involved in a virtually identical operation, conducted on the same timetable—Malcolm, the facts suggest, and I have prepared a report, for your eyes only, hypothesizing what I'm about to tell you. My opinion is that we've stumbled across what I'll call a 'rogue faction'—an unofficial alliance between certain extremists on the State Council and the government of North Korea. A new al-Qaeda, if we feel like using a sensationalist label."

"That is sensationalist, since your hypothesized group has, well, yet to do anything."

"Let's follow my theory all the way through. The rogue faction, presuming it exists, enjoys ties—or, greater than that, *influence* over more than one nation. There are joint preparations under way for potential simultaneous invasions of American allies, or, to be more accurate, nations whose independence is critical to our foreign policy and therefore our national security. What do you think will happen if I look elsewhere? We should establish a task force, Malcolm—it will take time if there are other participating nations, or other connected extremists within nonextremist regimes, but if further documentation exists—I realize that I am again being sensationalistic, but these could be the first signs of, well, you could call it a new form of world war, Malcolm."

"That's just not likely."

"When the plans to use hijacked passenger jets to destroy commercial buildings turned up in an apartment in the Philippines, it seemed unlikely then that anything—"

"Enough!"

Laramie quieted down at his tone. Rader leaned back, lifted his macchiato, and sipped. He swirled the coffee in the cup. She liked that he was mulling it over, or at least giving the outward impression that he was mulling it over. She suspected she should enjoy the moral victory. She could sense defeat looming.

Rader coughed. "You and I," he said, "are far from privy to the policy-making issues faced by our administration."

Laramie couldn't decide whether she wanted to strangle him, or yawn.

"Nor," he said, "do we have any exposure to the administration's intel docket. It could be, for instance, that Peter Gates had prior knowledge of your discovery, and evidence in favor of, or possibly against your theory, perhaps presented to him by another analyst, or agency. You've done some good work here, but the key to assessment lies in the chain of command. Your initial findings and the style of your original report were a bit inflammatory, no?"

"So I've been told."

"I believe that your ideal strategy, that which will allow your findings to be most effectively considered, is to offer this additional intel as a private gesture."

"A private gesture? Malcolm, I'm coming to you so you can take this in the right direction, but considering what I'm coming to you with—"

"A peace offering," Rader said, continuing. "'Memo to Peter Gates: Here's something more. I leave it in your hands.

I conclude nothing. I leave policy decisions to you. Thank you for your guidance.'"

Laramie was favoring strangulation.

"Better yet," he said, "I'll take a look at the document you mentioned. Why don't you slug it as a confidential brief, addressed solely to me. Do not duplicate the document. Do not forward to file. I'll suggest any formatting changes you'll need; you tidy it up; then we feed it to Rosen. Perhaps only verbally. This allows him, in turn, to present your findings to Gates, who will, based on history and experience, know what to do and when, guided by his judgment of the most appropriate timing." Rader was nodding at the good sense his plan made. "We work it this way, and Gates is pleased. Rosen comes off as handling his staff like a champ, and you and I get some credit. You, specifically, show that you've learned from your earlier brush with—well, disaster."

Laramie looked at him. She thought about how many people she was discovering were concerned not only about their own careers, but also those of others, including even her own, when, oh, by the way, there appeared to be a couple more important issues at stake. She thought about taking her frustrations out by giving Rader some kind of harsh, sarcastic reply, decided against it, and thought instead of the punch line delivered by Eddie Rothgeb in his Saturday morning lecture, and the fax that followed.

Politics: give them what they want to hear.

"That," she said, "is a pretty good idea, Malcolm."

"Hey, it's how we work around here. I don't need to tell you that." He smiled, the patronly boss, and Laramie offered a smile in return. Two happy, career-minded professionals, she thought, sharing coffee in the commissary.

"No," she said, "you don't, Malcolm. Thanks for hearing me out."

"Anytime," he said. "Anytime you're buying, that is." He chuckled.

Laramie yawned.

She knew a place in Annapolis. It took her ninety minutes from Langley; leaving early didn't spare her the usual rush-hour traffic, but she didn't mind the drive. It helped to clear her head, and she wanted to do this far from home, and certainly nowhere near the office. She parked in the public lot tucked behind the town's main drag, walked two blocks to the waterfront, and turned into a narrow shop with the word MORPHEUS painted on its green awning. It was six-fifteen when she arrived, toting the same bag she'd brought with her to O'Hare on the Rothgeb trip. She took the bag everywhere—used it like a purse, but it was big enough to throw just about anything inside. Today it held her wallet, keys, makeup, and the one-page fax from Eddie Rothgeb.

Morpheus looked like a narrow, single-store version of Starbucks, only lit like a nightclub; its small waitstaff offered coffee, a few pricey pastries, and, on a rental basis, T3 Internet time. Use your own or take a spin on one of the house computers.

Laramie had endured a tedious dinner date about three months ago; they'd eaten around the corner at an Italian place with white tablecloths. The dinner conversation had stunk, but she'd wandered in here to split a slab of cheesecake with the guy afterward. Not her usual menu choice, but Laramie usually ate big if she was having a terrible time with men. If you aren't interested and the date is already under way, there's nothing much to do or talk about, and you aren't worried about how you look anymore, you know you won't even consider swapping bodily fluids—why not blow out the diet for the day and give yourself something to be annoyed at later? A reason to run a couple extra miles in the morning.

It turned out that her busted-date dessert spot had been a cyber café, and she'd remembered that walking out of the commissary following the sissy-drink session with Rader.

She talked to the coffee jock behind the counter and paid for an hour on one of the computers in cash. She picked out a Mac, clicked onto the Yahoo! portal, and created a new account under a fictitious name. Trying a few clever code names, she discovered all of them to be taken. In the end she settled on EastWest7.

Then she confronted the blank screen.

There was, she supposed, only one question that remained once all the secret-agent, leave-the-office-early-and-drive-to-Annapolis excitement was over, and she was forced to figure out what to say to Senator Alan Kircher: had she really found something that warranted the clandestine whistle-blower routine? Rothgeb and his theories aside, the minute she engaged in a dialogue with somebody outside the Agency on the topic of classified intel, her future with CIA would probably prove instantly and drastically shortened. Somebody, somewhere, would eventually find out what she was up to; they always did. Laramie thinking she could last two weeks or two years, but sooner or later, send this correspondence and she'd be pink-slipped.

She composed a note on the screen before her:

Dear Senator Kircher,

Our friends in the East may not be as friendly as your friends are telling you.

An intelligent source

And there it was. The whistle-blower's first correspondence—Deep Throat's opening salvo. Eddie Rothgeb's screenplay, she thought, proceeding as outlined.

Her right hand depressed the mouse and the cursor sent the e-mail, Laramie thinking her fingers possessed the courage that she did not. No matter.

Whichever part of her had done it, she thought, that was all it took.

18

There came the cold sweat—the sheen that chilled his skin. He burrowed into the sheets, hiding from the wrath of the ceiling fan, its wind biting icily at his sweaty skin. In the fitful, restless circuit that followed, he would fall into the dream, exit it shivering, cover his perspiring skin from the elements with the sheets, and fall again into the dream.

Brief, abrupt segments of the forgotten period of his life would appear in different ways, from different angles, so that even within the cycle of the same three nightmares, he would learn something new about the portions of his life his conscious mind required him to forget. The visions came in blurred, stunted images, each snapshot bringing another, bursting into his mind's eye then retreating—never clear or complete.

Naked, running, seeing the blood on his naked body, he knew there was too much of it to be solely his own. He felt the lingering stab of pain from the bullet they had put in his back; he sliced his bare feet on the gravel road. Brain fogged, vision blurred, he peered into the searing sun and sharp blue sky, trying to piece together direction. North, south, *east*—he was headed *east*. He couldn't be sure—he didn't know where they had taken him—but if they'd kept him imprisoned anywhere within miles of the assassination team's drop point, then he knew there was a chance, going east, to reach the Sulaco. Río Sulaco—his promised land, that river a highway to his freedom.

He barreled into the jungle, never slowing, feeling the whip and sting of branches, of vines, thorns, nettles, the itch of insect bites—and still he ran, measuring the sun through the trees. Continuing east. East, to the Río Sulaco.

He ran for hours. Nothing remained within—nothing. There was only exterior pain, throbbing, sharp; if he'd been able to see himself he'd have given up, Cooper a swollen mass of red welts. His naked, blistered, bleeding feet had lost their skin, propelling him eastward as little more than raw, seeping stumps.

No river came. No highway, no power lines, no homes, no crops. Only jungle. He fell at least a hundred times, flying headlong over logs, roots, stumps—anthills—each time rising more slowly than the last. After a particularly rough tumble, he felt death's cool breath on his hot neck.

Enough, he remembered thinking. *I've gone far enough.*

They couldn't be following him, not after the hours he'd spent running, his journey taking him across tens of miles of all-but-impenetrable jungle. He set his face into the dirt, closed his eyes, and slumped. It was time for sleep, the fatigue too great for consciousness. Even, perhaps, too great for life.

He heard birds, and insects, and wind.

Wind.

It was a steady wind—too steady a wind, so steady that he knew it was not wind. It was *water*. Moving water, rushing like the wind through the trees.

He rose again. Scarcely capable of standing upright, he shuffled forward, attempting to run but managing little more than a crawl. Soon, he smelled it and, finally, saw it—that wide, lazy road of black water—and he stumbled, plodding down the muddy riverbank, tripping again and falling head-first, plunging, and then he splashed, his head sinking beneath the surface and bobbing up like a float at the end of a fishing line. He had found his salvation, his escape—he would ride the current a hundred miles, a thousand if he could.

The river was warm. It stung the welts, the bites, the blisters and sores, but it felt good. It felt like freedom. The mosquitoes came off his skin, drowning in droves, and a short-lived euphoria consumed him. The excitement robbed him of the last remaining energy in his body, and he found himself slipping beneath the surface. The current began to sweep him downstream, and it was all he could do to keep his mouth out of the water, and then he could no longer manage even that, and he went under. His consciousness faded, the world blinking out as it passed by, the banks of the river moving past with greater and greater velocity in shorter and shorter flashes.

In a section of whitewater, one of his legs struck a rock and snapped like a twig, and he felt his head crack against something hard. He lost his bearings, suddenly forgetting how he'd come to be here. He tried to gasp but couldn't find any air; there was only water, which he'd inhaled and could not expel. Panic struck him, but there was no physical strength remaining for him to tap into. He struggled, flailing, trying in vain to push his head above the surface—sucking, heaving. The world began to fade around the edges, then crumble to blackness, and finally, with no remaining hope, he felt a deep sense of calm.

Cooper always welcomed the calm. When it came, he

knew the second of the three dreams in the cycle had finished. He would open his eyes and find the welcome confines of his bungalow, surviving to await the third dream.

When he opened his eyes tonight, though, he found that he hadn't awakened in the bed of his bungalow. He hadn't been pulled from the delta of the Río Sulaco by a kindhearted fisherman, either, in the way that his third dream usually began.

Instead, he saw rocks. He reached for an object that was hard to see, buried as it was beneath a set of smaller stones, and as he pulled on it the object broke free, and he saw that it was a plank of wood. He looked up, frantically now, in hopes he wouldn't see what he suspected he would—but, to his horror, he saw precisely what he knew he would see.

Standing around his broken body, doing their little dance, were Cap'n Roy's band of Marine Base cops. They kept on with the show as Cooper watched them from his nook in the rocks, Riley and the others doing their best to distract any wandering eyes with the illusion that work was being done out here, so that the wandering eyes would fail to notice the pile of rags and rotting flesh and bone that had washed ashore.

19

One year before the USS *Chameleon* was sunk by the Vietnamese mine, a group of London businessmen each kicked in five thousand pounds sterling and purchased one-half of a private island in the British Virgin Islands. Another twenty-five-hundred U.S. dollars built each partner a two-room bungalow, and the partners had themselves a nifty investment property. Part vacation time-share, part tax shelter, it allowed its owners to split up the high-season calendar among themselves and rent out the rooms for the remainder of the year. On paper, the resort lost money; in reality, it provided the partners a small but undeclared cash dividend at the end of each year.

To manage the property, the investors found a suitable candidate when a graduate student named Chris Woolsey applied to the ad they'd posted at Oxford. At the end of his first summer of work, Woolsey accepted the investors' offer and dropped out of the two-year masters program he'd beat out thousands of candidates to attend and opted, instead, to turn his first few months spent at the place called Conch Bay into an endless summer.

It didn't take much of Woolsey's time or energy to tend to Conch Bay's guests. Woolsey made a daily run to Tortola on a rickety skiff, retrieving enough in the way of food and supplies to keep his charges drunk and fed; he cleaned the outhouse seat every night, turned down the cots, and threw the old set of sheets in the wash and hung them out to dry in the sun each afternoon. A cistern collected and filtered rainwater for the showers; a septic-tank service boat came to do the dirty work every three weeks or so. After his supply run in the morning, Woolsey, meanwhile, spent the remainder of each day one of three ways: on the beach, at the bar, or in the water. He read virtually every literary classic still in print.

Easily the oddest of the many odd guests ever to stay at the rustic resort was a visitor who'd arrived about three years into Woolsey's tour of duty. The guest introduced himself with only one name, arriving one morning on a water taxi and renting one of the ramshackle bungalows by paying six months' rent up front, in cash; he added five thousand on top of the rent to cover whatever meal-and-alcohol plan Woolsey could muster for the same stretch of time. He then, to Woolsey's amusement, proceeded to do little more than stay in his room, sleep on the beach, and get schnockered for three months running. The guy didn't talk once. Still, Woolsey provided him with a plastic cooler, ducking into the man's quarters whenever he went out to the beach, Woolsey keeping the cooler loaded with tuna sandwiches and whatever fresh fruit he'd brought over on the skiff. The man always ate all the food, so Woolsey kept filling it up.

Five months in, the guest took to snorkeling out along the rim of the bay, staying out for two or three hours at a time,

Woolsey once timing him at four hours and thirty-three minutes. He began jogging on the beach, the shortest beach Woolsey had ever seen a man run on, no longer than a quarter mile, but once he'd started the habit, in no time at all the guest was out running the length of the beach fifteen to twenty times each morning around dawn.

The guest paid for another six months, Woolsey wondering where he'd been keeping the cash all this time. When the man offered Woolsey a thousand-dollar tip, Woolsey waved it off and said the proprietors paid him just fine, but thanks for the thought just the same. The next day Woolsey told him about some good snorkeling he'd done over on Virgin Gorda, in a place called the Baths, Woolsey saying that maybe he would want to come along with the other guests he was taking over there on the skiff. The man went, and on the ride back, passing the bigger island's marina, asked Woolsey if he knew anybody running a deep-sea fishing charter, maybe one with a captain who knew where the marlin ran. Woolsey told him he knew a guy who could take care of him, and a couple days later—after a morning at sea—the man came back with ten pounds of swordfish filets. Woolsey grilled up a batch of steaks for the guests, and the extras kept the cooler full of sandwiches for a week.

One afternoon the man was taking up three feet of the six-foot bar and working on the seventh glass of his new favorite drink, Puerto Rican rum and Coke with a lime wedge, Woolsey serving him the Cuba libres, when Woolsey said, "Got some bad news, Guv. Proprietors are looking to sell."

Cooper, clearly not wishing to be disturbed, said, "That right."

"Figure they can get top dollar for the real estate," Woolsey said, "all these cruise ships doing so much business down here. Owners don't come around anymore anyway—

bunch of old fogeys. One of 'em even died, I think. Bloody shame, you ask me."

Cooper asked why he thought it was such a shame, that people died all the time, and Woolsey shook his head and waved his arm out at the beach, where the bay's two-inch wavelets were busy lapping at the white sand. "Look at this effin' place," he said. "Anybody with half a noggin and five pounds," he said, "he'd put up a restaurant, throw a thatched roof over the bar, build a bigger dock—in fact, he'd get some old bugger like you to dive down, pour some concrete moorings out in that bay—and there you go."

Cooper said, "Where?"

"What?"

"You just told me 'there you go.' Where?"

Woolsey looked at him and said, "I'll tell you where you go. You go to a few travel magazines and invite 'em to visit you free of charge. Spread the word that if you've got a sailboat and you're coming through the BVIs, well, stop by this little island down here, and they'll serve you conch fritters and mahimahi steaks. If you want, you can fly in through Tortola and they'll taxi you over free of charge, then put you up for a week for next to nothing. More than we charge now, but still a fair price. Throw up some palm trees, couple of tropical bushes, make it look like a real resort—and make a bloody fortune doing it."

Woolsey said, "Place may cost a hundred grand, not a big ticket for a place like this, but you've gotta spend another hundred to make it worth your while, otherwise nobody who can afford the higher price is staying here. Marriott or Westin could afford to do it, and therein lies your problem, Guv—they'll put up a high-rise, replace this whole bleedin' lagoon with a swimming pool, put in some fake waterfalls with fuckin' water lilies."

Woolsey told Cooper he'd been saving plenty of money, skimming whatever he could off the top, but no way in hell could he drop two hundred grand into this place. Not even the first hundred.

"So that," he said, "is why it's a bloody shame." He looked out at the bay again and shrugged. "Thought you'd want to be the first to know, Guv. Let me know, you want some help finding another island to hide out on."

"Thanks for telling me," Cooper said, then did his best to ignore Woolsey for the rest of the night. He fell asleep on the beach with his naked feet brushing the edge of the water in the dark.

Just under five weeks later, a short, heavyset man wearing a navy blue business suit arrived at Conch Bay on a water taxi at ten in the morning. When he told Woolsey he'd just flown in from the Caymans and was looking for a man named Chris Woolsey, Woolsey shook hands with the man, who introduced himself as Jacob Bartleby, attorney-at-law. Bartleby said he represented a holding corporation out of Grand Cayman specializing in resort investments, and Woolsey, long since accustomed to such inquiries, told Bartleby to come over to his office, where he would provide the information on how to contact the proprietors.

When they reached the office—a converted outhouse with a pair of folding metal chairs—Bartleby said, "Mr. Woolsey, my clients have already contacted the proprietors."

Bartleby withdrew a cashier's check from the briefcase he'd brought and handed it to Woolsey. Woolsey read the check, which was made out in the sum of $140,000 to a company called Conch Bay LP.

"This cashier's check reflects my clients' estimate for the

costs of renovation, marketing, and maintenance that would be required to keep this resort running, profitably, for the foreseeable future. Do you feel this number is realistic?"

"Realistic?" Woolsey shook his head. "I don't know, Guv. Asking price is a hundred K, and that'd leave you with forty. Could be done, you could dress the place up a little, I suppose, but you'll lose money, probably a lot of it in fact, if that's all you're puttin' into it."

"I'm sorry," Bartleby said, "allow me to clarify. My clients have already purchased the resort. Or to be precise, they have had the ninety-nine-year lease from the local government assigned to them. And you're correct—the price was one hundred thousand U.S. dollars."

Bartleby pulled a sheet of paper and a pen from his briefcase and handed both to Woolsey.

"This is a limited partnership agreement. If you sign it, my clients' rights to the ninety-nine-year lease will be assigned to the partnership. In exchange for such assignment, and the check I've just given you, my clients would like to retain a forty-nine percent stake in the limited partnership, which obviously would entitle them to the equivalent share of any profits generated by the partnership, in perpetuity."

Woolsey read the document, where he discovered the odd feature of his name, printed in the text of the agreement. He looked up at Bartleby with a forced, lopsided grin intended to mask his confusion.

"Look, Guv'nor, I'm not sure your clients understand how—well, bloody hell. Mr.—Bartleby, is it?"

"Yes."

"You see, well, I'm not sure I understand, mate."

Bartleby offered a firm grin.

"The fifty-one percent share goes to you, Mr. Woolsey, as managing partner. In exchange, of course, you would need to be willing to run the day-to-day operations of the resort on a continuing basis. My clients," he said, "intend to be passive partners in this venture."

Later that afternoon, Woolsey found Cooper out on the beach, sipping a Cuba libre on a lounge chair. Woolsey pulled up another chair, clicked it back to the same angle as Cooper's, and sat beside him.

"Listen, mate," Woolsey said. "A pesky little man representing a Cayman Islands holding firm came by to see me this morning."

"That right," Cooper said.

"Seems they've bought the resort," Woolsey said. "Want me to run it, seems."

Cooper grunted. Woolsey was silent for a moment.

Then he said, "You have any ideas about that?"

Cooper looked out into the bay, reaching up with his right hand to shield his eyes from the glare of the sun. "Sounds to me," he said after a long while of looking out at the bay, "that things may just stay the same around here."

Woolsey nodded, and the two of them stared out at the bay, sitting in the two lounge chairs, the sun glaring down at them from the sky, careening off the water and the sand, keeping the air warm as the wind rustled the trees behind the bungalows.

"I've given this some thought," Woolsey said.

Cooper didn't say anything.

"I get through putting this place together, I'm thinking it'll have nine bungalows. I'm thinking the one I'll build over there, the one with the most privacy, I'm thinking you ought to stay in that one."

Cooper kept looking out at the turquoise bay. Soaking up the sun.

"I'm thinking you ought to stay there free of charge,"

Woolsey said, "and I know you like to drink a lot, so once I get the restaurant going, remodel the bar, maybe put up a thatched roof, then you'll also be able to eat and drink for free. That sound all right to you?"

After a while, Cooper nodded, said, "I don't see why not," and fell asleep.

After a while Woolsey stood, but didn't leave. Cooper woke up, feeling Woolsey's annoying presence behind him as he attempted to relax. Woolsey shifted his weight from one foot to another in the sand. Finally, Cooper shaded his eyes from the sun with a hand again, craned his neck to look up at Woolsey, and said, "What do you want?"

"What I told you that day," Woolsey said, "that part about skimming off the top. I just wanted to let you know I won't be doing that any longer."

Through with what he had to say, the gangly young man walked away and left Cooper alone with the sun.

20

For his first exercise since the long haul up the hill, Cooper took one of those twenty-lap runs on Conch Bay's quarter-mile beach and swam across the lagoon a dozen times. Afterward, he collapsed into a chaise lounge under the shade of a palm tree. After almost a week of zilch, his legs and back still ached. The salt water and sand had stung the healing blisters on his feet, but he could feel the water's purifying effect on his wounds, the exercise clearing his arteries. Opening his lungs.

Trudging up the hill, he'd dropped Alphonse only five times. Upon reaching the summit, he found that nobody had stolen the pickup, so he put the vehicle to use and got Alphonse to a hospital in Port-au-Prince. The journey had taken maybe eighteen hours, cemetery-to-door. In the end, they hadn't been able to save Alphonse's arm, but when the docs said it looked like the kid would make it, Cooper had a specialist flown in from the U.C.L.A. Medical Center, assembled a wire transfer covering the treatment, and arranged to have the kid outfitted with the latest version of a prosthetic arm. He wired enough to cover a few months of recovery in the hospital room, food included, Cooper thinking it meant better living than Alphonse had ever known, but still came up short of the boy's natural-born right arm. At least the kid would get three squares for a while, and maybe even get laid, thanks to the conversation piece they'd be hooking up to his shoulder.

It was easier, Cooper thought, to help somebody when the person was actually alive. Somebody's dead, you can bust a few caps in the witch doctor who offed him and still wind up with the kid's ghost banging around your head. *Ce n'est pas fini, mon ami,* Marcel's ghost saying to him, Cooper hearing him more clearly in his mind's ear now, knowing the accent he'd have after listening to Simone—*Non, mon ami, you not finished. Not yet. You still all I got, Cooper. Et wi, c'est vrai—I still got more for you, too.*

He'd left a bag beside the chaise lounge before embarking on his morning workout. The beige canvas sack was stenciled with the words UNITED STATES OF AMERICA OFFICIAL GOVERNMENT BUSINESS.

The regularly scheduled diplomatic pouch that Cooper received as chief of station for the British Virgin Islands came every three weeks. International law specified that customs officials weren't allowed to examine diplomatic pouches, and some countries actually observed this rule. BVI customs officers rarely even opened personal luggage at Terrance B. Lettsome International, let alone a U.S. government pouch; Cooper figured he could probably run dope with the bag if he ever ran low on funds.

Usually the contents of these shipments meant nothing to him. On days when the pouch arrived on the launch, typically accompanied by food supplies and a handful of guests, Cooper had a tradition going: he would sit on a lounge chair, smoke a cigar, and burn each of the papers as he withdrew them, reading a line here, a paragraph there, brushing the end of the cigar against the page, blowing to get the flame going, then flipping the burning page into the sand. Nobody bothered him when he sat out here lighting fires. Not even Ronnie. He figured he looked dangerous, or possibly even insane. It gave him some space.

Today, he fired up a cigar, opened the sack, purged it of its contents, and lit up a half-dozen documents without reading anything past the heading of the cover page. Toward the bottom of the pouch, Cooper came across a DI memorandum which, as with the others, he nearly burned without reading. It was a standard memo, sent to all stations, not much different from the documents he'd already torched. Cigar butt held beside the corner of the page, Cooper took a closer look, almost out of coincidence, and saw that after a few meaningless introductory sentences, the memo said:

> Unauthorized international or extranational transport
> of substantial military weaponry, including but not
> limited to large handgun shipments, antiaircraft guns,
> armored vehicles, missiles, warheads, or lethal
> substances with possible military use, even by nation-
> states, may have special significance. Please report on
> a priority basis.

Cooper wondered about a couple of things. First, he wondered whether "lethal substances with possible military use" could include U-238/U-235 uranium. Second, while an oceanic voyage of uranium molecules aboard a supposed menial laborer's body didn't necessarily qualify as "transport of substantial military weaponry," there was something that Cooper understood about memorandums like this. What you had to ask yourself was the reason some deputy director or other, most of whom were highly educated, would authorize the distribution of such a ludicrous letter. Come across an inane memo like this and it was a safe bet something serious was afoot. You just had to translate, maybe ask around—make a couple phone calls, for instance.

Cooper figured he'd be able to discover who'd written the memo with no more than a single call.

Once he'd identified the author, he could ask a question or two of him, or her, in hopes of finding additional reasons to ignore the plea for help from the ghost of Marcel S. Maybe he could even bolster his case against digging out those business cards he'd lifted from the witch doctor's desk. He knew Barry the fucking *bokor* had killed Marcel the first time around, that much was obvious—but once that fat fuck had resurrected the boy, the odds were he'd passed the kid onto someone else. Someone who'd gone on to kill the kid again.

Wi, Cooper-mon, ce n'est pas fini.

He also knew the longer he put off avenging the second murder of Marcel S., the greater the chance his natural laziness would overcome him. That laziness would tend to keep him sequestered along the quarter mile of white sand, in the snorkeling holes, among the reefs, at the bar, in his bungalow, or on the chaise lounge under the palm tree.

And calling around Langley to unearth the nasty little secret behind the plain vanilla memo, he thought, was as good a form of procrastination as any.

You know something, Marcel, he thought—wondering whether he was talking aloud as he thought it—if I'm all you got, then you, *mon ami,* are fucked.

21

Peter M. Gates hadn't joined the Agency to fool around. His first exposure to CIA had come from political science textbooks as an undergrad, when he was bitten by the bug—the feeling, reading about the great spymasters, that he'd found his calling. Dulles. McCone. Schlesinger— men who'd hashed out deep-cover operations, pondered war strategy, run intelligence webs over fine tobacco and brandy. Gates could see it happening to him, knowing it was his destiny to become a *spymaster*, a strategy guru, a sophisticated gentleman spending his evenings in the richly furnished surroundings of a men's club—Gates thinking, even then, that Cleo's, the club in Dupont Circle, might just do.

The moment he obtained a position in government—a low-level slot at State—Gates sought out people at other agencies, and on the Hill. He made these people his friends, and he did it by finding what they aspired to and helping them get there. In a few years he had his loyal set, and he was soon able to persuade those who could afford it to join him at Cleo's. They developed a rhythm—play a few sets of squash, shower up, get together in the lounge for dinner, smoke a cigar, maybe a pipe, sip an after-dinner drink. Probe issues of foreign policy—*define* foreign policy. Make some quiet vows to *run* it.

When an acquaintance and casual member of his power network received a political appointment as director of central intelligence, Gates spent a cool four hundred dollars on a steak dinner with the man and gleaned a deputy directorship in CIA's Directorate of Operations. Because of his influence he was given two Central American countries, and just like that—fewer than five years in—Gates was running operatives from the shadowy corners of a men's club, just as he'd envisioned it.

He took pains to ensure that the job security, and, where appropriate, physical well-being of the people reporting to him were directly tied to his own supremacy within the Agency. All significant information originating from his unit reached the top of the food chain only through his office; he controlled every management decision down to the secretary and intern level with a maniacal, vengeful supervision. Slash, burn, and rule: make the eagles feel rewarded yet never allow them to take more than forty percent of the credit for any particular accomplishment, while you punted the turkeys, or, as was necessary in government, buried them with a transfer or lateral promotion. Final maxim: exert total control over the release of all information so as always to apply the appropriate spin.

He'd risen to second in command in six years.

Given his seniority level, Gates was required to take a car service everywhere; the black Lincoln assigned to him this morning came equipped with both driver and bodyguard.

The driver got the door for him as Gates exited the building through the executive tunnel. He settled into the leather seat in back.

The driver climbed behind the wheel and turned to face him.

"The Hill this morning, correct, sir?"

Gates nodded and opened a folder. Unlabeled, it contained a two-page surveillance summary written entirely in code. He was accustomed to the encryption, and knew the file to be an eight-day summary of the activities of Julie Laramie as gathered by a man named Sperling Rhone. Rhone possessed the clearance to snoop just about anywhere; outside of these essentials, the security man understood he was on his own, that there existed no record of any relationship between himself and Gates, and that Gates would deny any assertion to the contrary. Rhone followed, bugged, monitored, and occasionally intimidated any Agency employee—or non-Agency person—Gates chose to keep an eye on. The reports he generated from these activities were hand delivered, and backup records were not kept.

The report indicated that Laramie's daily routine consisted of a morning visit to a local Starbucks; a three-mile run; until recently, a fairly typical workday that included on-campus meals and commissary coffee breaks; after, she'd go directly home, sip from a glass of Chardonnay, and inevitably fall asleep in the same oversize L.A. Lakers T-shirt on her couch with some twenty-four-hour cable news channel blaring on the television. She had deviated from this routine four times—twice, she skipped the morning run; once, she met a female friend for dinner near her home; and on another night she'd driven to an Annapolis coffee house that sold Internet time by the hour.

Gates would have to instruct Rhone to watch for another

visit to the cyber café, and if she went there again, Gates would have his security man employ some reverse-keystroke software. Most of the time, suspected moles conducting such activity turned out to be nothing more than serial Internet daters or porn-surfing junkies. Gates didn't peg Laramie for a mole, but he didn't see her as a cyber-sex junkie either.

Reading Rhone's report in the back of the Lincoln, Gates chuckled at Laramie's utterly predictable behavior. It was always the same, at least among the good ones. Duly informed that Big Brother was watching, they responded by insisting on proving their point: *I'm on the radar now; if I crack the case and deliver the goods, I'm redeemed.* Those with an expansive ego took it one step further. They got ticked off, and usually worked to show him they were smarter than he was. Such employees generated deeply thorough follow-up intel and analysis, which Gates quickly took the credit for finding.

The bad ones sulked, coming to work late or calling in with too many sick days, self-justifying a demotion or transfer. Transfers worked best, since this enhanced the profile of his pervasive authority: the sulking employees delivered the message to their newly assigned departments that they'd fucked with Gates and lost.

Following her Korea score, Laramie had examined months of SATINT, working her way around the Middle and Far East in a kind of outwardly expanding semicircle. At first she'd stayed late intermittently to accomplish this, but in the last few days had worked long hours more consistently, the girl clearly less concerned about arousing suspicion. She'd kept on, searching through an ever-wider swath of images in the general portion of the world to which she was assigned, but following her initial pair of discoveries, had found nothing further.

Rhone noted for Gates a limited number of outside calls Laramie had taken in the office. None of them seemed relevant to the private investigation she had decided to conduct, except one: a conversation with a professor of political science from Northwestern University. Gates read the transcript and could see from the first part of the conversation the man knew about her predicament. This was illegal, but not alarming or uncommon; lower-level DI staffers weren't held to the rules as stringently as their DO counterparts. The remainder of Laramie's conversation with the professor was vaguely worded; this too was common—people knew they were being monitored and worked at maintaining a degree of privacy.

Considering what Julie Laramie had found, her "rogue faction" theory—as explained to Gates by Rosen and Rader—was not unreasonable. But this, Gates knew, was not the time to fire up the troops. The president was engaged in initiatives Laramie could never have known about, including a protracted negotiation with the premier of the People's Republic of China on a U.S.-China free-trade initiative. Find the right moment to deliver Laramie's intel to the president, and Gates knew the discovery could serve as significant leverage to the president in his negotiation and allow Gates to reap some kudos in the process. If it worked out that way—if he extracted enough mileage from her discovery— he'd recognize her work, Gates thinking he'd even push her right past that nitwit Rader.

Now, however, was not the right moment to bring the goods to the table.

"Shall I get your door, sir?"

Gates looked up. They'd reached Capitol Hill.

"Park it for a minute."

He closed the Laramie file and opened a second folder, labeled S.I.C. MONTHLY. He spent five minutes rereading the documents within, enough to reassure himself that he already knew exactly what to say. Then he shoved both files into his valise and opened the door himself.

"See you in an hour," he told the men in the front seat.

When Gates finished his briefing, the senators seated on the panel asked a dozen meaningless questions, which Gates's boss, Lou Ebbers, fielded on behalf of the intelligence community with twelve substance-free answers. As DCI, Ebbers was the direct contact for the committee, and was only interested in delivering presentations with sufficient substance to retain his budget. Given the Republican majority in Congress, the Senate Select Committee on Intelligence had no intention of providing anything but support for CIA, even when the president recommended differently.

When the rubber-stamp question-answer charade concluded, the senator seated in the middle of the dais whacked his gavel against its base. He removed his reading glasses and cleared his throat. A nameplate on the desk before him was engraved with the words SEN. ALAN R. KIRCHER, and below his name, the word CHAIRMAN.

"With that, gentlemen," he said, his lazy Carolina drawl resonating through the committee hall, "we're gonna go ahead and adjourn for the day."

Kircher rose, gathered his papers, handed them to an aide, and stormed out. He stormed everywhere he went. Six doors from the committee hall, Kircher stormed into his office, returned fourteen calls, held his weekly staff assembly, hosted seven back-to-back campaign-related meetings, and sat at his desk to read. He read most of the afternoon, primarily bill synopses written by his senior aides, along with selected press clippings, poll results, and the occasional correspondence from a wealthy campaign contributor. No contribution over a thousand dollars, he'd learned, had ever been provided to an election campaign without an accompanying demand for a chunk of one's soul—though this presented no particular problem for Kircher, whose soul had been for sale beginning just after birth.

At the tail end of Kircher's reading session, he unlocked a file drawer and examined its contents: a stack of photographs, mostly head-and-shoulders shots, all of stunningly beautiful women. There was a note attached to each photograph, which Kircher ignored unless he liked the picture. He flagged a pair he liked with green Post-its and returned the file to the drawer.

At a quarter to five his male assistant barged in on his reading session and handed him the evening's calendar. It listed three on-camera media appearances and one call-in interview, the first appearance booked for five-thirty. Following the interviews, he had a dinner at seven with an attractive lobbyist whose agenda he would pretend to entertain to see if he could get laid, then a party fund-raiser at nine he'd be cohosting with the Senate majority leader. Kircher dismissed his assistant, who reminded him he would need to be ass-down in his Town Car in four minutes if he hoped to keep his schedule.

Waving off the departing assistant's running commentary, Kircher logged on to his home Internet provider's site. His wife frequently left him reminders of one kind or another; it was most wise, he found, to make sure and check for such nagging demands before leaving the office. He deleted some spam and opened a note from his wife: a demand for Redskins tickets for a friend from the racquet club. "Her husband is a die-hard fan," went the note. "It would mean the world to him, hon." Kircher forwarded the note to his assistant, wrote, "Call Durso and take care of this," replied to his wife with a "No problem, sweetheart," and was about to delete another piece of spam when he noticed the sender's name, which he found to be atypically straightforward for a junk-mail correspondent. The sender's name was East-West7, and the subject line said EXERCISE.

"Senator," came the voice of his assistant from the door.

His back to the door, Kircher nodded and waved. He opened the e-mail.

Dear Senator Kircher,

Our friends in the East may not be as friendly as your friends are telling you.

An intelligent source

Kircher read it again. He did not have time to think about what it could have meant, other than the obvious. And while there was the chance of the note being nothing more than a prank, he couldn't immediately think of any punch line the note might have led to.

"Senator."

He hit Reply and wrote:

Be nice to know who you are regardless of what you are talking about.

He hit Send, logged off, pulled his jacket off the hook behind the door, and left, wordlessly snagging the bag his assistant held aloft in the hallway as he stormed out of the office.

22

The clock in the corner of her monitor told Laramie it was 12:37 A.M. She'd stayed this late, or later, the entire week. She'd stopped concerning herself with the issue of whether late nights were cause for alarm with Agency management types, mainly because she wasn't getting anywhere. She had found nothing new, so what did she care if somebody questioned the odd hours? There was nothing for them to find if they dug—no secret intel revealing the onset of World War III, simply a rebellious junior analyst working long hours to get ahead.

Or behind.

Already thinking about the glass of Chardonnay she'd knock back in three gulps the minute she got through the door, Laramie logged off and began gathering her things. She had not yet risen from her seat when the phone in her cubicle gurgled.

She tapped the speaker button.

"Yes," she said.

"Laramie."

The voice sounded a lot like Eddie Rothgeb's, so it made sense, she would later think, that in responding to it, she let his name roll off her lips.

"Eddie?"

Once the sound of his name vanished into the phone line, Laramie's impression of the voice began to register. The caller was certainly not Eddie Rothgeb. It was a man's voice, silky and deep—she didn't recognize it in the slightest.

"Yes," the voice said. "It's me."

She felt a flush of heat rush into her face. Whoever it was had just lied, and he'd thought about the lie before giving it.

Her first thought was that it might be Senator Kircher, but she knew she'd recognize his southern drawl instantaneously, and she hadn't. It could be a ruse—one of Gates's stooges keeping an eye on her. Maybe they'd found her e-mail to the senator and Gates had ordered her tested. Find out how much classified intel she was willing to part with.

"Hello, professor," she said carefully.

"Loved your memo."

Laramie's father had told her that whenever you didn't know what to do, you should count to three. He'd recommended the *one-Mississippi, two-Mississippi* technique, and also claimed that if you didn't figure something out by the time you counted to three, you never would; she thought that her father had probably added his own flair to it, something like, *If you can't figure something out by then you're still an idiot,* but the first part had stuck.

One-Mississippi.

The voice hadn't mentioned any e-mail, at least not yet. It could still be a Gates crony playing games with her, but she'd have to assume it was not, since the caller had directed the conversation toward the memo.

Two-Mississippi. She knew the memo had been released—Rader had done her the favor of blind-copying her on the distribution—and it had probably hit all stations as of a couple days back. What confused her was how the caller might have known she'd written it.

"That's very kind of you," she said. "How did you know?"

"I've got people in the right places," the voice said. "I say people, because I don't consider them friends."

Laramie needed to figure out what was going on, but she also needed to be brief in what she said. In fact, she thought, you probably shouldn't have asked him how he'd known, since you just managed to give away the fact that you'd written the memo, which the mystery caller might not have actually known without your confirmation. In any event, she had to remember Agency people would later be listening to the recording of the call. And if this wasn't one of them on the horn with her now, the roster of eavesdroppers would no doubt include a posse of Gates's cronies. *Be careful.*

"Anyway, I'm in town," the voice said. "Thought I'd give you a call. Maybe we could get together."

"Really."

"Hell, you know, catch up some. I'm curious what you've been up to."

After a moment, Laramie said, "Me too."

"While I'm in town, I'm staying with our old buddy WC. You remember old WC, don't you?"

Laramie realized something: this was her opportunity to protect herself from the people who would later be reviewing the tapes. All she had to do now was contradict what the voice was feeding her. *No,* she could say, *I never knew the guy, and while we're at it, I don't know you either.*

She knew, though, that if she were to say that, the mystery

behind the call, and the mystery of the caller's identity, would aggravate her no end.

She said, "Of course I remember WC. So he's in Washington now?"

"Yeah, how about that. You know something else? I think that after all these years, old WC's still a virgin. You believe it? Anyway, he's in the phone book. Give me a call on your way home. I'll buy you a cup of coffee.'"

Laramie was thinking what to say next in this oddly calculated conversation when she heard a click and the line went dead.

By the time she reached her car, Laramie the puzzle solver was on the case.

She considered the clues deposited by the mystery caller. He had wanted her to call him on an outside phone, that part was easy enough: *Give me a call on your way home.* And since, unless she knew what number to call, no call would be made, it followed that he'd provided enough information for Laramie to determine where to reach him.

The mystery man had also read the memo. While the memo had gone to all stations, still, such documents were only distributed to duly cleared staff; this meant the mystery man could be working anywhere in the world, but it also meant he was probably no less senior than a case officer, and considering that he had been able to pinpoint Laramie as the author of the memo, chances were he ranked pretty high on the ladder—or, if nothing else, he'd been around for a while.

He hadn't sounded like a younger man in any case.

He'd picked up on her blunder of using Rothgeb's name and run with it, working that angle into everything he said, making it sound like a perfectly normal conversation while giving her enough to figure out how to reach him. He'd repeated the initials *WC*—their *old buddy WC;* their *old buddy WC* was *still a virgin*—these, she knew, were the bread crumbs he wanted her to follow.

She released the emergency brake and made for the gate.

The names of case officers were highly compartmentalized, generally not available to DI analysts without specific need-to-know clearances. But if he knew she'd written the memo, he also knew she didn't have the kind of clearance that would allow her to look up the contact information of a typical field officer outside of her assigned projects, even a chief of station whose identity might have been more publicly known. Pulling up to the gate and waiting for it to rise, Laramie considered the two territories she knew to be called *virgin*—the U.S. and British Virgin Islands.

"Shit," she said, gestured to the guard in the booth through her closed window that she'd forgotten something, drove out the gate, turned around, and came back in, the guard raising the gate and waving her back in with a smile. She parked closer to the entrance, tempted to borrow the slot reserved for the Peter M. Gates Town Car before thinking better of it. Back in her cubicle, she logged back in, navigated to the internal telephone directory, and clicked the Index icon. She typed BVI into the empty field— Laramie figuring that for the appropriate abbreviation— and got a fresh screen headed by the words BRITISH VIRGIN ISLANDS.

There was a post office box listing in the city of Road Town, Tortola, a phone number, and the name W. COOPER alongside what appeared to be the man's cover job: PUBLIC RELATIONS/COLLEGE RECRUITER.

Laramie wrote the phone number on a Post-it, shoved the Post-it into the breast pocket of her blouse, logged out, and trudged back down to her car. She got a salute from the guard on her way out.

23

"That Laramie?"

"Why," Laramie said, "would we need a public relations officer in the British Virgin Islands?"

Cooper had a Cuba libre in his left hand and his sat phone in his right, reclined as he was in the chair on the deck of his bungalow. It was dark, the swish of the trades soothing against the palms, a distant stream of voices and music floating over from the restaurant. He could just see the bar through the garden; tourists were telling stories there, Cooper thinking gleefully that Ronnie was getting what he deserved, serving the sunburned drunkards and cleaning off their tables with a wet rag when they were done.

"Image is everything," he said.

"Who are you?"

"Mere fact of the call," Cooper said, "indicates that you already know my name."

"I don't mean your name, which I assume isn't your real name anyway. I was asking who you are. Meaning why you called, and why you wanted me to solve your little riddle and call you back."

"Which you did."

Laramie was silent.

"I," Cooper said, "would be what the BV Islanders refer to as the 'spy-a-de-island.' Chief and sole officer of station, British Virgin Islands."

"And the 'college recruiter' portion of your title?"

Cooper thought about that for a moment and said, "Not a great number of schools down here, Laramie."

"Can I ask how it is that you know my name?"

Cooper took a sip of his drink. "No," he said.

"Then I suppose I also won't hear how you know I wrote the memo."

A mechanical female voice said, "Please deposit one dollar and seventy-five cents to continue your call for two minutes." Cooper heard the sounds of Laramie inserting the proper change into the slot.

"This is an expensive call," she said.

"Pay phone." Cooper left it at that.

"Meaning you're pleased I'm playing this game of yours?"

"I'd like to ask you a question," Cooper said. "That list of materials—those I'm supposed to report on a priority basis. Would that include non-weapons-grade uranium, specifically a U-238/U-235 combination found in older power plants?"

After considering the question, Laramie said, "Based on my limited understanding of nuclear weaponry, fuel rods can be processed to create bombs, but non-weapons-grade uranium in and of itself cannot be used, practically speaking, as explosive material in a nuke. Not that it shouldn't be reported if you've discovered the illegal transportation of uranium, Mr. Cooper."

"So your list would or would not include that substance?" Cooper twirled the ice in his drink. "You *did* write the memo?"

"You know that I'm not officially allowed to comment on whether—"

"It was a rhetorical question, Laramie."

Cooper wondered what the analyst was thinking on the other end of the line, Laramie standing in a random phone booth, probably bolted into the corner of a convenience store's parking lot. The enigma from the Caribbean getting under her skin.

"Who's Eddie?" he said.

"What?"

"Your buck-seventy-five is running low."

"An old professor," Laramie said.

"Old?"

"No, not *old*. Old as in *former*. A former professor of mine."

"Where?"

"What is this?"

The hiss of the connection rose in Cooper's ear.

"Northwestern," she said.

"Good school."

"Mm-hm."

"Good professors."

Dig around enough, Cooper thought, and you find dirt. Even with this junior analyst and her former college professor. He was thinking—

"You're drunk."

Cooper heard a *click*.

The wind had begun to die down, and there wasn't as

much noise floating over from the bar. Cooper could still see a few people milling about—the sunburned faces, tank tops, Bermuda shorts and flip-flops, one or two of them wearing slacks, probably somebody told them long pants helped fend off the no-see-'ems. Watching all this in silence, Cooper thought that perhaps Julie Laramie the junior analyst wasn't so junior after all.

She had just taken him to the cleaners.

After draining the Cuba libre, Cooper ducked into his bungalow and found the two business cards he'd pilfered from the box on the witch doctor's desk. Trying the easy way first, he dialed both numbers with his sat phone. The Puerto Rico number was no longer in service, Cooper yanking the phone from his ear when the annoying triple-tone blare jolted him and a woman's recorded voice told him in Spanish that the number had been disconnected. The second number, which he'd figured for a Kingston, Jamaica, area code, went right through and gave him three short beeps. He punched in his number and the pound sign.

It took about fifteen minutes—not a bad turnaround, he thought, for two o'clock in the morning.

"Yes," Cooper said into his phone.

A muffled male voice mumbled, "Yeah, who this."

"It's me," Cooper said. "Eddie."

A second or two of static. Sounded to Cooper like another pay phone call.

"You page me, yeah?" the voice asked.

"I'm calling about the Haiti thing," Cooper said. "My talking to the right guy?"

Static ruled. Finally, in its mumble, the voice said, "What you need?"

Cooper hesitated a beat longer than he'd intended. He was well aware that lies worked better when you were fast on your feet, but Julie Laramie, he thought, stripped me of my bulletproof vest. Took away my edge. Her distracting effect has been to make me consider whether this moron with the pager can see right through the game.

"I need somebody," Cooper said. "Another Haitian—know what I mean?" Wincing, he knew he'd blown it the second the words escaped his mouth.

"Fuck you, pig."

Pager-man hung up.

Cooper shook his head. That was ridiculous—he'd had the guy going, should have been able to set up a meet, and he blows it that fast. Practically a seamless fuck-up, in fact.

He set the sat phone on the kitchen table, came over to his bed, picked up the Louisville Slugger, and took some practice swings. Thinking things over.

He'd tried the easy angle first, and if nothing else, he'd found his boy. Pager-man had bitten on the Haiti ask—hadn't told him to fuck off till he'd blown the improv later in the conversation. Now he'd just have to track the man down—maybe meet up with him wherever he made his phone calls, ask him a few questions about witch doctors. About zombies and business cards, no need to play charades any longer with the Browning pinned to Pager-man's eyebrow.

Without even seeing him yet—without asking enough questions to know anything for certain—Cooper had the impulse to hunt down Pager-man and whack him with the baseball bat. Maybe it was the guy's cocky, mumbling tone, Pager-man sounding stoned out of his gourd, ready to deal some crank, or hell, maybe a recently exhumed Haitian, dial one-eight-hundred, *Z-O-M-B-I-E-S*—

Cooper tossed the Louisville Slugger on the bed and migrated to the chair. He fired up his PowerBook, worked through some firewalls, and got himself to the inquiry page of Interpol's reverse-telephone directory. He pulled the business card and punched in Pager-man's phone number. It took about five minutes for the system to spit out the phone company—Verizon. Easy enough, he thought. Exiting the Interpol database, he worked his way into an Agency site, filled out the appropriate online form, and e-mailed a request. This one would take two or three days to get an answer, but when the drones working the night shift in the basement in Langley got back to him, they'd deliver on his request and provide the correct billing address of the Verizon account coinciding with the number he'd dialed to get a hold of his new, though somewhat rude, phone pal.

Laramie knew of a Kinko's near the turnaround point on her morning run. Since finding the China intel, she was only running twice a week; while this meant her weekly exercise quota had been halved, she'd nonetheless been able to check her new e-mail account twice while out on the runs. Outside of a canned WELCOME, EASTWEST7! from somebody called Mail Services, the in-box had remained woefully vacant.

She thought about the odd phone call from W. Cooper on the outbound segment of her morning jog. Maybe she was becoming a mean-spirited person, but she had to admit her most enjoyable moment in weeks had come when she outed the inebriated, so-called college recruiter. She'd easily been able to tell he was hammered, the man working hard enough against slurring his words to give it away, but Laramie had an unfair advantage on reading such mannerisms after spending the first twelve years of her life with a similarly and consistently inebriated father. No matter how frequently W. Cooper tossed 'em back, Laramie thought, it was unlikely he could have hung with Dad in the consumption department.

W. Cooper's voice had sounded familiar to her. Not because she had met him before—she knew she hadn't—but there'd been an ease between them, the kind you shared with a friend you'd been holding daily water-cooler conversations with, bonding in the copy room of some high-stress office environment. It occurred to her now that this was largely due to the fact that W. Cooper actually sounded a lot like her father—though this, she thought, probably stemmed from the fact he'd have tested out at somewhere near the blood-alcohol percentage Dad would have registered the last time she'd seen him.

Or maybe he was just an asshole, and because of this, she'd enjoyed coming out ahead in their little sparring match.

She came around a corner and slipped into the Kinko's. She checked her watch and saw it was almost six-forty-five; as with the two other mornings she'd visited, the store was just opening for the day. It said OPEN TWENTY-FOUR HOURS on the window, but for reasons on which Laramie chose not to speculate, the place usually opened at six-thirty and closed before midnight.

She bought a computer-hour in cash, logged on, and found Senator Kircher's reply. She read his request a few times and still couldn't figure out how to answer.

Did it make any sense to continue the game? After Korea, she'd been unable to find even a shred of additional supporting evidence. Rogue faction, my ass, she thought. Rogue analyst, yes—sitting here like a buffoon in my running bra, digging for trouble where none exists. Still, she thought, at least Kircher might be able to tell me whether this connect-the-dots guesswork of mine has any legitimacy, or whether I'm simply full of shit.

She composed an adaptation of the pair of reports she'd filed during the prior two weeks. She included all of it—everything she'd written, all the material she'd presented totally against Agency protocol, even the speculative guesswork she'd shared with Malcolm Rader in the commissary.

When she'd worked up a draft, she reread it four, then five times, editing nearly every word on each pass. She nearly deleted the entire document twice, then ultimately decided the whole thing needed an introductory statement, which she added as the first line of her note:

It's better for the both of us if my identity remains confidential. Look at it this way: I'm an informed source, privy to the following intelligence, which you may or may not find useful. Some of this is theory, in fact most of it is theory, but my voice is not being heard in the community you oversee. Thus it occurred to me you might want to hear what I'm about to tell you.

She inserted a paragraph break between her introductory statement and the body of her document, reread the entire thing a sixth time, and decided to add some closing remarks:

Since I find it useful to remain gainfully employed, chances are you will not hear from me again. I leave what I am disclosing for you to do with as you see fit. Thank you for your time.

She resisted the impulse to read the document a seventh time, further resisted the impulse to delete the entire composition, clicked Send, logged off, waved to the clerk at the counter despite the fact that his eyes lingered too long in the vicinity of her sports bra, and set out on the return leg of her run.

24

One day a nineteen-year-old named Travis Malloy was a petty officer in the U.S. Navy; the next day he wasn't. It had been as simple as that.

With the ship leaving Kingston after his three days of leave, Malloy just didn't get back on. He didn't have a choice: get back on and they'd have busted him, Malloy getting word they'd found him out. And who cared? Malloy didn't need the navy anyway, the whole deal a sausage fest, thousands of homos sleeping side by side in bunks a regular guy like Malloy wouldn't even share with a *woman*.

Now he could share his bed with any woman he pleased.

Travis Malloy had strange, pale freckled skin and short, shockingly red hair. Technically, Malloy was of African-American descent, but aside from a slightly blunted nose and the thick texture of his hair, Malloy was an albino. He fit no single previously defined ethnic category.

Light-complected though he happened to be, Malloy preferred women with skin so dark it gleamed. Get a whore like that, and he'd ball her all night. Yeah, he could sure ball 'em all night, Malloy banging away like the girl was lifeless, which made sense, since by the time he had the girl in bed, she usually was. Malloy mostly asphyxiated them, though sometimes broke their necks, generally doing it as he pulled them through the doorway of whatever room he'd procured for the night—paying in cash to keep his identity a secret. Having performed this morbid act in nearly a dozen ports of call, Malloy figured somebody would eventually make him, so when he finally got word they'd caught on it didn't surprise him at all. Malloy overheard some idle talk from a couple of the navy fags during leave in Jamaica and bolted immediately.

Kingston was his favorite city in the world anyway, a town overflowing with dark-skinned prostitutes, Malloy finding they were a dime a dozen here, about all Malloy was looking to pay, anyway. He could get all he wanted, pick hookers up everywhere he went—lost souls, wanderers, enough of them here that Malloy had to be careful not to kill too many, since he found he wanted to stay. He met one girl, just the kind he wanted, her mind blown to kingdom come from so much weed Malloy got high just sucking on her lips. She was into some sort of freaked-out religion, a form of voodoo. Initially, the only reason this mattered to Malloy was that she and her religious practices represented an easy way for him to score weed—some good shit in fact. He found the dope was a part of the religion. They smoked it during the ceremonies.

During the time he was balling the voodoo girl, Malloy did pick-up day labor to pay the bills, using a fake name so the navy wouldn't send the marines after his AWOL ass. He found plenty of jobs, Malloy discovering that labor laws weren't quite as stringent in Jamaica as in the States; he was, however, getting a little tired of the day-to-day grind, waiting around before the crack of dawn, hoping the labor truck would cruise by with enough empty seats for him to squeeze in. Get work, and you had enough money for drugs and parties; get passed over, and you starved.

From this desperation was born in Travis Malloy an idea, an entrepreneurial scheme that occurred to him mainly because he misunderstood something at work.

Malloy overheard his foreman saying something about the good old days of slavery, a time when you could buy your labor and the labor wouldn't talk back. The foreman had been telling a joke, his way of complaining about some local hooligans who were trying to form a labor syndicate, but to Malloy the man's comment contained a different and deeper meaning.

That night his voodoo girl took him to one of her parties. It was a wild one this time, crazy, the whole deal taking place in a vacant warehouse. The thing Malloy noticed was a group of guys, skin dark as asphalt like his girl—maybe six or seven of them, guys so doped up they were comatose the whole time he was there. They stood in corners, sometimes swaying to the music but never doing anything more than that.

It gave him one hell of an idea.

Malloy suckered three of them, one by one, into coming outside. He gave each a line—something about the sweet pussy he could arrange for them in the joint next door—and once outside, he bound, gagged, and shoved each of them into the back of his van. He stopped at three—any more than that, and even the stoners at the party would have noticed these losers missing. Plus, three bodies were all he could fit into his van without stacking them. He figured three would be plenty anyway.

The next morning he drove up to the quarry where he'd been working and found the foreman he'd overheard the day before. He pulled the foreman aside.

"I heard you talking about slavery yesterday," he said.

The foreman, a thick-limbed West Indian with a gut like Santa Claus, looked Travis Malloy up and down.

"What about it?" he said.

Malloy asked, "Ain't you the man does all the hiring here?"

"Most of it."

"What about some shit needs doing, nobody needs to know about it? Anybody ever want you to find people can do that kind of work?"

After a moment, the foreman said, "Maybe."

Malloy said, "Probably something you might need, you got a job like that you need to fill, is disposable labor. The kind you can use up and throw out when you're finished."

The foreman stared at this strange-looking, light-skinned, vaguely African-American freak with the short-cropped red hair.

Malloy said, "If you're interested, I got some contacts could hook you up with somebody provides that kind of labor pretty cheap."

After another short while the foreman said, "I'll think about it."

Malloy told the fat-ass foreman to have somebody call him. Scribbling his beeper number on a brown paper lunch sack and handing it to the man.

The acquisition of the three stoners presented a small problem: it kept Malloy apart from his voodoo girl while he waited it out. He had to keep the three guys tied up in his house, couldn't risk bringing the girl by and having her find out. Lucky for Malloy, who couldn't afford to feed his captives, the wait only lasted a day and a half. The page came directly from the foreman, who asked whether Malloy would be able to come and meet with the foreman's associates, so they could discuss that concept of his, what did he call it?

Malloy said, "Disposable labor's what I called it," and agreed to meet.

He had to go out to a rural park in the middle of the night, but he took a gamble and brought his three captives along in the van. This allowed him to close the deal on the spot—no questions asked, hand over the trio of starving drug addicts for two-fifty cash, more money than Malloy could have made working in the quarry for five or six weeks.

A few months later, about the time his finances were running low again—Malloy thinking about going back out to wait for the day-labor truck—he got another page. It was a new voice, not the foreman and not the people the foreman had brought him to. The voice asked whether he had access to any more of the sort of labor he'd provided to an acquaintance of his. Malloy said that he did and asked how many they were talking here. The voice said two, or maybe three. Malloy thought for a moment before saying, "Going rate's five hundred a head."

The voice told him that wouldn't be a problem.

Malloy had some difficulty this time, had to cruise the hard-core party scene for a few days before he found some suitable addicts. He even had to work the Kingston homo scene to get his third man, but his navy days gave him some experience with that, so he got it together and delivered the goods just the same. Five hundred bucks a head, cash, and Malloy was fucking *loaded*.

As word got around there was a serial killer preying on homosexual users in the Kingston underground party circuit, it wasn't long before demand had outstripped his basic supply. A few calls from such sources as the contractors of a South American airport expansion, some shadowy weapons manufacturers, and a pair of rogue strip-mining investors made it clear to Malloy how much fucked-up shit was going down. He had raised his price to fifteen hundred a head by the time his girl taught him more about the voodoo ceremonies, telling him some of the traditions, including the one in which local medicine men drugged up the town retards, rattled off some mumbo jumbo, and turned them into zombies. Fucking real-life zombies, some in Jamaica, a hell of a lot more up in Haiti. Malloy was a businessman, and he saw in this new product source an opportunity to lower his risk, accountability, and cost. The logic was pretty simple: find some people other people thought were already dead, and you had yourself some *truly* disposable labor.

Malloy soon had to off the voodoo girl, figuring she'd have too much on him if he didn't, but once she was out of the picture, Malloy got back into a rotation of dark-skinned hookers, fresh ones, boning 'em all night like he used to—putting some of his ingeniously earned money to use. In fact, he was taking care of a frail one, bony, rocking her from behind in something like his fourth hour, when dawn broke one morning outside the rental house he kept near Belle Acres, one of the rare middle-class neighborhoods in Kingston.

Parked discreetly on the street in front of Malloy's house was a green Ford Taurus. Since Malloy couldn't see the car while balling his girlfriend inside the house, he obviously couldn't see the man inside the car, either; seated behind the wheel of the Taurus was a gruff, deeply tanned American with bloodshot eyes and a few days' stubble.

Bored out of his skull and half asleep, Cooper wondered when the hell he would see something that would indicate what the sexual dynamo inside the house did for a living, and why a witch doctor in the Haitian badlands would have kept this freak's pager number on a blank business card behind his desk.

The Verizon account inquiry CIA made through the company's USVI-based regional headquarters had kicked back a name and billing address. The name on the account was James Beam, which joke Cooper appreciated immediately; the address turned out to be only that, matching a shithole local equivalent of a Mail Boxes, Etc. store. Cooper had first parked his Taurus near the store, begrudgingly arriving by way of American Eagle to San Juan and then American, no Eagle, on to Kingston. He had no idea what he was looking for, but hadn't partaken of the utter boredom of a good old-fashioned stakeout in years. It hadn't seemed so bad, Cooper sitting on the Conch Bay beach thinking about doing it, but after seventy-two hours of observing box number nineteen through the facility's dirt-spattered window, chubbing up on a variety of Blimpie sandwiches while planted in the driver's seat of the Taurus, he began to think that there might be a better way of going about this. Pulling around the corner every four or five hours to take a leak in the alley behind a grocery store, heading downtown to pass out in a room at the Crowne Plaza when the mail center's closing time came around, only to start the routine from the beginning again.

He tried to avoid thinking about Marcel S. and Cap'n Roy

while he sat in the car, working at different methods of throwing up a mind block when thoughts of them entered his head. One way that worked, he found, was to allow his mind to wander northward. To Langley, or at least to some suburb nearby.

To wherever it was that Julie Laramie lived.

He kept thinking about the way she'd spoken to him. She'd carefully and consistently taken a moment to think about anything she said before saying it, Laramie putting the extra time she bought into thinking about what to say or what not to say, maybe into calculating the reason he'd called her with his annoying probe in the first place. She'd handled the first call effectively, considering he'd caught her in the Professor Eddie mistake—well enough to tell him to go fuck himself, at least in her own way. Lot of people, Cooper thought, are coming up with highly creative ways to tell me to fuck off.

It's funny, he thought: I spent the whole call trying to get under her skin, and in the end, she's the one who burrowed under mine.

Early in the seventy-third hour of his stakeout of the mail joint, Cooper got his first look at Barry the witch doctor's distributor of the undead. The guy who opened box nineteen was one of the strangest-looking human beings Cooper had ever seen—there was no doubt he was African-American somewhere back in the family tree, but his lunar skin and tiki-torch hair made for a brutal departure from that side of his family. To get a grasp on what he was looking at, Cooper decided he would have to make up a new racial-profiling term and called the man a redheaded albino black.

Cooper had pulled into traffic behind the guy's sputtering Mitsubishi minivan and followed him home; a little later he followed him to a bar with an address on a particularly sleazy avenue called the Half Way Tree Road. Later still, Cooper followed ol' Jim Beam—along with the dark-skinned girl he'd picked up at the bar—back to Jim's house. The home was a two-bedroom job on a decent street, Jim doing all right for himself renting here—assuming he was renting, which Cooper figured he probably was.

Camped outside Jim's place, Cooper's knees were in danger of catching frostbite, so cold was the air-conditioning flow from the vents beneath the dash. The A/C was uneven, so that while his knees were turning blue, sweat ran in a constant stream down his neck, back, and ass. The subject of his stakeout didn't emerge from the house for sixteen hours following the time he'd entered it with his dark-skinned date, though two events did occur during that time. Around 6 A.M., immediately following the Caribbean's rapidly brightening dawn, a taxi crawled up the street, stopped in front of the albino's house, and parked until the girl came out and got in. The cab drove off. Later, just after four, Cooper burning up the engine in the Taurus to keep the air-conditioning going, a young Jamaican arrived in a beat-up four-door Civic—the car reminding Cooper of Manny's SJPD-issue detective mobile.

The visitor wore a shiny Adidas sweat suit, going with the full outfit even in the ninety-degree heat. He cool-walked it to the albino's front door, and then they were pretty obvious about it: Jim answered the door, came out on the porch, handed the Jamaican some money, and the Jamaican handed Jim a bag of weed. Neither of them looked around or otherwise displayed any cause for concern, just standing out there on the porch doing a drug deal.

There, Cooper thought—that, in a nutshell, is what the Caribbean is all about.

The Jamaican cool-walked it back to his Honda and

zipped off down the street. After dark, around nine, the albino started the circuit all over again, Cooper pulling out to follow the Mitsubishi minivan, actually moving some air through the Ford's radiator for a change, following him to the bar, where the albino came out with the same dark-skinned girl and took her home with him again. Cooper took the opportunity to change clothes, procure more Blimpie sandwiches, relieve himself somewhere besides the tree at the end of the block, and refill the fluids in the Ford. He didn't have too much faith in the car, its thermometer rising one notch closer to the red zone each day he spent in the afternoon heat.

For four days running, the albino followed this routine, almost to the minute. The lone deviation was that the dope supplier came every *other* day, which was still pretty frequent, given the hefty size of the Baggies the albino was buying from him.

Without some indication as to how the redheaded albino black worked, if at all, with Barry the Haitian witch doctor, Cooper didn't know how long he could sit out on this fucking street watching some freak get off and get high. On the fifth day of his surveillance of Jim Beam's home—presented with no sign of a break in the routine—Cooper gave up on his current angle and decided to try out one of the two leads he'd ingeniously unearthed from the seat of his rental car.

25

In the far eastern reaches of the Lesser Antilles lay one of the more exclusive resorts on earth. Built into a sloping hill on the leeward side of an island called Mango Cay, the resort grounds included the most luxurious rooms, a secluded private beach, and adjoining world-class coral reefs. For any traveler affluent enough to stay here during the high season, the nightly room rate might have run in excess of five thousand dollars—except for the fact that no rooms were ever rented to anyone.

There were poolside cabanas, all near the beach, all with sweeping ocean views. The furniture was imported from Europe, costing hundreds of thousands of dollars, and the beach had been formed of the purest white sand, the water in the lagoon the clearest blue. Mango Cay was densely wooded and mountainous, a particularly lush volcanic isle. Many of the islands in the neighboring Antilles were volcanic in origin; many were lush.

But not like Mango Cay.

Fully half its land mass seemed eternally shrouded in

mist, a thin, lingering fog that hung low over the steep, jagged cliffs of the windward side of the isle. A single, thick rain forest, painting the hills emerald green, squatted beneath the eternal mist. On the leeward side of the island was the horseshoe-shaped bay that held in its clutches the exclusive resort and its glassy lagoon, untouched by the mist.

There was an unwritten law in the Caribbean: if you were rich enough to buy one of these islands, you wouldn't be bothered. Not by the local citizenry, not by the authorities. And so, as mysterious as this particular island happened to be, nobody paid any mind to Mango Cay. Outside of their receipt of the chunky quarterly property tax deposit from the isle's proprietors, officials of the island's governing territory—Martinique, controlled ultimately by France—simply ignored the place, unobtrusively providing Mango Cay with the privacy its clandestine proprietor sought.

Local rumor had it that the reclusive proprietor was a famous multibillionaire, a quiet captain of industry so rich he could afford to have the island meticulously kept year-round simply for the one or two weekends a year he and his family came to visit.

This, however, was not the case at all.

Once he had found the *Chameleon,* Deng positioned two teams of frogmen in the vicinity of the wreck on an indefinite basis. He was able to do this by building the small but exorbitantly expensive underwater equivalent of a space station, and by outfitting the frogmen with custom-designed deep-sea dive equipment capable of withstanding pressure in excess of 9,000 p.s.i.—depths of nearly four miles. He had the station built in dry dock and submarined in modules to its home south of the Bermuda Triangle; Deng designed it with underwater stealth technology, stolen, as usual, from a U.S. defense contractor.

Operating a set of limited-range salvage pods out of the underwater docking station, Deng's teams took almost three years to penetrate the *Chameleon*'s skin, isolate its missile bays, and move, piecemeal, each of the submarine's full inventory of twenty-four C-4 Trident I intercontinental ballistic missiles from the submarine to the station. The frogmen worked six-month shifts, Deng having them picked up or dropped off by a PLN submarine pass a few miles off. By September 1997, at the annual break his team was forced to take during hurricane season, Deng had disassembled and transferred to a nearby uninhabited island twelve complete Trident missiles, and—of equal importance in Deng's long-range scheme—the *Chameleon*'s nuclear power cell.

To maintain secrecy over the life of his project, Deng was presented with various concerns, the first being where and how to secure, and then conceal, his astronomical budget. Had Deng used Chinese military or intelligence allocations to fund the operation, fellow State Council members would have found out about it. Deng knew that as surely as Mikhail Gorbachev had assassinated the Soviet Union, it was only a matter of time before some fellow council member coined his own term for *glasnost*, or, worse, *perestroika*—and were any one of the cowards now thinking up such words to stumble across Deng's modest clandestine scheme, he wouldn't be around to enjoy any weekly polo match: he'd be holed up in solitary in Inner Mongolia, freezing his ass off. And that was only if he were able to convince enough of his political allies to keep him away from the firing squad.

Accordingly, Deng decided to reach out to a few supposed ideological comrades around the Orient. He never took a meeting directly; he used Li and, later, a Caucasian associate as his front men. Once the operation was moving forward and the Trident missiles were found intact, he extended his recruiting effort beyond the Pacific Rim. If there weren't such a stark prerequisite of secrecy, he would have welcomed every would-be revolutionary into his gala scheme, but instead settled on a dozen organizations, most of them nation-states, all with declared communist or socialist intentions, all totalitarian in their management style. He instructed his middlemen to speak grandly of the New World Order, a revolutionary brotherhood that would return the leadership of the world to its people. The working people. *To each according to his needs.*

Sending his front men to hold secret, face-to-face meetings, he would have them pose a single question. Imagine, his script went, if we could guarantee you that the military superpower now standing guard against your imperialist intentions would be rendered impotent, immobile, and blind. That, say, if you were to march your army straight down into South Korea and annex that country into yours, and in the process receive no resistance whatever from that superpower—what, Deng's men asked, would that be worth?

Early on, Deng asked for comparatively minuscule membership fees—sixty million a pop, divided into semiannual payments—and provided comparatively vague promises. He also discovered a flaw in his scheme and scrambled to correct the error: anybody who heard this question and happened to decline to enroll in the brotherhood presented an immediate problem, even with the buffer of the middlemen. Fortunately for Deng, though, the three leaders who rejected his vision died soon after the rejection: one in an airline crash, one in a hit-and-run automobile accident, and another who'd managed to drown while swimming alone in a private pool that lacked a deep end.

Finally, just under four years ago—or about the time Julie Laramie was signing the requisite thirty-month commitment letter making her a trainee of the Central Intelligence Agency—Deng asked Admiral Li and the Caucasian to convene his revolutionary brethren inside of a bank vault in Zurich, where they were told that the yet-to-be-identified visionary behind the operation would, in fact, make good on his promise.

They were told they could now take the final preparatory steps to prepare for their military operations. They were told that their investment would now, imminently, yield the sought-after freedom from the evil capitalist superpower they despised—the freedom promised in those very first meetings. Deng also had his middlemen tell the brethren they should gather a few hundred million dollars so that they could afford the final installment of their membership dues.

After an additional year of delays brought on by a Caribbean hurricane—and about the time Laramie spotted the first invasion simulation—Deng sent the official invoice for one final, whopping payment from each member of the revolutionary brotherhood, graciously extending an invitation along with the invoice. What Deng offered as bait to warrant delivery of the final payment was an opportunity for each investor to witness history in the making: the members of the revolutionary brotherhood would be invited to observe, first-hand, the facility the investments had enabled their mentor to construct.

Upon deposit of their invoiced payment, Deng would bring his league of revolutionary leaders to see the launch headquarters for the project he had not yet named in correspondence with the brotherhood, but had privately come to call Operation Blunt Fist.

The customary flourish of an appearance by General Deng Jiang was dampened by the logistics of Mango Cay's lagoon: to get from the pontoon of the seaplane to the dry sand of the beach required a calf-deep, three-step wade through the Caribbean. Deng, who had been here before, had come prepared: he'd removed his shoes and socks and rolled up his khakis to the knee while still inside the float plane. Ill-prepared by comparison, PLN Rear Admiral Li Zhu strode into the water in his tennis shoes and jeans. Li, at least, unlike Deng, had dressed in the assigned disguise— Levi's jeans, Nike T-shirt, Reebok sneakers. He looked as American as a man like Li was capable of looking.

Deng and Li were met on the beach by the island's security director, a grotesquely muscle-bound man with oily black hair and perhaps the thinnest neck ever seen on a man of his bulk. With dark bags under his eyes, whitehead zits spread across his forehead, and an upper body befitting a winner of the World's Strongest Man competition, he represented a rare dichotomy of both sickly, blemished weakness, and near-ideal physical health. There was no one on earth who resembled this man.

His name was Spike Gibson.

Gibson gave General Deng a halfhearted bow.

"*Lou bahn,*" he said, Mandarin for *boss.*

Deng nodded at his middleman and kept walking, barefoot in the sand. "You have taken care of our guests, I gather," he said.

"Eleven strong, most of them relaxing in the cabanas. The first six came in last night, the other five an hour ago." The oddly disproportionate muscles in Gibson's chest were nearly splitting the fabric of the tropical print shirt he wore, but when he spoke, his neck stretched even thinner than its normal, scrawny state.

Deng looked sternly about the resort.

"I don't see any of them utilizing the facilities," he said. "This is not what I ordered."

Two steps behind, Li peered past Deng to take in the pool, the bar, the racks stacked full of plush towels, the rows of portable lounge chairs, the cabanas, the bartender, the maid. The sun was oppressively hot; Deng and Li had each already begun to sweat.

"Our guests are a little shy, General," Spike Gibson said, telling a bald-faced lie. "Most of them are staying inside—looking to keep cool." In fact Spike Gibson had instructed the men they were not allowed on the beach for longer than five minutes at a time.

Deng grunted. "Tell them that while they're here, the point is to appear that they are vacationing. Tell them I expect all of them to take full advantage of the resort and all its amenities."

Gibson said, "Of course, Comrade General. As you want it."

"And your other projects?"

Gibson returned Deng's gaze without speaking.

Deng didn't budge. Gibson shrugged.

"All is well," Gibson said.

Deng turned and walked onto the poolside tile, Admiral Li in tow. Gibson summoned the maid, asking that she show the leaders to their rooms.

Passing Gibson, Li caught the security director's eyes and kept hold of them as he crossed the poolside patio. Just before turning the corner, he bowed officiously, the act meant to emphasize that Li was the honored guest, and Gibson, his subservient host. Gibson jerked his chin at Li—a bow in Gibson's language—and watched as he walked away, Li's wet tennis shoes squeaking on the tile as he went.

Deciding he needed a break from the stakeout routine, Cooper took a drive to the bar where it might have appeared, to the untrained eye, that the albino's dark-skinned girlfriend was working as a cocktail waitress. He parked the Taurus around the corner from the place around six-forty-five, which gave him a good two hours before Jim came to collect his woman for another night of rapture.

The minute he came through the door, Cooper, private-eye-for-the-dead, confirmed the obvious: the girl was working there, all right, but not as a cocktail waitress. The only legitimate employee in the place was the bartender. He stood behind the bar, facing a pair of rummies, who sat on two of the pub's four stools. The joint was a dump—a couple of naked bulbs dangling above the bar, some reggae playing on a boom box behind it, a handful of seats and tables in the narrow corridor between the bar and the opposing wall.

Seated at one of the tables were four girls. One of them was Jim's woman; all four wore skirts that bottomed out around mid-ass and tops about as modest as Saran Wrap.

They wore cheap jewelry that dangled from ears, wrists, ankles, and waist, Cooper figuring there were some dangling from places he couldn't see too. There was the rich scent of weed, wafting to him from the hazy cloud of smoke over their table, starting to give him a buzz just from standing in the doorway.

Cooper took one of the vacant stools at the bar and ordered some bourbon. When the bartender finished pouring the watered-down, unlabeled selection of his own choosing, Cooper said, "How much for more?"

The bartender looked him over, shrugged, and said, "That depend on what you want, mon." He had that accent, Jamaicans always sounding to Cooper like they were ready to party. Every little thing goin' to be all right.

Cooper put a hundred-dollar bill on the counter and said, "I like the skinny one."

The bartender's eyes gleamed, staring down at the bill. Cooper could sense an inner turmoil. He guessed the man was thinking how to make a buck off him, since Cooper was obviously loaded, laying down a C-note like it was nothing. But the man didn't want to lose his top client, either.

The bartender-pimp completed his inner battle and said, "That get you two hours."

Cooper frowned, giving him an acting job, *Man, tough decision, all that money.* "All I get is two hours then?"

The bartender-pimp flipped his hands upside down and shrugged again. "Understand, any other time you get more than that, but Rhonda here, she got a regular kind of thing, mon. Friend of hers coming by 'round nine o'clock."

Cooper nodded. He said, "Rhonda."

"We got a deal, mister? Or you want another maybe."

"No," Cooper said, "Rhonda's my kind of girl."

Rhonda didn't say or do anything different from what

she'd been doing since Cooper had come into the bar: eyes closed, she pulsed slightly to the music, sitting on her chair, toking absently on the joint each time it came around to her.

The bartender-pimp swiped the hundred bucks off the counter.

"Nine o'clock," he said. "Don't be late, mon."

Coming across the busy lobby of the Crowne Plaza around seven-thirty, Rhonda's skirt showed an under-crescent of her skinny ass with every step, first one side then the other. She was so stoned that Cooper gleefully antici-pated at least an "Ex*cuse* me, sir" from the concierge—or *somebody* on the hotel staff—but sadly, they made it through the lobby, into the elevator, and all the way into his room without incident.

In his suite he watched her shed the halter top and unzip the miniskirt. Lying on the bed then, eyes half-shut, one knee raised, arms splayed out with her palms outstretched, Rhonda telling him to come and get some, Cooper thought that the sight might have been appealing to him had his tastes run to anorexic, comatose preteen boys. Holding back from tearing off his clothes, he took out his wallet and fanned about fifty bucks in fives and tens on the table beside the bed. He was obvious about it, crumpling then unfolding the bills to help release her from the anticipatory trance she had going.

"Nice as that looks, Rhonda," he said, "I've got some-thing else in mind."

Rhonda had her eyes open now, the girl counting the money he was showing. "What that you lookin' for den, mon," she said.

"Tell you what. Why don't I just ask you some questions,"

he said. "Any answers you give sound true to me, I'll pay you five or ten bucks. We're done and I feel like you haven't been making everything up, you get a fifty-dollar bonus. After that, I take you back to the bar and the albino comes and picks you up just like he did yesterday, and the day before that. Two or three weeks go by and I find out you can keep a secret, nobody knows we did anything but fuck like bunnies up in here, there's another five hundred bucks coming your way free of all commissions to your pimp daddy bartender."

She didn't say anything, just stayed splayed out on the bed, lips moist and parted.

"How's that sound, Rhonda," Cooper said.

Rhonda shuffled her feet to push herself back up against the headboard. She pulled on the halter top, zipped up the miniskirt, brought her legs up against her body, and clasped her arms around her knees. Eyes no longer hiding under their lids, Rhonda looked at him, fully alert.

"Yeah, mon," she said, "that sound pretty good to me."

According to Rhonda, Jim had gone through two of the other girls in the bar—spend a few weeks tagging one, take another for the same price, switch back once in a while, depending on the mood. He always did it the same way— come in, get a drink or two, bring the girl back, pound away like a madman for something like five hours, this guy a sexual piston, sleep a couple hours, wake up, call a cab, kick the girl out. Rhonda told him there had been the occasional visit from a friend, sometimes expected, sometimes not, somebody swinging by once every two or three days. This Cooper knew: Jim's supplier. He asked her what she thought he did to make his money; Rhonda said she knew he didn't ever leave to go to any particular job, Jim having her stick around well into the day a few times, and all he ever did was buy more dope and come back inside and smoke it.

He asked if Jim kept anything around the house that had something to do with a career of any kind; Rhonda thought it over before saying there was nothing she could remember, except that she'd seen him fiddling with a chain.

"You know, mon," she said, "pendant and chain, but the kind a man keep," and Cooper thought of something and said, "You mean dog tags?" and she said that was it.

He asked if she knew where he kept them, and she said he had a jewelry box—she'd seen him taking it in and out of the top drawer of his dresser. Cooper asked about his real name, or at least the name he used with her, and she said he went only by Jim. He asked if she'd ever seen his full name on anything, maybe on a utility bill, and she told him he never left anything out for her to look at. When he asked whether she'd ever seen what it said on the dog tags, she said she hadn't.

The only other interesting revelation, in which Rhonda made about a hundred bucks, was that whenever Jim was paged, he announced it was time for Rhonda to leave. It had happened twice, late at night both times, Jim pulling out of her, checking the pager, telling her it was time to go, let's get you a cab, then walking out the door with her and driving off in that van of his before the cab arrived. When Cooper asked how late at night this was, she said it had happened sometime after 2 A.M. each time.

He took Rhonda back to the bar around eight-forty-five and hung around until Jim showed up. Cooper watched Jim sip some rum and Coke from a straw, reach over and do one of those brother-man handshakes with the bartender-pimp, the kind Cooper could never keep up with, always something new with these guys—then Jim took Rhonda by the hand and led her out to his van. It looked to Cooper as though Rhonda actually gave him a wink as she walked out the door, but with those swollen, bloodshot eyes it was hard to tell for sure.

Cooper stuck around for another half hour, left a five-dollar tip for the one-dollar beer he'd been sipping, and trudged out to the Taurus, thinking if he kept having to sit in that goddamned car he was going to have to get out and run a couple hundred laps on the quarter-mile beach when he got home.

27

The next time Jim left to pick up Rhonda for the night, Cooper climbed out of the Taurus and made his way up Jim's porch. Seeing no visible sign of an alarm system, he went ahead and took the grave risk of breaking and entering a home in Kingston, Jamaica, and upon snapping open the lock was promptly assaulted by the smell of reefer. Coming in, Cooper thought that the guy had to be smoking morning, noon, and night with the odor as thick as it was in the house. Maybe he would grow dreadlocks by the time he left.

The house was poorly kept, with rumpled dirty laundry obscuring much of the floor in the front hall. Cooper moved into the kitchen, which told the same story, crumbs and half-eaten fast food on the counter, a couple weeks of crusty dishes stacked in the sink. There were no pictures on the fridge, and only American cheese, Wonder bread, peanut butter, ketchup, mustard, mayonnaise, whole milk, and three cans of Bud inside it. Working through a pair of closets, he found the usual Caribbean attire.

The bedroom was the center of Jim's world, all the necessities packed in there—the weed spilling out of a plastic bag on the side table, some joints beside it, a Magnavox TV, a boom box, a full-length mirror angled against the wall. On the unmade bed he found a remote control, a dank towel, and a cigarette lighter. The dirty laundry scheme for this particular room included underwear, socks, and T-shirts; Cooper couldn't find a single photograph of Jim, and nothing at all hung on the walls.

He went through the drawers: low on clothes, a few magazines, neatly stacked—*Penthouse, Hustler, Oui*—Cooper thinking the *Oui* must have been tough to get, living in Kingston. He found a pistol under a pair of jeans, a basic revolver, Smith & Wesson .38 Special. It was loaded. Another drawer had a box of bullets and a knife, a big serrated hunting knife in an olive green sheath. Military issue. He found no jewelry box, nor anything like one.

In the drawer of the side table, Cooper found some cash, a spare set of keys, a gold chain, some women's hair clips, a scuffed Yankees cap—but still no jewelry box. It began to occur to Cooper that Jim didn't use condoms, not unless he kept them hidden in one hell of a hiding place.

He opened the closet, where he found the other half of the various pairs of shoes that Jim kept distributed across the rest of the house. Sweat suits, shorts, belts, shirts, a rolled poster—Cooper unfurling it to find a *Sports Illustrated* photograph of Tyra Banks in a bikini—boxes stacked in the bottom of the closet, some of them shoe boxes, Cooper pulling out the most accessible one and opening it, finding the only sign of life yet, a short stack of old snapshots, mainly of Jim on the beach with different black girls. Cooper moved a pair of broken sunglasses out of the way and saw something he thought Rhonda might consider a jewelry box: a bare pine cube about six inches across, lid secured with a hook and eyelet.

Inside were some identification cards, all with Jim's picture but under a variety of names—driver's license, a couple U.S. passports, some local picture IDs Cooper didn't recognize. The names on the cards were Allan Rodriguez, Robert Jackson, James Haggood—Cooper thinking that could be the real version of Jim.

He spotted the flimsy chain peeking out from under the identification cards and pulled. The U.S. Navy dog tags that came out of the rubble displayed the engraved name of TRAVIS JAMES MALLOY.

Cooper took a moment to memorize all the names and numbers on the cards and the tags. He replaced them in their original order and walked out, trying to decide whether to refer to the man as Jim the Redheaded Albino Black, or whether he should switch up and just call him by his real name of Travis.

Jim, he thought, suits the man better.

He drove back to the Crowne Plaza, slept for ninety minutes, brewed some coffee at the minibar and drank it black while he shot for and caught a wireless signal with his PowerBook. He logged on to one of the seven secure law enforcement databases to which he had access and, twenty minutes later, made the discovery that Travis James Malloy packed quite a resumé.

A three-year-old picture of Jim, or Travis, stared out at Cooper from the computer screen, where, beside the picture, there ran a list of warrants, charges, and indictments that took him three minutes to read. Malloy was wanted for murder, rape, sodomy, sexual battery, armed robbery, aggravated assault, child molestation, and absence without official leave.

U.S. Navy AWOL.

Cooper saw that until four years ago, when the authorities had quit charging him with new crimes, Malloy had been a card-carrying member of the FBI's Ten Most Wanted. He'd fallen off the list after no leads had been found. Cooper read the rest of it, noting the sites of the alleged murders and rapes, figuring it meant that Malloy's idea of a tour in the navy was to use the various ports of call for a serial rape-and-murder spree. He wondered whether there had been a similar series of murders and rapes in Kingston these past few years, but culling through the local missing persons and homicide case files didn't jump out at him as a productive use of his time. You're either a serial killer or you're not, and he figured it for a good bet Travis James Malloy was a prolific one.

Cooper was getting to the end of his rope. Camping out in a rental car in Belle Acres, watching a ten-time serial killer screw a drugged-out anorexic hooker night in, night out—Christ, enough. He decided that if this guy didn't give him something to go on in the next few days, he'd pay a visit to the U.S. embassy, ask a couple of marines to follow him back to Jimbo's love nest, and retire from his position as private-eye-for-the-dead.

He downed the last of the coffee, gathered his gear, and headed out for another night of sex-machine surveillance.

That night Jim was paged twice.

At least that was how many times he took off in his mini-van, destined for two pay phones in separate neighborhoods. He hadn't sent Rhonda home either time, just slipped out, made a phone call, returned, and come back out an hour later to repeat the routine. Afterward, Cooper assumed his position in the Taurus outside the house while Jim slipped back inside and things returned to normal.

Cooper checked the clock on the dash—almost midnight, and midnight in Jamaica meant either eleven or midnight in Langley, he could never remember. Depended on the time of year. Either way, when two shots with his sat phone got nothing but her answering machine on the home line, Cooper made a third call to retrieve the number he was looking for, then tapped out the digits to Julie Laramie's cell phone.

When Laramie answered, Cooper said, "How we doing, Lie Detector?"

Cooper could hear road noise from Laramie's end of the line.

"Hello, Professor," she said.

Cooper thought that she had to be wondering what he meant by that, why he was goofing around with her at all, but she wasn't asking about any of it. Laramie: cool as a cucumber.

"You couldn't be coming home from the office this late," he said.

"Ah, but I could be. And am."

"You skip dinner?"

"I had a salad from the commissary, if you must know."

"A salad person."

"Sometimes."

Sometimes, my ass, Cooper thought. "What about breakfast," he said. "You eat a big breakfast?"

"Only coffee," she said. "Maybe a banana."

"Banana." Cooper said the word as though it summed up all.

"I take it you're not a salad eater."

"No."

"Or a fruit person.",

"Nope."

"What did you mean by 'Lie Detector'?" Laramie said.

There we go.

"I mean," Cooper said, "you have a way of seeing past the surface."

Laramie didn't say anything for a minute, Cooper wondering whether the silence stemmed from indifference, distraction, annoyance, or something else.

"The drinking thing," she said. "That's what you're talking about. That I knew you'd been drinking."

"What's making you burn the midnight oil?"

"Nothing I'd be permitted to tell you, of course."

"Maybe I could help."

"Maybe not."

Cooper waited.

"Even if you could," she said, "I'd probably refuse your sage advice and do things my own way, making decisions guaranteed to flush my career down the toilet."

"Professor Eddie," Cooper said. "Professor Eddie gives you advice and you don't take it."

"Yes. Mr. Lie Detector."

"Was he right?"

"What do you mean?"

"I mean, was it good advice?"

"Yes."

"And you didn't take it."

"No. Listen—what can I help you with?"

Cooper thought for a moment.

"Not sure," he said.

The road noise on the other end of the line evaporated. Cooper heard the yank of an emergency brake, the *ding-ding* of the car telling Laramie the door was open with her keys in the ignition, the jangling of keys and slamming of a door.

"So I'm home," she said.

"Tell me about the memo."

"What do you want me to tell you about it?"

He heard more jangling of keys, a door opening and closing. He imagined Laramie turning on the light as she came in. He found he couldn't picture either her or her house. Maybe she had an apartment. Condo—a salad person would own a condominium.

"It came from something you found," Cooper said. "As with every widely distributed Agency memo, it made a generic statement which obviously didn't reflect what you found, but which came from something you found nonetheless. What was it you found?"

"What do you care?"

"The long hours you're clocking have something to do with your discovery?"

Laramie stayed quiet and so did Cooper. The chill from the car's air conditioner, Cooper sitting there in the Taurus, felt as if it had frozen the cartilage beneath his kneecaps. Nonetheless he could still feel the sweat oozing from his back, causing him to stick, like a suction cup, to the seat.

Laramie said, "I found something, and I'm looking for something more, but I'm not finding the something more I'm looking for. Actually I found a *little* something more, but I'm not finding anything else."

"That's vague."

"I can't talk about this."

"I'm cleared higher than the head of your department, Laramie."

"Well that's very impressive," she said, "but isn't the issue."

"No?"

"I'm not—"

"Ah," Cooper said.

"Ah?"

"You're not supposed to be working on what you're working on, are you?"

Laramie hesitated.

"Fuck them," he said. "Tell me what's going on."

"Tough talk," Laramie said. "You know, Professor, 'fuck them' isn't the kind of advice professors usually give."

Cooper heard a few rustling noises. Keys being dropped somewhere. And maybe, way in the background, the sound of feet kicking off shoes.

Then Laramie sighed, the sigh loud in his ear with Cooper busy straining to hear what she was up to.

"Look," she said, "I analyze satellite intelligence. I found an unscheduled military exercise in the province they've assigned me in China. Shandong. The base there has mobilized and added troops in sufficient numbers to indicate there are plans in store for the real-world version of the exercise. The simulation I saw was a sea-to-land assault."

"Taiwan."

"That was my deduction too," she said. "But perhaps you're not aware of the recent strides we've made in Sino-American relations."

"No," Cooper said, "I'm not."

"Suffice to say that if you were to write an internal Agency report documenting the deduction to which we just came, you might get a reprimand from pretty high up the chain of command."

Cooper thought, *Gates,* but didn't say anything.

"The reason I'm not officially working on what I'm

working on is a little more complicated. I'm a China analyst. I *know* we're growing our relationship with the PRC; it's happening precisely due to the ideological makeup of the State Council. I *know* that plans for the annexation of Taiwan don't fit the profile of eight, or even nine, of the eleven council members. I *do* realize the likely situation is that a couple of the most extreme vice premiers are doing it on their own. Or not alone, at least internationally speaking. So I check around and find the same thing going on in another country."

"Where?"

"North Korea. And superanalyst Julie Laramie's knee-jerk concluding hypothesis? A multinational 'rogue faction' exists. I believe it is possible that the members of the faction are jointly planning independent military actions, each hostile to U.S. interests."

Cooper digested this for a moment. "Sounds like a reasonable hypothesis," he said.

"Fortunately—or unfortunately—depending on whether I'm looking at it from the perspective of national security or personal job security—I've been checking other countries for similar exercises and seem to be finding zilch."

"Burning the midnight oil."

"Burning my career to a crisp. And by the way, if they didn't have enough to go on to pink-slip me already, this phone call ought to wrap things up nicely."

Cooper thought he heard a cork *thuk* gently from a bottle.

"Cell phone conversations are more labor-intensive to review," he said. "How old are you?"

"Old enough."

"How old are you?"

"Twenty-six."

"You don't remember the cold war then."

"You must be joking. I've studied—"

"When the wall came down, you were what, eleven? Go back another decade or so. Around when you were born."

"What do you mean?"

"The Soviet Union was beating our pants off. They had fifty, sixty countries lined up, the Comintern's revolutionary brotherhood, ready to gang-tackle us. You know how we won?"

"Are you going to give me a Ronald Reagan speech?"

"They ran out of money, and we didn't. They couldn't keep funding the brotherhood that had signed up for the revolutionary gravy train."

There was silence for a moment.

Then Laramie laughed. She laughed pretty hard. Hard enough so that it took her a couple minutes to settle down.

"No kidding, Columbo," she said, finally.

Cooper frowned.

"My dad used to say that—'No kidding, Columbo.' I'm an analyst, mystery man. I already thought to select the countries I was checking based on ideology. If I can be so bold as to presume that's the advice you're suggesting I follow."

"Well—"

"I'm in the midst of examining SATINT from a handful of Marxist-Leninist, socialism-espousing, or otherwise anti-American, capitalism-hating countries for similar military exercises. But I can only review so much of the world per week—at some point I need to know where to look, and even then it's still the needle-in-the-haystack thing, presuming there's a needle to find in the first place. My one semi-discovery is in Yemen, where there is a broad troop buildup by the rebels in the southern part of the country. They're led by a terrorist you may know of—nickname's the Arabian

Bulldog—and they want to secede. This, however, pretty much reflects exactly what's been going on in that pocket of the world at least once per decade for the past fifty years. Conclusion? My hypothesis is bullshit. My bosses are burying my findings because they're wiser than I."

Cooper sat there, stuck to the seat, thinking for a moment.

"You know," he said, "and some of us can speak from experience on this—one thing most of your bosses are not is wise. In fact, I can think of one of them in particular who happens to be a horse's ass. And about as wise as a horse's ass too, while we're at it."

Cooper saw the door open across the street. Jim came out hurriedly, a protesting Rhonda in tow. He looked down at the in-dash clock. It said 12:33.

"Gotta run, Lie Detector," he said. "Go easy on the Chardonnay."

It was a guess, but Cooper took the lack of any reply before the *click* when Laramie hung up as affirmation of the guess. He wondered if she'd been smiling as she broke the connection—Cooper the fellow lie detector, figuring her out.

Jim didn't bother to wait for the cab he'd presumably called for Rhonda but instead simply left her on the stairs, strolled over to his van, gunned the engine, and pulled out.

Figuring he might need the help if Jim had any excitement planned, Cooper had borrowed from a bit he'd seen in the movie *Chinatown* and busted one of Jim's taillight covers a few minutes after the night's first pager run. With the added luxury of the naked white bulb shining from the rear of the minivan, Cooper let Jim pull out and get a good way out ahead before he fell in behind. Once they hit the main drag Cooper stayed about a half mile back, easily able to see the beacon of the busted taillight up the road apiece.

He tailed Jim into one of downtown Kingston's worst

slums, about thirty minutes from the Belle Acres love nest. Jim drove around for a while, seemingly aimless, before parking his minivan in an alley. Cooper pulled the Taurus against the curb across the street from the alley, parking at an angle, so that he could see the van itself, but that was about it. He saw from the sign at the corner of the alley that they were on East Queen Street. Jim exited the van and walked out of the alley and onto East Queen, Cooper getting a good look at him as he passed under the splash of the streetlights, that bright red hair of his cut high-and-tight.

There were a couple of nightclubs and some shops on this segment of East Queen. Long since closed for the night, most of the shops were protected by the usual articulated metal cage doors; there were enough winos and junkies sleeping in the storefront alcoves that Cooper lost count trying to figure out how many were living here.

Jim went up the street, away from Cooper, and seemed to decide on a particular alcove, Cooper seeing it was a pawnshop. He disappeared into the pocket of darkness and was in there long enough for Cooper to think Jim might have shaken him when a tiny orange flame flared from the alcove. After that a similar orange glow appeared from time to time. This went on for a while, maybe twenty-five minutes, Jim having a smoke under the awning of a pawnshop at one-thirty in the morning on one of the worst streets in all of Kingston.

Then Jim came out of the alcove. Cooper watched as he flicked the remnants of his last cigarette into the street, turned, and began to walk with a deliberate stride back down the street, moving in the direction of the van. Cooper was ready for a confrontation, figuring Jim would easily have made him from the alcove, Cooper sitting in a gleaming

Ford Taurus with four hundred miles on the odometer in a neighborhood littered with vehicle carcasses. Jim didn't come his way, though, and instead paused on the other side of the street and looked around the interior of another alcove from his spot on the sidewalk.

Cooper realized what it was Jim had in mind just before he did it.

Turning suddenly into the alcove, Jim leaped on the bum sleeping against the wall and unleashed a series of savage, pistonlike kicks into the man's head. The attack was silent, brutal, and quick. Once the violence subsided, Jim checked his victim over, grabbed him by his hair to take a look, confirming the knockout. Then he threw the wino over his shoulder, shifted his posture to get comfortable with the weight, and carried the comatose bum back to the van. Cooper had the urge to get out of the Taurus, walk across the street, and kick Jim's teeth in, but he knew it wouldn't do him, or his twice-dead client, any good. He still had to find out where Jim was headed, why, and to see whom. Among other things.

Jim drove a few miles on a main thoroughfare before making another turn. Cooper was completely lost, but he discovered this didn't matter, since Jim wasn't going anywhere—he parked on a quiet side street and simply remained inside the van. After a while, Cooper saw him duck into the back; after another while, he returned to smoke another cigarette in the front seat before leading Cooper onto the highway.

At 3:11 by Cooper's dashboard clock, Jim exited the turnpike. Cooper burned some fuel catching up as the Mitsubishi vanished from the throughway, and as he followed Jim's route off the exit ramp he saw a sign displaying the

words CANNERY and MUSEUMS. He caught the broken taillight around a corner between what appeared to be a pair of
abandoned warehouses before the minivan's brake lights
flared and Cooper could see Jim easing the Mitsubishi out
onto a dock.

Cooper parked the Taurus and got out. He could smell the
Caribbean immediately. They'd come to a run-down waterfront district where some of the buildings had been pre-
served and repainted as museums, others either abandoned
or used anonymously, streaks of grime and rust evident
along their corrugated metal siding. Two piers stretched out
into the bay; rows of creosote-laden pilings supported the
fat buildings the way giraffe legs might hold up an elephant.
Cooper could see the van out on the first pier, the southernmost, so he found his way out to the end of the other.

Cooper heard the thrum of an approaching engine and
pegged it, without being able to see the boat, for a Bertram
or a Chris-Craft, Cooper guessing at least a forty-five-
footer. He found a small depression in the planks of the pier,
a place where he could sit, adequately camouflaged, and still
enjoy an unobstructed view of Jim. Jimbo, he saw, was leaning against the front grille of the minivan, having another
smoke. Cooper wondered whether it was tobacco or dope
he'd been smoking along the way.

The boat approached the dock sideways, giving the pilings a brawny bump, Cooper thinking the boat's captain
couldn't keep a freight train on railroad tracks. It looked a
little bigger than he'd thought, maybe fifty feet, but definitely a Chris-Craft like he'd guessed; it was hard to tell,
given the boat's severe weathering. What he *could* see, even
in the half-moon darkness, was that the hull was swollen
with barnacles and stained with blooms of rust.

A thin white guy wearing foul-weather gear and a baseball cap emerged from the rear of the boat. He secured the lines, climbed a ladder that Cooper hadn't noticed was connected to the pier, and pulled himself up onto the dock. He and Jim came together, Jim still smoking; there was conversation which Cooper had no way of hearing, and then the white guy went back to the edge of the dock and waved. A second man, also white, appeared in the back of the boat holding something small and dark. He tossed it up to the guy on the dock and went back inside the boat. Cooper could see that he had thrown his companion a canvas athletic bag.

The first white guy handed the bag to Jim, who unzipped it, checked inside, then zipped it closed again and tossed the bag into the minivan through the open passenger-side window. Jim then opened the rear hatch and proceeded to remove the wino, now bound with duct tape. Jim carried him to the edge of the dock, where the first white guy, now positioned on the ladder, grabbed hold. Struggling to hold the wino's near-dead weight, he climbed down the ladder to the boat. His companion came out again and helped take the wino into the cabin.

Then the two of them were back inside the boat, Jim was behind the wheel of the minivan, and everybody left.

Cooper stayed where he was for a moment, not really sure whether he wanted to get up at all. He thought about what this meant, presuming he could extrapolate—or whatever it's called, he thought, when it's the opposite of extrapolation—and apply this odd turn of events to recent history. If he could, then perhaps Marcel S., once-dead and then exhumed and revived, had been delivered somehow to Jim, who then passed him on, as with the wino, in exchange for whatever was in the canvas bag. Maybe to the same pair of white guys in the Chris-Craft; maybe not. It seemed unlikely—and, given the rest of Cap'n Roy's mystery ride, too easy—for the owners of the boat he'd just seen here at Cannery Row to have procured both the wino and Marcel from ol' Jimbo, but it was certainly possible. This logic therefore made it worth his while to make a call he'd been thinking about making for one hell of a long time anyway.

In the meantime, though, there was something he needed to do.

He caught up to the minivan just shy of the highway on-ramp, using some good old-fashioned American horsepower to overtake it. Once he had, Cooper cut in front of the van and stood on the brake pedal, giving Jim a choice: lock his own brakes or ram headlong into the Taurus. Jim hit the brakes.

Cooper, who was already out of the Taurus, was able to get over to the driver's-side door of the minivan before Jim had figured out what was going on. When he got there, he smashed his fist through the window, grabbed Jim by the neck, and slammed his head against the steering wheel. Jimbo's eyes rolled back in his head, pretty much the way Cooper had seen albacores' eyes do when you whacked the suckers with the deep-sea charter-issue kill-stick. Cooper then opened the door, reached over, unbuckled Jim's seat belt, got hold of the back of Jim's sweat suit top, and pile-drove him through the front windshield. He pulled Jim's head back inside, raking his face through the jagged glass, then bashed Jimbo's forehead against the steering wheel until his arm hurt, Cooper losing count of the number of times Jim's bleeding face hit the hard plastic of the wheel after maybe twenty whacks.

Winded, he hoisted Jim, long since comatose, out of the minivan and over his shoulder, then loaded him into the trunk of the Taurus. He crawled inside the van and found the duct tape, came back, and mummified Jim about the way Jim had done with the wino.

Consulting the map provided by the rental agency, Cooper took the Taurus to the front entrance of the U.S. embassy on Oxford Road. He pulled up to the barricade blocking car bombers from direct access to the front stairs, rolled down his window, and showed the stone-faced M.P. standing there his fraudulent DEA identification card. He told the M.P. there was a man tied up in his trunk who'd gone AWOL and was wanted on fifteen counts of first-degree murder, requested that the guard return his car to Hertz when he had a chance, then got out of the Taurus and walked away.

The M.P. shouted after him a few times but decided he ought to check to see whether the DEA man was telling the truth before giving chase. By the time he looked up from the bound, bloody, unconscious, odd-looking sight of Travis James Malloy, the M.P. couldn't see Cooper anywhere on the road. Even after he'd summoned additional marines for the search, the M.P. quickly developed the sense, which turned out to be correct, that he'd seen the last of the driver of the Ford Taurus claiming to work for the Drug Enforcement Administration.

28

Eleven revolutionary leaders stood behind the resort on Mango Cay in freshly pressed hiking gear.

Arriving here over the course of two days, the dignitaries had traveled through four different regional hubs—San Juan, Kingston, St. Lucia, and, for some of the higher-profile leaders, Havana. From these hubs, arrangements had been made for clandestine transportation to six different Antilles harbors, where private float planes, free of all customs inspection or other unwelcome review, completed the trip to the resort. Each man's personal security detail, if any, was disallowed for this last leg of the journey, as had been agreed.

On the third morning of their visit to the resort, the leaders were told to meet at 8 A.M. sharp in front of the Greathouse. The men were told to wear clothes suitable for a hike in the woods, such clothes having been set out for each man in his private cabana.

Not accustomed to being made to wait, the men lingered uncomfortably until the sound of thrumming motors approached from the woods. It was then that Spike Gibson and a man the leaders had come to know as the resort's bartender appeared from a trailhead at the base of the island's lone hill. Each drove his own stretch golf cart, three rows of seats per cart, outfitted with all-weather tires and raised suspensions. Gibson and the bartender, whose name was Hiram, pulled the carts to either side of the trail.

Gibson made small talk with some of the men, speaking to several in their native languages. Then, at five past eight, General Deng and Admiral Li arrived on a smaller—though equally equipped—cart. Deng and Li wore hiking gear too, and when they exited the smaller cart, Hiram and Gibson boarded it and drove off, disappearing around a corner on their way up the island's rainforest hill.

Deng invited the men to board the limo carts and took the wheel of one; Li took the other. With Li following directly behind, Deng led the two-cart procession along the same route taken by Gibson and Hiram.

This was the first time the brethren had seen their mentor, and Deng knew one or two of them would still be wondering who he was, while others must have been bursting at the seams with surprise, even awe. *China!* he figured much of the brethren to be thinking. *And not just a midlevel officer, acting alone, but a vice premier, overseeing the entire military of the greatest revolutionary nation on earth!*

He began a disjointed narration as they drove, his speech aided by a wireless translation system, its software rendering his Mandarin into Korean, Vietnamese, Spanish, Portuguese, Arabic, Russian, and a pair of African dialects. The system required his guests to wear earpieces and receivers resembling iPods; running on a three-second delay, Deng's words were delivered into the ears of his guests in their native tongues.

Deng told the men about the salvage operation. He told them how *he* had shown patience where the Americans had not. How *he* had taken one of the C-4 Trident I missiles and shipped it in pieces to a laboratory in Hangzhou, where a team of military scientists created an exact, working replica. How he had shipped the replica to another lab, where a second team of scientists assembled another dozen replicas based on the prototype. The circuit was repeated until, in addition to the full complement of twenty-four missiles he'd ultimately recovered from the USS *Chameleon,* Deng had another twenty-four replicas on his hands. He told the guests that each of the forty-eight missiles was, in theory, fully functional, with each C-4 ICBM loaded with four 100-kiloton W-76 thermonuclear warheads and Mk-4 MIRV re-entry vehicles. Six of the forty-eight missiles—all six part of the inventory of originals pilfered from the *Chameleon*—had been partially damaged from the American submarine's sinking, he reported, and were being repaired in a secondary cave.

One of four African revolutionary leaders in the procession inquired as to how Deng had kept the work quiet. Deng answered through the translation headsets.

"We keep the work quiet," he said, "with something our security director prefers to call 'disposable labor.'"

He did not explain further, and nobody asked for clarification.

The gravel path had become a skinny dirt road, then a muddy trail, and in due course they were ducking palm fronds, snapping twigs with the rearview mirrors, and spinning out in muddy sections of the road. They reached another trailhead, and Deng parked, locked the foot brake, and turned to face his passengers. Some of the men appeared bewildered, others suspicious.

Deng said, "If you continue past this point on the trail,

your last payment will be immediately drawn and posted to the operation's account. The banking information and preauthorization we required from you will be used to execute the wire transfer, and the transaction will be executed within sixty seconds of Admiral Li's e-mail notification." Li held aloft a BlackBerry-like device. "You could, of course, turn around and walk back to the resort and the float planes there. If you decide to do so, bear in mind that Mr. Gibson knows how to find you—and always will. Your silence is not only expected, but will be strictly enforced. In a sense, if you withdraw now, you will become as 'disposable' as Mr. Gibson's labor pool."

When no leader took the exit option, Deng steered down a brief, steep slope. He worked the buttons of a handheld key-code remote, which, as they drove past a grove of squat palms, opened a hidden, reinforced steel door. He made a sharp turn to the left, and with Li following in the cart behind, the two loads of dignitaries found themselves in Mango Cay's transport tunnel, an eight-foot-wide passageway with muddy gravel beneath the wheels of the carts. Timbers—not unlike those found in a mine shaft—spanned the ceiling at fifteen-foot intervals. They came shortly to another reinforced steel door. Deng stopped his cart, and Li did the same.

"Behold," Deng said, "the supreme weapon of the Revolution. Though I, of course, prefer to use its code name: 'Operation Blunt Fist.'"

He punched another code on the remote keypad and the door slid open to admit the procession into a vast cavern, its wide expanse carved by the hand of God but outfitted with man-made artifacts including at least two hundred ceiling-mounted floodlights and, most notably, forty-two white-and-black pillars of steel. Uniformed mercenaries, roving the facility in pairs, appeared from time to time behind one missile or another.

Each missile had its own freestanding silo, resembling scaffolding, reaching halfway to the cavern's domed ceiling. There was a series of what looked like storm drains in the ceiling immediately above each silo, and numbers were painted on the cavern floor, the numbers climbing in sequence across each row of missiles from 1 to 42.

"All forty-two missiles in this cavern," Deng said over the translation headsets, "will be operational within the week. The replica C-4s will—even upon detonation—be indistinguishable from authentic U.S. Navy–issue C-4 Trident I ICBMs. We have purchased metals from the supplier for Lockheed, stolen and duplicated guidance system components from Martin Marietta, constructed the warheads using uranium and plutonium with a signature matching that produced in Los Alamos. We have even used the same brand of paint for the exterior markings. There will be no accountability."

The dignitaries followed Deng through the maze of silos, most of them dumbfounded that, at least by all appearances, he had actually succeeded with his plan.

Deng described the targeting strategy in general terms, naming a number of American military installations, and finished by saying, "The American military-industrial complex will be rendered impotent for at least months, and possibly years. As though struck," he said, "by a blunt fist." Deng liked this part, so he repeated it, trusting that in some form the translation would take:

"As though struck," he said, *"by a blunt fist."*

Deep in the cavern, near the back, stood a guest who had forgone the walking tour. He leaned against a wide opening in the wall of the cave where, behind him, there stood the calm waters of an underwater docking bay. The conning tower of a medium-size submarine bereft of national insignia protruded from the water in the bay.

This man, like the others, wore a headset. He had been following the tour on audio, but had only come as far from his submarine as the position he occupied now.

In the world of the communist brotherhood Deng had recruited, there were few VIPs, and even fewer men—including those found throughout history—who qualified to function as royalty. The man leaning against the cavern wall, however, was to these men, as Deng well knew, quite literally a symbol of revolution itself.

An aging fossil of defiance in the face of capitalism, friend to all Marxist-Leninist regimes, the man had now, thanks to Vice Premier General Deng Jiang, inherited the role of royal mascot for the next phase of the revolution. As Deng's tour came around the forty-second silo, the man stepped forward and raised a hand to his brethren. One by one, the faces of the other dignitaries in the procession registered precisely the look Deng had sought: a combination of shock, awe, and self-satisfaction. The man's beard was thick and gray—even unruly—but he didn't look nearly as old as most of the dignitaries had pegged him for.

At that point the mascot from Cuba grinned through teeth yellowed from too many years of gluttonous cigar consumption and joined his comrades for the conclusion of the tour.

29

Pete, you stay for a bit?"

The remainder of CIA's senior staff departed the conference room adjoining Lou Ebbers's executive suite, leaving Peter M. Gates alone with the DCI. Gates replaced his ass in the seat he'd held for the past two hours as Ebbers stood at the head of the table and waited for the last deputy director to leave.

When the door had closed, Ebbers slid a photocopy of a letter across the table.

"Inquiry from Senator Kircher," Ebbers said. "Came to me."

Ebbers was a man who looked more virile at sixty than he had at twenty-five. He had a stripe of gray stretching back from each temple but was otherwise bald. A pair of wire rims rested high on his nose.

"Copied the president," Ebbers said, "and most of the NSC. It's a request, as you can see, for a 'comprehensive summary of all CIA intelligence related to China's readiness and/or intention to annex Taiwan.' Wants it in a week, report to remain classified, his eyes only. No committee review. He'll accept a blacked-out version."

Gates immediately understood the letter to be a warning shot intended for the president. When requests like this were made, it usually meant the congressman in question already had the goods, and sought either verification of what he already knew or, more likely, to make a point. Kircher, in copying the administration, was telling the nation's chief executive he knew something the president didn't, or that he knew something the president hadn't wanted him to find out about. Either way, Kircher was going back-channel to fight a skirmish the senator was confident he would win, Gates hearing it in the trademark accent of the ubiquitous guest star of prime-time cable debate shows: *Just puttin' it out there, Mr. President—lettin' you know a conversation's comin'.*

The way Kircher was playing it, Gates guessed the senator intended to pressure the president into backing out of his proposed U.S.-China corporate-partner initiative, which Kircher opposed, though the senator could have been shooting for any of a number of benefits serving the citizens of the great state of North Carolina.

None of this was out of the ordinary—routine Beltway activity. What disturbed Gates was the topic of the inquiry.

Could he possibly have so grossly underestimated her?

Following his reprimand, had Julie Laramie gone off-rez and handed classified intel to a senator known to be the president's arch-rival? If so, he'd slap a treason investigation on her ass so fast her head—and career—would spin.

When Gates looked up from reading the letter he found Ebbers looking at him.

"If the gentleman from North Carolina is doin' some fishin'," Ebbers said, "my guess'd be he knows where they're bitin'. We have any idea what he's got?"

Gates shook his head, giving the impression he was trying to think of anything he might have heard about.

"Think I'll need to check, Lou," he said.

"You got anybody sitting on anything, now's the time."

Gates didn't think he hesitated, but it felt that way to him. Ebbers wasn't always so direct. "I'll dig," Gates said, "and whatever he's got, if it's anything at all, we'll find it."

"I want whatever you have in three days. We clear?"

"As ice. This will not be a problem, Lou."

"All right, then." Gates knew this to be Ebbers's standard end-of-meeting remark. "Lemme know."

Gates procured a tall coffee from the Starbucks kiosk and returned immediately to his office. On his way through the executive waiting room, he fired an order at Miss Anders without looking at her.

"Get Rhone up here," he said, then stopped before charging through the door to his office. Miss Anders, he realized, had not reacted to his order with her usual fervor. In fact, she hadn't reacted at all.

The typically stone-faced assistant was flush with either embarrassment or anger, the color of her face approaching the shade of her candy-apple-red blazer.

"What is it," Gates said.

"There's a caller holding."

She didn't say anything more.

"Well?" Gates said. "Who?"

"He says his name is 'Lunar Eclipse.' He doesn't seem to accept that I'm not able—"

"Fine."

"I've told him you're not—"

"I'll take the damn call, Miss Anders."

For Gates it hadn't been the worst day of his life, but it sure as hell wasn't his best.

During his third year in the Directorate of Operations, he'd been trying to install a leader his staff had told him would be the right man for a certain Central American nation. The problem was that there was no election in that particular nation for another four years, and the nation's current prime minister, who had no interest in America's views, was in perfect health. For Gates the solution was simple: remove the misguided leader and install the correct one in his place.

It was a complicated operation, but in Gates's view he orchestrated it brilliantly, even in failure. At least this was what he had come to believe once he'd consumed the gushing round of compliments fed him by his men's club comrades after the fact.

In one of the few successful covert CIA assassinations in history, his team had succeeded in taking out the errant leader, doing it, in fact, under the cover of night at the very palace where he slept. Unfortunately, Gates had overlooked the leader's very powerful minister of defense who, upon getting wind of the assassination attempt, allowed the American agents to waltz into the leader's palace and take him out with no resistance whatsoever. The only resistance that occurred came after the minister of defense confirmed the prime minister was *muerto,* at which point he sealed the palace perimeter and captured or killed the entire American team.

Rather than leave anything to chance or election returns, the minister of defense decried this terrible tragedy, declared himself prime minister for the length of the former leader's term, and promptly imprisoned the opposition leader and all the top members of his party. The opposition leader, of course, was Gates's man.

Gates quickly moved to reduce CIA's presence in the region and bagged any further plans to install a new leader, switching instead to a grassroots strategy of antigovernment propaganda. He had cargo planes dump leaflets on the country's bigger cities, blasted the regional airwaves with powerful radio broadcasts, and coordinated with anyone willing to participate in a domestic disinformation campaign documenting whatever fictional atrocities he felt were appropriate to sully the reputation of the former minister of defense.

Encouraged by his men's club comrades to do so, Gates shelved his concerns for the twelve-man team he'd sent down to engineer the coup. They were an extreme liability, especially as Gates had undertaken the operation on his own initiative, but in time he felt safe concluding that all twelve had died. A month after the botched raid, Gates had notified the media that a DC-3, sent on a relief mission to Zimbabwe, had crashed in a treacherous African mountain range, killing all twelve passengers. The names on the manifest mysteriously matched those Gates had sent to assassinate the Central American prime minister.

Gates was promoted shortly thereafter to deputy director of operations.

That put him at sixteen years ago, coming out of Cleo's on a Thursday afternoon, having just finished a lunch with a particularly well-connected undersecretary of state.

Gates hadn't met anyone on the team he'd sent to Central America, so there wasn't any reason for him to recognize the tall, deeply tanned man who bumped him while Gates was making for his car outside the club. The man apologized, then followed him the block and a half to his car, Gates driving a big Buick that year.

That's when the man, back then, said, "So you're Gates."

The man had short black hair. He wore a suit and over-coat. Despite the wardrobe selection, he failed to come off as one of the men's club set.

Gates recognized him as the same man who had bumped into him outside of Cleo's. He felt a surge of fear, wondering whether he should duck into the driver's seat and speed off while he still had the Buick between them.

"Well, yes," he replied.

"We should talk," the man said.

The stranger had a baritone voice and cold, vacant eyes. Gates pulled himself together, thinking the guy could be a re-porter—that he should be careful what he said, or admitted.

"What about?" he said. "What do you want to talk about?"

The stranger jerked his head, said, "Over here," and walked off past the hood of the Buick and across the street to Dupont Circle, a brief expanse of green packed with con-crete benches and a fountain. He waited for Gates to make up his mind. This took about ninety seconds, the stranger just standing at the edge of the park, appearing more inter-ested in the circle's pivotal fountain than in Gates's decision-making process.

Gates dodged a car or two and brought himself even with the stranger as the man strolled along the trail encircling the fountain. After about a quarter-loop on the path, Gates felt compelled to speak.

"Why might I want to talk?"

The stranger looked at him. "I didn't say you'd want to," he said, "only that we should."

They strolled on, the stranger quiet for another quarter-loop. "I'm officially dead," he said eventually, as casually as though he were discussing the flora. "But it should be obvious to you that I am alive."

Gates wasn't firing on all cylinders. He said, "Right."

"'Eclipse,'" the stranger said.

Jesus! Gates nearly jumped out of his skin.

How could he—Christ, how could *any* man have made it, and why hadn't he heard from him before now?

Eclipse.

It was the term he had used as the internal memo coding for the flubbed Central American assassination effort: Operation Eclipse.

Gates realized he had clammed up and, in order to say something, said, "You're being somewhat vague," and was already thinking about how much it was going to cost him to keep this son of a bitch quiet when the stranger spoke again.

"Don't bullshit me." They were halfway around their second loop of the park. "But don't panic, either."

Gates looked ahead, behind, to the side, seeing no one but the usual derelicts loitering in defiance of the city ordinance, draped across the benches like they owned the place. There were no members of Cleo's to come to the rescue, so Gates continued walking.

"Why shouldn't I?" he said.

"Because," the stranger said, "I've got a solution."

"Oh?"

"What we'll do," the stranger said, "is find a nice posting somewhere. I'm seeing a small place—lots of sun, some sand, water, not much going on, maybe some fishing to pass the day. There's a spot I'm thinking of that might just work.

They call them the British Virgin Islands—the BVIs. Why not? Then let's tenure me. You can finance it out of, oh, I don't know, pick a fund. Call me a GS-14 and pay me that plus hazard pay. Any GS-14 in the British Virgins is likely to be chief of station, so let's go ahead and assign me that title too. This sound all right so far?"

"It sounds difficult," Gates said.

"But not impossible. I'm in the BVIs, hell, there probably isn't much else to do—I'll even work for you. Keep a keen eye out for any intel, routine or otherwise, coming out of the strategically significant Antilles region. Even better are the things I won't say to—"

"I get it."

The stranger stopped and stared at Gates with those vacant eyes.

"If you get it," the stranger said, "then I'll see you in your office tomorrow morning at nine, at which time you'll provide me all necessary documentation on the numbered account which will already contain the trust. The trust should be of sufficient size to afford my salary for a minimum of forty-five years, including cost-of-living increases, periodic promotions, and hazard pay. I will control the trust, not you. I'll be using the name Cooper, first initial W., because I like the sound of it, and will expect a pass waiting for me at the gate, along with my Agency ID and a manufactured employee-history file under that name. Do we need to go into the 'attorney-at-law who's been instructed to release such-and-such to the Justice Department and news media under the following circumstances' crap in order to keep you from sending your goons after me?"

Gates said, "No."

The stranger didn't nod, acknowledge that he was leaving, or otherwise announce the end of the conversation, but, instead, simply walked away.

Before he reached the fountain in the center of the park, the stranger turned. Gates caught a flash of his hollow eyes.

"There's something else," the stranger said. "If I ever need you, I'll call under a code name. Could be an emergency, something I need taken care of, or maybe just a favor for a friend I'm looking to impress. When I call, you'll do as I say, no questions asked, and if I'm using the code when I make the call, then you'll know I'm not calling just to chat."

Gates said, "Fine. What's the name?"

"Lunar Eclipse," the stranger said. "I like the sound of that too. You?"

Back in his seventh-floor office, Starbucks still in hand, Gates listened to the caller.

"Snorkeling's great this time of year," Cooper said. "You ought to come down and visit."

"I don't particularly like the Caribbean." He pronounced Caribbean with the emphasis on the *be*.

"That's odd," Cooper said. "Then again you're an odd one, aren't you, Pete?"

"What do you want?"

"A favor."

Gates felt a prickly sensation, his skin starting to sweat underneath the fabric of his suit. He took a sip of the coffee. He wanted to say, *You've got some nerve,* or something like that, but there was nothing like that he could say. Nothing that would get him anywhere.

"Go ahead," he said.

Cooper talked for two minutes, providing a detailed set of instructions, then hung up.

Standing behind his desk, Gates set the phone back on its cradle. After another minute or so, he pulled the lid off the coffee, took one last sip, then dumped the remainder on his telephone. He held the overturned cardboard cup above the receiver until the last dark drop slid from the rim and splashed against the phone.

Then he picked up the telephone console and threw it against the wall.

Following a two-minute stare-down with the brown dent he'd made in the white wall, Gates relented, walked around his desk to the guest telephone on the other side of his office, and buzzed Miss Anders.

When she answered, he told her there was a call he would need her to place for him.

30

When Cooper got back to Conch Bay, the satellite shots he'd ordered via the Peter M. Gates delivery service were waiting for him. Ronnie had deposited the fat enclosure from the diplomatic pouch on his front porch.

Cooper had ordered Gates to send him images captured by various military intelligence satellites during a seventy-two-hour period. The period commenced with the approximate time of departure of the fifty-foot Chris-Craft from the pier outside of Kingston; Cooper knew he could order printouts of another day, week, or more if he needed to.

Looking over the spread of glossy black-and-white prints on the table in his kitchenette, he saw little more than a strangely uneventful voyage by the mystery boat. Each massive print was folded into an eight-by-ten rectangular stack, an oversize version of a folded glove-compartment map, which, when unfurled, blossomed into some thirty-six square feet of high-definition, mostly featureless ocean. Cooper thinking that if you knew how to examine the photos properly—as Laramie surely did—you could find the boat in there with your naked eye. Cooper had to dig out a magnifying glass to see what he was looking for and verify the relevant speck was in fact the boat he was tracking.

He'd ordered shots of virtually the entire Caribbean Sea and adjacent Atlantic but was able to narrow his choices, throwing out one map stack after another as he kept his eye on the boat's progression. There was little for him to see outside of the unerring course of the boat: a handful of other ships passed within twenty or thirty miles, none close enough to make contact; the boat did not appear to dock anywhere; the vessel simply steamed east-southeast for some eight hundred miles, hove to in calm seas twenty miles east of the island of Martinique, then retraced its course back toward its apparent home port in Jamaica. The odyssey lasted forty-plus hours on the outbound route, and, following a pause lasting about two hours, the boat headed back along the same course. Cooper ignored the remainder of the prints once it appeared likely the boat was destined to return to Jamaica.

It didn't make any sense. One thing for sure—that boat had some fuel tanks to kill for. Maybe the captain of the boat preferred to eat human steak with his morning eggs; maybe the vessel's crew had some dirty work to handle and needed some form of slave labor on board. If so, he decided that the only way to learn anything, if there was anything to be learned at all, was to take his own boat along the course he'd just tracked. Follow the coordinates he'd scribbled on the edges of the photographs, sail out to where the mystery boat had turned around, fire off a memory card's worth of digital photos with his Nikon, and see if there was anything he could find offering some explanation.

He could also ambush the Chris-Craft, check it over, and interrogate the two guys he'd seen on it—but he had a pretty good idea the wino would be nowhere near that boat by now, and as for the guys piloting it, he knew the type. They were hired hands, guys who've been told nothing by nobody.

He set out at dawn on his second day back from Jamaica.

It took him three hours, going south, to intersect the course the boat had taken to Martinique. From there it took him another four hours—Cooper's Apache over three times faster than the mystery boat, even when he was taking it easy. He saw little of interest along the way—nice weather, a few birds, some flotsam. He planed over the rolling swells and crashed down into the ocean on the other side of them. Every two or three hours he would ease up and consult the charts to confirm his course, have a sandwich, or nod off for fifteen minutes.

When he got to where the Chris-Craft had turned around, there was nothing but open sea. Cooper flipped off the Mer-Cruisers and let his Apache drift while he took a look at his charts. He checked his GPS-11, marking his position precisely, examined the relevant blown-up satellite photograph, and cross-referenced the GPS numbers with the notes he'd taken. When he was through with all this there was no question about it: he was exactly where the spy satellite had registered the Chris-Craft at its journey's farthest point from Jamaica.

Cooper's depth finder told him the water here was 210 fathoms deep. He cruised around for the better part of two hours, continuing to read the depth finder; the numbers fluctuated between 190 and 220 fathoms, about 1,100 to 1,300 feet deep. There was no shoal or sandbar, no way anyone was out here diving on a reef, Cooper beginning to think he was wasting his time, that he should have shot dead the captain of that goddamn boat and pulled the wino back up the ladder when he'd had the chance.

Since he'd already come all the way out here, he decided to take another look at the navigation charts he kept aboard and see whether it made any sense to nose around. The nearest land was just under four miles to the east, where a small island chain, geopolitically part of Martinique, occupied a ten-mile crescent of sea. The main island lay at the northwest end of the chain, closest to where he now drifted on the open water.

Cooper rode over to the archipelago. It was conceivable, he thought, that the mystery boat had zipped over to one of the islands, then quickly returned between successive satellite photographs, but the positions of the boat in the two shots, taken one hour apart, were virtually identical, and the boat hadn't shown it could move fast enough to make it there and back in much less than an hour, no matter which neighboring island it went to visit.

He found the chain's main island to be a steep chunk of land rimmed by cliffs and similarly steep terrain, with dense vegetation spilling from the lip of the cliffs. When he reached it, he was facing the eastern side of the island; there was a fine mist, even in the hot afternoon sun, covering somewhere around two-thirds of the land mass. To Cooper the place looked to contain five or six square miles of forest, maybe more. There was a small dock at the base of one of the cliffs that faced him, but no visible structures above. He made a wide swing around the island, keeping an eye on the depth finder—you weren't wary of reefs in these parts, your boat would wind up as another underwater home for prowling barracuda and maniacal free-divers seeking to hold their breath like the kids of the South Pacific. As he reached the leeward coast, the depth finder started to bleep—five fathoms, three, two, one. The sand was coming up on him through the clear blue water, and Cooper could see rocks poking at the surface a few meters away.

On this, the western side of the island, there lay, some six hundred yards from his boat, a protected lagoon. Cabanas, a white sand beach, an artificial preponderance of coconut palms amid the indigenous Caribbean forest, a few tourists in the sun. He saw a pair of float planes moored in the lagoon, but no boats, Cooper thinking the planes provided the only access to the shallow lagoon—that no fifty-foot Chris-Craft would be pulling in there. But then again, he thought, there were other ways of getting a mummified wino off a boat and onto an island.

For the hell of it, he snapped a few pictures. He used his Nikon's big zoom lens but still couldn't see much through the viewfinder, not from this far out. He didn't really care about getting close-ups of sunburned fatties lying around like beached whales anyway. What he could see looked no different from any of the usual Caribbean corporate retreats: guests lounged around the bar and the beach, drinking, eating, a couple of them knee-deep in the water of the lagoon.

Cooper poked around the rest of the chain, made up of three smaller islands, two of which were small and barren enough to be uninhabitable, though Cooper had seen beach-front bed-and-breakfasts built on worse. The bigger of the three displayed a handful of private homes, some rickety docks, but little else besides trees and rock.

He popped off enough shots to fill out the remainder of the memory card and powered back to the mystery boat's holding spot. Seeing nothing further that convinced him to stick around, he whacked the Apache's twin throttles all ahead full with his elbow and shot a rooster tail of whitewater out behind the boat as he hauled some westward ass on a course for the Virgins.

31

Spike Gibson peered through a set of Xenon binoculars from his suite in the Greathouse. His massive biceps twitching lazily, he watched the Apache speed away until the racing boat was a speck appearing above one swell, then another, and then could no longer be seen.

He wondered whether this was another round in General Deng's charade. In the past five days there had been four other passing boats and one private plane, meaning that in the span of less than a week, Mango Cay had seen a three hundred percent increase in casual passersby as compared to the entire last two and a half years. Gibson knew this had nothing to do with coincidence: while the increased traffic flow, arriving at the worst possible time for the project, might have been the result of a leak from one of the general's guests, or even a freak occurrence of chance, the more likely scenario was that Deng had planned it. Either the general was conducting a test or, Gibson thought, worse.

This latest drive-by felt different, though. It wasn't

Deng's style. This one felt to Gibson like a visit from some dumb, oblivious asshole in a noisy speedboat snapping random shots of a beautiful tropical isle, or better yet, the opposite: a visit from somebody who knew exactly what he was doing and just happened to be *acting* like a dumb, oblivious asshole.

Gibson deposited the binoculars on the bar between the lounge and the kitchen in his suite and fired up a Black & Decker blender. The blender was racked full of sliced fruit, which the maid, whose name was Lana, knew to leave for him three times a day. He shoveled six ounces of creatine powder into the blender along with ice, nonfat milk, and the fruit, downed the protein shake in three tremendous gulps, stretched his massive arms above his head, and flipped off the kitchen's ceiling fan on his way out of the room.

It was time for a workout.

In a meticulously designed circuit, iPod blasting N.W.A. in his ears, Gibson pumped iron for ninety straight minutes. He worked with massive stacks of weight in endless sets. While he pumped, he cleansed his mind of impurities and focused solely on the dumb asshole in the Apache racing boat.

While he was fully capable of detecting and tracking such passing boats anywhere within miles of Mango Cay, he was generally forced to allow these visitors to take their look and move on. It was only when he suspected something sensitive had been revealed—say, for instance, the dozen fucking commie pinkos funding the whole project being photographed frolicking together in the water of the lagoon—that Gibson was forced to take additional measures. He always made sure the additional measures took place back on the visitors' home turf—as far away from the island as possible.

The pilot of the Apache, whoever he was, had taken photographs of people who could never be photographed together, and that meant that Gibson would now have to deal with the man.

He hit the climax of his workout with a series of lat pull-downs, veins nearly popping from his arms as he mimicked pull-ups in a seated position with over two times his body weight. He polished off the last rep with ease, stretched on the aerobics mat he kept in the corner of the room against a mirror, then made his way through a set of double doors at the back of the weight room. It was necessary for him to punch in an entry code to pass through the doorway.

It was here—and in the daisy-chained series of dual-G5 processor-based desktops functioning as the system's central processing unit—where the software was housed for Gibson's $168 million surveillance system, the cost of which he knew to the nickel, since he'd been the one to commission its installation.

With a few keystrokes he had on the monitor in front of him the full array of data that the system had already gathered on the topic of the Apache racing boat. Radar and sonar readings, 360-degree infrared photography, 1,200-millimeter zoom lens snapshots, background checks on any registered owners—all automatically conducted by the software while Gibson had worked out. Also there were the Apache's registration data; numerous close-up photographs of the asshole piloting the vessel, in which photographs Spike Gibson was able to see that the man had been reviewing maps, not simply taking photographs; and the precise location of the boat every five minutes following its departure, made possible by the private satellite aboard which Gibson rented camera space. He saw that the Apache was steaming west-northwest across the Caribbean Sea, on a course, the system speculated, for either the Virgin Islands, Puerto Rico, or Florida. When the trace on the vessel's owner popped up on his screen, Gibson saw that the boat was registered to Albert Einstein, listed under an address in Paris, France.

Funny guy, Gibson thought. Funny fucking guy.

The stench of trouble wafting from the man behind the wheel of the racing boat was, he thought, nearly overwhelming—but if nothing else, it had become obvious the dumb asshole had nothing to do with General Deng and his fucking games.

Gibson returned to the balcony and stared out at the Caribbean, across which his new acquaintance Albert Einstein had arrived, and then left.

Albert, Gibson thought, you'll soon see that I can be a pretty funny fucking guy too.

The revolutionary leaders attending Deng's Mango Cay missile seminar were permitted to carry firearms. The weapons allowance would make the guests more likely to accept Deng's invitation, and attend, as the invitation stipulated, solo. No security detail was permitted—not for the final segment of the leaders' voyage, nor for their time on-island—so the firearm policy served as a security blanket.

This sense of security proved useful when, near the conclusion of a celebratory meal arranged for the men on the final night of their stay, Hiram the bartender flipped the knob on a rather large canister lodged beneath the poolside bar.

His introductory remarks concluded, Admiral Li—who, following Deng's departure the prior day, had assumed the duties of host—excused himself from the dinner. Lana the maid quickly served the hors d'oeuvres, depositing seven platters of food on the long table before moving into the kitchen and out its rear door. This left Hiram alone behind the bar, at least until the point at which he turned the knob on the canister and strode calmly off in the direction of the Greathouse.

While it appeared to supply the bar's soft-drink gun, the canister actually housed a batch of the nerve agent VX. The canister was charged with sufficient supply—assuming the gas was administered judiciously—to exterminate most of the inhabitants of any major metropolis.

The premixed VX took approximately forty-nine seconds to flow from the canister, down its tubes, and out through the heater stands beside the dining table, the stands tripling as the source for illumination, nighttime heat, and the thin, odorless, amber mist of the world's deadliest airborne nerve toxin. It took fewer than thirty seconds for the concentrated dose to paralyze every leader seated at the table.

Four of the men managed to draw their personal firearms upon being struck by the initial physical symptoms of the fog—seized lungs, immediate vomiting, defecation, and seizures—but the guns fell from fingers or froze in clutched hands as full paralysis followed. The remaining complement of guests perished within one minute of the initial emission. Only two men remained conscious for longer than fifteen of these sixty seconds.

Just over an hour later, outfitted in a Gulf War–style chemical warfare suit, Hiram returned to the poolside party. Wheeling in on one of the resort's golf carts, he removed an industrial-strength, oscillating fan from the vehicle and stood it facing the lagoon behind the dinner table. He stepped behind the bar, shut off the VX canister, and proceeded to crank the fan to its highest setting. He returned after another two hours armed with a hose from the pool house; still wearing the suit, he left the fan running as he hosed down the entire poolside deck, including every body, chair, utensil, and scrap of food that occupied it.

Another two hours after Hiram's initial cleansing, Gibson, Li, and Lana arrived aboard the pair of limousine-length carts. An emaciated black man rode in the rear of Lana's cart, and when Lana braked to a stop, he rose as though she'd ordered him to do so, which she had not. He exited the cart and stood before her on the poolside tile wearing no protective gear. At Lana's command, the former wino from the pawnshop alcove on East Queen Street then loaded the bodies collapsed around the dinner table aboard the pair of limo carts.

When the wino was finished, Gibson pulled a second hose from a cabana and began working its spray across the deck for a follow-up wash-down. Hiram and Lana climbed behind the steering wheels of the two carts; the wino slinked aboard, draping himself across the feet of the last body he'd transferred.

"Any chunks wind up as floaters," Gibson said, "pull them out and try again."

Hiram and Lana steered the limo carts up the hill. Gibson knew their destination to be the underwater lagoon in a secondary cavern he referred to as the cargo cave, which Deng preferred to call the Lab. It was in the waters beneath the cargo cave where a local gang of sharks had learned to feast upon Gibson's disposable labor pool.

When the carts vanished behind the Greathouse, Gibson noticed Admiral Li standing on the main trail some distance back from the pool, looking like a misplaced astronaut in his beige-and-green chemical suit.

Gibson switched hands, flipping the hose to his left, and saluted the admiral with his right. Since Gibson too was wearing one of the haz-mat suits, he figured Li might not have seen the grin Gibson was hiding behind the mask, but Li didn't respond to his salute, either, so the security director left it at that and continued his work with the hose. Per its manufacturer, the VX would take about two more hours to break down once he had soaked whatever remained of it.

32

Dottie, the blonde waitress, was taking dinner orders from the yachting contingent at the Conch Bay Bar & Grill with a mildly haggard look of exhaustion and a satisfied kind of glow. Cooper had spent some time with her—they'd shared a drink at the bar two or three times, Cooper feeling he had a pretty good read on her, but he figured he didn't need to have spent any time with her at all to understand the look on Dottie's face tonight. He peered around the restaurant over the lip of his Cuba libre, trying to get a sense of who might have landed her. He saw nobody giving her rather ample bosom the fond eye of remembrance, or of regret, Cooper first thinking he'd got it wrong, and then thinking finally of one word:

Ronnie.

Apart from their difference in age and station in life—which hadn't ever stopped him before—Cooper thought about why he hadn't pursued Dottie himself. The girl's hulking schnoz didn't bother him; there were equally hulking breasts that came along for the ride. She was nice enough, and reasonably intelligent. No, Cooper decided, he'd ignored the occasional open door simply because he still preferred to dine from a menu of the betrothed. Working from a pool of brides got him a little more space in which to operate—whoever she was, whenever he did whatever he did with her, a married woman was more likely to leave him alone afterward. Stay out of his personal real estate—read the KEEP OUT sign he had chipped into his shoulder.

Keep out, he thought, sipping the last of his drink: as good a two-word phrase as has ever been coined.

Dottie slid him his appetizer order of conch fritters and a tall, fresh glass of rum and Coke. He stared across Sir Francis Drake Channel, where, a mile away, the steep, sparsely populated hills of Tortola revealed themselves only by the occasional dot of artificial light beneath a sky of stars. When he was through staring out there thinking of nothing, he opened his PowerBook. Cooper was sort of celebrating tonight: he'd decided this would be it, that he'd review the photographs he'd taken, and—presuming the yield would be the usual dead end—call this case closed. There simply remained no other worthy leads; besides, what was so bad about having some new neighbors in the world of his dreams? He and the ghost of Marcel S. could hang out on the trip down the Río Sulaco, for the torture sessions, for his blood-spattered escape from the chamber of horrors. Hell— he could use the company.

He clicked on the Photoshop icon and opened the folder of pictures he'd downloaded from the Nikon.

He knew he could always nose around for the title deed on the island he'd photographed—referred to as "Mango Cay" on his navigation charts—or maybe order some follow-up SATINT and pin down the mystery boat's home dock, but this was getting ridiculous. That fucking witch doctor had killed the boy, and Cooper had dealt with him; Albino Jim had bought the resurrected kid for a few bucks and probably sold him at a healthy profit to somebody else, but Cooper had dealt with good ol' Jim Beam too. And the bastards pumping Marcel's back full of armor-piercing shells? Sons of bitches would just have to remain anonymous, and so the fuck what. His learning their identities wouldn't do squat for Marcel anyway.

He activated the software's slideshow feature, which he played intentionally in reverse order. As suspected, the scenics he'd snapped of the smaller islands east of the resort isle were useless. One or two of the houses he saw looked all right, but he still wouldn't think anybody but a terrorist on the lam, or maybe a California crook fleeing the ramifications of his third strike, would want to live there. No beach, no running water, the structures rickety, perched high up on steep, rocky slopes, Cooper guessing they'd be floating toothpicks by the end of hurricane season.

Moving over to the resort island, the rest of the shots featured an all-male cast of uncomfortable-looking beach bums. He let the slides play uninterrupted, fading in and out on their three-second-per-picture cycle, Cooper eyeing the multicultural beach bums as they came and went.

Then the slideshow ended and the folder of thumbnails retook the screen.

"Christ," he said.

He double clicked on five of the pictures in the same order in which they'd appeared in the slide show, carefully studying each. When he opened the fifth, he outlined a section of the photo, blew it up, and leaned in for the closest possible view.

There was no mistaking the two male guests reclining on

the lounge chairs in the shot. One was East Asian, terribly out of shape, sporting a potbelly and an odd pair of sunglasses; the other, a dark, bearded man, possessed an unnaturally large head, broad shoulders, and thick knees. The broad-shouldered man had a distinctive enough appearance, in fact, for Cooper to grasp why the international news media had christened him the Arabian Bulldog.

There was a third man in the shot, standing behind the other two, his image grainy and mostly out of focus, given the short depth of field of the long lens. Cooper couldn't summon the man's name immediately, but he recognized him, a prominent senior lieutenant, he thought, in the Chinese military. Lean and fit, his skin dark for his ethnicity, the man had the unmistakable look of a career soldier despite the casual shorts and tropical-print shirt he was modeling in the photo.

An old habit that died hard among spies was the constant review of news related to foreign affairs. As much as he'd made a game effort at checking out, once he'd settled on a permanent residence in the form of Conch Bay, Cooper had fallen back into the routine of keeping up. He routinely peeked through most major periodicals, and was, at the time he was enjoying the slide show, more or less current on international affairs. So while there seemed no apparent relation between the pictures and the plight of the late Marcel S., Cooper was nonetheless easily able to discern a rather stark connection between the three men in the photograph and the three countries Julie Laramie was investigating:

Two of the men on the lounge chairs ran them, and the third had a pretty good chunk of the military of Laramie's primary SATINT assignment reporting up through him.

Laramie jumped when the phone rang. She'd already put on her nightshirt and was sipping the evening glass of Chardonnay, a rare night where she'd actually settled in prior to the stroke of midnight. But she was getting this way lately—jumpy.

The annoying words RESTRICTED NUMBER blinked rhythmically on the caller ID screen. Laramie decided to roll the dice.

"Yes?"

"I need your e-mail address."

Laramie felt the stiffness in her shoulders ease but she didn't respond until she'd returned to her seat on the couch.

"Why?"

"You'll see when I send these pictures. Could be nothing, random coincidence, but coincidence is overrated, if you ask me."

"What are you talking about?"

"After China, you found the same sort of exercises in North Korea. Your other lead was in Yemen, where the rebels take their orders from quite an odd-looking man, correct?"

Laramie hesitated. Given how little credence she now gave her theories, any discussion of classified topics from her home phone no longer seemed worthwhile.

"I still have no idea what you're talking about," she said.

"Ah," he said. "Disciplined."

Cooper broke the connection, punched Laramie's cell number into his sat phone, hit Send, and waited for Laramie to find and answer the mobile phone.

"Is this really going to make any difference?" she said.

"You're being smart—if they even care about you at all, it's likely they're only into your hard line. Now give me your e-mail address."

Obviously she couldn't receive the photographs at her office; nonetheless, she'd made an effort to avoid using the fabricated Yahoo! account. The whistle-blower swallowing the whistle, returning to obscurity while she still had the chance.

"Fine," she said, and gave him the EastWest7 address. "But I'm not sure how soon I'll be able to access it. Also, this probably isn't the best—"

"I took some pictures," Cooper said, "of some people you're familiar with. Together."

Laramie wasn't precisely sure what he meant, but if he was talking about the countries she'd been surveying, then she *really* didn't know what he was talking about. What *could* he be talking about? Pictures? It didn't seem possible.

"Who," she said, "and where?"

"Have a look and call me back."

Laramie knew he was about to hang up, W. Cooper playing the mystery man game, so she jumped in before he could do it.

"Um," she said.

Silence—make that static. But she knew she hadn't lost him.

"What do you do," she said, stopped, put the phone in her lap, thought for a moment, lifted the phone again, and said, "how do you know when you're being followed? Technically, I mean. How would you go about finding out, if you thought you were?"

More static. Laramie felt the mild warmth of frustration rise into her cheeks. She didn't like the feeling it gave her, asking her odd new phone pal for serious advice. But who else could she ask? Eddie Rothgeb came loaded with a formidable knowledge base, but one thing he certainly didn't bring to the table was operations experience.

"The first rule," Cooper said, "is when you bust them, don't let them know you've done it."

"Fine, but maybe you could offer a couple, you know, technical—"

"Second rule: if you think somebody's on you, then somebody is. Easiest thing to do, if you want to make them, is chop up your routine. Not the whole thing, just parts of it."

Laramie thought about that for a moment. "All right," she said.

"Where did you have dinner tonight?"

Laramie didn't answer right away, which bothered her— and which also explained why she didn't like asking W. Cooper questions like this. It put her at a disadvantage, Laramie knowing he'd somehow seize the opportunity to ask more personal questions than she cared to answer.

"Koo Koo Roo," she said.

"Chicken?"

"Chicken."

"Skinless?"

"I'm not finding the humor here, so if you—"

"Regular stop, maybe you get it to go, coming home, a couple nights a week? When you aren't knee-deep in SATINT till two A.M."

Laramie eyed the plastic bag with the restaurant's logo on the kitchen counter near the phone.

Cooper said, "Keep the restaurant in the routine, but change it up. Dine in-house instead. Read a book for an hour while you eat. Visit the restroom five or six times—and keep an eye peeled while you do it. Do the same thing for every segment of your routine, and you may see the same face a couple times. You run, right?"

Laramie resisted the urge to sigh. "Yes, I run."

"Head out the same way you always do, then change the loops. Log an extra mile or two. You get it by now."

"I do."

"Call me when you've looked at the pictures," he said, and clicked off.

Laramie tossed the phone on the other side of the couch, lifted her wineglass, sipped, and noticed the blinds covering her living room window weren't entirely shut. She closed them, came back to the couch, and tucked her bare legs beneath her. She pulled a blanket from the armrest, covered her legs with it, found the remote control, and punched up *Headline News*. She'd make her way through the gamut of 24-hour cable news networks, and maybe a few minutes of E! or Style before she crashed, but she usually chose to start things off with the twenty-two minutes as peddled by the *Headline News* marketing campaign.

W. Cooper, Laramie thought, is a fucking smart-ass—but I suppose I picked the right guy to ask.

33

When Cooper's eyes opened in his bungalow, he did not feel as though one of his dreams had awakened him. Ordinarily he felt that way—he would burst awake sucking wind, soaked in sweat, gasping for oxygen after drowning in the river, or grasping at the locked dungeon door. Tonight, though, there was no such desperation. One moment he had been lost in the void of drunken slumber; in the next, he was awake, silent, and sober.

It might have been the sound of a twig, broken unnaturally; possibly it was a series of actions—breathing, walking, moving—audible only when performed by heavy mammals or the occasional oversize reptile. Whatever it was that had awakened him, it was not organic to the island, to the resort, or, for that matter, to life as he had lived it for what would soon approach two decades.

In a place even Ronnie could not find, Cooper kept something in addition to the Louisville Slugger. He had not used it once during his time in the Caribbean, but tonight, he knew, would be different. He found and withdrew the TEC-9 assault pistol from its hiding place and, checking over his senses, found himself to be strangely sober. It was as though he hadn't tasted an alcoholic beverage in years, when in fact he had been blistering drunk when he'd passed out for the night a mere couple hours back.

He left his bungalow through a gate attached to the outdoor shower, neither noticing nor caring that he was stark naked as he did it.

Then Cooper was out in the night.

Shreds of moonlight allowed him to identify the black-clad shapes, hard shadows against the more inconsistent lines made by the palm fronds, the shadows creeping along the side of his bungalow. They were headed for his porch.

Wraiths, he thought. Always wraiths.

Without sound, in no rush, he strolled casually along the stones of the garden path and, with a cap-gun set of cracking spits, tagged two of the three wraiths with unerring head shots, reflexively averting the potential complications of body armor.

Wraith number three contorted his shadow into a turn-and-shoot motion and got a bullet headed in Cooper's direction. Despite the wraith's speed, his shot only lashed a burning stripe of pain across Cooper's right shoulder. Otherwise it failed to affect the more deliberately aimed round from Cooper's gun, and then there were no more wraiths, and in their place only unseen lumps in the unlit garden.

Cooper grabbed at his right shoulder and found his arm to be functioning. He continued his self-check, finding his entire body, notwithstanding the shoulder, remained in whatever moderately good health in which it had found itself prior to the incident. Then he took another form of inventory, realizing, among other things, that he now stood nude in the garden, and that the sound of gunfire must already be delivering every last one of the club's occupants for a look-see. He slipped into his bungalow through the back, redeposited the gun in its hole, pulled on some Adidas shorts and the Tevas, found a bandage and some athletic tape, strapped the bandage over the shoulder wound, covered the dressing with a T-shirt, found his sat phone, and went back out by way of the porch.

As Cooper had known he'd be, Ronnie was already waiting for him on the path below the stairs. He came down and they talked for a minute, Cooper making some suggestions on what to tell the guests who would probably be swarming the bungalow in seconds.

Once they'd agreed on what Ronnie should tell them, Cooper noticed Dottie standing quietly on the path a few yards back from his porch, arms folded across her breasts, which, unfortunately, he wouldn't have been able to see anyway, since she seemed to be wearing a tank top. She also seemed to be wearing a bikini bottom, or maybe just panties—either way, the Dottie-spotting, coinciding as it did with Ronnie's zippy arrival, confirmed his suspicion. She'd been in the putz's room when the firecrackers had gone off.

"Oh, look," Cooper said, "Dottie."

Ronnie shrugged and turned to head off the resort's guests at the pass.

From the confines of bungalow nine, Cooper dialed Cap'n Roy's home number with his sat phone.

"Yeah, mon," Roy muttered.

"Roy," Cooper said, starting right in, "I've got three dead commandos in the garden outside my room."

It took a minute, but then Roy said, "How they get there?"

"I haven't really thought it through, but I feel pretty safe making the wild guess they came to see me after I talked to the wrong person, or took a look around the wrong place, while working in my capacity as detective-for-the-dead."

"What you talkin' 'bout, mon?"

"What I'm talking about is, I've been asking around about that twice-dead zombie from your Marine Base beach," Cooper said. "I assume you knew our boy was a zombie before handing him over to your unsuspecting friend the spook, by the way. His name, in case you wondered, was Marcel. Marcel S."

Roy didn't say anything for a while. When he did, he had that clarity in his voice that Cooper took to mean he'd sat up in bed, maybe even rolled his feet off the edge of the mattress and planted them on the floor while he thought things through.

"That right?" Roy said. "Marcel?"

"Uh-huh."

"Where he from, then? You know that too?"

"Haiti," Cooper said. "Kid was also engaged when he died. Additional fun fact."

Roy *cluck-clucked* with his tongue. Cooper envisioned him shaking his head while he did it—*What a shame,* Roy thinking over there in Road Town, *dat poor fella, then.*

"Anyway," Cooper said, "reason for the call, Roy, is one, to inform the authorities that I've just shot and killed three individuals who, in seeking to off me in the peace and quiet of my bungalow, wore body armor and carried automatic weapons."

"'Off you,' eh?" Roy said. "And how 'bout two?"

"Thought you'd never ask. Mainly I wanted to see what

you thought about the idea of my stuffing these boys into some SCUBA bags, dragging them out to my Apache, and paying an early morning call on that pair of makos and their barracuda pals in Eastman's Cove."

Cooper waited. It didn't take long.

"Hungry sharks," Roy said, "be a menace to us islanders."

Cooper held on for any further pronouncement; receiving none, he broke the connection.

Cooper returned from Eastman's Cove just before dawn. Heading inside, he retrieved a pinkie-thick joint from the drawer of his reading table, fired it up, and mourned the passing of the three commandos in a more mellow state of mind from one of the chairs on his porch.

Pondering their connection to his recent adventures, he concluded, about two-thirds of the way through the blunt, that since it couldn't be Jimbo, couldn't be Barry the witch doctor, and probably wasn't within the means of either the Cat in the Hat or the parrot-voiced quack from Hôpital H. L. Dantier, it was almost undoubtedly somebody on that fucking island.

The island hosting the convention of Communist dictators, who must, he decided, have appreciated his visit to such a degree that they'd sent him the thoughtful gift of the three somewhat ineffective G.I. Joe impersonators.

While he smoked, Cooper waited patiently for his muscles to calm. The part of his dispatching of the commandos that he didn't particularly want to acknowledge was that his muscles—particularly one of his quadriceps, just above his right knee—had been trembling since the bullet nipped him. Been a while, he supposed, since I've been shot—not, however, long enough for my nerves to be shot too.

He tried to focus on something else. He could hear the

water breaking against the reef in the distance; there was a warm breeze that brought with it the smell of the sea, and palm trees, and a flower he couldn't place.

When his muscles firmed up he killed the joint, ducked inside, and went back to sleep.

34

He reprimands her in his very office—in the presence of her direct supervisor and the head of her directorate—and Laramie has the ovaries to leak her entire report to a *U.S. senator?*

He *had* underestimated her.

Laramie, Gates thought, would be subjected to suspension, intimidation, interrogation, indictment, and one hell of a momentum against her ever again finding gainful employment—unless, of course, she wanted to upgrade to drive-through jockey at Burger King. This much was self-evident, since it was widely known that to defy Peter M. Gates without suitable leverage meant it was time to get ready to pay a heavy toll. He'd begin taxing her before the day was out.

None of this, though, would alter his newfound predicament.

Not in the slightest.

He'd grossly misjudged the girl, and the president—the

fucking *president*—would, as a result, either be publicly embarrassed or privately mugged. Senator Kircher would see his way to victory in some form. Somebody would in turn be made to pay the price, and the moment Gates read, in Rhone's report, that Laramie had been the one to spill the beans to the senator, Gates knew his own occupational death to be as imminent as Laramie's.

His only hope now was to delay his demise, and the only way he'd be able to pull *that* off was to prevent Kircher—and subsequently Lou Ebbers and the White House—from learning the true identity of "EastWest7." If the senator got hold of Laramie's name, he'd undoubtedly track her down, and Gates had the feeling Laramie wouldn't be shy about disclosing his own role in quashing her findings.

Stop the Kircher-Laramie conversation from taking place, and Gates knew he still had a shot at covering the president's ass, and therefore the national security advisor's ass, and therefore the Agency's substantially exposed ass, and therefore his own, on the matter he figured Bill O'Reilly and company would soon be calling "the Kircher letter."

Regardless, he'd underestimated the zeal of a *junior analyst*—and fucked himself accordingly. And perhaps, Gates mused, he might even be able to stomach this second major error of his career—the error that would surely prove his undoing—were it not for the horrific revelation contained in the transcripts of Laramie's phone conversations.

Rooting through his bag in the back of his Town Car, Gates found the first Laramie file his security man had provided him and reread the encrypted summary of Laramie's second recorded telephone conversation. It had been with her so-called former professor, but Gates felt a churn roil through his gastrointestinal tract as he read with a newfound understanding. He could practically hear the bastard's voice as the words popped out at him from the page:

MALE VOICE: While I'm in town, I'm staying with our old buddy WC. You remember old WC, don't you?

(pause)

LARAMIE: Of course I remember WC. So he's in Washington now?

MALE VOICE: Yeah, how about that. You know something else? I think that after all these years, old WC's still a virgin. You believe it? Anyway, he's in the phone book. Give me a call on your way home.

Giving her sophomoric clues to locate him in the Agency's internal directory—*fuck*! Fucking mosquito that he was, the man must have spent half his idle time—of which Gates knew he possessed a great deal—concocting ways to *fuck* him. Bite him, pass on some deadly viral disease, disappear for ten years to plan the next chomp. What was it—had *Lunar Fucking Eclipse* sensed an opportunity to destroy him simply by reading a copy of the all-stations memorandum he'd ordered Laramie to write?

Gates read on, seeking a stream of logic to answer his fury:

LARAMIE: I'm not—

MALE VOICE: Ah.

LARAMIE: Ah?

MALE VOICE: You're not supposed to be working on what you're working on, are you?

(pause)

Fuck them. Tell me what's going on.

LARAMIE: Tough talk. You know, professor, "fuck them" isn't the kind of advice professors usually give.

Later the mosquito e-mailed photographs to her—Gates
reviewed the pictures and instantly ID'd every face at the resort. Then Laramie had called him, Gates reading the date as
the night before last, the time of the call 4:17 A.M. He noted
from the report that Laramie had placed the call following
another long night of unauthorized SATINT-viewing:

LARAMIE: How did you, what I mean is, why did you take
them? The pictures? Do you live near there?

MALE VOICE: It's a few hours from here by boat. By my boat.
Longer on others.

LARAMIE: Where is it?

MALE VOICE: About twenty miles east of Martinique.

LARAMIE: Do you know what these—it's Kim Jong-il, Fatah
Duwami from Yemen, and an admiral in the Chinese
navy, Li Zhu, did you know that? And—do you know
what they were doing there?

MALE VOICE: I know who they are. I've got no idea why
they're there.

LARAMIE: You know what I did after you sent me these pictures?

MALE VOICE: No.

LARAMIE: I worked from the other faces. Not the three in the
shot you cropped, but the other ones, you understand
what I'm saying?

MALE VOICE: Yes.

LARAMIE: Do you know who the others are?

MALE VOICE: Just about every one of them.

LARAMIE: I spent eight hours in the lab tonight examining
the home countries of the leaders in your pictures. How
did you do this? Find them?

MALE VOICE: Wild luck. You're saying your theory remains
intact?

LARAMIE: I haven't had the time to check them all, but at this point—

MALE VOICE: At four a.m.—

LARAMIE: Every nation I've checked has some form of military buildup, an exercise, plus significant and unusual troop movement. These countries are preparing for simultaneous military action. It's as simple as that.

MALE VOICE: Sounds like you were right. And your bosses weren't.

LARAMIE: My God.

MALE VOICE: Quick question. You find anything related to twice-dead slave-labor zombies in those satellite photographs?

LARAMIE: What?

MALE VOICE: Thought I'd give it a shot.

LARAMIE: You're joking about this? Do you understand what this could amount to? For all intents and purposes—

MALE VOICE: Actually it's pretty serious, this thing I'm stuck with, and I don't particularly feel like going back to the Island of Dr. Marx to find the answers I think I need to find.

LARAMIE: The Island of Dr.—oh, I get it now.

Gates, fuming behind the desk in his office, reread every document on Julie Laramie he'd received over the course of the surveillance he'd ordered. Then he read them again. Finally he buzzed Miss Anders and told her to usher in Sperling Rhone, his security man, whom he ordered to sit in the chair with the thin rubber cushion then promptly fired. He told Rhone he was an ignorant shit for delivering his report too late for Gates to find any use in it, then had him forcibly escorted from the building by a pair of marines.

Lou Ebbers finished reading the executive summary and raised his eyebrows without saying a word. Gates didn't like the feeling the DCI's expression gave him.

"Be nice," Ebbers said, "if we could have been out ahead of this one."

"No question, Lou," Gates said.

Gates, Rosen, Rader, and Ebbers sat at the conference table meant for twenty adjoining Ebbers's office. Gates had provided his boss with what amounted to a cut-and-pasted version of Laramie's two reports, the wording essentially unchanged. The memo's header, proclaiming its classified status, stated that it came directly from Gates—the DDCI's personal stamp, meant to reassure Ebbers that Gates had personally seen to the compilation and verification of the report.

Gates knew this would do him no good now.

Ebbers was reviewing the report. "A new al-Qaeda," he said, "with, in the very least, circumstantial evidence documenting the sponsorship by, or collusion of a minimum of three nations, likely more." He looked up from the document and straight into the eyes of Gates. "Not the best scenario, considering the president's intelligence chief will be delivering him this rather groundbreaking information only as the result of a prompt from the president's leading ideological combatant. In fact, when I present this to the national security advisor in about fifteen minutes, I expect it will be transparent to him, and thus the president, that our friend from North Carolina had his hands on the intel well before the senior leaders of the Central Intelligence Agency.

"Were I the president," Ebbers said, "this would give me pause as to why the people currently holding the senior leadership positions at CIA in fact have these jobs. Frankly, gentlemen, this is an embarrassment."

He leaned back from the report and took his time passing his eyes over each of them.

"We sitting on anything else, say, might help keep my ass out of the sling it'll occupy beginning some thirteen minutes from now?"

Gates felt an ulcerous boil at the base of his gut. Even as the spymaster he'd become, Gates could not conceive of any strategy that could offer Ebbers salvation from appearing foolhardy, late, and ineffective in the upcoming meeting. And considering that shit, in the nation's capital, flowed downhill with frictionless efficiency, the current circumstances meant to Gates that his job was pretty much shot to hell.

He could—and would, of course—take measures to shore things up. He would dig up and provide another white-hot chunk of intel he'd been sitting on and lay it out for Ebbers and the NSC somewhere out ahead of the curve instead of woefully behind. But even if Ebbers didn't drop him like a sack of wet sand immediately following the pending NSC wrist-slap, Gates knew that any measures he took at this point would only amount to a four-corner stall. The fact was, unless he was prepared to bind and gag and leave Julie Laramie to rot in the corner of some overgrown park—which he'd given some thought to doing—Kircher would ultimately track the bitch down, the remainder of the truth would be exposed, and that would be all she wrote.

When neither Rosen nor Rader piped up with any helpful suggestions that might aid their boss, Gates performed a combination nod and shrug—meant to indicate he was being a man here, taking personal responsibility for Ebbers's predicament.

"Sorry to say, Lou," he said, "I think you've got just about all we know on this one."

After a long while, Ebbers closed the file, rose, and left.

35

They sent a woman. That, she knew, was how they did it: match you up with your physical equal to avoid the intimidation factor, giving the impression you were being summoned for nothing more than a conversation.

Laramie had been through this before, at least a routine variation of it. Anyone working above the intern level in the Directorate of Intelligence was subjected to the "Scuds," CIA's routine psychological profile-refresher and lie detector exams. Laramie was long since in on the meaning behind the nickname: they hit you with annoying, hastily launched, generally ineffective missiles, hoping to put you on the defensive and force a mistake in case you might have something to hide. If you didn't, the semiannual, four-hour sessions were a joke.

Since she'd endured her most recent bout with the Scuds only six weeks back, it was fairly evident to Laramie that the thirtysomething woman whose reflection appeared on a darkened portion of the monitor in her viewing cubicle had not come for another routine inquisition. The purpose of the visit was clear as day: they'd discovered her e-mails to Senator Kircher.

She wondered what it meant that they knew what she'd done. What they had in store for her. Then she wondered what they were doing with the intel they must have known she'd discovered—were they acting on it? Or just punishing her for leaking it? If history were any indication—

The woman asked Laramie to accompany her and led the way up the elevator to the fourth floor, home of the Internal Investigations Unit. The woman took her into an enclosed room equipped with a mirror, encouraged Laramie to take a seat in one of the room's two chairs, and left, closing the door behind her and locking Laramie in.

Considering that Scud sessions typically began with a lie detector exam, that an investigative officer accompanied you through the entire process, and that the officer, until now, had never failed to offer up a cup of coffee to kick things off, it occurred to Laramie there was a pretty good chance she had one hell of a long day ahead of her.

Cooper found there wasn't much in the Langley database on the topic of who controlled the real estate on the island called Mango Cay. Abandoning the ostensibly far-superior CIA search engine for plain old Google, he verified from the chair on his porch that real estate falling under the jurisdiction of Martinique could not be owned by foreigners, and, as in the British Virgins, a lease-hold system had been established to circumvent such revenue-killing nationalism. Property secured by foreign interests in both Martinique and the BVIs involved the transfer of what was usually a ninety-nine-year lease, ultimately rented from the federal government of France or the United Kingdom, respectively; it was the lease rights that were purchased or transferred by private property "owners" in the case of a local sale.

Cooper made some calls and ultimately found a clerk in the appropriate records hall in Martinique. The midday sun had begun to bear down on him, the old porch oriented poorly when it came to the blistering afternoon heat. Nonetheless, he managed to score from the clerk the reasonably uninteresting and possibly useless ownership history of Mango Cay. The current leaseholder was a Delaware corporation called Global Exports, whose signatory officer was somebody named Spencer H. Gibson. Global Exports had bought the Mango Cay lease just over ten years ago. The prior owner, according to the clerk, was a Liberian firm called Freedom Partners, LLC, which had controlled the land for nine years. Two individuals held it prior to that; Cooper jotted down the names as the clerk rattled them off. Before the clerk's list of four ownership entities, the land had apparently been classified as uninhabited public property.

By the time he'd hung up on the clerk, Cooper had already clicked back into cyberspace and determined that no particular Agency record existed on anybody named Spencer H. Gibson. He was also unable to find any CIA-originated intelligence on either Global Exports or Freedom Partners, and the earlier owners, two American multimillionaires, were now deceased. Cooper dialed up the phone numbers the clerk had given for both Global Exports and Freedom Partners, reaching a disconnection notice for Global Exports and a loud, repeating *bratt-bratt* noise when he tried Freedom Partners. He tried the number a few more times and kept getting the same sound.

Annoyed and overheated, Cooper leaned his head back and fell asleep in the chair, the sun stinging hot on his face.

They kept her in the Scuds unit for thirty-eight hours. Sleep was not permitted and no food was provided. The throbbing headache that resulted from Laramie's inability to quench her caffeine addiction would have made it impossible for her to sleep in any case, but with the added irritation of the headache, enduring the last hours of the interrogation nearly did her in. There were moments—for instance, the utterance of the thousandth repeat of the identical question, queried by the sixth interrogator of the session, with Laramie strapped into the lie detector seat, EKG stickers adorning breasts, belly, hips, wrists—when Laramie was forced to dig her fingernails into the skin of her palm, even to bite a bleeding incision into her tongue, in order to keep from leaping from the chair and bashing the interrogator's brains in.

Ironically, it was the interrogation simulation they'd given her at The Farm that gave her the chops to survive the thirty-eight hours intact. One of the first lessons they'd conveyed to the fresh batch of recruits back then had been simple enough to remember now: *never go belly-up*. No matter what they had on you, never admit that you did anything wrong, who you worked for, or whatever it was they were trying to get out of you—or so went the lesson. The principle was intended for use in the unlikely event a DI analyst subjected to torture in a Syrian prison just happened to possess the secrets underpinning America's national security, but it proved particularly useful as a guide on what to admit, and what to deny, as the Agency's own investigators sought to pry various confessions from her on the topic of her supposedly treasonous activities.

They had everything—she wasn't sure how they had it all,

but they did—everything she'd said into a pay phone, cell phone, home phone, some things she'd said aloud to herself at home, the text from each of the e-mails she'd let fly to Senator Kircher from Kinko's and Morpheus. They knew about her relationship with Eddie Rothgeb, they had transcripts of every conversation she'd had with the mysterious W. Cooper, and they had meticulous documentation of her precise whereabouts within the confines of the headquarters building, pretty much minute by minute.

What Laramie decided to do was admit to divulging classified intelligence to Eddie Rothgeb and W. Cooper; she chose not to go belly-up on the Kircher e-mails. She'd devised this strategy on the walk over to the IIU wing from her cubicle, and stuck to it for the duration of the session. She found she had some ground to stand on, since she'd never put her name on anything, had never sent or received anything relating to the senator from home, or the office, or anywhere tied to her real name; she'd been careful with her language in the summary she'd sent, steering clear of names, departments, and specific intel and analysis that could be directly tied to her. She didn't actually see how it really made any difference that she refused to own up to the cyber communiqués with a U.S. senator who supposedly oversaw the government's intelligence operations, but stonewalling the interrogators at least gave her something to focus on during the caffeine-deprivation marathon. She also guessed that anybody inside or outside CIA contemplating bringing criminal charges against her would see the Kircher leak as the most egregious of the offenses she'd committed over the past three weeks of her life, and any physical evidence they'd have linking her to Kircher would be dicey at best. She'd passed the lie detector tests with flying colors.

While she chose not to own up to the Kircher notes, she

found, oddly enough, that the line of questioning pursued by the roster of interrogators focused almost solely on her correspondence with W. Cooper. Between bolts of pain from the caffeine headache, she found this emphasis disturbing, presuming Cooper was in fact who he purported to be. She had a pretty good hunch he wasn't anything or anybody different than he claimed, and at least until recently she'd done all right sticking by her instincts. Cooper himself had pegged her as a human lie detector machine. Why, then, the fourth degree on her phone calls with an Agency operative?

At 11 P.M. the day after they'd come for her, the last interrogator in the succession of faces told her she was free to go. She was made to sign a document agreeing to the fact that her employment status had officially been categorized as "suspended without pay pending internal investigation" and that she was now legally required to notify the gentleman listed on the document if she intended to leave the greater Baltimore-Washington metropolitan area for any period of time whatsoever. Laramie knew from the expression on the last interrogator's face that she wasn't free to go anywhere—they'd follow her everywhere she went, as had now been bluntly pointed out to have been the case for some time.

On the way home she pulled into the same 7-Eleven where she'd first used a pay phone to call Cooper and bought a vial of Advil, a Diet Pepsi, and a PowerBar. She swallowed eight hundred milligrams of ibuprofen between Power Bar chunks and drove home, noting with neither surprise nor concern that one particular set of headlights seemed to find its way into her rearview mirror regardless of where she turned or how fast she drove. The car would drop back, vanish when she made a turn, then reappear, never coming closer than a few hundred yards behind.

As she pulled into her condo complex, she observed the

guest parking lot adjoining her unit now featured three black sedans and one minivan, no single one of which she had ever seen parked here.

The garage door opened at the base of her town house and she slid inside.

It wasn't until she pulled on the emergency brake and killed the engine that Laramie acknowledged how hungry she was. Still behind the wheel, she punched 411 on her cell phone, connected to Domino's, and ordered a large pepperoni-and-green-pepper pizza. The delivery took a great deal longer than thirty minutes, and Laramie had a pretty good idea why. She didn't ask the guy delivering the pizza whether he'd been pulled over by the police halfway through his run, or whether, when he was pulled over, the cops searched his Altima bumper to bumper, but figured that was about the size of it. The boy drove off—subject, no doubt, to another stop-and-search, probably for that same ineffective blinker.

She tried to make a phone call and got nothing in the way of a dial tone. She tried her cell phone, and got a message saying her service had been temporarily interrupted. She nodded, assuming they'd realized she could make calls with it once the pizza boy showed. Unfazed, she booted up the Dell desktop she kept in an alcove between the kitchen and living room, took a shot at checking for any e-mails, and failed to get an Internet connection. The Explorer status bar explained itself by saying, CANNOT LOCATE SERVER.

She changed into her nightshirt and looked in vain for a bottle of wine until she stumbled upon the jackpot of an un-opened bottle of champagne in the back of the fridge. She shot the cork at the ceiling, kicked the lid off the pizza box, and never quite got around to turning on the television set while she sat on the couch and polished off all the Dom and seven-eighths of the pie.

She was thinking something to the effect that both Cooper and her father, when he'd been around, really had something with that alcoholism bit as she leaned her head back into the cushions and passed out for the night.

36

The hardware behind Spike Gibson's perimeter security system required so much processing capacity that Gibson had been forced to invent a daisy-chained combination of servers to support it. He initially bought Crays, then later switched to Apple/IBM dual-G5 processor-based CPUs; he acquired the equipment through a ladder of American shell corporations, none traceable to the next.

His software oversaw a vast web of data capture, including military-grade radar and sonar systems, surface and submarine motion sensors, closed-circuit digital video feeds, and online control of a private satellite outfitted with spy cameras. The complexities of the system were such that during each twenty-four-hour period, the system required a short period of time—seven minutes and twenty-two seconds, to be exact—to reboot.

During the reboot window, the system's data-capture inventory was tested in its entirety; all hardware, including processors and memory, were examined and updated; and all data collected during the prior twenty-four-hour period was digitally archived. Emergency power capacity for the island was tested—the power grid fed by the nuclear power cell in the main cavern was switched for five minutes to a gasoline-powered generator, then for another two minutes to a battery cell. In order for the system to work without any error whatsoever over the course of more than a decade, the daily reboot was a necessary evil, which Gibson attempted to minimize but still found imperative.

At least that was how he had explained matters to General Deng.

Gibson thought it more effective to spare General Deng the details, and thus had informed him of the daily reboot as a side note. Deng had never asked for clarification, and his apparent indifference to this minor nuisance worked particularly well for Gibson, who had, due to the window of darkness offered by the preposterously redundant daily reboot, conducted a highly regimented salvage operation of his own.

Over the course of the past eighty days, the daily increments amounted to just over nine hours of cumulative time, which proved plenty for Gibson's team—Hiram, Lana, and the rotation of disposable laborers—to make significant headway toward his aim of pilfering four W-76 thermonuclear warheads from the Trident missiles in the cavern. The extraction involved a transfer of the warheads to the cargo cave—or in Deng's parlance, the Lab—located three-quarters of a mile from the main missile hall.

The work had to be performed during the main transfer phase of the reboot session, since it was during this period that the cavern's floodlights popped off and the cavern-based closed-circuit video cameras closed down to facilitate the daily archiving function. Had Gibson conducted his operation at any other point during the day, Deng could have seen what he was doing; the mainframe simulcast all data streams to an encrypted hard drive in whichever of Deng's War Rooms the general planned to occupy next.

To date, Gibson had succeeded in extricating 2 of the cavern's 168 warheads from their homes inside the Trident missiles.

On the afternoon of the second day of Julie Laramie's interrogation, the daily reboot commenced on schedule at 3:52:38 P.M. A second later, the bank of floodlights lining the ceiling of the missile cavern doused. Pale yellow emergency lighting, emanating from bulbs built into poles lining the walls of the cavern, flickered to life.

Two seconds after the pale yellow darkness had consumed the cavern, a pair of figures emerged from the tunnel entrance through which Deng had brought his guided tour. While impossible to detect by the digital cameras' dormant chips, the two figures were Hiram and the wino. Hiram drove one of the carts and kept a black rod draped across his lap. The wino carried a heavy black duffel bag.

As the duo approached missile 6, Hiram exited the cart and opened the cage door of the two-person platform secured to the outside of the missile's external silo. When the wino didn't walk into the lift unprompted, Hiram zapped him with the rod, the cattle prod doing the trick. Hiram retrieved a chunky harness, an apron, and a rope-and-pulley assembly from the cart—affixed, on one end, to a winch at the rear of the cart—and followed the wino aboard the lift. As the lift reached the twenty-foot mark, Hiram doffed the heavy apron, opened the lift, and gestured for the wino to get to work.

The wino hastily withdrew a rubber plate and series of tools from the duffel bag; he used the plate as a shelf, affixing it to a length of pipe and dumping the tools across it. It took him thirty seconds to unscrew and open an access panel on the side of the missile; with Hiram and his cattle prod lurking behind the metal skin of the access door, the wino conducted a meticulous, though not precise, series of tasks, on which Hiram had instructed him earlier.

Including the wino, a sequence of three slaves had been working for weeks at removing one of this missile's four warheads, extricating the warhead rivet by rivet, seven minutes at a time, from the Mk-4 MIRV to which it was secured within the missile. Inside the access panel, the wino chewed through struts with saws, whacked at chunks of metal blocking the extraction path, and hammered and chiseled at rivets, all the while sucking down metal sawdust and soaking up enough radiation to peg a Geiger counter against its stop. The heroin Hiram had been injecting into the wino's bloodstream did not appear to affect the performance of his assigned tasks.

Though Hiram could not see the re-entry vehicle from his protected vantage behind the access door, he knew the MIRV to resemble a cruise missile without the wings. Having logged nine cumulative hours of such extraction work, Hiram also knew each C-4 Trident I to contain four such MIRVs. This meant that each of the forty-two Tridents was therefore capable of delivering four one-hundred-kiloton nuclear detonations to four independently targeted locations of up to one thousand miles apart. On this particular W-76/Mk-4, Hiram's slaves had logged two hours, thirty-one minutes, and forty-two seconds to date, leaving Hiram with what he estimated to be one minute and fifteen seconds before the wino got the last rivet out.

Hiram swung the rope over a strut and clipped the hook at its end to the harness. At the three-minute mark in the reboot sequence, the last extracted rivet made a *ping* against a sheet of metal somewhere inside the projectile; Hiram reached around the access door, handed the wino the harness, and took the lift down to the floor.

Nearly five minutes of the reboot had elapsed when the wino signaled as instructed that the harness was ready. Gloved now, and strapped to a portion of the scaffolding, Hiram used the rope to begin hauling the 375-pound warhead out of the missile and into the lift, aided by minimal guidance from the wino. With a minute thirty to go, Hiram swung the warhead into the rear of the golf cart. He let the rope go slack; the warhead, settling, sunk the vehicle against its axles. Hiram quickly unfastened the rope from the harness.

With Hiram's foot to the floor, the cart inched back across the cavern, gaining enough momentum to make it into the transport tunnel just before the elapsing reboot sequence resulted in the closing and locking of the tunnel door. The wino ran, stumbled, then finally managed to fall into the passenger seat beside Hiram as the door slammed shut behind them, neither of them able to see the bank of floodlights pop, click, and flutter to life within the cavern on the other side of the door.

Hiram parked the cart and ordered the wino to follow him on foot out of the transport tunnel.

The naming of the supreme leader of the People's Republic of China—who traditionally held the titles of both president and premier—generally occurred by two methods: first, and officially, by a vote of the Central Committee of the Communist Party, the CPC; second, and more important, the ascendant to the throne must, unofficially, have been given the thumbs-up by both the sitting premier and the most revered of the elder CPC leaders. Historically, the former process had followed the latter like a rubber stamp.

While the man holding the offices of president and premier since Deng's rise through the military was now only fifty-eight years old, it was common practice to tab either a single successor or a pair of competing candidates from the beginning of one's tenure. In keeping with this tradition, the premier had identified two men with the potential to succeed him when the time came and had elevated each to vice premier. The first man, named Lu Azhau, oversaw all domestic law enforcement and served as the general secretary of the CPC; Deng was the other man, and while he had effectively navigated the maze of party politics to position himself as the leading contender, the general believed there to be a number of perfectly viable, and speedier, alternate means of succession.

Unfortunately, the critical first step of the means Deng had decided to employ was falling dangerously behind schedule. Five minutes behind, in fact—five minutes he wasn't sure he could spare. He *was* sure that if another ten minutes passed and his motorcade continued along at its current route and pace, he would not survive to see the eleventh minute.

The convoy, composed of Deng's bulletproof limousine with the old man at the wheel, two jeeps, one armored vehicle, and a police sedan, found itself two hours in on the three-hour trek from PLA headquarters in Beijing to the seaside village of Beidaihe. Deng couldn't remember exactly when the decision had been made, but somewhere along the line, Beidaihe had become the permanent site of a number of annual governmental summits. The legislature convened in Beidaihe each summer; the CPC held a larger convention, inclusive of almost all party members, in the spring; the third summit, held in October, was considerably more exclusive. Each year on this weekend, the Standing Committee of the State Council came to town.

There were only eleven members of the council's Standing Committee, China's equivalent of the former Soviet Politburo, a body with a function similar to but having much greater domestic control than America's National Security Council or the president's cabinet. Council members included senior party leaders, bureau chiefs, the nation's two vice premiers, and the president and premier himself. The group gathered in Beidaihe to clarify the government's official platform. Coming out of this meeting each year, the CPC invariably adopted a broader version of the council's views. Attendance for council members was mandatory.

Some, however, were scheduled to arrive later than others.

It was a Thursday and, by Deng's watch, twenty minutes after five in the evening—six minutes late. An aide of Deng's had verified by phone that eight of the eleven council members had arrived in their rooms, including the premier and Deng's fellow vice premier. While the other late arrivals happened to be two of Deng's most staunch political allies, this arrival pattern nonetheless fit the standard schedule. All members were required to be in their sleeping quarters by midnight; sessions began the following morning at seven.

Deng was beginning to wonder whether he had misjudged the timing. The American W-76 warheads were powerful, and he'd been assured by his chief scientist that the warheads, even after a decade underwater, were likely to reach a yield approaching their original capacity. This led Deng to his current predicament: allow his motorcade to draw much closer to Beidaihe, and the succession order he had in mind wouldn't quite work out—and yet there had been no choice, since if he didn't cut it close, he would arouse suspicion. Still, the thought clung to Deng that even where he now rode in the convoy—seventy miles from Beihaide—there remained a significant chance that he wouldn't survive. And what if the weapon failed to work at all? A dud, lying worthless beneath—

An odd pressure shift lifted him slightly from his seat. He felt instantaneously claustrophobic and noticed that he couldn't hear. He flexed his jaw to pop his ears; they cleared, but he sensed that something else was wrong, and it took him a few seconds to realize it was the limousine's electronics. The reading lights in his compartment, the dashboard up front, the radio that had been playing—all had gone out as though from a blown fuse. The computer monitor providing him constant military readiness updates, the television screen he kept tuned to an international satellite telecast of CNN—all had gone dark.

The electromagnetic pulse! Deng's heart accelerated—the EMP had killed the instrumentation in the vehicle, wiping clean any active electronic activity. The W-76 had gone off.

As the vehicle slowed, Deng saw it first against the treetops a mile ahead of them on the highway, then felt it strike suddenly against the front of the limousine—a wind blast, powerful enough to rock the convoy, lifting the limo's wheels three inches from the surface of the highway yet too weak to overturn the vehicles. This, Deng knew, represented approximately, if not precisely, the forecasted effect of a one-hundred-kiloton nuclear detonation seventy miles from ground zero—the closest point, his chief scientist had told him, at which one could be positioned without sustaining fatal or near-fatal effects from the blast.

As panic struck among the soldiers, his loyal driver, and the security detail in the convoy, Deng savored a moment of pride—of utter satisfaction. He had judged correctly, and, based on the series of events he'd just witnessed, the first step of his master plan had advanced without a hitch.

Tomorrow, he thought, is upon us. Today.

37

When the phone chortled its usual two rings and the machine picked up, Laramie came awake with the sense that something was out of place. Asleep in the same position in which she'd passed out, she wasn't sure what it was that bothered her while Eddie Rothgeb's voice blasted from the answering machine and banged around her aching head.

"Laramie, where the hell are you? Pick up! Are you seeing this?"

She knocked the phone off the hook, fumbled for it, picked it up, said, "Enough," and heard a click. Then nothing.

"Eddie?"

There was no answer. No noise at all—just dead air.

Maybe she had disconnected the call with her butterfingers maneuver, but Laramie doubted it. She hung up, clicked back on, and got no dial tone. She tried this a few times with the same result before her headache began to reassault her. .Groaning, she leaned her forehead against a palm, and in so doing, caught an angle on the open pizza box. Sprawled on the floor, it contained only the lone remaining slice. She noticed that she had even consumed the crusts of the missing pieces.

Last night, there hadn't been a single message on the answering machine. Not even any she had previously saved. She usually had four or five waiting for her at the end of each day and knew for a fact she'd had at least fifteen saved on the chip, so she was confident they hadn't been letting any calls through.

Meaning this morning, they would have kept the intercept going. The call from Rothgeb, cut short though it had been, didn't make sense.

She crossed to the front window and peered outside; it was still dark. She checked her watch, which they'd let her wear for the length of the interrogation, probably just to annoy her further. It was 5:15 A.M.

Two of the sedans appeared to have abandoned the assignment. There remained only one black sedan and the van. She thought of Eddie's words.

Are you seeing this?

Laramie found the remote. The BREAKING NEWS headline registered before the full screen image came up on the tube:

NUKE BLAST AT CHINA SUMMIT

She kicked up the volume. It appeared she'd clicked on to the Fox News Channel. Brit Hume had the desk.

". . . acted immediately. In an emergency vote of the surviving leaders, former vice premier and military general Deng Jiang has been appointed premier.

"The high-intensity detonation had initially been confirmed by a U.S. intelligence source, and has now been officially characterized by China's ambassador to the U.S., as a nuclear explosion. Our American intelligence source is also referring to the size of the detonation as, quote, 'significant.' The Chinese Ambassador in Washington states that China's own intelligence wing has ruled out accidental detonation, and suspects terrorism as the cause. Tens of thousands are suspected dead, including eight of the State Council members, the ruling body of the People's Republic of China. Among the confirmed dead at this hour is China's president and premier. We'll go again to a statement made by the PRC moments after news of this tragedy was confirmed."

Laramie now had a pretty good idea why her personal surveillance detachment had been depleted by fifty percent: half-assed treason investigation notwithstanding, she figured she'd be safe in placing herself a little lower on the global-crisis pecking order than the world's first act of nuclear terror.

Crap.

She knew China with the same familiarity she had with the tiny birthmark on the side of her neck. The territory, the tendencies of every key leader, the way they reacted in a time of crisis. All of it. She could have predicted to the second—in her sleep—the process and result of the immediate-succession vote installing General Deng Jiang as premier. She would have been able to predict who it was who called the vote, who voted, who voted for whom, what actions would be taken, what the State Council and the CPC's public statements would be, and who would issue the statements in the wake of the bombing.

And here I am in my living room. The morning of the worst terrorist act ever to hit the PRC—the worst terrorist act ever—and I'm stuck here under house arrest.

Hung over, no less.

Hume was back on her television screen.

"Interim Premier Deng Jiang issued a written statement to the global news media minutes after the ambassador's press conference." Hume read from a prepared statement while its text appeared over a map of China.

"'The most horrible of tragedies has been wrought upon the People's Republic of China. The destruction was not accidental—this atrocity is almost positively an act of international terror. And while the terrorists did not use a Chinese weapon, I assure you that China possesses suitable weapons to combat this act of war. I can tell you that we are in possession of strong intelligence indicating the presence of a well-funded international terrorist organization hostile to the interests of the People's Republic of China, which was fully capable of perpetrating this murderous act. If and when we determine this organization's responsibility, China will strike defiantly and supremely. The People's Republic of China is now at war, and we will vanquish our mortal enemy with furor, vengeance, and haste.'"

Hume came back onscreen, looked up from the page he'd been reading, and held the gaze of the camera for a long moment of reflection.

"Eerily reminiscent," he said, "of a day in September, not long ago."

Laramie returned to her couch. She sat cross-legged on its cushions and stared blankly at the images on the television for a long time. The phone rang once. The answering machine did not pick up. It rang again, this time as a clipped half-ring.

After a while she went into the bedroom, changed into a sweater, jeans, and running shoes, packed her preferred travel bag with a couple days of things, found the vial of

Advil and downed a trio of tablets. She turned on the lights in the bathroom, kitchen, and bedroom, and turned up the volume on the television. Then she grabbed her purse and bag, returned to the garage, and, working in the dark, used a key to open the door normally reserved for the egress of her garbage bin.

Outside, she found herself face-to-face with the purple plastic monstrosity the city required its residents to use for refuse. Behind it lay the condo village's service road and the fairly ugly rear view of a dozen townhomes backed up against the road.

Crouching, she slid sideways into a bed of bark chips and periwinkle. From this unobstructed, crappy hiding place she listened and watched. Somebody's alarm clock wailed; a local morning news show blared; a phone rang. The tendrils of dawn had not yet reached into the predawn sky. As her eyes adjusted, she tried to see into the cavities at the rear of each townhome—see whether one of her house-arrest squad was out here keeping an eye on the back of her unit. The light from her bathroom window was bright up above her; maybe, she thought, if one of them is watching and is too incompetent to have spotted me already, his eyes would be drawn to that window.

Since she didn't see any figure in the shadows, didn't see any smoke rising from a cigarette, or hear the muffled static of a security radio, Laramie crept around the corner of the unit next to hers. Then, hearing no shouts demanding she stop in her tracks, she started out on the service road, slinking along the garage walls of her neighbors.

After keeping close to the buildings of six or seven units and still finding no objection, she stepped out onto the road, clasped her bag and purse against her side, and set off at a jog.

Security was beefed up to post-9/11 levels every-where in town, let alone at the entrance to the building where fifty-one of the nation's most senior elected represen-tatives happened to work. Nonetheless, when asked by the security man whether she had an appointment with the sen-ator she'd come to see, Laramie gave it her best shot.

"I don't have an appointment," she said, "but Senator Kircher is expecting me."

The guard offered her an amused look as he examined her driver's license, and suddenly Laramie wondered whether Gates's goons had managed to get a warrant issued, or an APB, and that the mild-mannered security officer was play-ing games with her, buying time while he contemplated how best to leap around his desk and cuff her.

But the man merely returned her license, and when she took it, Laramie saw that he'd stacked atop it a visitor's pass.

So much for security on Capitol Hill.

The metal detectors offered no further resistance; when she asked a page for directions, he too offered a bemused ex-pression and directed her down the building's main hallway.

"Fourth office on the left, Miss," he said with a smile.

She came into the waiting room outside Senator Kircher's wing of offices and approached the fiftysomething woman behind the reception desk. Laramie identified herself, told the woman she was here to see the senator, and said, "He may not know me by name, but he'll be familiar with my e-mail address. It's EastWest7. I believe he'll be interested in hearing from me."

Laramie almost blew a gasket when the woman gave her the same sort of inside-joke look offered by the security guard and page.

"Sure," the receptionist said. "'EastWest7,' is it?"

"Correct. I'd like to see him immediately."

"Do you have any information?" the receptionist said. When Laramie stared uncomprehendingly at her, the woman said, "A résumé?" and pushed an eight-by-ten head shot of a very attractive woman across the countertop, not all the way over to Laramie but far enough for her to see.

Laramie examined the photograph from her upside-down perspective. The receptionist looked Laramie over and smiled a motherly smile. "Tell you what," she said. "The senator isn't meeting with constituents today, but one of his aides is here. Why don't you go ahead and wait over there and I'll put a good word in for you." When the woman tilted her chin toward the chairs behind her, Laramie turned to see that there was another woman seated in the waiting room. The woman was stunning. Tall. And thin. Laramie also noticed, connecting the dots now, that the woman did not exactly possess the demeanor of, say, a lobbyist, or a fellow representative.

It was the same woman she'd just seen in the head shot.

A door opened behind the reception desk and a man who reminded Laramie of Rob Lowe leaned out. The receptionist turned and handed him the other woman's head shot and an accompanying sheet of paper. Rob examined the photograph, nodded, and looked across Laramie until his eyes landed on the other woman in the room. He smiled.

"Sherrie? Come on in," he said.

When the stunningly beautiful woman had strolled through the doorway and Rob Lowe closed the door, Laramie, feeling somewhat short and plain, looked at the receptionist.

"You've got to be kidding me," she said.

The woman smiled.

Laramie said, "The reason I'm asking to see—"

She abandoned the explanation midstream. She dug into her purse for a pen, and in as polite a tone as she could muster, said, "Would you happen to have a pad of paper back there?"

"Of course."

Laramie chose a seat as far from where the other woman had been sitting as she could find. Fighting a gag reflex at the prospect of another "constituent" coming in and mistaking her for a fellow aspirant to the Rob Lowe preinterview, she composed with her pen and the receptionist's pad a six-page letter that would bring Kircher up to speed on her findings since the last whistle-blower e-mail. She included her theories on the topic of collusion between General and now-Premier Deng Jiang, North Korea, and the remainder of the declared or aspiring Marxist-Leninist dictatorships Cooper had photographed on the remote island resort. She also included her hypothesis on Peter M. Gates's apparent systematic model of withholding important intelligence from his superiors until the moment of greatest political expediency—expediency for his own career.

When she was through, she checked the document for mistakes—an impulse she rarely possessed the strength to buck—and folded the pages in half. She wrote the following words across one of the blank sides:

TO: SENATOR KIRCHER
FR: EASTWEST7 (AKA JULIE LARAMIE, CIA)
RE: CHINA AND OTHER MATTERS

She had started to write her cell number below the subject line when, deciding the disconnected number would do her, and Senator Kircher for that matter, no particular good, she crossed out the prefix and composed, instead, a three-word note:

HAPPY CASTING, SENATOR!

Thinking that once her ordeal ended, if it ever did, she might consider paying a visit on Mrs. Alan Kircher, or perhaps the assignment editor at *60 Minutes,* Laramie stood and handed the folded pages of her makeshift essay to the receptionist.

"Please give that to somebody on the senator's staff," she said, and jerked her thumb toward the door Rob Lowe had used. "Preferably somebody besides him."

Then Laramie walked out of Kircher's waiting room and exited the building.

38

Admiral Li came down to the poolside lounge and found a stool at the bar. He wore the Bermuda shorts and tropical-print short-sleeved shirt he'd found in one of the revolutionary brotherhood gift bags. Spike Gibson, biceps protruding obscenely from a white tank top, sat three stools from Li, sipping a creatine shake. Hiram stood behind the counter, wiping down the glassware.

Gibson grinned as Li took his stool.

"Afternoon, Admiral." As he always did in the presence of Li or Deng, Gibson spoke in Mandarin.

Li bowed from the shoulders up. Hiram moved over to draw even with him at the bar.

"Buy you a drink?" Gibson said.

Hiram's long, narrow fingers, exuding the false impression of sluggishness, combined a series of juices and rum over ice, sprinkled the selection with nutmeg and cinnamon, and, on a small white napkin, pushed the glass across the counter into Li's palm.

Li took a sip, savored the flavor of the drink, and nodded.

"Painkiller," Gibson said.

"Yours?"

Gibson shrugged, taking a tremendous gulp of his shake. "Creatine and nonfat milk with pineapple and banana chunks."

"Creatine?"

"Highly refined protein."

Li nodded. "Steroids, then."

"Not in my temple, Admiral. I prefer all-natural foods."

"Such as bananas and pineapples."

"Correct."

"But this 'creatine' is a steroid, no? Certain American baseball players come to mind."

"That's Andro. Or worse."

"There is a difference?"

"Vast."

"Mister?"

Li turned sharply at the bright, light voice and watched, first in delight, then in increasing disgust, as a young American girl in a bikini, not a day older than fourteen, came out of the bright sun into the shade of the bar's thatched roof. She was so drunk she could barely walk, but she made her way to Spike Gibson's side nonetheless. The girl wore diamond earrings, a pink iPod Mini, sunglasses, a bracelet on each wrist, and an anklet above one foot. Her bikini top had slipped off one shoulder to expose a nipple; she was slick with a blend of tanning oil and perspiration, her blondish hair held back with a clip.

Gibson said, "Pardon me, Admiral."

At that point the girl leaned in, and Gibson kissed her with a sloppy, tongue-ridden kiss, Gibson fondling the girl's exposed breast with one hand, cupping her hip and ass with the other. Li stared. The girl removed an earpiece, twirled a loop of hair with her finger, and said something close-in to Gibson. Gibson said something back, turned to Hiram, said, "Rum punch," waited for Hiram to hand him the drink, gave it to the girl, then squeezed her tiny ass as she turned and stumbled back to the pool. She ducked out of view and into the lounge chair in which she'd been planted before her approach.

"Spoiled rich girl down from New England," Gibson said. "Connecticut. Parents think she's on a boat ride. She likes to party."

Gibson polished off his creatine shake and reached above his head, stretching his massive arms.

"Listen, Admiral," he said. "I'm scheduled for a forty-minute exercise circuit in my gym. You look like a man who's in excellent physical condition. You're welcome to join me for the workout."

Li, expressionless, stared into Gibson's beady, blackish eyes.

"Perhaps later," he said.

Wordlessly, Gibson rose, ducked behind the pool house and, a moment later, emerged on his personal off-road-grade golf cart. The cart's electric motor thrummed as Gibson sped around the corner of the last poolside cabana and vanished.

Li drained his painkiller and pushed the glass of remaining ice cubes across the bar to Hiram.

Deng was in his Mobile War Room, seventh and smallest of the series of custom command centers, housed aboard the most recent generation of People's Liberation Navy nuclear attack submarines. He'd built this partic-

ular suite expressly for the final stages of Operation Blunt Fist, and none of the crew, including the captain, knew what went on inside it. A trio of communications officers sat immediately outside its walls, fulfilling various actions ordered by way of the general's command buttons inside the suite, but all communications Deng conducted with the outside world were encrypted before the communications officers could access the signal.

It had been sixteen hours since the Beidaihe detonation, and the Mobile War Room was currently serving in its official capacity as China's equivalent of Air Force One. For the past six hours, Deng had been holding wall-to-wall video teleconference sessions with his newly appointed vice premier, who, in his absence, was executing various decisions generated by Deng.

Within two hours of being secreted into his submarine lair, Deng had ordered his vice premier to read his initial statement to the global media. An hour ago he allowed his own face to appear, taping a statement in the War Room and beaming it to Beijing. In the recorded statement, Deng announced that he had "personally confirmed" the intelligence captured by PRC operatives that represented "hard evidence of culpability" for the nuclear strike. His static-ridden, head-and-shoulder videoconferencing image had been re-telecast across the world's news channels:

"We have determined," his image said, "that the responsibility for the act of mass murder committed against the People's Republic of China rests with a highly organized, well-funded international terrorist organization. While we must acknowledge our intelligence failure in allowing this cabal of evil to conduct the first act of nuclear proliferation within China's very borders, we will not fail again. Our intelligence operatives have made significant progress in isolating those nations responsible for the funding and strategic management of this organization, and once we determine with finality the authenticity of the evidence, vengeance by the People's Republic of China will be exacted. That vengeance will be harsh. It will be swift, and it will be severe."

Deng took note of a flashing indicator light on the main wide-screen monitor, the centerpiece of the War Board. He was afforded the luxury of positioning his submarine anywhere in the world, since no one knew where he was. He ordered the captain of the sub to approach the surface for a better signal, and the vessel's communications array nipped the swells about eight hundred miles east of Miami and two hundred miles north of Mango Cay. This location happened to position him squarely within the generally accepted confines of the Bermuda Triangle.

He punched a command on his keyboard and Admiral Li appeared immediately on the monitor. Li bowed deeply. Deng could see that Li, as instructed, wore one of the gift-bag-issue tropical-pattern shirts.

The admiral began immediately.

"Preoperational status: all systems go," he said. "System mainframe and redundant processors active. No security system failures. Primary power cell currently running at ten percent of capacity, backup online generators one through four fueled to capacity. According to all hourly reports from security director, perimeter alarms have remained active and silent, with radar traffic normal, during the past forty-eight hours."

Li's mouth twitched—not, Deng saw, from the static of the transmission.

"What is it, Admiral?"

"Comrade Premier," Li said, tendering a brief bow of submission, "I recognize the importance of this assignment to the revolution."

Deng suppressed a chuckle—he knew this had been coming and was surprised it had taken the career soldier this long.

"Go on," he said.

"Thank you, Comrade Premier. It is just that as an admiral in the People's Navy I am compelled, at this time of national crisis, to serve in, forgive me, but I'm not sure how best to put this—"

"A more traditional role?"

"Yes."

"There is no more critical mission to the fabric of our nation's future than the assignment I have entrusted to you. I recognize your more . . . *standard* instincts, but we no longer inhabit a standard world. Stay the course, Admiral. I will see you for your next status report."

Deng killed the connection. He sipped from a cup of tea he'd had delivered through the room's food-dispensing window, savoring its flavor, prolonging the tingling sensation he felt in his belly. In fact he felt it even in his soul, though Deng didn't believe particularly in souls.

This was a moment for which he had been waiting a very long time.

In the upper left-hand corner of Deng's control board was a hinged Plexiglas cube. He flipped it open, revealing a key-hole. Removing from around his neck a thin chain resembling the kind affixed to dog tags, he seized the lone key affixed to the chain. He inserted the key in the hole the open cube had exposed and twisted.

A red light began flashing beside the lock. On two of the monitors on the War Board, a set of numbers blinked to life.

For the first second of their display on the monitors, the numbers read:

72:00:00.

Then the numbers changed immediately to 71:59:59, 71:59:58, and so on.

A smug grin creasing the hard lines of his face, it was somewhere around T-minus 71:56:22 when a thought crystallized in General Deng's mind—the rallying cry he'd instructed Li and Gibson to use in the recruitment of Operation Blunt Fist's pool of Marxist-Leninist investors:

Long live the Revolution!

Then he gave the order for the PLN captain to retreat.

The submarine dipped beneath the swells.

39

Stabbing the fish with a barbed hook, the boy held it aloft and watched the tortured fish wriggle. Satisfied, he heaved the whole assembly over the side of the boat and paid out the line. Once the line was out where he wanted it, he used rubber bands to clip the filament to an outrigger.

Cooper hadn't got the kid's name and didn't care. He squinted into the glare of the sun, its blinding rays banging off the sea as the boat rolled with the swells. The kid had three lines in the water for him, one a long way out, maybe a hundred yards behind the boat; one with no outrigger, forty, fifty yards out; and now this third line, which he'd positioned about one-fifty back. That also made three live bait fish. It had taken them an hour to hook that many, Cooper pulling them in while the boat made for the narrow band of sea where the captain knew the big game fish were biting this week.

The captain of the charter was a man so dark from the abuse of years of ocean sunshine he looked like a splash of high-gloss black enamel against the white fiberglass boat.

He sat under a canopy in the crow's nest, allowing the boat to drive itself while he smoked a Cuban cigar in the breezy ocean heat.

His name was Abe Worel.

Worel had once owned a single boat. Unable to afford any advertising outside of word-of-mouth, he scraped by on the inconsistent deep-sea bookings he got from the more adventuresome visitors who happened down the pier where he moored his boat. He knew the waters and could find the game fish better than anyone, but the chief problem Worel encountered was that right when he had begun to build some steady referral business, hurricane Hugo took his boat and turned it into kindling. Worel hadn't even contemplated the notion of securing insurance, meaning he was left, following the unleashing of Hugo's wrath, with nothing but a two-thousand-dollar debt on the loan he'd taken out to buy the boat.

A few months later, Worel had been ready to disconnect his phone and return to work as a first mate, humping for tips at forty-six years of age, when a baritone-voiced guy tracked him down on the phone and asked if he was available to head out and scare up some marlin. The man indicated he'd chartered from Worel once before.

Worel remembered him, a gruff son of a bitch, nothing like the usual tourist. The man hadn't said a word in the eight hours they'd spent on the water when he'd chartered the now-defunct boat that first time out.

"Been running that boat for twenty goddamn years," Worel said to him over the phone.

"Yeah?"

"Yeah, mon," Worel said. "Too bad some bastard name of

Hugo take it away. There ain't a single plank o' wood re-mainin'."

The man told Worel thanks anyway and that he was sorry about the boat. A moment of silence played out, neither of them hanging up. Then Cooper said, "You make a living, running a deep-sea charter?"

"Sure you do, mon. Way that happen is, you buy four, five boats, give the fat cats what they really want for the bulk of your business—cushion under their big ass, cooler full of rum and beer. Take 'em out on tours, catch a couple tuna for kicks, and save the deep-sea game for the fellas come down here to do it for real. Keep the boats in different places—that way there ain't no goddamn storm—ain't *nobody*—gonna take all them boats from you. And there somethin' else too, mon: make sure when you buy them boats, you get yourself an insurance policy. Do that, or do nothin' at all."

When Cooper didn't say anything in response, Worel said, "Yeah, shit, mon, that fucking Hugo," and hung up the phone.

Two days later, Worel was stepping off the boat of a friend who'd given him a day of first-mate work when he found himself confronted by a short man wearing a navy blue business suit.

"Pardon me," the man asked, "but would you be Mr. Worel?"

Worel asked him who wanted to know.

"Jacob Bartleby," said the man.

"Can't say the name mean anything to me, mon."

Bartleby nodded his understanding. "Mr. Worel, I'm an attorney representing a Cayman Islands investment firm specializing in resort and recreational properties."

He handed Worel a slip of paper, which Worel took, ex-amined, and discovered to be a cashier's check, made out to cash, in the sum of $250,000. Bartleby asked Worel if he would be able to procure four boats for that amount, assuming the inventory of four vessels included both pleasure yachts and deep-sea fishing vessels.

"What the hell you talkin' 'bout, mon?"

Bartleby said, "Well, I ask because if so, my clients are looking to take a forty-nine percent interest in the boats."

Worel narrowed his eyes and reached out to return the cashier's check.

"Seem to me," he said, "that if them clients can afford to buy 'em, they'd be best served takin' a hundred percent stake. Also, for that price you probably get five, you know who to call."

Bartleby explained to Worel that in exchange for the check he'd handed him, his clients would receive a forty-nine percent stake in the fleet of charter boats Worel would procure and manage with the investment capital represented by the amount of the check. He told Worel that he would remain the controlling partner, retaining a fifty-one percent ownership interest in the fleet. Without another word, Worel walked directly across the street to the local savings and loan. Upon hearing that the bank had cleared the check, he hired the best boat builder in the Caribbean to make him five thirty-four-foot boats for $200,000 cash. He used the rest to set up an office with a fax machine, two phone lines, and a voice mail service, and to outfit the pleasure yachts with all the amenities and a killer insurance policy. He even got himself a sonar unit, a fish-finding secret weapon, for the boat he'd use purely as the deep-sea fishing charter.

Six months later, the man with the baritone voice called again and asked Worel whether he had ever been able to replace that smashed-up boat of his.

Worel said, "Just so happen I've been able to procure a few of them boats, mon. You looking to do some fishing?"

"I am."

"Reason I ask," Worel said, "is if you looking to do some fishin', we goin' to do some fishin'. Matter of fact that be the case anytime you call. Anytime you want, we go out. Refreshments on the house. Matter of fact," Worel told him, "you ever get any idea 'bout payin' for any of these trips, then you should call somebody else. Seein' as I'm sure anybody else out there probably be happy to take your money. But not me, mon, no sir. Not me."

Cooper said that was all right by him and booked an all-day fishing trip for the following week.

There was a tug on the shorter line. Worel spotted it from the bridge, upward of twenty feet away, and eased off on the throttle. Silence flooded the boat with the drone of the engine off a few decibels.

"Look like he coming in again," Worel said up top, when *bang,* the tip of the pole shot down toward the water.

Cooper clambered to the chair. The kid took the pole, adjusted the drag, and set the rod in the cup between Cooper's legs, Cooper now buckled into the chair that always reminded him of the kind they used in prisons to execute convicts. Only this chair was the opposite kind of chair: one built for redemption. A seat in which he could rediscover some of the broken-off pieces of his soul.

He waited for Worel to set the hook, the old man gunning the boat to lock the barb in the fish's mouth. Then the fish took off, the reel screaming in Cooper's hands. Cooper knew what was coming, and only a few seconds passed before it did—about a hundred yards away, back behind the boat on the starboard side, there she went. Worel was looking back at her too, the old captain's outstretched arm pointing out to sea.

It was a marlin, her side bluer than the ocean in the sun as the graceful fish got airborne, reaching skyward, bucking, infuriated at the presence of the hook in her mouth. Cooper knew the fish was sending him a message as clearly as if she had called him to deliver it on his sat phone: *Go ahead, try and bring me in, Cooper, you old sack of shit. Look at my lines, a world-class athlete of the deep—go ahead and try to drag me in with that useless rod.*

Cooper thinking he was ready, knowing what he had in store for the next four, five, or who knew, maybe eight hours, judging from the size of that bitch offering up her challenge. What he had in store was the chair, the rod, the fish, and pain. Lose your concentration three hours in, let up on the tension, and that marlin would burn you for your moment of weakness. She'd shake the hook and be off for a tuna dinner that didn't feature a hidden hook in its gut.

Up top, Worel worked the boat backward, chasing the fish as it ran. The kid pulled in the last of the other lines. Chalking up his palms in the attached bin, Cooper settled in for the unique form of bliss he knew he'd find—the physical exhaustion, the sharp pain, muscle failure, dehydration, blood loss, and sunburn, combining to deliver a sensation more liberating than even the purest chemical high. Peaceful, floating nothingness—the ultimate painkiller.

Beginning the cycle, Cooper fell into the rhythm of his own thoughts.

During the past few days, he had found some interesting stories in the seven newspapers Ronnie always delivered to his porch. He probably wouldn't have given a flying leap about any of these stories had it not been for the whispering prompt from his omnipresent comrade-in-arms, the ghost of Marcel telling him, *Regardez-vous, mon ami—there something here I'm thinking you maybe wanna see.*

It wasn't the nuke blast he and his supernatural comrade found intriguing—though once he'd seen the story, Cooper had logged a few calls to Laramie's numbers and found her oddly unreachable. Instead, it was a series of articles, each failing to make the front page, that Marcel nudged him to examine. It seemed a number of heads of state, along with the occasional minister of defense, had gone missing. Each affected country had released its own version, in a different way and at an alternate pace, but the story was the same. Joe Leader of Such-and-Such Nation had been traveling on business or pleasure, and failed to reach his scheduled destination. In fact, he had failed to reach any destination at all.

Ordinarily, Cooper simply notched such news in his memory banks, looking forward to the day when one of the missing leaders turned up on some adjoining island with a botched face-lift and a few billion bucks of extorted dough. This time, though, he found the stories more relevant. The men who had gone missing, he found, were the same people he'd captured in the digital photos he'd sent to Laramie before she too had gone MIA.

What this meant—at least the way Cooper saw it—was that something stunk on that fucking island.

It was early in the seventh hour when the marlin, worn out, attempted and failed to make another run at freedom. Cooper delivered the sluggish fish to the kid's waiting gaff with one final heave of the rod, and the boy swung the hook and stuck it in the marlin's side. It was a shallow stab, not deep enough to hold, and with its remaining fumes of energy, the marlin slipped the gaff, moving back from the boat, a gentle weave all she could muster. That was when the fading fish took a look at him.

The fish stared right into his eyes—the old girl spent, still putting up a fight, weaving in the swells while some punk kid sought to jam a gaff hook in her back. He heard her speak too, and when she did, her words floated to him in the soothing voice of Simone, Marcel's widowed lover. That fish, or Simone, he wasn't sure which, pleading to him, to her corrupt soldier of honor:

Wi, monsieur, she said—*somethin' done come to pass on that island.* Then Simone's voice shifted deeper, becoming more masculine as the boy approached the marlin with the hook again. *You the only one can deliver justice, Cooper-mon.*

Oh yeah, she said, *the truth, it shall set us free.*

"Leave her alone," Cooper said.

The boy looked over his shoulder at him, hook held aloft. Halted midswing.

Cooper motioned to the boy with a flick of his bleeding, blistered hand.

"Get my line out of her mouth," he said, "and let that old bitch go."

From up top, Worel said, "May die anyway, Cooper."

"Let her go!"

The boy shrugged and did as he was told.

40

In the Virgin Gorda marina, Cooper had Worel pull alongside his Apache. He stripped, heaving his short stack of soggy clothes into his own boat, and dove into the tranquil waters of the marina to cleanse his body of the fish-battle grime. He boarded the Apache, kicked on the MerCruisers and, nude and upright, rode at full throttle, blow-drying himself in the usual manner.

When he'd completed the ten-minute trip to Conch Bay, he secured the bowline to his mooring and ambled to the rear of the boat. Balancing on the very edge of the stern, toes wiggling beyond the edge of the fiberglass, he pissed long and far into the sea.

Since there appeared to be the usual amount of business under way at magic hour in the Conch Bay Bar & Grill, Cooper obeyed some sense of decorum and clothed himself in tie-dyed shorts and a tank top adorned with a sketch of three Charlie's Angels–looking women riding the same surfboard. He rode his dinghy to the dock and jumped off without tying up; he passed Ronnie on the way in.

"Hustle up," he said as Ronnie sped by him to secure the skiff.

He noticed that Ronnie displayed an oddly self-satisfied look as he ran past; Cooper also found it strange that the putz hadn't fired back with some retort or other and concluded that something fishy was under way. Stepping behind the bar to pour himself some bourbon, he was sure of it. He told the bartender to have Ronnie bring the usual sandwich to his bungalow and made his way out of the restaurant.

He was halfway up the stairs of his porch when he noticed a well-toned set of legs, naked from mid-thigh down and crossed in that supremely feminine knee-over-knee way. The legs were visible, but just barely, in the dim postsunset twilight. Ordinarily Cooper would not have taken issue with a woman seated on his deck chair, awaiting his arrival while showing some of the best legs he'd ever seen. Today, though, he knew there to be the high probability the owner of the legs was playing a role in Ronnie's, and hell, probably also Woolsey's latest idea of a practical joke.

"Don't get your hopes up," he said. "Whatever it is they convinced you is going to happen, it's been a long day. Too long. So it's not going to happen."

"Your hands are bleeding."

Cooper recognized the voice but wasn't immediately sure where he'd heard it; since he couldn't yet see the woman's face in the shadows of his porch, he looked down at his bandaged hands while he tried to figure it out.

"They'll do that for a while," he said. "Maybe a day or two."

"You always sail nude?"

Her voice kind of drifted out to him. The feeling it gave him was somewhat disturbing—warmth, familiarity, imbalance. It felt good, but he felt immediately off guard. There'd only been one woman, a long time ago—

Wait a minute.

He tried to take back the thought he'd been in the midst of having, his mind's hand reaching out, clutching, grasping for it in his attempt to reel it back in. He'd just realized who it was seated there on his porch, and he wasn't about to acknowledge *that* kind of effect from *her*. Try as he did, he couldn't grasp the thought—it hung there in his mind, evading him, the impression caused by her voice lingering.

He moved to the top stair, and through the inky shadows caught a flash of white from her eyes. He saw that her skin was nearly as bright as her eyes—woman needs a tan, he thought, like nobody's business.

"Yes, I do," he said, answering her question, "but that isn't a sailboat, Laramie."

He saw more white—a flash of teeth. Laramie was smiling.

Realizing she'd seen him pissing off the edge of the boat, Cooper felt suddenly childish. Everybody at the club, of course, was forced to regard that particular spectacle on a frequent basis, but having Laramie there to witness the nude blow-dry-and-piss session actually gave him the feeling he'd made a fool of himself.

"When you say your hands will do that for a while," she said, "how do you know?"

"I did it while deep-sea angling." Cooper wasn't sure why he used the term *angling,* since he couldn't remember ever having called it that. "Bring in a game fish the size we got today will usually take you six or seven hours. You're out of practice, you'll blister up in the first hour. Start bleeding before you've got the fish halfway home. I'm out of practice."

"What did you catch?"

"What exactly are you doing here? Unless you'd prefer to beat around the bush for another hour or two."

"Come on, what did you catch?"

"A marlin."

"How big?"

"Hard to tell. Four-fifty, five hundred pounds."

"Five hundred? Where is it?"

Cooper looked at her. The lie detector.

"I let her go."

"Her?"

"Why are you here, Laramie," he said.

Laramie stood. She brushed her shorts flat, and he saw she was wearing a pair of Conch Bay–issue knee-length khakis, part of the merchandising line Woolsey had launched the year before. Meaning maybe she'd come down in a hurry—packed light. Cooper thought of how she'd been difficult to get a hold of.

He could see her in full now, the recently set sun casting her in a glow he placed somewhere between crimson and sepia: buttery skin, pink from a couple hours of sun, compact features with little to nothing amiss, longish hair he'd call something like brownish blonde pulled back in a ponytail. She had the trim frame of a runner—fit and lean, but not about to go out and win any Puerto Rico bikini contests.

"Tell you what, W. Cooper," she said. "Why don't you bop into your room and shower off those little waves of salt."

She pointed to his chest, where there were, indeed, crusted white wavelets of salt, distributed in the approximate pattern of sand on a beach. Cooper knew the salt water to dry that way when he started wet and rode home in the breeze.

"After that," she said, "maybe we can have something to

eat. I'll buy you a dinner at the restaurant down there and answer your question of why I'm here. In fact, I'll do you one better: I'll make you a proposition."

When it became apparent she wasn't going to tell him the nature of the proposition, Cooper said, "If I were to hazard a guess, I'd say you're down here on the sly. Maybe you even had your cute little rear end handed to you by some of those supremely wise bosses of yours. Meaning that the thing you're probably interested in, I'm not necessarily capable—"

"Thanks for the 'cute little rear end' thing, just then," Laramie said.

Cooper found he'd run out of fuel for whatever thought he'd been in the midst of conveying. He stood there at the top of the stairs, looking at Laramie's particularly bright eyes with what he figured to be as blank an expression as he'd seen in the marlin's half-dead stare.

"Just take that shower, mister," she said, then sat down and recrossed her legs.

41

Cooper figured out what Ronnie's smart-ass look was all about. The errand boy pulled a bottle of Chardonnay from a nest of ice beside their table, poured Laramie a glass, and replaced Cooper's melting tumbler of tinted ice with a fresh pour of Maker's Mark. Then Ronnie stood tall, hands clasped behind his back, and announced he was ready to take their orders, flaunting his smug gleam of pleasurable contempt in a way that made Cooper want to kick him in the shin.

Cooper knew that Ronnie was thinking there had never been a legitimate dinner date hosted by the occupant of bungalow nine, not that he'd seen in his tenure anyway. Ronnie was well aware that Cooper spent plenty of time helping women get drunk and enticing them to sneak up to his bungalow—leave your husband and his Izod shirt at the bar—but now, in the presence of Laramie, Cooper knew Ronnie could smell his vulnerability like a shark on the scent of blood. And the kid thought he was succeeding in delivering his implicit threat: *Give me a few minutes with the lass and I'll have her hightailing it for the States in no time, mate. Tell her a story or two about her knight in shining armor, few of the things been said to have gone down over the years in good old bungalow number nine.* Cooper resisted the tangible urge to grab Ronnie by his ponytail and inform the putz he didn't give a shit about either Ronnie's implicit threat, or the woman Ronnie was evidently so impressed with.

Laramie ordered a seafood Caesar salad and asked for the dressing on the side. Cooper told her nobody eats a Caesar salad with the dressing on the side, since that would keep it from being a Caesar salad. Then he ordered a Cabernet to accompany the Maker's Mark, conch fritters, and the house burger with cheddar.

Once Ronnie had tenderfooted his way back to the kitchen, Cooper looked at Laramie, whose face was growing pinker by the minute from whatever sun she'd got while waiting for him to return. She was staring back at him with a look he couldn't interpret, something between skepticism, fascination, and determination.

"Shoot," Cooper said.

"Hm?"

"What's the favor?"

"Proposition," she said, and smiled, and Cooper felt a funny twitch in his stomach. Laramie grabbed her glass of Chardonnay and peered around the place—beach, lagoon, stars, garden, bungalows, torches. The warm orange glow of the fire-lit restaurant.

"Your home," she said.

Ronnie came with Cooper's glass of Cab. "Everything all right here?"

"Fine, boy. Now leave." To Laramie, Cooper said, "This,

along with a few hundred thousand square miles of ocean I consider the better places to dive and fish, a couple dozen miles of various white sand beaches, sunrise, sunset, an ivory moon, that precision-engineered machine you call a sailboat, the humid heat that burns your skin, plus whatever whiskey, rum, vodka, and women are available, along with the credo of 'live slow, mon.' That, and an occasional visit to the handful of casinos within 'sailing' distance—yes," he said, "this is my home."

He drank a slug of the Cab.

"Now let me guess," he said. "You want me to take you to Mango Cay."

"The island, you mean?"

"The island."

Laramie put her fist under her chin and leaned the weight of her head against her fist. Cooper wondered if she were considering how savvy he'd been in determining her reason for being here, or maybe admiring how sharp his features looked around the eyes.

Laramie said, "Let me ask you a question."

"Go right ahead."

"Is there maybe a little friction between you and the esteemed deputy director of our nation's intelligence operations?"

Cooper raised his eyebrows once he thought about this for a moment, deciding Gates's goon squad must have determined he'd been the one on the other end of Laramie's phone calls. The DDCI would not have liked seeing that.

"'Bad blood,'" he said, "may be the more appropriate term."

"It probably wouldn't have been a bad idea," she said, "to provide at least *some* indication of the shitstorm I'm sure you knew would hit once Gates figured out it was you I was talking to."

Again Cooper had the sensation of mild embarrassment, that feeling of foolishness—as though he'd behaved like a five-year-old and been caught at it. Before he could interject in his own defense, Laramie said, "Wouldn't have mattered anyway. You illegally obtain access to classified SATINT you're not cleared to review and proceed to leak an even more highly classified analysis of the intel to a senator hostile to the foreign policy platform of the president—which analysis had previously and personally been compartmentalized by the CIA's chief operating officer—and I suppose it's inconsequential, relatively speaking, that I've befriended the COO's arch-nemesis in the process."

Ronnie delivered the conch fritters and Laramie's salad. Once he'd topped off their wineglasses and departed, Laramie took a bite of her salad, the bite consisting of a morsel of sea bass and one square of romaine lettuce but no dip in the side dish of dressing.

Cooper ate three conch fritters slathered in Thousand Island sauce, took a thick sip of his wine, and said, "Who's the senator?"

She told him about her notes to Senator Kircher, leaving out the casting couch episode.

"And yes," she said, "I'd like you to take me to that island."

Cooper drank some Maker's Mark.

"I'll pay you for your time," Laramie said. "I'll pay you to take more photographs while we're there too. I have to warn you that I'm not sure what I'm looking for, or what we'll accomplish in going there, but I can't do nothing, and given what I know, nothing is something that shouldn't be done. Nobody in Langley, or anywhere else that I can tell, is doing anything to connect the dots. The only dots anybody seems intent on connecting are those that would establish beyond a reasonable doubt that I showed classified intelligence and analysis to Senator Alan Kircher—and, above all, that I was secretly talking to you."

Cooper had polished off the fritters; wordlessly, Ronnie swiped the empty basket and delivered Cooper's burger and an array of condiments.

"The leaders," Laramie said, "the ones from your pictures. Are you aware of what has happened?"

"That they're MIA, you mean?"

"Yes. And the rhetoric from China's premier—new premier—Deng Jiang—"

Cooper, observing that he'd nearly polished off the burger, said, "Education, tax cuts, and war on terror. Everybody uses the same line of bull the minute they take office."

"Yes, but he's specifically identified a 'well-funded international terrorist organization.' Do you understand what I'm saying?"

"No."

He noticed Laramie had drunk a reasonable dose of Chardonnay, consumed all the lettuce, but failed to eat even half the seafood or any of the dressing. He considered asking whether she was planning on finishing her dinner and was going to reach over for the strips of swordfish and rings of calamari she'd left untouched, then thought better of it and devoured his fries instead.

"I'm saying," she said, "that Deng has the same theory I do. Or that I originally did. I call it a 'rogue faction'; he calls it an international terrorist organization. Same thing."

"Possibly."

"Don't you find it odd that the international terrorist organization Deng has mentioned—assuming it's run by the people you photographed and who are now missing—played host to an admiral from Deng's navy?"

"Yes."

"Okay, well these supposed enemies of China have also been conducting military exercises that coincide precisely with Deng's Taiwan simulation. You could, if you thought of it this way, interpret the simulations as preparations for attacks best conducted once a change in political climate has taken place. Such as, for instance, the change that just happened with the Beihaide nuclear warhead blast. Did you know that now-premier Deng was one of only three council members who was late to the meeting where the bomb detonated? He happened to have been the first in line for succession were the premier to die, and his political allies happen to have been the other survivors of the blast. Why is nobody talking about these things?"

Knowing his brain to be significantly more sluggish than it once had been—and knowing it hadn't exactly started out as a fighter jet—Cooper took the time to glance into the sky above Laramie's head while he put her theory through the motions a few times.

"You're drawing some pretty brash conclusions," he said when his mind had finished the workout.

"Thus far," she said, "every ludicrous conclusion I've reached has pretty much proven to be accurate. Or close to it."

"I didn't say they were ludicrous. I said they were brash."

"I'd say it's pretty ludicrous operating under the theory that a Chinese vice premier detonated a nuclear weapon in his own country to succeed the sitting premier and, further, knows more than he's letting on, or his lieutenant knows more than he's letting on, about the leaders of the terrorist league he's publicly identified—though still anonymously—as the perpetrators behind the detonation."

"I'll come back to what I was going to say when you interrupted me on my porch: you *do* realize there are maybe five thousand people better suited—"

"What do you propose I do," she said, "besides attempt to get my hands on hard, physical evidence that I'm right?"

Cooper thought about that, then said, "One option would be to retire to a tropical isle and do approximately nothing for the rest of your life."

Laramie's neck and cheeks had turned, and held, a ruddy shade of pink. Ronnie came, took away their plates, then returned to solicit their dessert order, that same annoying expression on his face throughout.

"Despite the lack of decent help here," Cooper said, "I think we should order dessert."

"I don't usually order dessert," Laramie said.

Ronnie took a long step backward but otherwise remained stationed in the vicinity of their table. Cooper glared in Ronnie's direction, then returned his gaze to Laramie without the glare.

"You should eat up," he said. "There won't be time for breakfast if we want to get to the island before dusk, because if we do, we'll need to leave at dawn."

"Do we?"

"Do we what?"

"Do we want to get to the island before dusk?"

"Yes," he said.

"Good."

Laramie eased back in her chair. She reached for her glass of wine and took a sip.

"How much?" Cooper said.

"What?"

"How much are you offering? You said you'd pay me to take you there."

"Um, well—how much will you charge?"

"Nothing."

She looked at him in a way that made Cooper think she

was weighing whether she should throw a punch across the table.

He said, "Would you like to know why?"

"Sure, Professor." She appeared to be amusing herself with a joke he didn't understand. "Why?"

"The ferry was already headed there."

Laramie thought about this.

"You were there taking pictures for your own reasons, of course," she said.

"Correct as usual, Lie Detector. And while there may or may not be a connection between your brash theories, the owners of the Mango Cay lease, or even the second death of a young man named Marcel S., the fact remains I've got some unfinished business to handle, and the place it's looking like I'll have to handle it is out on that fucking island."

Laramie smiled a little bit, causing another, somewhat alien twinge in Cooper's belly.

"Who," she said, "is Marcel S.?"

"Long story. I'll fill you in on the ride over." He twirled the thinning bourbon and melting ice in his glass. "You should know," he said, "that the thing I'm taking care of, if it turns out that's the place to take care of it—there's a pretty good chance it'll get ugly. Very."

Laramie didn't react one way or the other.

"Ronnie," Cooper said.

Ronnie, who had held his position at the expense of various other tables—ostensibly to await their dessert order, but primarily to eavesdrop—stepped forward and inclined his chin.

"Mud pie. Couple spoons."

"Aye-aye, Guv."

42

Once the mainframe's reboot sequence began for the day, Hiram and the wino returned to the cart they had hidden in the tunnel the afternoon before. If the cart's motor and the wino's measly muscles cooperated, it would take them just over one minute to pilot the warhead-laden cart down the length of the tunnel. Hiram had done this before, and the key was the morning rain: when the rainfall was light or nonexistent, the tunnel was dry, and transport relatively easy. Following a storm, it took some serious muscle to move the cart through the mud. Gibson had sunk over two hundred grand into sump pumps and other contraptions, but nothing seemed to work.

Today had been a dry morning, so Hiram was optimistic—he figured he wouldn't need to use the cattle prod more than half a dozen times on the minute-plus journey.

Though Gibson preferred his own label of "cargo cave," Deng had originally called the island's secondary freight cavern "the Lab" for fairly self-evident reasons. The Lab was less than half the size of the primary missile cavern and significantly less organized, strewn with industrial equipment, spare parts, and the six defunct C-4 Trident I missiles that had yet to pass inspection. A dust-free, sterile laboratory, built in the cavern's back room early on, had been used by Deng's scientists for adjustments to the barometric pressure units serving as the detonation triggers for the W-76 warheads, earning the cavern its nickname.

Gibson had used the cargo cave as a clandestine freight entrance during Operation Blunt Fist's construction phase, and while only substandard-size submarines could access the cave, due to the lesser dimensions of its docking bay, much of the operation's more important cargo had been delivered here. Gibson, for instance, had seen no need to expose the arrival of shipments of enriched uranium, explosive caps, or completed warhead-MIRV replicas to the mercenary guards and construction staff working in the main cavern when, at times, crews there had numbered as many as fifteen or twenty men. Most of these workers had already been or would soon be killed, but Gibson never saw reason to take undue risk.

Standing this afternoon on the catwalk that rimmed the cargo cave's underground lagoon, Gibson touched a button on his wristwatch to check the time under the dim illumination of the safety lights. The reboot sequence had begun almost a minute ago; if Hiram and the slave arrived on time, he would have just over six minutes and twenty seconds to fulfill the day's objective.

Just past the 1:05 mark, the door connecting the transport tunnel and the cargo cave eased open and the overloaded golf cart emerged, its suspension dragging with every bump.

Gibson climbed into the control seat of a squat yellow crane positioned in the corner of the cavern. A miniature version of the sort found at container terminals, the crane's body formed a cube of some twelve feet in width. It stood on a set of rails beside the dock; with its long arm, the crane was capable of accessing nearly any portion of the cave from its home on the rails. A hook was affixed to a cable that dangled from the arm.

Gibson fired up the crane's two-cylinder diesel engine and steered the machine to one end of the rails, where a series of spare rods, struts, and storage boxes lay against the far wall of the cavern. As Hiram brought the cart to the same spot, Gibson rotated the crane, dipping its hook until it bumped against the roof of the cart. Hiram grabbed the hook and secured it to the harness he and the wino had wrapped around the warhead earlier.

With a surge of its engine, the crane lifted the warhead as if it were a pillow, and at Gibson's direction maneuvered it out across the field of equipment. Hiram leashed the wino to the side of the golf cart with a dog chain; after yanking on the chain to make sure it held, he walked through the debris to the rear wall of the cavern, where the largest of the room's cargo boxes sat in apparent disrepair against the wall. He crouched before the first of the box's eight locks and waved to Gibson. On his cue, Gibson punched a lengthy code into a remote control device, and the first in the sequence of locks clicked open in Hiram's hands. He removed it, hooked it around his belt, and moved to the next. Once all eight locks had been remote-unlocked and removed, Hiram flipped aside a pair of latches and, feet planted, clean-and-jerked open the box's thick lid. This act exposed the contents of the box: two W-76 warheads, resting side by side in protective foam padding. The warheads looked like stretched versions of the standard bombs portrayed in Road Runner cartoons—long, rounded, bullet-shaped projectiles with a four-spoke fantail at the rear. There were two remaining warhead-shaped spaces in the padding that filled the crate.

With the help of Hiram's guiding hands, Gibson worked the controls in the driver's seat of the crane and lowered the third warhead into one of the slots. Hiram released the hook and unbuckled the harness from the warhead; the bomb rolled into its nook. Hiram replaced the crate's lid, snapped shut the eight locks, and began his return trip through the mound of industrial debris.

Gibson was off the crane and aboard his private golf cart when he noticed something and motioned to Hiram.

"Looks like we lost another one," he said. "Toss him in."

Hiram came around the corner of his cart to see the wino collapsed on the cavern floor. Still leashed to the cart, the former occupant of the alcove on East Queen Street had nonetheless fallen hard on the lava rock floor, which fall seemed to have resulted in the puddle of blood beneath his head. The blood had drained from his ears.

Hiram unleashed the body, dragged it to the edge of the underground lagoon, and heaved it into the water. He hung back a moment to watch as the water roiled in a froth of bubbles and blood, then jumped aboard his cart and drove out on Gibson's heels.

He cleared the surface exit of the transport tunnel with twenty-five seconds to spare.

43

They reached the waters off the western shore of Mango Cay around four-thirty. Cooper anchored where the water was deep, outside the reef that ringed the lagoon. There was no way he could get his Apache in over the reef, but he spotted a narrow channel where the water looked to be three or four feet deep, Cooper thinking the two float planes he'd seen last time had probably used the channel to enter the lagoon after landing on the open water. He lowered the Apache's skiff into the water, and once he had it there, climbed in and offered Laramie a hand. She took it with a shrug, Cooper reading the shrug as Laramie's way of saying she didn't need the help, but since she appreciated the gesture she'd do him the favor of accepting his assistance. He knew, however, that she could use the help, since Laramie, having refused his offer of Dramamine at sunrise, had turned green around seven, falling into a repeating thirty-minute cycle as Cooper drove them southeast: lean over the railing at the stern, try to find the horizon, lose track of it as the boat planed over a swell, heave whatever was left of the seafood Caesar salad over the edge, feel completely better, stand, return to the seat next to Cooper at the bow of the boat, feel it coming on again and retreat to the rail at the stern. Eventually she'd settled permanently into the copilot's seat, resigned to her useless state, a glazed, sickly expression on her face. After a while of watching her sit there, Cooper had asked Laramie what she planned to do with whatever evidence they retrieved from Mango Cay.

"What do you mean?"

Laramie had to yell over the roar of the MerCruisers and the wind.

"Say we find Saddam Hussein's weapons of mass destruction," Cooper said, "and swipe one. As evidence. You'll take it where?"

Laramie shrugged, then realized he couldn't see the shrug given the motion of the boat. "Nobody in Washington seems to care what I have to say," she said, "so maybe CNN will."

Cooper steered.

"Since we don't know what we're going to find," he said, "and don't have much of an idea what to look for in the first place, I'm going to recommend that when we get there, we abide by my tried-and-true, supremely sophisticated espionage technique."

"That," she said, "being what?"

"Cause trouble, fuck with people, and generally operate as a pain in the ass."

Laramie thought about that, then said, "See what shakes out?"

"See what shakes out."

After a few minutes of nothing but the roar and the roll, Laramie had looked over at him.

"Nice strategy," she yelled.

With Laramie now loaded into the skiff, Cooper fired up

the forty-horse outboard and steered them into the channel. Coming around a bluff, he could see there was a man waiting for them on the beach. From the size of the man's upper body, it appeared to Cooper that this was the Herculean individual he remembered seeing in one of his photographs, pretty much the only person in the set of photos, outside of the bartender and maid, he hadn't been able to ID.

Cooper went as far as he could go with the engine. When he heard the outboard begin to clip the coral at the bottom of the shallow lagoon, he tilted it out of the water, slapped the skiff's oars into place, and came into the lagoon under manual power. Cooper was wearing a short-sleeve beige-on-black Tommy Bahama silk shirt, and wondered whether Laramie was impressed with his physique, rowing the boat into the cove like a local fisherman who's been doing it for fifty years. When they cleared the coral, Cooper flipped the oars back into the boat, lowered the engine, and broke the glassy surface of the lagoon at a marina-friendly five knots or so.

As they approached, Cooper could see, as he hadn't observed fully in the photos, that the man waiting for them on the beach wasn't simply bulked up, but grotesquely musclebound—and yet the man's neck seemed far too thin to secure the head above it to the thick musculature beneath.

Another man, much taller and darker—the bartender from the pictures—came down the white sand slope and took Cooper's bowline, pulled the boat onto the beach, and tied the line to a nail protruding from the sand. He wore a white polo shirt and khaki shorts, with a small knapsack strapped to his shoulders.

Cooper came off first and Laramie followed, stepping unsteadily. Outside of their two-man greeting party, the resort's beach and poolside patio beyond were empty. There was a single remaining float plane and three cedar deck chairs dotting the beach; the plane looked as though it had made a few too many drug runs.

Cooper led Laramie up the beach to greet their muscle-bound host, extending a hand as he approached. The man shook.

"Welcome to Mango Cay," he said. "How can we help you?"

"We," Cooper said, "as in the royal 'we,' or 'we' meaning you and the baker's dozen of so-called communist dictators you had staying here last week?"

Laramie looked at Cooper; Cooper watched as the bartender glanced sideways at his boss Mr. Muscle-head, doing it in a way, Cooper saw, that allowed him to check Muscle-head's expression but still keep Cooper and Laramie in full view.

Muscle-head smiled and said, "Dr. Einstein, I presume."

Cooper nodded. "Warmer here than in Paris," he said, "don't you think?"

Since it wasn't much of a stretch to assume somebody who had taken the time to track his registration could also track his return course, Cooper decided to go ahead and flip Gibson's ID of the Apache's registration info into a confession: the man may as well just have told him he was the one who'd sent the commandos to visit him outside his bungalow at Conch Bay.

"Well, Albert, my name's Spike Gibson. I have no need to hide my identity. Buy you a drink?" He motioned to the poolside bar.

Cooper extended his elbow for Laramie to latch onto, which she did. They walked together up the beach to the pool and sat in two of the stools against the bar. Gibson took the stool beside Cooper; Hiram went behind the bar.

"Choose your poison," Gibson said.

"Maker's Mark, rocks."

"And the lady, whose name we didn't get?" Gibson looked at Cooper. "The royal 'we,'" he said.

Cooper started in on an answer then stopped when Laramie put her hand on his forearm. The way her hand felt gave him that familiar twinge, which he chose to ignore for the moment, considering that what he was doing required at least nominal concentration.

"My name's 'EastWest7,'" she said, "and I'll take something sweet please."

Gibson nodded. "Odd name. Hiram—painkiller."

Hiram, his voice gruff and thick, the accent falling somewhere between that of Barry the witch doctor and the screeching ghost of Marcel S., said, "Maker's Mark. Painkiller. Shake for Mr. Gibson."

He made the drinks and served them.

"Creatine shake," Gibson explained.

"For the workouts?" Cooper said.

"For the workouts."

Gibson drank, but Cooper did not. Laramie watched Cooper hold the glass, twirl it, push and pull it, but never drink from it. She followed his lead and left the painkiller on the bar, observing the posture and behavior of Cooper and Gibson while she fiddled with her glass.

"The way your shirt drapes in the back," Gibson said, "I can't tell for sure. Browning?"

"Correct. You, I'm betting Glock."

"Absolutely."

Given the size and weight of his knapsack, Cooper figured Hiram for an Uzi or MAC-10 but didn't verbalize his guess.

After another sip of his shake, Gibson said, "This resort is private property, and while we don't mind the occasional visitor, we would prefer that visitors not take photographs."

Cooper nodded. "Unfortunately," he said, "if I feel like taking pictures, there isn't much you can do about it."

Neither of them spoke for a moment. Cooper twirled his drink on the bar.

"Spike," he said, "—or do you prefer Spencer?"

"Spike will do."

"Well, Spike, as you might expect, we popped over here to ask you a couple questions."

Cooper jerked his head toward Laramie. Laramie noticed that Cooper did not take his eyes off of Gibson as he did it. "To begin with, my friend here—'EastWest7'—asked me to inquire as to the business purpose, or theme if you will, of the convention held here by the aforementioned dictators."

Gibson gulped most of the remainder of his shake. Hiram watched. "We don't divulge the identity, itinerary, or agenda, if any," Gibson said, "of our guests."

"I didn't think you would answer that one. It was somewhat broad in nature. *My* question, however, is a little more specific."

Gibson inclined his head.

"You ever get any boats around here, running forty-five, maybe fifty feet? I'm thinking specifically of an old Chris-Craft, kind of a shitty, rusting gray. Pretty sure it operates out of Jamaica. In fact, the boat I'm thinking of stopped a few miles west of here, and drifted for maybe two hours before turning around and heading back to Bob Marley's homeland."

Spike Gibson turned his head to the side and shook it a little. "This is the West Indies, friend, so we see quite a few boats come through here," he said. "But some like that? Hell, I couldn't tell you."

"See, that particular boat was loaded up on the Jamaica side with a half-dead Kingston rummy, who, it seems, had been abducted and sold as a kind of modern-day slave, at least the way I'm figuring it. It's funny—I find this to be an interesting coincidence."

"Oh?"

"See, it just so happens that another guy, actually a resurrected, well, zombie, recently turned up dead for the second time—I know this sounds complicated, but I think I have it right—on a beach in Road Town. This would have been one day after a hurricane passed southeast to northwest across your resort and was downgraded to a tropical storm as it made its way up to the British Virgins. Road Town, of course, being part of the BVIs."

"Of course."

"The Road Town zombie appears to have died from an intriguing combination of causes: burn wounds caused by direct contact with non-weapons-grade uranium, and gunshots to the back. Put another way," Cooper said, "what do an illegal nuclear power plant, zombie slave laborers, and a dozen disappearing communist dictators have in common? Besides you, me, EastWest7, and Hiram here with the assault pistol in his backpack, that is."

A high-pitched girl's voice peeped from the vicinity of the pool. To Cooper it sounded as though the voice had said, "Spike?"

Gibson excused himself and walked toward the pool. Between bar stools and cabanas, Cooper and Laramie caught glimpses of Gibson and what looked to Cooper like a sixteen-year-old girl talking, gesturing, and finally touching, as the girl handed Gibson a vial of tanning lotion and Gibson proceeded to take a full fifteen minutes to lube her sunburned body from head to toe. The girl was topless and didn't shift her position—face-up—on the poolside recliner for the duration of Gibson's massage, including the grip she had on what appeared to be a mai tai. When Gibson completed the massage, he slapped the girl on the side of the ass and came back over to his stool at the bar.

"I don't really have an answer to your question," he said.

Cooper nodded; Laramie said and did nothing. The resort's maid floated past, dropping a short stack of bright white towels on a table near the bar. Cooper and Laramie noticed separately that for a member of the housekeeping staff, the woman leaving the towels on the chair was exceedingly muscular. Her appearance, from the black coffee skin to the sinewy neck, was strikingly similar to Hiram's, though she was considerably shorter. Once she had deposited the towels, the maid moved off to busy herself with some other task on the opposite side of the pool.

Cooper said, "Mind if we have a look around?"

"Yes," Gibson said, "we mind."

"Private property," Cooper said.

"Private property."

Cooper stood. Laramie stood. Gibson stood. "Thank you for the drink," Cooper said. "Are you still a signatory for Global Exports?"

Gibson smiled, said, "Nice having you," and motioned toward the beach. Cooper and Laramie followed his cue, Cooper keeping his head turned at an angle that kept Gibson and Hiram in full view for the full stroll.

When they reached the boat, Hiram helped untie the line. He waded out to the boat, helped Laramie aboard, and stood, prepared to push the boat back from the shallows as Cooper faced Gibson.

"Spence," he said, "at some point you and I will have a conversation about the boys who stopped by for a drink at the Conch Bay Beach Club."

Cooper flung a leg into his skiff, and when Gibson didn't say anything to him, Cooper said, "Live slow, mon," and pushed the boat out into the lagoon without Hiram's help. He got the outboard humming and sped across the lagoon, churning up enough sand and coral chunks to form a wedge of dirty water, the skiff painting a nasty stripe of brown across the otherwise pristine bay.

44

Admiral Li found Spike Gibson in his private gym, where Gibson was on his fourth repetition on a bench press of 360 pounds. The rippling musculature of Gibson's upper chest was striated with a spiderweb pattern of blue veins, a beastly, unnatural feature that looked somehow appropriate beneath Gibson's acne-scarred, grease-spattered face.

Gibson had been made aware of Li's approach by a series of indicator lights on a wall-mounted console that would pass for a thermostat to the untrained eye.

"Admiral," he said in Mandarin during the exhale phase of his twelfth rep.

"Who were those people?"

"Random visitors." Gibson exhaled with a hiss and pushed up number thirteen.

"You seemed to know each other."

"Did we?" Fourteen.

"What did they want? Why did you have them up for a drink?"

"It's resort policy to be cordial and unassuming," Gibson

said. He concluded the set with no discernible effort and sat upright solely with the use of his abdominal muscles. He massaged his hands, then separated his arms and reached backward, stretching his chest.

"They knew something," Li said. "I watched, and understood some of their words."

Gibson enjoyed watching Li's transformation, slight though it was—no man, he believed, could resist it. Island life influenced you like a gravitational pull, and however imperceptibly, Li's hard-nosed attitude was under the influence. The rear admiral of the People's Liberation Navy, standing there with his assigned tropical-print-shirt-and-khaki-shorts disguise, unwittingly allowing it to affect his manner. Gibson remembered a beer commercial he'd seen, two people sipping a cold one on a tranquil beach, a caption beneath them saying "Change your whole latitude." He liked that commercial; that was what had happened to him, and that was what he was seeing develop in Li. Not that the admiral had taken to doing laps in the pool, or baking on the beach, but it was still there, more in the angle of the man's shoulders than anything else. Stay long enough, Gibson thought, and it mellowed you out—that was what the islands did.

They changed your whole latitude.

"Those visitors," Gibson said, "will be taken care of. This is nothing you or General Deng need concern yourselves with."

Li stared at the grotesque, inhuman figure before him.

"It is Premier Deng now," he said.

Actually Gibson had lied again: he had no intention of risking exposure by sending another assault team to deal with Albert Einstein. Gibson's time on Mango Cay had just about concluded, and he'd decided he no longer gave two shits whether Einstein and his girlfriend ratted out Deng. As long as they didn't do it in the next twenty-four hours, it just didn't matter. He didn't think they would anyway. In fact, it didn't seem to him that Einstein and friend knew anything besides what they'd seen in the photographs. The speculation the man had tried to bait him with on the topic of his disposable labor pool meant nothing, since as long as Einstein and his bicoastal babe were here alone, it was only that: speculation.

He stood, popped another ten-pound ring on each side of the overloaded barbell, and returned to his bench press position.

"Premier Deng, then," Gibson said. "I stand corrected. Now if you'll excuse me, Admiral."

He began the next set of fifteen reps.

Li watched through the ninth repetition of the set before turning away and leaving the suite.

Just past 5:40, Deng ordered his submarine to the surface and sent his third official statement to the international media via a single, mass-burst e-mail. In addition to the inclusion of more aggressive language about the antiterror response the PLA had in store, Deng provided a series of attachments with the e-mail missive and indicated that his intelligence unit had now identified definitive evidence of culpability for the nuke strike. The attachments included a series of photographs documenting a meeting held by the chief architects behind the attack, men whom Deng described as the leaders of the international terrorist organization his intelligence officers had managed to infiltrate. The meeting of these leaders had taken place, the statement said, at an undisclosed warm-weather location. As Deng completed his distribution of the e-mail, the countdown clock in the Mobile War Room ticked from 36:00:00 to 35:59:59.

It was six o'clock even as he flipped a switch and watched Admiral Li's face pop up on the monitor. Li did not appear unduly nervous or agitated.

"Status at T-minus thirty-six hours: all systems go," he said. "One perimeter breach this time, occurring at sixteen-thirty-eight hours. Vessel: pleasure craft. Passengers from the craft inquired about the resort. Inquiries were fielded by Mr. Gibson and the visitors dismissed. I have not been fully informed of the response strategy, but believe that Mr. Gibson will deploy a two-man surveillance team to dispatch with the visitors as he has done before."

While Deng could tell that Li was acting differently from usual, he had neither the time, nor the empathy, to bother monitoring Li's day-to-day mood shifts. Thus, following an initial pause, Deng concluded that Li's report satisfied him, at least to the degree that he needed satisfaction from his Mango Cay staff and the security perimeter they kept this late in the game.

"See you at oh-six-hundred tomorrow," Deng said.

Li bowed as Deng zapped him from the screen and ordered the submarine beneath the surface.

45

That was one hell of a strategy," Laramie said, "that tried-and-true espionage technique of yours."

Cooper took the pizza box and nodded for Laramie to lead the way.

"It appears," he said, "your case has reached the same dead end as mine. Either that, or the cases are one and the same, and between the two of us we lack sufficient IQ to figure the whole deal out."

They strolled along a grubby asphalt lane in Sainte-Anne, Martinique, about two blocks from the marina that Cooper had picked to moor the Apache. It was almost dark; they'd made the twenty-mile trip from Mango Cay, and Cooper had recommended pizza as a meal Laramie might be capable of keeping down. To his surprise she'd agreed, so he'd taken her to the joint across the road, which he'd heard a little about.

They came down a long dock and climbed aboard the Apache.

"U-238/U-235," Laramie said.

When Cooper figured out what it was she'd just told him, he said, "Ah."

"The reason you called me about the memo."

"Also, I was bored."

"The uranium could connect our . . . cases," she said. "It might be a stretch, but follow me for a second. Your guy, um—"

"Marcel."

"—could have been exposed to fuel rods on Muscle-boy's island."

"Head," Cooper said. "I think of him as Muscle-head."

"Head sounds fine. Nuclear power is quiet, of course, and invisible if you run it right, except for maybe steam."

Cooper thought about this and said, "There was a fog over the woods behind the resort when we were chatting with Muscle-head. Looked the same way when I was out here taking pictures. According to this latest brash theory of yours, the missing dictators, if that's who Muscle-head is working for, would be using the power plant for what purpose?"

"It's remotely possible they could be using it to create plutonium, or highly enriched uranium, which they in turn—no, that's a stretch."

"In turn what?"

"Used to build a nuclear warhead, which they then detonated in Beidaihe, China."

Cooper set the pizza box on the Apache's copilot's seat. "Definitely a stretch," he said.

He ducked into the cabin and came out with a pair of ceramic plates, on which he stacked stainless steel utensils, cloth napkins, and a pair of highball glasses. He reached into a minifridge and came out with a pair of Budweiser longnecks.

"You're eating pizza, you need to have beer," he said.

Laramie was sitting cross-legged on the deck. She tugged on the pizza box until it slid off the seat and landed beside her. She opened the lid.

"Agreed."

Laramie put a slice on each plate. Cooper found he liked her better over pizza than Caesar salad without the dressing.

"What were you talking about," she said, "when you mentioned the 'boys who stopped by for a drink' at the club?"

Cooper chewed a bite of pizza and slung back some beer. "Believe our friend Muscle-head sent a couple mercenaries my way. They didn't really plan for me to survive the visit."

"What happened to—" Laramie thought better of where she was headed and decided to leave the question hanging. "This was after you took the pictures?"

"Yes."

"So he figured out where you live."

"Pretty easily."

"But your boat isn't registered locally."

"Paris," he said.

"So Muscle-head probably has some sophisticated tracking equipment. Or he could have had you followed."

Cooper nodded. "But he didn't," he said.

"You'd have known?"

"The Caribbean is largely flat and featureless."

"So he may have access to satellite imagery, then," she said.

"That'd be my guess."

"What's he protecting?"

Cooper took a swig of his beer, then shrugged.

Laramie said, "You think Muscle-head's going to send somebody else to pay us a visit?"

"Didn't work before."

"What if he does?"

"Well," he said, "you may not have noticed that I'm doing so, but I am in fact keeping an eye out."

Laramie looked at him. "I see."

Cooper took another bite of pizza, the beginning of his third slice, and said, "I've got a riddle for you."

"Okay."

"Boat loads up a half-dead wino in Kingston. Sails, as you might put it, five hundred-plus miles east. Stops and drifts for maybe an hour, about five miles west of Mango Cay. Doesn't head over to the island. Doesn't come here to Martinique. Just sits, then turns around and goes back. What happened?"

Laramie thought for a moment. Cooper noticed she wasn't half-bad at putting away pizza—she too had consumed the tip of her third slice.

"The half-dead wino," she said.

"Yeah?"

"Did he come back with the boat?"

"I'm not totally sure, but I think we can assume no."

"I hate to admit it," she said, "but for the moment, at least, I'm stumped."

Cooper went into the cabin, came out with two more beers, set them on the deck, then turned and opened the box where he kept his navigation charts. He pulled out one of the accordion-folded satellite photos Gates had sent him, made some room on the deck by moving aside the pizza box and the plates, unfurled a few folds in the photo, and draped it across the space he'd cleared on the deck.

"SATINT," he said.

Laramie sort of half-frowned. "No kidding, Columbo."

"Your dad."

"Right."

Cooper pointed at a beetle-size image on one of the squares, the only visible variation from ocean in the huge photo spread.

"The boat," he said.

Laramie rose to her knees and leaned over the square. She didn't look only at the place where he'd pointed.

"Where did you get these?"

Cooper flattened a second square about half a chessboard from the square that featured the boat, and knelt beside it. He ignored Laramie's question.

"The night after Muscle-head's pals stopped by to say hi, I took another look at these things. They were just about all I had to go on. Except maybe your memo, that is."

When he found what he was looking for, he set his finger against the photo.

"You're the analyst," he said. "What's that?"

Laramie hesitated. Cooper didn't grasp why at first, then understood what it was—the way he was sitting, facing her, and the place he was asking her to look, could have meant he was planning on showing her something in addition to the satellite shot. He adjusted the position of his leg; she lowered her eyes and crawled over.

When she'd examined the place in the ocean where Cooper was pointing, Laramie rose to her knees, looked around, found Cooper's unused glass—he was drinking from the bottle—flipped the glass upside down, and set it on the surface of the photo. She checked, found it did what she wanted it to do, and, using it as a magnifying glass, leaned over the place where Cooper was pointing and took as close a look as she could under the circumstances. When she was through, Laramie leaned back on her heels and looked at him.

"I think that's the conning tower of a small submarine," she said.

Cooper nodded. "Pretty good, Lie Detector. That was my guess too."

Cooper watched her as she thought of the same series of things he'd thought of when he'd made the discovery of the submarine.

"Go ahead," he said, "ask."

"All right, I will. How the hell are we going to take a look underneath Muscle-head's island?"

Cooper smiled. He realized as he did it that it wasn't something he did often.

"Let me see what I can do," he said, and pulled his sat phone from his waist.

46

When Carlos Muske, the president's national security advisor, had finished reading the Julie Laramie surveillance reports compiled by Sperling Rhone, Gates's former private security man, he closed the file and said to Lou Ebbers, "The motives of your deputy director are somewhat difficult to grasp."

Ebbers said, "Yes."

They were seated in Muske's office in the West Wing.

"And the suspended analyst," Muske said. "Laramie. Appears she ain't bad at this."

Ebbers had already known Laramie to be quite an analyst, for reasons unrelated to the current predicament.

"Agreed," he said.

Muske looked at Ebbers across his desk. The national security advisor cut a leaner form but otherwise gave the impression somebody had performed a visual effect morphing together Colin and Michael Powell.

"You could have taken this straight to the president."

"Could have," Ebbers said.

"Probably would have helped repair your profile with him."

"Might," Ebbers said. "Though at the moment I'm not particularly concerned with that."

"No?"

"No."

"You're concerned with the matter of"—Muske licked his thumb, leafing through one of the documents Ebbers had given him—"Mango Cay."

"Yes."

"And the missing dictators."

"And the speed," Ebbers said, "of any actions we might undertake in these matters."

Muske thought about that.

"I suppose you mean, among other things, the president," he said, "would have taken a while to schedule the meeting once you contacted him."

"At which point," Ebbers said, "once he'd read those reports, or heard me out, he'd have contacted you."

Muske inclined his head. "And you figure I would then have . . ."

"Called the secretary of defense to request a navy reconnaissance team be dispatched to investigate the island where the missing dictators were photographed."

Muske nodded.

"Be damned," he said, "if you didn't save yourself twelve or thirteen hours."

"If not a whole day."

Muske said, "Give me a minute," punched the intercom on his phone, and when the voice of his assistant floated from the speaker, he said, "Could you get Wally on the horn please."

Ebbers knew Wally to be Walter Parke, the secretary of defense. He listened to Muske's conversation with Parke, in which it was decided that the nearest navy vessel equipped with a marines recon squad would be redirected to Mango Cay.

Muske hung up and Ebbers stood.

"You don't mind," Ebbers said, "I've got a little family business to tend to."

Muske rose and shook Ebbers's hand.

"Give my regards to Deputy Gates," Muske said.

Cooper's call from the deck of his boat had been to an extension at the Pentagon.

When a thick female voice with a Louisiana lilt answered with the words, "Admiral Sullivan's office," Cooper identified himself and said that he would need to be connected to the admiral immediately.

"Chop-chop," he said.

After a stretch of blank air, the secretary said that she would check whether Admiral Sullivan was available. In fewer than five seconds, the crisp, reserved voice of Robert C. Sullivan, Admiral, USN, punched into Cooper's right ear.

"What do you want?"

Sullivan had the acronym CINCLANTFLT affixed to the tail end of his rank. Sullivan hadn't always been commander in chief of the U.S. Atlantic Fleet, and in fact had spent some time in Cooper's neck of the woods a little over a decade ago. He'd been the captain of a destroyer pulling regular calls in Puerto Rico, Guantánamo Bay, and St. Thomas, and during his stops at these various ports, Sullivan, who was married with three then-teenage children, had been prone to frequenting local massage parlors. The former captain made sure that he cultivated a reputation as a generous tipper, provided, of course, the services were sufficient to warrant the gratuity. The menu offered to Sullivan at these parlors always included happy endings, and Sullivan had been happy enough to lose count somewhere between four and five hundred sexual encounters, a hundred bucks a pop plus the tip. Cooper had always been curious whether Sullivan's wife ever asked her hubby why he'd withdrawn so much cash during his tours of duty.

Cooper had occasionally visited such establishments himself, mainly in Puerto Rico and St. Thomas. During his visits, he'd come to note some familiar faces among the clientele out in the waiting rooms. Accordingly, he came to see the shops as a lucrative opportunity to build his list. He found that for a small fee, for instance, the proprietors of the various parlors were more than willing to install an automatic digital camera in each therapy room, and even agreed to handle the arrangements for monthly delivery of the data files to Road Town One-Hour Photo for convenient printing.

On the occasional night under the stars on the porch of his bungalow, Cooper would peruse the inventory of photographs, and found, to his delight, that many clients of the St. Thomas and San Juan massage parlors happened to work for such interesting organizations as the U.S. Department of State, the U.S. Senate, 354 of the Fortune 500, the FBI, CIA, Russian military intelligence, and, as in Sullivan's case, the navy.

One autumn morning, Cooper had landed at Washington National, driven to Annapolis, and telephoned then rear admiral Robert C. Sullivan at home. He introduced himself as a lobbyist for a PAC seeking higher military budgets, offered to buy Sullivan a lunch, and Sullivan took him up on the offer the following day. At lunch, Cooper ordered a cheddar bacon burger and a Bass Ale, waited for the burger and Sullivan's chicken parmesan risotto to arrive, then slid a pair of eight-by-ten black-and-white prints across the table.

In the first shot, though Sullivan was hard to identify, a "masseuse" had her hands wrapped around Sullivan's not-insignificant member as he sat upright during what might have been referred to as a massage. In the second, Sullivan's face was clearly recognizable, the navy man's neck flexed and his trim waist slightly blurred as, in the picture, he fucked his masseuse, doggie style, one knee atop the table for balancing purposes.

Sullivan didn't quite spit out his first bite of risotto, but did halt midchew. He coughed gently and set down his fork, then lifted his glass, took a sip of water, set it down, rested his elbows on the table, looked at Cooper without moving his head, and said, "Who the hell are you and what is it you want."

After telling Sullivan he was merely a colleague on the federal payroll who might, someday, call upon him for a favor, Cooper raised his glass and toasted the unfaithful future CINCLANTFLT.

"May we all achieve happy endings," he said.

Cooper was hearing Sullivan's voice tonight for the first time since the lunch. Laramie watched him from her cross-legged position on the deck of the Apache.

"What I want, Admiral," Cooper said, "is a favor. The favor I'm looking for shouldn't present much of a challenge—not considering your rank, anyway. Congratulations, by the way, on your rise to glory."

"What is it, then," Sullivan said. "*Tell me*. I've been waiting for your call for *nine years,* you sadistic prick!" He lowered his voice to a whisper. "I haven't committed marital infidelity since our lunch. You've driven me into a born-again, self-imposed puritanical hell. I see cameras every-where I go—even looking up some slut's skirt from across a conference room. At least you've called—maybe now I can get you and your little cameras out of my head."

"I'd like to know the selection of nuclear submarines cur-rently at sea in the vicinity of the Windward Islands. Mar-tinique, specifically. I'm fairly certain you've got three, maybe four down here with the feature I'm looking for, pro-vided my bedtime reading is accurate. Which it probably is, since I wouldn't be reading it if I didn't have the twenty-first-highest security clearance in the United States. What's your ranking?"

Sullivan remained quiet.

"Basically, Admiral, I could use a UUV and an MSLC. Both of which I assume you understand come as standard equipment in your typical SEAL Hole."

Sullivan again said nothing.

"We both know how the Holes work—as a result, and for-tunately for you, nobody will know a thing. Hell, Admiral, for a man like you, that might have a couple of meanings."

"I'll take a look at the available inventory," Sullivan said.

Cooper said, "Do it in the next ten minutes and deliver the submarine by dawn."

"Fine."

"Got a pen? I'll give you directions."

When the pizza, and most of Cooper's stash of beer, was gone, Laramie curled up on the deck beside the copi-lot's seat and dozed off. Cooper set a hand on her shoulder.

"There's a bed downstairs," he said. "All yours if you

want it. Probably isn't a bad idea for me to stick around top-side. Muscle-head may still send friends."

A combination hum and grunt came from Laramie's throat, but she only curled into a tighter ball. Cooper pulled a jacket from the compartment beside the box where he kept the charts and draped it over her shoulders and back. He found one of the Apache's life preservers, slipped it beneath her shoulders and head, and sat upright on the deck beside her. He leaned his back against the railing along the copilot's side of the boat.

He'd just begun to realize how uncomfortable a position he'd chosen for his lookout duties, and lifted a foot to stand, when Laramie, asleep, repeated her hum-grunt sound, pulled herself a few inches off the life preserver, moved it aside, then resettled her head and shoulders on his thigh. With Laramie's cheek against his leg, Cooper reconsidered the discomfort he was feeling in his back muscles.

In another hour it began to rain. It came the way it did in the Caribbean, a few fat drops, then nothing, followed by a curtain blast of water hurtling downward. Laramie woke up sputtering, slightly confused, maybe even a little perturbed, he thought, after realizing she'd been sleeping on his leg.

When she put her weight on one arm to lean up and get her bearings, Cooper leaned down and kissed her. He did it hard, pushing through the rain that had already coated the smooth skin of her face. Oddly, considering they'd both been drinking beer, she tasted to him like the distant fruit of white wine. She also tasted like coolness, and warmth. As she kissed him back he could feel that her tongue was smooth, like her skin, Cooper getting the overwhelming sensation he'd been engulfed by wet flower petals.

As they fell back onto the fiberglass deck, the torrential

rain soaking through their clothes, Laramie pulled her lips from Cooper's, leaned her mouth against his ear, and said, "What about keeping an eye out?"

Cooper pulled her on top of him, pressing her lips back against his by grasping the back of her head with his palm. Through their cemented lips, he said, "Fuck it."

The way their mouths muffled the words, he wasn't sure whether she'd been able to understand what he'd said, but he soon developed a theory that Laramie didn't really care.

He had those lie detector powers down to a science now.

47

The rotors of the helicopter shot a streaming gust of wind against the quiet harbor, compressing a circular section of the ocean's surface, the water churning, then breaking into white spray as the chopper cleared the lagoon's edge and settled on the soft white sand of the Sainte-Anne marina. It continued to rain hard. A spotlight roved around the marina, directing its beam from one boat to the next, finding, leaving, then returning to Cooper's Apache, the boat's registration number highlighted in the center of the blinding white cone of light. The chopper was a UH-1N "Huey," standard U.S. Navy issue, its olive exterior at peace with the moonless Caribbean night.

Ignoring the pounding rain, Cooper rose on the deck of his boat, hand shielding his eyes from the searchlight. Laramie emerged from the cabin door behind him wearing a pair of Cooper's sweat pants and a T-shirt that didn't come close to fitting. The black shirt had the words FEEL ALRIGHT emblazoned in white across her chest.

"Our ride," Cooper said, yelling to be heard over the roar

of the Huey. The two of them, he decided, had been doing too much yelling.

Laramie looked up at him. Cooper decided she looked like a very appealing wet rat.

"Nice night for one," she yelled.

When Cooper and Laramie boarded, the Huey's copilot turned in his seat, formed a rectangle with his hands, and confirmed that Cooper was the man they'd come for when Cooper handed him one of his identification cards. The copilot then rose and distributed a pair of wireless headsets to his passengers. Once he saw they'd put them on, he said, "Good morning, sir. Ma'am. Please take a seat and buckle up. I assume you're aware that our instructions are to deposit you in the open ocean on a safety raft approximately fifteen miles due south of Diamond Rock. That would be the southwestern corner of this island. The rain will continue, but we expect calm seas. The trip should take approximately twenty-five minutes. I'm Lance Corporal Miller, and I'll be conducting the drop once we reach our destination. Any questions?"

Laramie looked around the cabin. Cooper saw her doing it.

"Got any barf bags?" he said to Miller.

Miller produced a pair and nodded.

"Even I use 'em sometimes, ma'am."

"Thank you," Laramie said. Cooper wasn't sure who she was talking to when she said it.

"Appreciate the lift," Cooper said.

"No problem, sir." Miller nodded at Laramie. "Ma'am." He reached back, slammed the side door closed, secured its latch, and returned to his seat.

When the pilot saw that Miller had buckled himself in, he applied some fuel to the turbines and left a white sandstorm in their wake as the Huey rose out of the marina and vanished upward into the downpour.

At the drop point, the pilot let the Huey nose up and hover in a lazy circle. Laramie forcibly swallowed a few waves of nausea as the chopper settled into a stationary position thirty feet above a patch of dark sea.

Miller flipped a switch, and the interior of the cabin lit up with a pair of dull red bulbs, one on either side of them. In a flurry, Miller hauled open the Huey's side door, released a pair of nylon safety handles, removed a yellow cube from a storage container, grasped and pulled a red tab on the yellow cube, and tossed the cube through the open door. The cube self-inflated wildly, bursting into a circular life raft six feet in diameter and floating through the thirty feet of altitude like a glow-in-the-dark parachute until it flopped lazily onto the ocean's surface. Through the open door, Cooper saw the hard Caribbean rain popping off of the ocean's surface in a hundred thousand pinpricks of white foam. The water's surface was otherwise flat.

Miller hand-cranked six feet of slack from a cable system behind a small door built into the cabin, found a pair of knapsacks in a square of netting, opened them, withdrew a slicker and a harness from the first knapsack, and flipped them to Cooper. The slicker and harness landed on Cooper's lap.

"You first, sir," Miller said over his headset. He looked at Laramie with what was intended, and which Cooper figured she regarded, as a respectful nod. "Ma'am, rule of this procedure is the reverse of a rescue operation: women and children last. We don't want you landing alone on that raft."

. Miller looked outside. "Looks like you'll get a little wet on the way down, sir," he said.

Cooper slipped into the harness. Miller snagged it with a hook affixed to the cable he'd paid out, set a hand on Cooper's shoulder, and gave the hook a short, violent tug. Satisfied, he guided Cooper to one of the safety handles dangling from the open doorway. He laid out a brief set of instructions before taking back Cooper's headset.

Cooper leaned backward into the rain and sunk out of sight.

A rumbling rush of water sounded out in the blackness, giving the impression of approaching bulk. A tremor passed through the raft beneath them; a large swell followed, with smaller, choppier waves behind it, and then the sea returned to its prior peaceful state. The raindrops had become fewer and less bulky in the past fifteen minutes.

Cooper looked at his watch. Three-thirty.

A spotlight hit them with hot white light, then doused. Another light popped on fifty yards off, this one more faint, a yellow floodlight bathing a section of the black sea with incandescence. It offered sufficient illumination for Cooper and Laramie to notice a small group of men approaching in a Zodiac. The light, Cooper saw, was affixed to a stationary black column featuring a small deck, a series of antennae, and a white number painted on its side. Beneath the column, just protruding from the water, a swath of black steel stretched far enough in each direction to be lost in the darkness before it ended.

The Zodiac approached the raft, and in fewer than five

minutes, Cooper and Laramie were deposited on the deck of the nuclear attack submarine USS *Hampton*. Their raft was quickly deflated and hidden by the men as Cooper and Laramie were escorted through a hatch at the base of the conning tower.

Eight minutes following its arrival, the sub slipped silently beneath the surface, its new and unofficial cargo of two civilian passengers safely aboard.

48

Inside the *Hampton*, Cooper and Laramie were taken to a minuscule cabin equipped with two doors. There was little between the doors other than a pair of cots so small they appeared to have been designed for children. Their escorts left, closing and locking the door they'd entered through, leaving them alone inside the room.

After a moment the bolt shifted in the opposite door. The seal popped, and the door eased open an inch or two. Nobody appeared; nobody reached through. Cooper watched the door, waiting, but nothing else happened. Finally he reached out and opened it, revealing, when he peered through, a hallway that from all appearances matched the one through which they'd just arrived. Noticing an unmistakable, pungent scent, he took a step into the passageway and saw, maybe halfway down the hall, the back of a short, beefy man in a blue T-shirt and the lower half of a wetsuit. Cooper could see as the guy walked away that he possessed forearms the size of a running back's thighs. A wisp of smoke lingered in the hall, leading in a curlicue contrail to its source: a joint, lodged in the man's mouth, of a size falling somewhere between a Cuban cigar and the state of Texas.

About twenty paces off now, the man turned a corner and ducked through another doorway, massive left forearm extended above his head in a wave Cooper figured was meant for him. Laramie stepped into the hallway behind him.

"What have we got?" she asked.

"What we've got," he said, "is some very good weed."

U.S. Navy SEAL submarine-based diving platforms, or SEAL Holes, were technical operations rooms housed aboard every U.S. Navy nuclear attack submarine built after 1992. The two-room compartments were isolated from the rest of the host submarines, accessible only by way of a sub-surface dive port and one interior entrance, an example of which Cooper had seen the thick-limbed SEAL turn into from the passageway inside the *Hampton*. None of the ordinary crew members could access the Hole without an encrypted code-key which, in most cases, was only provided to the SEALs working the Hole, along with the captain and executive officer of the boat.

The sole function of the Hole was mission control for clandestine operations. If so ordered, the captain and executive officer of the submarine would steer the boat according to the needs of a SEAL Hole operation; even in such cases, though, none of the submarine's regular crew possessed any idea of the purpose behind the submarine's change in course.

Just after 4:15 A.M., twenty-two miles east of the southern tip of Martinique, the USS *Hampton* inched along at a depth of four fathoms. She maintained a speed of six knots at a distance of approximately two thousand yards from the windward shoreline of Mango Cay. Along this shore, the island's primary geographic feature was a sheer cliff face. With only a brief, scraggly pause to deposit a short, black sand beach, the cliffs plunged sharply below the ocean's surface, creating a depth of many hundreds of feet of ocean in as short a horizontal distance as twelve feet from shore.

Inside the SEAL Hole, planted in a seat with his back to a wide control board, the man who had opened the hallway door for them sat smoking his cigar-size joint, alternately pulling in the reefer and taking in gulps of fresh air. He canted the joint to the side when he sought the fresh air between tokes, but otherwise kept it lodged between his teeth.

"Code name's Popeye," the man said, facing his audience of two. He'd just offered them a pair of stools. "I'll call you Olive," he said to Laramie, "and you Brutus. That's who we'll be for the duration."

He sucked in a lungful of Colombia's finest.

"Chief tells me I work for you the next eight hours. I take orders from you," he said to Cooper, "not out of any disrespect to you, Olive, but simply because I work best with a direct chain of command, and it's you, Brutus, I'm choosing." He clasped his hands behind his head and leaned back, the cigar-size blunt curling smoke into the sub's otherwise highly controlled atmosphere.

"Now what," he said, "can I do you for?"

Cooper said, "We're wondering if our friends running the resort up top have anything to hide. Specifically, we're wondering if they've got a way of getting in and out—or off and on—from underwater. Maybe with a small submarine."

"Good people, your friends?" Popeye said. "I ask 'cause

I'm wondering if they mind us snooping around. In other words, how clandestine," he said, drawing out the *stine,* "we need to be?"

Laramie said, "Pretty clande*stine.* Not to speak out of turn, of course."

"You can assume they've got it all," Cooper said. "Sonar, cameras, motion detection of one kind or another. I'm figuring a Hole run by a guy named Popeye, though, comes loaded with the latest devices engineered to circumvent such security systems."

Joint between his teeth, Popeye said, "Correctamundo."

"After looking around, we find anything interesting, we might need to get inside. You get us in and you've got an all-expenses-paid three-week vacation on a white sand beach a few miles from here. You name the time."

Popeye looked at Cooper, then Laramie, then back at Cooper before pulling the joint from his mouth and rolling it around between his fingers. "I don't know who you are or where you come from, Brutus," he said, "but for you to get a free ride in my room, you must be one well-connected *hombre*. And come to think of it, I could use a little R & R next month. Maybe bring along the missus?"

"She's invited and we're paying for her too," Cooper said.

Popeye jammed the thick joint back into the corner of his mouth.

"In that case," he said, "lemme introduce you to my little friend."

SEAL Hole data was fed to a segmented large-screen plasma monitor, so that images from the equivalent of eight television screens were visible at any given time on the single monitor. One segment, the largest, was dedicated to digital video playback, and in this portion of the screen Popeye had activated the moving image of a sheer face of underwater rock wall. Cast in a red hue symptomatic of the infrared lens capturing its images, the picture moved slowly from right to left on the screen. There was little to see besides rock, seaweed, uninteresting groupings of rock-based plant life, and the occasional small fish.

The video rolling across the monitor had been shot fifteen minutes prior by the Hole's unmanned underwater vehicle, or UUV. Popeye had loaded up the drone with commands, sent it out to fulfill its data capture mission, and digitized its video to the Hole's hard drive upon its return.

"UUV hung a left here," Popeye said. He pronounced the acronym *uve*. "Puppy's got artificial intelligence in its chip. Following the curve of the wall." The sheer rock face on the monitor dropped out of sight, then appeared again as the camera made a sharp turn and the infrared spotlight affixed to the lens reilluminated the cliff. A number of times, the UUV had found its way into underwater caves, something that took Cooper about two minutes of surveillance to learn were a common geographic feature beneath Mango Cay. In one such cave, the images recorded by the UUV showed the flat surface of the water above the drone's lens, but aside from an unusual preponderance of looming tiger sharks, the cave was featureless.

It was another three-quarters of a mile along the rim of the island's submarine strata where a more interesting feature presented itself on the monitor.

"More fish here," Cooper said.

Schools of small fish, gray in the infrared video image, surged in and out of sight of the camera's eye.

Cooper watched the monitor as the image progressed

from blank rock wall and three fish, to a dozen fish, then a hundred, and then suddenly the screen was filled with thousands of fish of all kinds—Cooper seeing the same set he got in the Conch Bay coral beds, wrasse and damselfish, a few sergeant majors, the bigger bar jack, yellowtail snapper, even barracuda. The rock wall became difficult to see behind the teeming mass of sea life.

Once he was able to catch a glimpse of the wall again, Cooper pointed at the monitor.

"More seaweed too," he said.

Popeye said, "Water temperature's kicked up about ten degrees." He pointed to one of the data segments on the monitor.

"How deep is the drone?" Laramie asked.

"No change in depth." Popeye eyed another segment on the screen. "Four fathoms."

As the drone turned back to the right—knifing between what Cooper thought might have been a million fish—the video image revealed a massive hole in the face of the rock wall. The opening was entirely natural in its contour, but it was the glow emanating from the rear of the cave—brightening as the UUV entered the cavern—that they could see wasn't the least bit natural. In fact, it was quite obviously man-made.

"Aye, aye," Popeye said when he saw the bright cone of light.

Cooper's first impression was that they'd found an underwater ballpark, that glow you got when you saw a distant baseball diamond at night. Or, he thought, an underground cave housing an illicit nuclear power plant. As the video image relayed the UUV's continued trek along the shoreline, the diffuse white light moved to the left, faded, then vanished. Popeye banged out a series of commands on his keyboard and the image of the underwater cliff popped off the monitor. The squat man turned to look at them.

"I'm guessing," he said, "you'd like our friend the *uve* to take a deeper recon tour inside that cave."

Laramie nodded.

"Correctamundo," she said.

In surveying Mango Cay for the location of the operation's nuclear power plant, Deng's civil engineering team had pinpointed the island's largest cavern as the ideal clandestine depository for contaminated runoff, primarily due to its considerable underground lagoon. Surviving intact from its days as the power cell aboard the USS *Chameleon*, the nuclear plant generated power in sufficient quantity to run the facility's day-to-day operations, but also generated a hundred thousand gallons a day of scalding, highly radioactive runoff, plus a steady seep of mildly radioactive steam.

Due to the resulting swath of irregularly warm water, there was, outside Mango Cay's underwater docking facility, a splash of sea life more concentrated than that inhabiting the most photographed coral reef in the hemisphere—a preponderance of creatures that ultimately punched a hole in Deng's otherwise bulletproof security blanket.

The underwater docking station within the missile cavern was canvassed by both closed-circuit video surveillance and sonar-based motion sensors. By their nature, the closed-circuit cameras positioned at the entrance to the underwater cavern were basically useless, since the images fed to the mainframe's software were composed of nothing but wall-to-wall fish. The routine presence of sharks and other predators required the sensitivity of the sonar package be set to near infinity in order to avoid hundreds of false alarms daily.

This meant that the methodical, preprogrammed second voyage through the cavern by the *Hampton*'s UUV went undetected outside of the shiver of fear it inspired in countless fish. Despite this, it appeared there wasn't much to see: the cove contained what appeared to be some sort of dock, a thick pipe that opened into the cove, a series of other, smaller pipes, and little else. The cove itself, Cooper could see on the display, was huge.

Laramie watched Popeye as he studied a data window alongside the video playback.

"Water coming out of that pipe," he said, "is just under two hundred degrees Fahrenheit." He clicked the mouselike tool that allowed him full control of the console, checking another readout. "It's also highly radioactive."

The video images concluded their playback on the monitor. Popeye reclined in his seat and eyed the instruments. He was still smoking. Laramie looked at Cooper.

"You know," she said, "if we were to send a sample of that water to the appropriate lab, I'd bet the tests would come back with a positive ID on a familiar combination of uranium-235 and -238."

"Mm," Cooper said.

"And unless somebody suddenly appears in a patrol boat now that our drone's been in there, it seems we've found a flaw in whatever system Muscle-head is using to safeguard the island from intruders."

"Like us," Cooper said. He watched her as she spoke.

"If the system can't tell the difference between a three-foot-long *uve*," she said, "and, say, a barracuda, then it probably can't tell the difference between a seal, or a shark, or a six-foot person, either."

Cooper said, "And you aren't even six feet tall."

"I'm five-four, in fact."

"So," he said, "if we want to see what's going on at the underwater ballpark Muscle-head is trying to hide, you're saying we skin-dive in there and find out?"

"Besides the fact that I can't swim?"

"Besides that."

"Yes."

Laramie looked at Popeye. "What do you think, Popeye? That is, if you don't mind answering a question from Olive."

Popeye grunted and stood. Cooper could see he wasn't much taller than Laramie, even with Laramie sitting in the stool.

"No need for skin-diving up in here," Popeye said. "You got me for another five hours and forty-five minutes, and as long as I'm on the clock, we got us a special SEAL Hole bus service, take you anywhere you want to get within a travel radius somewhere near five nautical miles."

Laramie said, "You need some spinach to back that up?"

Popeye grinned, sucking in another lungful of Colombia's leading agricultural product as he flashed his smile.

"Olive," he said, "I got all the spinach I need right here."

49

Peter M. Gates had his morning routine nailed. As DDCI, he was one of six officials who received a preview of the daily intelligence briefing, which would in turn be shown to the president. The preview version went out to its limited-distribution roster via encrypted fax at four-thirty each morning. By 4:37, Gates would pull the fax off the machine in his study, set it on the kitchen table, pour himself some coffee—already brewed with the aid of a timer—then read the report while he drank two cups from his favorite mug. He then made any necessary calls, reviewed a trio of daily newspapers, hit the treadmill, shaved before a sink of water so hot it steamed up his bathroom mirror, and concluded with a cool shower. Choose a suit for the day, fill another favorite—his burnished metal travel mug—with a third cup of coffee, and he was on his way by seven sharp. Most days, Gates came out his door thinking he'd got a two-hour jump on the bad guys.

This particular morning, however—the same morning Cooper and Laramie were busy getting high off Popeye's secondhand ganja fumes—Gates didn't feel so hot about the two-hour jump.

It was on this morning that Gates's fax machine failed to ring. The coffee timer delivered his brew on schedule, but as he drank his two cups, the taste of the coffee seemed slightly bitter. He read the *Times* and *Post*, rode the treadmill, shaved, showered, dressed, filled his travel mug with his third dose of java, then, at the door leading from his kitchen to the garage, Gates stood, unmoving, until, slowly, he lowered his head almost to where his chin pressed against his chest.

He stood that way for a long time; while doing so, Gates found it odd that his thoughts turned to a place with no apparent relevance to the conversation he'd had in Lou Ebbers's office the day before.

The DCI had fired him unceremoniously. No one else had been present, and there was no call for a letter of resignation; Gates was simply dismissed. Let go like a middle-management drone, as though he were a man who had never held in his grasp history's greatest and broadest-reaching spy shop.

As though, Gates observed at the time, he were a common corporate loser.

Still, his head bowed as he stood before the garage door, Gates found that he thought not of Lou Ebbers, or of his firing, or even of his mistakes—but of marriage. His wife was not home this morning; she was almost never home in the morning. He assumed that this morning was no different from other mornings; that she was sleeping in the bed of whatever man she'd fucked the night before. He hadn't spoken to her in days. He might have seen her a week ago, but he couldn't be sure.

What occurred to Gates, standing there in the kitchen, was that he now had nothing. Previously it had not been an issue, taking the big house that came with his wife's money, taking all the shit she shoveled at him along with it. It hadn't been an issue, because Gates had his work. It was all he cared about; it was all he did. Now it had become the only issue: he was a married man bereft of marriage. A human being utterly without home.

He tried for a moment to determine whether he should affix the blame to Cooper, Laramie, or possibly even his own mistakes for doing himself in, but in the end, he found it didn't matter. A flash of brilliance surged through his skull, and Gates realized he did possess something after all. There was, he decided, one last action he could undertake to secure his rightful place in the annals of Washington diplomacy and intrigue.

He took a moment to think through the logistics.

The media would have to get hold of the story; this meant local law enforcement would need to arrive on the scene before Lou Ebbers and his crew got their grubby hands on matters. If Ebbers found out before the local police did, Gates knew that he didn't have a prayer of getting the story into a single newspaper.

The details now properly arranged in his head, Gates placed a call to the local 911 operator. To the woman who took the call, he said, "Christ, there's been a shooting!" He provided the address where he claimed to have heard the shots fired—his own—and hung up while the operator was asking for further clarification. He then retreated to his study, opened the drawer where he kept his Walther P99, exited through the kitchen to his garage, got situated in the driver's seat of the Lexus he rarely drove, and, inexperienced as he was with the device, somehow managed to put a bullet through his right temple.

50

Cooper breathed rhythmically through the regulator. The breathing apparatus he wore generated a noise only its occupant could hear and emitted no bubbles; the noise it made sounded to Cooper like the rushing of a brook through the woods. He heard it each time he exhaled.

Cooper, Laramie, and Popeye rode in the SEAL Hole's mini-submarine landing craft. Built in various sizes and launched solely from SEAL Holes, the skin of the minisubs appeared to all existing underwater detection systems as organic matter; they were also internally amphibious, so that their passengers could occupy and operate an MSLC with the cockpit either flooded with seawater, or empty and dry.

Popeye had them operating in wet mode along Mango Cay's eastern shoreline. Along with their wet suits, Cooper and Laramie wore masks equipped with infrared underwater scopes, so that even in the murk of dawn, they could observe the approach of the island's underwater cliffs in a splash of pale red light.

As Popeye took them into the cavern, Cooper looked

around through the windshield of the sub. The entrance, now passing behind them, was massive. The sides of the hole consisted of pockmarked lava rock, strewn with splotchy outcroppings of algae and seaweed. He looked over at Laramie. She found his eyes through the masks and shrugged.

Between the curtains of fish, he could see they were approaching the rear of the cavern, the glassy surface of the water a few feet above them. Cooper noticed he was sweating, then remembered the water temperature inside the cave. He guessed it was upward of ninety-five degrees.

The light source they'd seen on the video playback shifted—changing, as they neared the surface, from a single, diffuse glow to a series of crisp white circles. Popeye pulled back on the joystick and hovered.

"SEAL Hole bus service ends here," he said, speaking over their sonar headsets. He pointed. "When I get us around that corner, punch the yellow knob on the console. It'll release you below the sub. I'd get out ASAP—Geiger count doesn't bode well for the lymph nodes." He adjusted a knob on the control panel. "You've got four and a half hours on the clock, Brutus. The *Hampton* will remain within SEAL Hole range of this location for no longer than that time period. Your knapsack contains a remote homing device; if you need a ride before the carriage turns into a pumpkin, press the button and I'll find you."

Popeye got on the joystick again and the MSLC nosed its way into the corner of the cove where the video playback from the UUV had registered a tangle of utility pipes. A cloud of fish darted from the nook; it looked to Cooper as though they were about three feet beneath the surface.

"Adiós, compañeros," Popeye said. "End of the line."

Cooper and Laramie followed Popeye's orders and punched their release buttons.

Free of the sub, Cooper watched as Popeye spun the MSLC around, waved at them through the cockpit glass, and motored toward the gaping exit hole.

"*Adiós*," Cooper said.

When the pager buzzed on his waist, Spike Gibson whipped his arms to their fully extended state, dropped the barbell on its twin hooks, and stood. He checked the pager and saw, among other facts, that it was 6:39 A.M.

There were two computer workstations on Mango Cay that were immediately and electronically notified in the case of a breach of the island's security perimeter. The first was the primary guard station; the second was Gibson's personal desktop.

Gibson unlocked the twin doors to his office, entered the appropriate codes on the keyboard, and checked the location of the breach. The half-crescent outline of a sector, highlighted in red, flashed lazily on the monitor.

The entrance to the missile cavern.

This sort of notification had happened maybe five or ten thousand times before, most frequently in the six months following the installation of the monitoring system. With the alarm ringing now, though—long after they'd made the changes in sensitivity—Gibson knew that whatever had breached the perimeter had to be, at a minimum, the approximate size of a whale. Examining the stat line on his monitor, Gibson saw that the object that had just slipped into the cavern was a great deal larger than that. The object, according to his monitor, was big enough to land a plane on, and was already surfacing inside the outer cove.

When this type of object had arrived in the past, Gibson had at least been given suitable advance notice. Today, though, there had been no such notification. No matter: he knew what—and who—had come. Playing back the relevant footage, Gibson confirmed his surmise: there, floating behind the usual canvas of teeming fish, was a colossal, cigar-shaped vessel of some five hundred feet in length.

The *Eagle,* he thought, has landed.

Considering that the next twenty-four hours represented the culmination of approximately fifteen years of meticulous planning, it occurred to Gibson that even a man so bold and vain as General Deng—*Premier* Deng—would be unlikely to commit so vain and foolhardy an act as to make an appearance now. At least not without something up his sleeve.

Gibson had already been giving a great deal of thought to the question Deng had asked him on his last visit. It had been a simple question, loaded with any number of meanings—*And your other projects?*—but Gibson figured he could translate the intended message with ease.

Deng had not previously referred to any facets of Operation Blunt Fist as Gibson's "projects"—in fact, Gibson hadn't heard Deng use that term for any purpose. Upon hearing Deng's question, Gibson had shut down his harvest operation for a couple days. He examined each of the archived closed-circuit feeds from the last couple of months to see whether something Deng had seen might have given him away; he examined everything else he could think of that could possibly have brought his "project" to Deng's attention. He found nothing.

Mildly uneasy, Gibson restarted the extraction sessions, and it wasn't until now, with Deng slipping his PLN submarine into the docking station of the main missile cavern, that Gibson admitted he'd been outfoxed.

Deng knew.

Gibson walked downstairs, jumped aboard his golf cart, and started up the trail to Admiral Li's bungalow. He figured the admiral would want to join him for whatever it was *Premier* Deng had up his sleeve.

51

Crawling down the ladder built into the submarine's hull, Deng stepped gingerly onto the missile cavern's narrow pier and turned to face his welcoming committee. Gibson, Li, Hiram, and four mercenaries stood watching him from their place on the dock; Li offered a deep bow, then, after a time, Gibson too lowered his head. Hiram and the soldiers made no gesture or expression, about what Deng expected, since none of these men was worthy of greeting him anyway.

"I've come," Deng said, "to conduct a prelaunch missile test." He had to shout to be heard over the sound of water cascading from the reactor's runoff pipe. "I am also here to announce an acceleration of the launch plans."

Gibson's face stiffened almost imperceptibly.

"We will now launch at noon, or eighteen hours ahead of schedule," Deng said, checking his watch, "and precisely five hours, seven minutes, and thirty seconds from now."

A second hatch on the deck made an unlocking noise, and the panel opened to emit the figure of an emaciated Chinese man wearing a white lab coat. It was hard to tell given his ill health, but the man looked to be seventy or so. He climbed from the hole, established his own footing on the deck, and bowed, first to Deng, then to the others.

Deng said, "I'm sure you remember Dr. Chu. This morning he will select four missiles at random and perform readiness tests on each. Mr. Gibson?"

Gibson raised his eyebrows.

"Lead the way."

Popeye had provided Cooper and Laramie with a pair of sea-to-land assault knapsacks, called "Silks," based on their commonly used, incomplete acronym of SLK. Strapped into each of the forty-pound knapsacks, Cooper and Laramie had found a hybrid assault pistol called a UR-14, twelve clips of ammunition, a suit of lightweight body armor, a change of civilian clothes, disposable military boots, a series of explosives, rations, and a sonar-based homing device. At Laramie's request, Cooper had stuffed his Nikon into his.

Equipped with a tutorial given by Popeye back in the Hole, Cooper and Laramie were able to remove their wet suits and pull on the body armor, clothes, and boots by the time Deng emerged from his sub.

With Cooper and Laramie watching from their hiding place, Deng and his entourage ambled through a massive set of cargo doors into the bigger internal cavern. The bigger cavern, Cooper observed, was the source of the ballpark-genre floodlighting they'd seen by way of the UUV.

"That," Laramie said, "would be Premier Deng Jiang of the People's Republic of China."

Cooper nodded. "Who would seem to be in charge, in fact."

"You have your camera?"

"I do."

"Please get CNN some shots."

Cooper snapped a few. When Deng's entourage was no longer visible, Cooper pulled Laramie from the nook and led her to the doorway the others had just passed through. They stuck to the walls but still needed to walk a good seventy yards completely exposed—crossing, in the process, the dock, a lava walkway beside the vacated guard station, and finally the broad gap beneath the arch of the doorway.

Coming inside the bigger internal cavern, Cooper stood still for an instant, gawking at the sight of the cavern and its contents. He nudged Laramie along the wall opposite the doorway; they ducked behind a section of piping wide enough to obscure them. Cooper could feel the heat popping off the pipe from a few feet away. From this hiding place, they could see the forest of white-and-black missiles in its full glory; there was also an odd, hourglass-shaped structure of ceramic, somewhere around twenty-five feet high, connected to the pipe beside them.

Seeing these things, Cooper considered that Julie Laramie had turned out to be one of three things: either she was the best SATINT analyst ever to set foot in the Langley headquarters building, the world's greatest organic lie detector machine, or simply psychic.

"Forty-two," he heard her say.

"I'd like to take back what I said before," Cooper said. "Your theory was ludicrous after all. Correct, but ludicrous."

"They're Tridents, by the way. They're supposed to be found in U.S. Navy *Ohio*-class and *Los Angeles*–class submarines."

Cooper looked around at the towering missiles, each touting an eight-digit identification code painted beneath a checkerboard stripe and an American flag about two-thirds of the way up its bulk.

"I'm no professor," he said, "but I'll hazard a layman's guess these particular Trident missiles weren't put here by the navy."

"At least not the American one."

Deng came to the base of the missile with the numeral 6 painted on the cavern floor beside it. The rest of the group gathered behind him in a loose semicircle, the mercenaries distributing themselves in a way that allowed them to keep an eye on Li, Deng, and Dr. Chu. By Chu's order, Hiram had gathered two boxes of tools from a maintenance cubicle.

Standing beside Deng, Gibson watched the leader of the most populous nation on earth examine the painted 6 on the ground beneath them and incline his head to take in the sight of the missile above. This, Gibson knew, was where Hiram and his just-keeled slave had most recently pillaged a W-76 warhead.

Deng lowered his gaze until it settled on Gibson. The premier eyed him in the same manner as when he'd asked the question, pre-tour, out by the pool, about Gibson's *other projects*.

Then Deng thrust his arm past Gibson's shoulder to point at a missile in the next row of silos.

"That one," he said to Chu. "We'll start there. Missile twelve."

Chu barked a series of orders; Hiram, following the commands, got to work unloading his dolly-bound equipment so the inspection of missile 12 could begin.

Considering that Deng was fucking with him, and doing it in so blatant a fashion, it had become evident to Gibson that Deng had been fucking with him for some time. Looking at the situation from this new perspective, it didn't take Gibson long to figure out the parts he hadn't already. At least not until now.

Strolling over to missile 12, he assembled the missing pieces of the puzzle and decided that he'd pretty much put it together.

All of it.

52

Cooper's instinct had been to do it the minute he saw all of them together on the dock. He'd suppressed it then, deciding to give current events a little breathing room—by seeing what went down, maybe he'd come to understand things a little better—but as the seconds ticked past, the two of them crouching halfway out on the open floor, he decided there wasn't much more to learn.

Sure, he thought, I've got a few questions I could ask these guys—maybe probe the topic of what it is, exactly, that Muscle-head does with the zombies once he brings them in here—but he was starting to feel exposed. It began to occur to him that even in his prime—presuming he'd ever *had* a prime—that he hadn't exactly been a crackerjack military strategist anyway. Back then, he thought, all you were was a goon: a highly trained, stupid goon, taking orders from people any idiot could have told you not to trust. And now? Now you're a flaccid, drunken beach bum, who ought to be out riding a wave, or taking a look at a starfish, or an anemone, or maybe some octopus hiding somewhere inside a shallow coral reef. You have no business tangling with these motherfuckers, and no intelligent reason to be doing it either.

Thinking that the opportunity for surprise rarely came around at all, he figured that once it had, maybe what was needed was a goon such as himself, stupid enough to be willing to seize the moment. He checked the clip on the UR-14, and, finding it to be in working order, leaned over until his lips brushed against Laramie's ear.

"The way I see it," he said, "right about now, we've got three options."

"Okay," she said.

Considering the look he saw in her eyes, peering past the pipe at Deng and his team, Cooper suspected Laramie was thinking the same thing he was, but he took her through it anyway.

"Option one," he said, "we do nothing and get caught."

She nodded. "Hang around another five minutes and we may as well just pick that one. How about two and three?"

"Use Popeye's homing beacon to bring him back, and, pictures in hand, get the hell out of here."

"If he can make it back."

"Yes—if."

"And if he does, it would probably take, well—at least five minutes of hanging around, wouldn't it?"

"I'd say longer," he said.

"How about door number three?"

"For the moment at least, we possess both the element of surprise and a pair of automatic weapons."

"We could look to hide out," she said. "You know— avoid option one for as long as we can while we figure out what to do."

"We could."

"My lie-detecting talents lead me to surmise that, if given your druthers, you would choose option three."

"Yes."

She looked at him. "I can't say that I've ever shot anybody. I *can* say that I've never killed anybody."

"Get on the floor."

"What do you mean, 'Get on the floor'?"

"I have."

"You—um," she said. "Both?"

"Get on the floor."

He moved across the phalanx of Gibson's rented soldiers, a staccato-firecracker echo caroming through the cavern as he went. Hiram popped up next in the shooting gallery—dropping his grip on the dolly he'd been wheeling along, Hiram stepped away from it and squeezed the trigger of his Uzi before the dolly hit the cavern floor, but only one of the shots he popped off came close before the last three shells from Cooper's first clip pierced the former bartender's neck, shoulder, and heart, and Hiram's body leaned sideways and draped itself lifelessly over the fallen dolly.

Having dispensed with the bodyguard contingent, Cooper ejected his spent clip, popped in another, and drifted out from his hiding place to seek a better angle on the principals. He continued firing as he moved; each of the others had found his way behind some obstruction or other, but as he rotated, pulling the UR-14's trigger, Cooper could see a few of his bullets landing. As he emptied the second clip, he saw a partially hidden body bounce from the impact of his shells, flopping sideways to the cavern floor. He couldn't tell who it had been.

He was in the process of ratcheting load number three

into the gun when his unprovoked assault on the denizens of Mango Cay came to an abrupt end.

Gibson spun to the cavern floor, reaching out as he spun, slapping Deng to the ground with an open palm to the side of the premier's head—the effect, due to Gibson's arm strength, that of a grizzly knocking a spawning salmon off its intended trajectory up a waterfall. Deng bounced across the cavern floor and tumbled out of sight into the hole beneath missile 36.

Gibson himself landed behind a transformer, which approximately forty percent of the bullets from Cooper's second clip proceeded to riddle. The transformer sparked, *whing*ed, *thwack*ed, and burst into flame, a narrow stream of black smoke curling roofward from its louvered vents. A bank of lights overhead doused, and half the cavern went dark.

Lacking the benefit of a Gibson grizzly swat, Admiral Li did not fare as well as his comrade premier. While he did manage to dive for cover and draw his pistol in a single fluid motion during the dive, the porous silo-housing he fell behind did little to stop the onslaught of the remaining percentage of bullets from Cooper's second clip. Li's pistol fell from his fingers as his body performed a spastic dance in objection to the rapid intake of bullets it was forced to endure. The forward momentum of his dive dissipated, and he collapsed on the cavern floor a few feet from Gibson.

Gibson took inventory of the sputtering, bleeding remainder of Admiral Li, the motionless lumps of the four mercenaries, and the prone, bent, and clearly dead Hiram splayed backward over the dolly. Two, then three seconds passed, during which time Gibson considered what he knew was about to happen next. Taking in the bodies, he did some math, and concluded that whoever was doing the shooting—not that it mattered now, but he had a pretty good guess—it would be more profitable, to the tune of an estimated two hundred million gross, were he to get the shooter to hang around for a little while longer.

He leaned back against the transformer.

"Alive!" he bellowed.

The sinewy muscles of his scrawny neck flexed and stretched as he elongated the word and repeated the wail.

"Alive!"

53

As Gibson's echoing plea reached her ears, Lana the maid pulled her finger off the trigger of the MAC-10 assault pistol she had been about to fire. Instead, she took two long steps, covering the remaining distance between her and the trespassing figures of Cooper and Laramie, and struck Cooper in the side of the head with a roundhouse kick that sent him sailing six feet before his body hit the cavern floor. When he did land, it was with a skull-carom across the lava surface and a back-bending bash against a silo joist. Lana then spun in a short, efficient motion and rammed her left elbow into Laramie's temple while Laramie attempted to rise from the floor of the cavern and fire back with her UR-14.

Laramie collapsed, sputtering, at which point Lana savagely and repeatedly kicked her, rolling her across the cavern floor until Laramie's body flopped against Cooper's at the base of missile 34.

Protection of Spike Gibson complete, Lana surveyed the carnage wrought upon the occupants of the cavern. Deng was nowhere to be seen; there was Gibson, alive and in perfect health; Li lay on the cavern floor, contorted, bruised, barely breathing; the four anonymous soldiers, dead and bleeding, were sprawled across the floor as though in formation; and finally there was Hiram, a six-foot-five-inch rag doll draped cold and dead across the dolly. Lana bent at the knees and touched Hiram's face, lingering for a few long seconds.

Then she stood upright, nearly at attention, and lowered the MAC-10 to her side.

"Clear!" she said.

Deng clawed his way up the side of the hole beneath missile 36 and peered over its top edge at the floor of the cavern. He could see Gibson's maid standing by the transformer; Gibson had just stood and said something to her. Everyone else was dead, dying, or comatose. Li was mortally wounded, but Deng didn't mind this much, since if Li died here, now, it would only serve to make things easier.

He scrabbled his way to a foothold and rose from the hole. Gibson and Lana watched him do it.

He thrust a finger toward the prone bodies of Cooper and Laramie.

"Who are they?" he demanded.

Deng didn't like the look in Gibson's eyes, the security director looking him over as though Gibson were the one controlling *his* fate.

"They're no one," Gibson said.

Deng shifted his gaze to the docking bay. He did so confidently, the threat implicit: *the military might of the People's Republic of China crouches within the skin of that vessel. I have ordered them to remain aboard, but defy me now, and pay.*

"I'm leaving now," he said. It didn't come out quite the way he meant to say it.

He could see Gibson was thinking something through, but the security director's expression hadn't changed, and he hadn't moved. Neither had the maid.

Deng started walking.

As he passed by, Deng heard the words that Gibson spoke, but he neither acknowledged them nor altered his stride as he walked from the interior of the cavern and out through the wide, arching doorway to his submarine.

"Bon voyage, lou bahn," Gibson said.

Li sucked at the air, sputtering, taking in as much blood as oxygen with every gasp. The admiral knew nothing but this simple task; occasionally, he would blink hard enough to clear the blood from his vision. After one of these blinks, the oil-greased, zit-scarred face of Spike Gibson loomed into view.

"How you doing, Admiral? You know, you aren't a bad guy, so it's a shame, isn't it, that you'll go down in history as the greatest all-time traitor to the people. Public enemies number two and one, my man. You and me. You figure this motherfucker out yet?"

Li's breathing stopped briefly. When it resumed, its pace was more frantic than before. The fogged look behind Li's eyes indicated to Gibson that the rear admiral of the People's Liberation Navy had just experienced something like an impulse to spit in his face.

"Your buddy the premier never took a meeting with any of his investors, Admiral. It was always you or me. And the terrorists behind the Beidaihe bombing—they had to have somebody on the inside, don't you think?" Gibson scratched his chin. "Deng does. He's got pictures. Evidence. Probably even some sources who'll squeal. What loyalist wouldn't, when it turns out a Chinese traitor by the name of Admiral Li Zhu held secret meetings in Bern with the chief architects behind both the Beidaihe bombing and the horrible destruction wrought upon America afterward."

Life was beginning to evaporate from Li's eyes. Gibson drew his Glock and examined the gun as if for the first time. Fascinated.

"But, Admiral, you're only number two. You realize who you're looking at? Bin-Laden's got nothing on me. I'm the new kid on the block—the mastermind behind not just one, but the *two* most brilliant and deadly terrorist strikes of all time. The chief assailant of *two* victimized superpowers."

Li coughed. It sounded more like a wheeze.

"Your comrade premier found out I was yoking his warheads. You know that? He should have taken me down too, because I had no idea. But he didn't. You know why? He didn't do it because your new premier is one smart puppy."

He waved the Glock skyward.

"As a loyalist, you should be pleased. When these missiles let fly, Deng will stand by America—China's fellow victim. America's military might will be shattered, but China's will not; the People's Republic will become the enforcer for the people of the world. All people—Americans too. The People's Liberation Army will effect regime change, as it is called, in the nations it has shown to be responsible for these twin acts of terror. China, while benevolent, will nonetheless become the world's supreme superpower. Pretty fucking cool, if you ask me."

Gibson racked a shell into the chamber.

"But even the most powerful nation on earth needs an enemy. And what your ingenious comrade premier figured out,

Admiral, is that if I get away—taking four thermonuclear warheads with me on my way out—then the great and benevolent Premier Deng Jiang will still have somebody left to fight."

Gibson grinned, grotesquely stretching the sinewy muscles of his upper neck and jaw. "A lethal, invisible force of evil," he said, "waiting to strike at any moment."

He pressed the tip of the pistol against Li's angular forehead.

"China must be vigilant!" he screamed.

The *crack* of the gunshot echoed through the cavern as the back of Admiral Li's skull painted the coarse lava floor beneath it.

54

The splash of water shocked him awake.

He knew immediately it was Caribbean water—lukewarm, with that mild, briny taste he knew all too well. He'd swallowed enough of it in the course of his free-diving escapades to fill a lake.

Cooper opened his eyes to a strange face—gaunt, harshly feminine, skin a wrinkled mahogany—and assumed he was having one of his nightmares. In his dreams, he would occasionally see faces he didn't recognize. He knew that he'd once known these faces, that he'd seen them before, and the dream was merely a visual playback of the memory that failed him during conscious thought. Usually, afterward, he could remember the faces from that dream permanently, so that, nightmare by nightmare, he was piecing together some of the missing portions of his life following his escape from the dungeon cell.

Cooper was trying to place himself in the dream, to figure out what this face meant and where it fell within the chronology of the usual three nightmares, when he realized that he recognized the face too keenly. He had seen it recently against a bright white pool, a background of bright sand and thatched-roof cabanas—

The face leering at him was Muscle-head's maid, and he wasn't anywhere near the comforting familiarity of his dreams. He was on the floor of the missile cavern beneath Mango Cay.

The maid had changed both her uniform and demeanor since their brief encounter by the pool. She was staring into his face with a sort of fanatical hatred, barrel of a MAC-10 pressed under his chin. She wore an olive green tank top that displayed naked shoulders and biceps easily bigger than his. The gun was secured with a strap slung over her right shoulder.

"Shithead, up!" she spat in a Haitian Creole drawl. Cooper thought immediately of Alphonse. *"On the feet!"*

She thrust a wrist beneath Cooper's right arm, lifted him effortlessly, said, "Against the wall!" and, using the muzzle of the MAC-10, pushed him backward against a web of scaffolding that Cooper figured she must have meant by "wall."

Through with Cooper for the moment, Lana crouched, lifted a second bucket of seawater, and dumped its contents on Laramie's face. Flat on her back as Cooper had been a moment before, Laramie shot immediately upright, gasping for air and clearing her eyes with both hands. She too got the muzzle of the MAC-10 against her chin.

"Fuck you!" Laramie yelled, lashing out in a reflexive burst that brought a smile to Cooper's face.

Lana shifted her weight from one leg to the other and kicked Laramie in the side of her head, reached out before Laramie could fall, and threw her against the scaffolding beside Cooper. Cooper grabbed hold of Laramie's shirt to hold her up.

Spike Gibson came into Cooper's field of vision and threw an olive green duffel bag at him. Cooper caught it with his free hand; it *clink*ed as he snatched it. The bag was heavy, maybe eighty or ninety pounds.

Gibson ignored the captives and spoke instead to Lana.

"Deng knows. He'll do nothing, so I've unlocked all the doors. All alarms are deactivated. Get in, bring me another two hundred mill, and get off the island. The U.S. Navy appears to be interested in us now—there's a destroyer fifteen miles east of Martinique and coming around. He does anything but break Hiram's record," he said, pointing at Cooper, then Laramie—"shoot her in the leg, then arm, and so on. See if that motivates him."

Gibson jumped behind the wheel of his cart, looked at Cooper, and said, "See you around, Albert."

Then he drove off.

Gun dangling from her shoulder, Lana positioned her own cart beside the nearest missile—38—and flipped the lever that summoned its silo elevator. She opened the cage door, returned to the cart, transferred a harness and rope to the elevator, and approached Cooper and Laramie.

Cooper could see that in addition to the assault pistol she now held a black rod.

"Get in," she said, and poked Cooper with the cattle prod. He jumped—fucking thing hurt, stinging him with a bone-jarring jolt. He pushed Laramie into the elevator, looking for an opening as he did it, but the maid didn't offer up any noticeable vulnerability.

Lana yelled to them from below as they rode the elevator up the length of the missile.

"*Maintenant* you open the bag! Listen and I tell you how to use!"

When they hit the twenty-foot mark, Lana flipped a

switch at the base of the silo, and the elevator jerked to a stop. Cooper listened, sort of, as she rattled off a how-to guide on the removal of your average nuclear warhead from a Trident missile. He wasn't sure whether she was through with the instructions when the *chukka-chuk-chuk* and *ping-ping-peow* of bullets from the MAC-10 *whing*ing past him gave Cooper a rough indication she'd completed the tutorial.

"V*ite! Allez-y!*"

Cooper attempted both to interpret and remember what he'd been told—thick accent like hers, he thought, wasn't exactly ideally suited for giving highly technical instructions. His time spent with Alphonse helped, but he still only understood about forty-five percent of what the well-muscled maid had to say.

Among the tools was a flashlight, which he handed to Laramie. As told, he installed a rubber plate to use as a shelf and set the other tools on it. Working quickly, he used a distant cousin of a Phillips-head screwdriver to remove the screws securing an access panel and opened the panel when he had the screws out. He grabbed two saws and a hammer and chisel and looked at Laramie.

"Do me a favor and keep as far back as you can," he said. "Just point the flashlight."

Laramie gave him a look, which he took for indecision on whether to be offended he thought he could handle the work and she couldn't, or flattered that he refused to expose her to unshielded plutonium, or enriched uranium, or whatever it was the warhead contained.

Cooper got to work, thinking that this is where his decision to take possession of Roy's body from the beach had proved a moderately bad call. Leading him here, inside a Trident missile, digging for radiation sickness at the order of a muscle-bound maid. Once he thought about this for a

bit, he made the guess that somebody else had probably
been doing this kind of work before him, and probably under the same exact threat. Gibson's words had been clear
enough: *he does anything but break Hiram's record* . . . Hiram, he thought, being the supposed bartender he'd recently
shot. Hiram must have had his own radiation diggers, and
maybe some time back, one of them had drawn some similar
radiation-exposure duty inside the nuclear power plant he
and Laramie had used as a hiding place. Considering that
the power plant appeared somewhat weathered and worn, he
assumed it generated its energy with the less modern
U-238/U-235 uranium fuel rods, and that an accident could
easily have happened while the radiation digger was doing
the work. Result: odd burn marks, severe pain, a hell-bent
escape for daylight, and a few gunshots in the back from
Gibson's goons. Thanks, Marcel, for all your hard work.

And there you have it. With the help of my associate, the
renegade entry-level analyst from Langley, the private-eye-
for-the-dead has just solved the second murder of poor,
sweet Simone's zombified fiancé.

Hell, he thought, maybe I'll give Marcel's widowed fi-
ancée a call and let her know everything's turned out just
fine. That there's a perfectly reasonable explanation for
Marcel's misfortune: exhumed following an overdose of
coup poudre potion, he was brought back to the living with
conconbre zombi serum and sold by your town wizard to a
redheaded, serial-killing albino black named Jim Beam,
who, in turn, sold him to somebody named Spike—short for
Spencer—Gibson. But if it's any solace to you, Simone,
Marcel probably commanded a minimum of a couple thousand bucks on the open market, at least judging from the
size of the bag of money Jim had taken in exchange for the
wino from East Queen Street.

Breathing lead dust and soaking up radiation inside the access panel, Cooper gave some additional thought to Gibson. With the man out here running Deng Jiang's missile factory, probably thinking after ten years of the assignment he could certainly get used to island life. Maybe even thinking he wouldn't mind securing a ninety-nine-year lease of his own. Maybe Gibson does the math, he thought, figures out how to snake a few of the warheads, and determines he can get somewhere around that *two hundred mill* he was telling the maid about each time he pulls a nuke out of its ICBM.

He couldn't see the whole docking bay from his cubby inside the missile, but it had looked to him, on the way up the elevator, that Deng's submarine was no longer parked in the underwater lagoon. Maybe the bullets from his UR-14 hadn't struck premier pay dirt, and the big fella had headed home. Cooper reached instinctively for his SLK, and the camera, homing device, and other goodies he had in it, but no such luck. Be good to find that camera with the pictures I took, now that they'd learned what they'd learned—Cooper figured even Peter M. Gates could put the pictures he'd taken of Premier Deng and his boys to use.

About an hour in, he gave the warhead-MIRV pairing one more whack with the hammer, and the twenty-fourth and final rivet fell from its anchor, *ping*ing its way down the interior of the missile.

As instructed, he stepped out from the hole and signaled to the maid.

"The harness!" she screamed. *"Maintenant!"*

55

When Zeke Sampson, captain of the USS *Hampton* nuclear attack submarine that housed Popeye's SEAL Hole, reported to Norfolk that his sonar man had spied a bogey in the waters near Martinique, he was ordered to track it. Sampson was also told to monitor and escort the arrival of the USS *Scavenger*, the navy destroyer assigned the investigation of Mango Cay. The captain's crew had long ago marked the approaching destroyer, which had reached its drop point some fifteen minutes back and would release its reconnaissance launch momentarily.

Sampson found it odd that it was now—only seconds before the *Scavenger*'s launch boat was set to splash down—that the bogey detected by his sonar man had turned up on their system. In fact, the vessel, which was clearly a foreign submarine, had made its appearance only two thousand yards from the island the *Scavenger* had been sent to investigate. When Sampson received confirmation that the sub they were tracking was a Chinese nuke, he made a simple call: the sub's presence was unacceptable.

Sampson did not view this as an exercise. For him, nothing was—he ran a tight sub, and, loose, tight, or otherwise, a U.S. Navy nuclear attack submarine always operated at wartime readiness.

He brought the *Hampton* to within seven hundred yards of the bogey.

In order to provide sufficient power to ignite forty-two Trident intercontinental missiles over a launch period of eighty-four minutes, Deng's engineers had recommended a five-plant in-line generator grid that, while spearheaded by an accelerated use of the nuclear reactor, had little resemblance to the clandestine power-generation the reactor produced in the course of its routine duty.

Stage one of the power boost involved the automated sinking of six times the typical count of U-238/U-235 fuel rods into the pool within the reactor; stages two through five supplemented that energy glut with the ignition of four massive diesel generators. The diesels providing the power for these generators had been diverted from a Chinese strip-mining site in Mongolia; each engine's twenty-four cylinders displaced 110 liters and burned nearly ten gallons of fuel per minute, belching an unfiltered cloud of soot.

Once the generators ramped up to the specified 4,000 rpm, the power grid feeding the missile-launch system contained sufficient juice to light the rocket engine propellant within a missile forty-two times in rapid succession, at least by aerospace standards. This process began thirty minutes ahead of Deng's revised launch time of noon and would hit full wattage nine minutes before the first missile was set to enter the history books.

In the meantime, with the reactor accelerated and the

diesels kicking on in sequence, Mango Cay was subjected to the kind of uproar normally associated with cataclysmic earthquakes and volcanic eruptions.

One of the fastest items to move off the shelf when the Soviet Union disbanded was a set of fourteen diesel-powered midget submarines that had operated out of Ukraine's Sevastopol harbor in the Black Sea. Upon dissolution of the empire, primary authority over Soviet matériel housed in the former republics was ceded to the newly independent republics—meaning, among other things, that various superpower-grade implements of destruction were placed in the hands of nations so poor and corrupt that nearly everything of value was sold within minutes, and the midget subs were no exception.

Sporting only a fraction of the beam of a typical nuclear sub at eighty-five feet, the subs had been built in the late 1970s as the Soviet precursor to SEAL Holes. They were designed as two-man vehicles, with a freight capacity similar to that of a forty-eight-foot shipping container. Twelve of the fourteen subs had been sold on the open market between 1991 and 1996 to various tourism companies; the thirteenth sub had been decommissioned and sold as scrap metal due to a series of accidents that occurred during its time of service.

The fourteenth had been purchased by Spike Gibson.

He used it sparingly, since he'd procured the sub primarily to get the hell off the island when the shit hit the fan—such as a time like the present—but he had applied its services from time to time. One use had been as a handy-dandy disposable laborer-retriever.

Gibson drove into the cargo cave and ditched his cart. Moving past the yellow crane, he ambled through a doorway that was normally locked, but which he'd opened along with all the island's other doors once Deng hit the road. He flipped a switch, and the pocket cavern housing his Ukrainian sub revealed itself under the lights.

He leaped aboard the sub's deck, scaled its six-foot conning tower, and boarded through the main hatch. When he started it up, the old contraption belched a cloud of black smoke but soon settled into a mellow purr. Gibson sealed the hatch, worked the crude controls, and navigated beneath the underwater ledge separating the pocket cavern from the cargo cave's main lagoon. He parked it against the dock before spending a laborious few minutes opening the sub's corrugated roof, a task accomplished by means of an ill-greased hand crank. When he had the roof open, he climbed out directly from the freight bay, stalked across the floor of the cave to the yellow crane, took the control seat, and started her up.

He maneuvered the crane on the tracks until its arm was positioned above the warhead storage container at the back of the cavern. There was a six-inch eye bolted to the top of the container; Gibson worked the crane's arm, causing the hook end of its cable to swing like an upside-down metronome, and jammed the left-hand lever forward and took a shot at the eyebolt with the hook. It clanged off the hole on the first couple of attempts, but he nailed it on the fourth. As the hook slipped through the hole, Gibson pulled back on the right-hand lever, elevating the arm. The cable tautened.

He gunned the engine and lifted the box, the rear of the crane creaking under the strain of the weight. When he had the container a few feet off the cavern floor, he steered his way backward and to the left, swinging the container across the stacks of equipment and debris until he had it hanging above the open cavern floor. Easing the container to the floor, he slackened the cable another notch and locked the crane in place.

Pulling the wireless remote from his belt, Gibson keyed the sequences on its pad, and the container's padlocks popped open one by one. He removed the eight locks, and then, squatting with a perfectly rigid back, slipped his fingers under the lid of the container and lifted the slab as though it were a cardboard stage prop.

Lid open, Gibson surveyed his merchandise: three W-76 warheads, each capable of generating an explosion equivalent to the simultaneous detonation of one hundred thousand tons of TNT. According to some casual probes he'd ordered up, Gibson estimated the market value of each of the warheads at just over two hundred million dollars gross. This meant that after the necessary but obscenely expensive middlemen and the various bribery, transport, and money-laundering-related expenses, Gibson figured he was now staring at a minimum of one hundred and eighty million bucks, net—free, clear, and tax-free.

Two-forty sounded even better.

He dropped the lid and examined his watch. Lana was late, and while it was certainly possible that good ol' Albert Einstein had caused her some difficulty, he was confident she could handle him, and instead attributed her delay to the mud that inevitably plagued the tunnel following a morning rain. Moving a golf cart holding a hundred-kiloton warhead through a quarter mile of mud, he thought, might just take their latest disposable laborers a little longer than usual.

56

Lana had the accelerator pinned to the floor, allowing her to kneel backward on the seat to monitor her captives while the cart's motor kept on. She had the MAC-10 trained on Cooper, the strap draped over her shoulder—if any bumps caused her to fumble it, the gun would spring back to her trigger hand.

Cooper pushed, Laramie beside him. The cart's fat wheels kept getting stuck in the mud, and there wasn't enough horsepower in the vehicle's battery-powered motor to lessen the challenge in the slightest.

The ordeal, though, was not as difficult as Cooper made it seem. Hanging his head, he made sure his movements took on a slow, exaggerated quality—Cooper, the beaten-down man. He grunted as he pushed, his chest heaving, face and neck slick with perspiration. Laramie watched him, initially trying to figure out whether he'd been wounded, but she soon caught his eye and found that the look he was giving her didn't match the show. Seeing this, she decided to join in, curious where he was headed but along for the ride wherever it took them.

Cooper began to experience a form of flashback. Slices of his recurring nightmares streamed across his interior field of vision, appearing as a kind of picture-in-a-picture, his normal vision the regular screen, the nightmare segments superimposed as a miniature moving image in the upper-left corner. The images were familiar to him—*the hands, guiding him through the tunnel—crescents of light searing his eyes through gaps in the blindfold—hacking swings with the machete, killing them all in a sea of blood.*

He wondered whether what he was seeing was some new variation of the post-traumatic stress disorder that had brought him to the Caribbean to start with, and kept him bathed in a cold sweat night after night—or just his soul's way of telling him this wasn't the way he wanted to cash out. Telling him he was just as fucked as he had been in that Central American dungeon, and if he didn't figure something out by the time they reached the end of the tunnel, he'd join Marcel in that place where zombies reside in the ever-after.

Listening to whatever message it was, broadcast by way of the picture-in-a-picture, Cooper continued to set the stage for the only play he held any hope of making, which was to lull the maid to sleep. He figured if he got her accustomed to slow movements passing before her eyes, if he convinced her he truly was dragging ass, then, when he made whatever move he had in him, he would at least have a fraction of an advantage going for him when he did it.

He noticed that the tunnel was beginning to fill with a black, sooty layer of smoke, laden with particles he could taste on his tongue. He assumed the smoke was related to the noise that had begun to pulse through the tunnel in waves—maybe it came from backup power generators, maybe from something else, he thought, but either way, it was getting harder to see, and breathe.

Which might have helped him, except that the maid was very good. The soulless black eye at the end of her gun never blinked, and the soulless hands that held the gun failed to waver. Cooper trudged on, playing his drag-ass game, all too aware of the approaching doorway at the end of the tunnel.

When they reached it, he figured their time was up.

The countdown clock in Deng's Mobile War Room told him that fourteen minutes remained until the first missile was airborne, but his sonar-mapping feed told him the U.S. Navy reconnaissance boat would reach the island in three minutes tops. This wouldn't give the navy much time before the first of the missiles got airborne, but while it was possible the American troops could wreck a few of his missiles, this didn't bother him. Enough of the missiles would make it out to accomplish the aims of Operation Blunt Fist.

What bothered him was the remote likelihood that circumstances would allow the U.S. Navy to discover something tying him to Mango Cay. The only way this could occur was through the slim chance that an operations team could sabotage the power grid prior to the ignition of the very last missile in the series.

The forty-third missile.

Deng believed he hadn't left a shred of evidence; except for the remaining presence of Admiral Li's body and Gibson's pending departure—both of which fit snugly into the strategy Deng had planned from the outset—he had been fanatical about keeping the People's Republic of China out of all affairs related to the island and its contents. He found it unlikely that his visit this morning, including his tumble into the exhaust hole, had blemished his carefully cleaned slate—Deng assumed Gibson would dispatch his captives and vanish with his maid in tow.

Had the navy boat been scheduled to reach the island an hour from now, or anytime toward the conclusion of the launch sequence, none of this would matter. At that late stage, Deng defied anyone to pry open or otherwise affect the unique lockbox he'd installed beneath another of the exhaust holes. Utilizing a final set of four W-76 warheads, Deng had arranged for the forty-third "missile" in the sequence—really just a warhead grouping buried beneath a slab of lava—to skip any form of launch and simply detonate.

At that point there would be nothing left of Mango Cay—or, for that matter, most of the Windward Islands. This, of course, meant that even the spinmasters running the American publicity machine would have nothing to work with. Risk vulnerability to some form of sabotage, though—including the possibility of a U.S. Navy reconnaissance team making landfall within minutes—and Deng knew he'd be exposing himself to exactly the sort of self-serving inquiry the American government yearned to make.

The crew of Deng's submarine had been monitoring the U.S. Navy destroyer's approach for hours, having first detected it prior to his visit to the missile cavern. Deng guessed that the Americans in the cavern had something to do with its presence, but he wasted no time speculating.

He connected to the captain of the sub with the War Room's hotline. When the captain asked how he could be of service to his comrade premier, Deng ordered him to activate the submarine's torpedo tubes.

"Fish on the loose!"

It was the first time Captain Zeke Sampson had heard the exclamation uttered for real. His crew aboard the *Hampton* had used the phrase endlessly during their quarterly exercises, the phrase signifying a live enemy torpedo had been fired into the water. The words now spread like wildfire up and down the chain of command, sparking the calculated, practiced series of actions forming the *Hampton*'s counterattack strategy.

Sampson immediately ordered a dual-salvo torpedo attack. Seconds after he gave the order, another call the crew had previously made only during war games came back up the radio grapevine:

"Shark out of the cage! Two! Two sharks out!"

Catchphrase delivered, the crew members aboard the *Hampton* braced for the concussion they knew would come almost instantaneously with the detonation of two nuclear-tipped torpedoes in fifteen fathoms of water at a distance of only seven hundred yards.

57

When Deng's twin torpedoes struck the hull of the PX-38 U.S. Navy reconnaissance launch boat, the vessel and its crew erupted in an explosion so overwhelming that within twenty-five seconds not a single scrap of shrapnel remained on the ocean's surface. One moment the thirty-eight-foot sea-to-land attack craft had been skimming the Caribbean at thirty-five knots; in the next, there was a thud; the third marked an explosion that blasted the boat into a cloud of shrapnel mist.

Then the Caribbean returned to the state in which it had found itself prior to the boat's arrival.

Deng was able to savor the destruction of the launch boat for two full seconds.

In the third, his War Room monitors told him two additional torpedoes had been released into the sea in fatally close proximity to his submarine lair. He knew immediately what this meant, and since he also knew there would be little time to do anything else, he simply set his jaw and stared with satisfaction as the last seconds of his life ticked off the countdown clock.

Now that he'd destroyed the reconnaissance boat, Deng knew the countdown would continue.

No one could stop it.

Eight seconds following the direct hit of Deng's torpedoes against the launch boat, the *Hampton*'s modified Mk-48 nuclear-tipped torpedoes commenced a dual-stage explosion that resulted in the complete disintegration of three-quarters of Deng's submarine.

The first Mk-48 detonated mid-hull on the starboard side of the sub, vaporizing most of the sub's steel skin. This resulted in an implosion; the submarine folded partly in on itself, sucking over a million gallons of water into its cavities, a brief underwater black hole. On the ocean's surface fifteen fathoms above, an oval-shaped area depressed by two inches.

Then the second Mk-48 struck; with so many of the sub's cavities flooded, the detonation blasted outward in all directions. At sea level, the ocean shot suddenly skyward in a geyser of salt water and shrapnel.

Because they took place beginning at T-minus 00:13:39 on the Mobile War Room's countdown clock, the twin Mk-48 explosions meant that Premier Deng Jiang would not live to witness the manifestation of Operation Blunt Fist.

58

Lana had no need to cock her weapon, nor pull back its hammer. The gun was already trained on Cooper's chest, a bullet positioned in its chamber, so all that remained for her to accomplish in order to dispose of Cooper and Laramie was the transmission of a signal from brain to index finger.

At the instant the cart nosed beneath the doorway to the cargo cave, her brain relayed this intention and her index finger flexed. The finger pulled the trigger of the MAC-10, and the inevitable followed.

At the instant Cooper felt the overburdened golf cart dip into a rut—the same instant in which Lana tugged the trigger of her MAC-10—reality adjusted itself within Cooper's being. The culmination of his picture-in-a-picture images, the images that came to him blurred, then eliminated what little remained of the line dividing the existence of his own being and that of the twice-dead Marcel S.

Over the course of a ten-millisecond span of time, an unimaginably long sequence of visions played out in the mind of the temporarily insane Cooper. He saw, in a continual, fast-forward band of muted colors, his torture in the Central American prison; his machete-fueled counterattack on his captors, followed by his flight; the usual content of his third dream—lost sections of his life afterward, the time spent in gutters, sewer pipes, drainage culverts and hospices; and, blended with the rapid-fire images from his dreams, there came images of a flight he had never known. *Jagged leaves, black in the wet night, whipped his cheeks as he ran; sores bled beneath a torn jersey. A gust of wind knocked him off balance and he slipped, fell, and rose again, only to flee, stumbling, over the edge of a cliff in the howling winds and rain of a hurricane. He smashed against the rocks below, felt bullets pummel him from above, and clawed his way across a thrashing dock to the tiny wooden rowboat lashed to its end.*

In this ten-millisecond instant, Cooper was not present on Mango Cay, but instead became lodged in an endless nightmare from which it seemed he would never awake or emerge, and in this endless instant he realized there was no other explanation except to admit that he and Marcel, both dead, had become enjoined, then arrived in hell, where Cooper had no doubt they would remain for eternity. Assuming it was his fault, not Marcel's, that hell was the prison to which they'd been sentenced, Cooper's mind burned through a thousand-year loop, a trap, an inescapable sentence stretching into a hideous, burning eternity, and then, in stubborn objection to this impossibility of instantaneously occurring eternal damnation, his physical being generated a counter-eternity of opposing energy.

His rage at the absurdity rose up against the images con-

fronting his mind—the equivalent of the jerking twitches
made by a sleeping man in his attempt to awaken from a
frightening dream—and Cooper's body, starkly aware of
the importance of this single moment of eternity, chan-
neled its counter-energy back into and out through the same
instant of real time through which the altered-reality vision
of hell had come.

In a flash of bloodred blindness, Cooper burst from his
nightmare with the propulsion of a shell launched from a
firearm, and he made, at least for the moment, an escape
from damnation. In the eleventh millisecond following the
golf cart's dip in the rut, Cooper's body shot forward, flying,
more catlike than human, across the three and one half feet
separating him from Lana. His body covered the distance in
so short a time that, for Lana, time did not pass between her
depression of the trigger and the impact of two-hundred-
plus pounds of conch-fritter-filled human projectile against
her solar plexus.

Cooper's leap was not quick enough to escape the pum-
meling strike of the first two bullets. As he got himself airborne, one struck the edge of the sheath-thin SLK-issue
body armor; partially ricocheting, it plunged into the flesh
of his shoulder but delivered no permanent damage. The
other succeeded in burrowing into the meat of his upper
thigh.

A pair of Lana's ribs snapped on impact and her body
flew backward over the cart's steering wheel. Landing on
the floor of the cavern, her head bashed against the unfor-
giving lava rock. The injuries would not have kept a soldier
of Lana's constitution from fulfilling her intent to kill were
it not for the speed with which Cooper then got his hand
around Lana's fingers, spun the MAC-10 into her bosom,

and put thirteen shells into her broken rib cage, thereby extinguishing the light that had, until now, burned within the muscle-bound maid.

At that point Cooper collapsed, landing facefirst beside Lana's body on the damp stone floor beside the doorway to the cargo cave.

59

Rusty since her training days at The Farm, Laramie still possessed a loose familiarity with the weapons they'd trained her to recognize. Stumbling past the golf cart over the prone bodies of Cooper and Lana, acting without conscious thought, she lifted the assault pistol from Cooper's bloody hand, found a loaded clip on Lana's ammo belt, switched it with the clip Cooper had just emptied, stepped out from the doorway into the cargo cave, took aim, and let loose.

Spike Gibson had been working the controls of the yellow crane to bring it over to the doorway, and while he'd ducked and drawn his weapon at the sound of the initial shots, he returned to his seat in the brief lull that followed. He'd got the crane back in motion when Laramie stepped out from the transport tunnel and threw down on the yellow machine with Lana's bequeathed MAC-10.

The automatic pistol's stream of bullets honed in on Gibson after Laramie's initially terrible aim. She wasn't sure whether she scored any direct hits by the time Gibson, aiming at her muzzle flash, pelted her first in the thin flesh of the upper arm just beneath the lip of the body armor she wore; Laramie's bone fragmented and she spun and fell from the impact, gasping as the breath shot from her lungs. On Laramie's way down, Gibson caught her with a second shell in the lower-right portion of her back. The thin body armor caught and deflected much of the bullet's force, but the shell was still able to penetrate Laramie's abdomen, and ultimately ripped an exit wound the size of a Ping-Pong ball just above her right hip.

The concussive momentum of the dual strike knocked her unconscious; Laramie, bleeding badly, was out by the time she hit the ground.

Once pushed through the doorway from the tunnel, Lana's all-terrain golf cart set forth on an independent, slow-motion journey across the cavern. Its accelerator still pinned to the floor, the cart propelled itself across the cave one inch at a time, the warhead load dragging its axles. The vehicle wasn't able to establish significant momentum along the way but still made steady progress and, in due course, passed through the open doorway of the pocket cavern normally belonging to the Ukrainian sub.

Once through the door, the cart encountered an impassable mound of industrial debris. Its electric motor hummed on, pressing stubbornly but to no avail against the stack of I-beams and engine parts.

Disengaging the crane hook from the container's eyebolt, Gibson reassumed the control seat in the crane and tracked the machine to the far end of its twin rails. He locked the arm in place, came over to the cart, affixed the hook to the harness wrapped around the warhead, retreated to the crane, and lifted the warhead out of the pocket cavern and into the container. He worked the levers until he'd managed to dunk the warhead into the fourth and final slot in the foam padding, then locked the arm and came around to switch the hook from the warhead harness to the eyebolt. Performing a reverse military press with no apparent effort, he lowered the lid into place. In the interest of time, he flipped and locked only three of the eight latches, leaving the rest for when he'd loaded the container into the submarine.

With Gibson back in the control seat, diesel engine whining like a possessed lawn mower, the crane's hydraulics tautened the cable holding the weight of the crate, and the sagging arm lifted Gibson's precious cargo from the cavern floor.

Face plastered against the soggy grit of the mud-coated lava, Cooper opened his eyes and observed the inert body of Gibson's maid—and, beyond the maid, Laramie. Laramie lay prone on the tunnel floor beneath the doorway. Through the doorway, he could see what appeared to be another cavern. The maid, he thought, had been trying to take them in there. The cart was now gone.

He could see that Laramie was unconscious. Fighting a spasm of pain from the movement, he crawled over to hold a hand above her nose and mouth. She was breathing, but he could see that she'd been shot: there was an exit wound above her right hip, and, from what he could see from his place on the floor, she was bleeding badly. He would have to find a way to stop the flow.

The booming *thrum* of distant engines throbbed through the cavern, the same rumble he'd heard during the journey over. He could taste the same layer of foul, black exhaust and saw that it hung lower now.

Cooper found he could move all of his limbs, which was good, but even the smallest motion caused searing bolts of pain to assault him from his two bullet wounds. He could move; that was all he needed to know, Cooper thinking that in the last ten years he'd sucked down enough medicine to last a hundred men a hundred years, so he shouldn't feel one bit of the pain.

Lifting his head, he felt such a crackling shock of agony that he determined his theory to be bullshit. Persevering, he crawled to a place on the tunnel floor from which he could see into the cavern.

Thirty or forty feet across the room was Muscle-head. Seated at the controls of a yellow crane, Gibson was using the device to lift a chubby container off the floor of the cavern. Cooper watched as Gibson inched the crane arm across the cave, and the brief expanse of water beyond, toward the submarine parked in the lagoon.

Cooper noticed something familiar about the sub's conning tower, and even in his semiconscious state, it didn't take him long to realize where he'd seen it before—it was the shortie submarine he and Laramie had picked out on the Gates-issue satellite photos. The rest, he thought, is obvious: Gibson is looking to remove his warhead bounty from Mango Cay by way of that submarine.

He checked for anybody who might be standing guard for Gibson while the weightlifting behemoth ran the crane. The pain from this simple act of swiveling his head sent debilitating convulsions down Cooper's back, but he saw nobody else in the cavern, so he reached over and got his hands on the MAC-10. He checked the clip, found it to be two-thirds full, and found another clip, spent, on the tunnel floor. Thinking about this, he looked at Laramie. It didn't make much sense, with Gibson nonchalantly operating his crane across the way, but if he had to guess, he'd say that Laramie had popped off a few rounds and been taken down by Gibson.

My kind of woman, he thought.

Straining through multiple bolts of pain, he lifted the gun with his healthy right arm, secured his aim with his injured left, and pulled the trigger.

60

Gibson detected the sound of the shots around the time Cooper's second bullet struck the crane's protective cage. He dove too late; Cooper's third bullet penetrated his massive latissimus dorsi, but had about as much effect on Gibson's health as a paintball pellet might have had on an elephant. Bullets four and five tore through the air precisely where Gibson's head had been positioned before his dive.

The evasive action got him safely over and behind the body of the crane, but also resulted in the violent jerking of the crane's control levers. The command was duly executed by the hydraulic system operating the arm of the crane, and under the propulsion of the violently whipping arm that held it, the fully loaded warhead container swung across the remaining expanse of lagoon Gibson had intended for it to cross. Packing tremendous momentum, the crate smashed headlong into the side of the Ukrainian submarine.

The stress brought on by the collision proved too great for the three padlocks Gibson had used to secure the container's lid. Had all eight been sealed, the lid might have held, but with only three locks struggling to contain the violence of the smash, the container's latches snapped clean off. Responding to gravity, the body of the container immediately dropped, yawing open at the hinges as it clanged a second time against the metal skin of the submarine. Two of the warheads tumbled immediately from their foam nests in the container and splashed into the lagoon; a third slid halfway out, its rounded head slipping from its slot but still holding. Having shed seven-hundred-odd pounds of bulk with the loss of the two warheads, the container then righted itself.

Held into the foam by the added width of the harness Gibson had left wrapped around it, the fourth bomb remained wedged in its slot.

Cooper stayed at it with the MAC-10, hammering another half-dozen bullets into the body of the crane in hopes it would blow, or maybe tilt over and fall on Muscle-head. Bullet holes cut into the crane's yellow skin; a rubber gasket snapped, releasing a geyser of hydraulic fluid; sparks flew, and a wisp of smoke rose from the crane's engine block. Finally, the engine sputtered, then died.

The instant Cooper paused, opting to save the remaining bullets in his clip, Gibson reached around the side of the crane with his Glock and took a pair of potshots. He missed by a few feet, and Cooper got off a couple more—realizing as the bullets *whing*ed off the crane and *pock*ed off the lava wall that he'd fired the last of the shells from his clip. He dropped, making sure to turn away from the place where Laramie lay, and ducked back into the tunnel. As he moved, he heard a series of shots fired by Gibson, one of the bullets clipping the SEAL-issue cross-terrain disposable boot on Cooper's right foot but otherwise coming up empty.

Gibson's next pull on the trigger, Cooper heard, resulted in a dry click.

The thrum of the four diesel generators groaned on outside the cavern, and the third of the W-76 warheads, tail dipping deeper from its slot in the container, finally slid, like a fish from a dock, into the water of the lagoon.

Given the relative silence, Cooper guessed that Gibson was doing something smarter than he was—maybe sneaking around behind him, for instance. Stumbling forward, Cooper folded the MAC-10 between his good elbow and his waist, and, grimacing, fumbled through the mess of blood, guts, and canvas jersey formerly composing the maid's stomach in search of another clip. He snagged nothing but muck until he heard the sound of metal against rock, and then it was heavy in his hand—full, loaded with all thirty-two bullets, and just about enough, Cooper thought, to remove Spike Gibson from cavern and earth.

He yanked the clip out of the mess of gore and struggled to get it into the gun.

Gibson came out from his hiding place and strode across the cargo cave.

As Cooper took his best shot at jamming the slippery clip into its slot, he was faced with the realization that he was completely fucked.

No way would he get the clip loaded in time.

Gibson stepped over Lana's body and grinned.

"Albert!" he exclaimed. "How are you, buddy?"

Cooper resorted to a pathetic surprise attack, ferociously whacking at Gibson's face with the butt of the MAC-10, a distraction that bought him about two seconds. Cooper felt the gun land on the hard bone of Gibson's left cheek at least once, but the bodybuilder soon threw his heavy forearm in the way of Cooper's thrashing blows and swatted the gun from his hands.

Then Gibson proceeded to unload on him.

Releasing the raw, sinewy power he'd stored in bulk form across years of exercise, Gibson pummeled Cooper with successive blows. Even with the bullet that had pierced his right lat, Gibson had both arms to work with, and Cooper's one-armed defensive maneuvers did nothing to stop the creatine-boosted onslaught. He tore open the skin on Cooper's face with the blows, loosened teeth with elbow shots, broke Cooper's nose for maybe the twenty-seventh time in Cooper's life with a succession of head butts. When Cooper could no longer stand, Gibson held him upright, grasping the collar of Cooper's body armor with his left fist while bashing Cooper's face with his right.

Finally Gibson let go, and Cooper dropped like a dress on the body of a woman who'd just had her shoulder straps snipped. Gibson straightened, inclined his head, breathed deeply of the foul air of the cavern, and, vaguely satisfied, turned and retraced his route across the lava rock floor.

61

The pool of blood from Lana's intestines seeped along the cargo cave's floor, moving along the same downward slope that helped the electric cart propel itself into the pocket cavern. The blood, however, failed to make the full trip. Instead, it dripped into a crack in the floor, where it found a new slope to follow, and flowed into the lagoon.

Accustomed to the routine deposit of expired disposable laborers and totalitarian dictators here, a school of eleven tiger sharks—roaming the region independently, but linked by hunger and conditioning—knew that when blood was released into the water in a certain location beneath Mango Cay, a meal was in store. Thus, once Lana's blood began to perfume the water—blooming outward from the crack in the floor where it emptied into the lagoon—the sharks arrived in short order beneath the belly of the Ukrainian sub. Soon, each shark, its nervous system confused at the lack of an available meal, began thrashing around and biting at random. The frantic pattern of cannibalistic abuse only worsened when the three lost warheads, splashing into the lagoon, proved inedible.

Prior experience, though, supported the possibility that more food was on the way, and so—driven by a primordial hope—the eleven sharks, each mildly confused and fully pissed off, remained within the confines of the lagoon.

Gibson vaulted from the dock to the nose of the sub and surveyed the damage. The collision between container and hull had put a wide dent in the side of the boat, but the dent was close enough to the waterline that it did not appear to have damaged the corrugated steel door he'd need to seal in order to keep the freight bay from springing a leak.

The container itself was lodged too low to drag or flip into the freight bay; it rested against the body of the submarine with its lid draped partially across the top of the sub, the main body of the container dangling nearly to the water. The good news for Gibson was that the fourth warhead occupied the slot closest to the sub, so that if he could get himself down to the main body of the container, it wouldn't be difficult to grab hold of the bomb. Of course there was the issue of the warhead tipping the scales at just under four hundred pounds, but Gibson chose not to acknowledge this as a factor.

He climbed out of the open freight bay onto the bent container lid. Scaling down to the container's main body, he lodged his left foot into the base of one of the empty warhead slots. Seizing the warhead's harness, he disconnected then reconnected the various clips, buckles, and Velcro straps, securing the harness both to the warhead and around his shoulders and waist.

Thinking he could buy the leverage he needed by wedging his right foot against the skin of the submarine, Gibson planted himself, legs splayed, as a bridge between container and sub. He tested his footing with a bouncing motion. It held.

Tightening the straps, he sucked in a series of thick, heaving breaths, and lifted. The warhead began to inch from its slot, Gibson the bodybuilder doing a single squat rep under a 375-pound barbell. In fact, he just about had the rounded head of the warhead's heavier side fully out of the foam padding when his right foot slipped on the wet steel of the submarine and he flipped sideways and splashed wildly into the water.

The warhead slunk back into its padded slot, so that the harness straps, affixed dually to Gibson and the warhead, prevented Gibson from dropping entirely beneath the surface. His right leg plunged into the lagoon, almost to the hip, but that was it. He flailed for one of the container's latches with his right arm, but since it took him two attempts to grab hold, his escape from the water was accomplished a fraction of a second late.

Battling for position once the splash had alerted her to the possibility of food, one of the tiger sharks shot directly toward the source of this agitation and clamped down on the first flesh she found. When she locked her multiple rows of teeth around the muscled ligament and bone of Spike Gibson's right shin, it took a few frenzied, thrashing jerks of her head to rip the bite off in her mouth, but, fiercely determined to eat, she succeeded in biting off a thick chunk, which she swallowed whole before spinning around to take another run at the offering.

Gibson screamed as his foot was torn from his leg midway up the shin, but when his ankle and foot separated from the rest of his leg, he popped high enough out of the water to grasp another, higher latch. Making a scrambling left-leg thrust into the padding, he pulled himself back onto the body of the container.

Seeing the stump where his right foot had previously been, Gibson first whimpered like a boy, then cursed at the top of his lungs, then screamed a level-toned roar of fury that echoed through the cargo cave.

Due partly to sheer brute strength borne of more than a decade of weight training, partly to unadulterated greed, and largely due to a freakishly large and instantaneous excretion of adrenaline into his bloodstream, Gibson, bearing down on his one good leg and pulling with bursting forearms from one latch to the next, somehow managed to uproot the W-76 warhead from its slot a second time and lift its immense weight fully out of the container.

Screaming and grunting in staccato bursts, every muscle popping with striated arteries, Gibson hefted the bomb across the six-foot gap spanning the container and the submarine's freight bay. He set the warhead on the rim of the freight bay, threw himself over the edge, and, warhead still tottering on the rim, body half inside, Gibson snatched an exposed interior length of pipe and pulled on it until both he and the warhead rolled down and in.

Like a tug towing a barge, the falling weight of the warhead towed Gibson the eight long feet to the bottom of the freight bay, where his dual collision with the bomb and the floor crushed one of his shoulders. The arm and collarbone on either side of his shoulder snapped with a dull stereophonic crunch.

Otherwise, Gibson survived the tumble unscathed.

His heart pounding to the bursting point, Gibson nonetheless had the presence of mind to detach himself from the warhead harness, stand, and hop to the rusted hand crank controlling the bay's retractable lid. One-armed and one-legged, he slowly turned the crank until he had the overhead door sealed shut. Taking an additional three minutes to tie off and wrap his stub leg with the shirt he wore, Gibson then ducked into the control room and executed the series of commands that would put the sub in gear.

A moment later, Spike Gibson, piloting his Ukrainian sub, dipped beneath the surface of the cargo cave's underwater lagoon and vanished permanently from the island called Mango Cay.

62

Cooper had always been able to take a punch; back in the world now relegated to his nightmares, it was one of the ways he'd been able to lull his original captors into complacency too. This time, though, like a stupid iron-jawed fighter who'd stretched his career one fight too far, he had the feeling the beating he'd just taken would eventually leave him harebrained or dead. If he didn't get himself to a very good hospital very soon, he'd be joining Marcel a little earlier than planned.

It wasn't long before a crushing pain replaced the numbness in his head and shoulders. He came out of the beating with a headache made for an elephant, but between waves of agony and nausea he started to be able to see around the cavern again. He wiped the blood, sweat, and grime from the narrow slits once known as his eyes and saw Laramie there beside him, exactly where she'd been before. He could feel that his face had been torn open across his cheekbones and lips. He could taste the blood flowing as he moved; he tried to move his jaw, couldn't, and decided it was broken. Feeling as though he weighed four thousand pounds, he performed a clumsy one-armed push-up and succeeded in pulling his good knee up under him. He shifted his weight from arm to leg and took a look around.

He could see—after another wiping of his eyes—that Spike Gibson, the fourth warhead, and the submarine were all gone. The lights in the cavern were failing, the black haze now so thick and low it reached almost to his face, crouched as he was on the cavern floor. He spotted movement through a doorway across the cavern, braced for another fight, then realized he was seeing the rear of the golf cart they'd pushed down the tunnel. The cart was bobbing against something that blocked its path.

He took about five minutes walking over to it, but once there, looked below the seats and unearthed what he remembered having seen on their journey through the tunnel: the maid had stowed their SLKs beneath the front seat. He slumped behind the steering wheel, solved the issue with the pinned accelerator, and drove back to Laramie. Once there, he opened one of the SLKs, found its first aid kit, and, through a remedy composed of strips of the shirt he was wearing, a portion of his body armor, and the contents of the first aid kit, did his best to stem the flow from Laramie's wounds. He pulled from the same SLK the homing device Popeye had told them to use before the carriage turned back into a pumpkin, and pocketed it. Not that it mattered any longer, but he found himself wondering whether his camera was still inside his knapsack and, figuring Laramie would want to know, checked, and found it there.

Then he zipped both SLKs shut and strapped them on.

Small and light though she was, as Cooper lifted and loaded Laramie's unconscious body onto the rear seat of the cart, he decided it was one of the most physically challenging tasks he'd ever endured—second only to his trek up the hill with Alphonse strapped to his waist. Still, he got Laramie aboard, fell into place again behind the steering wheel, and drove into the transport tunnel.

The mud made for slow going, but the lack of a warhead in the backseat helped. He found the side passage they'd passed on the way in, followed it for a while, eventually saw what appeared to be daylight, gunned the cart up a short slope, bounced through a rut, and shot suddenly into the blinding midday sunlight. He thought of the parable he'd heard about the man who saw only shadows on the wall of the cave in which he lived, until, years later, he turned around, discovering that the shadows had been caused by the sun he hadn't known was there. He tried to remember where he'd heard this, or read it, but couldn't.

Turning past the main building he'd noticed from their earlier visit with Gibson, he crossed the marble tiles of the poolside lounge and bounced onto the white sand beach. Reaching the beach's trio of cedar deck chairs, he stomped the brake into place and, fighting a set of back spasms from the effort, lifted Laramie from the cart into one of the chairs. He pulled the homing beacon from his pocket, punched the red button protruding from one end of it, set the beacon on Laramie's lap, and unloaded himself into the chair beside her.

It was as Cooper sat there, his swollen, pulpy head drooped, that the beach below him began to vibrate. From his limited perspective, staring down, he saw grains of sand tumble from the crests of the miniature hills built by the wind.

Then, against the sky behind him, a glorious explosion of white smoke and yellow flame burst from the peak of Mango Cay's lone hill. The roar of an immense fire raged,

Cooper feeling the heat of its flame against the back of his neck even from three-quarters of a mile away, and the first blunt-nosed C-4 Trident I missile blasted from its silo beneath the hill. The missile rose through the clouds of its own rocket fuel and the diesel exhaust until, as Cooper turned to watch, it cleared the smoke and sliced into the clear blue Caribbean sky. To Cooper the missile looked like a photograph of itself cut and pasted on a glossy, bluish purple background intended to represent the sky.

He blinked in the blinding yellow glare, turned away, and let his swollen head droop so low that his broken jaw almost touched his chest.

"Aw, crap," he said.

When the first of Operation Blunt Fist's missiles reached an elevation of five hundred feet above sea level, three simultaneous notifications were immediately transmitted by the North American Aerospace Defense Command's primary computer system. The first notification went to the staff manning a room on the grounds of Peterson Air Force Base, NORAD's headquarters near Colorado Springs. The second notification was sent by the equivalent of a multimedia instant messaging service to a series of government officials. Lou Ebbers, Alan Kircher, Carlos Muske, Secretary of Defense Wally Parke, the chairman of the joint chiefs of staff, the vice president, and the president were among those receiving immediate notification.

The third missive triggered an instantaneous escalation of the U.S. military's readiness status to DEFCON-1, known also as "maximum force readiness." Civilian agencies were placed on EMERGCON alert.

Under DEFCON-1, the required approvals for a counter-launch of American strategic nuclear assets could be granted, based on historical precedent from simulation exercises, no faster than seven minutes following the moment at which the president received notification that enemy missiles had got airborne. Transit time for the average U.S. ICBM to just about any worldwide target, including one in the Caribbean, involved a minimum of sixteen minutes, due to the ballistic trajectory of the weapons.

Thus, in all likelihood—if in fact it were ever ordered at all—at least twenty-three minutes would pass before any U.S. nuclear counterstrike could reach Mango Cay.

Sitting with his head slumped forward, staring blankly out at the lagoon, Cooper realized something.

Somebody had turned the float plane around.

It now faced the water, rather than the beach, and while this might ordinarily have held no particular meaning, with the fireworks show under way behind him, Cooper had been waging a brief internal skirmish.

It occurred to him that, depending on where the missiles were aimed, somebody was going to have to stop the launch before all forty-two caught air—and it didn't currently seem as if Washington, Langley, or anybody else was making any progress toward shutting this thing down. Cooper also considered that if Washington *were* to do something, the way the response might happen didn't bode well for anybody sitting on the cedar beach chairs along Mango Cay's blue lagoon.

He wondered how the hell *he* had drawn the shortest straw—that of all the expert, capable people who might have been perfectly suited to stop the ignition of four rows of Trident missiles aimed God-knows-where, it was an irascible, emotionally scarred societal reject with a made-up name who was the only conscious one on-site, and therefore the only one with any shot at doing a goddamn thing about bin-Laden's ultimate wet dream come true.

He wasn't sure what the new orientation of the float plane meant, but he knew it meant something, so he dipped his head and closed his eyes. He watched the backs of his eyelids as thoughts of Spike Gibson, Deng Jiang, the bartender, the maid, and Popeye floated past; he listened to what he remembered each of them saying, saw what he'd seen each of them doing. He gathered the sum of the impressions, splashed them into a blender, and let whirl. Some of the concoction spilled from the cylinder—blends of images, sounds, sensations—until, at length, one particular dollop splashed across the frame of the picture-in-a-picture window and stuck. What he saw, and heard, was Spike Gibson barking orders to his maid inside the missile cavern.

Get in, bring me another two hundred mill, and get off the island, he'd said.

In addition to the value of the fourth warhead, the bodybuilding behemoth had been talking about something else: they had planned for the maid to leave the island on her own. Presumably, of course, only to meet up again with Gibson and collect her share—at least presumably for the maid. That, he suspected, was not what Spike Gibson presumed.

Cooper had met people like Gibson before—at least somewhat like him. In the world of such people, he knew, there existed no such conceits as comradeship, brotherhood, or marriage; accordingly, Cooper understood as well as if he'd known Gibson his whole life that there was no way in hell the man would allow a single member of his staff to survive Mango Cay, let alone share the take.

And yet the maid had been instructed to take the plane.

He thought about this for a moment, Cooper considering Gibson's plan for the maid's ill-fated escape in the context of the highly boring reading he'd done some three weeks back on the beach at Conch Bay. He decided that the idea that came to mind represented, at best, an idiotic long shot—but that, he mused, is why we highly trained, stupid goons exist.

To roll the dice on the idiotic long shots no one else is dumb enough to try.

He stood and limped down the beach to the float plane. As he approached the plane's pontoons, a burst of artificial sunlight and billowing white smoke shot from the hill and another missile cleared its silo and tore into the sky. He checked his watch and placed the launches about two minutes apart.

Thinking about how many two-minute sets it would take him to accomplish his aim, Cooper began a systematic search of the plane. He explored every cavity where Gibson might have hidden what he was looking for, knowing full well that Muscle-head would need to have stowed it in a place where the maid would not have been able to find it. This said a lot, considering the haggard-faced bitch had looked like a person with some pretty good ideas about how to keep people from killing her. There was a chance, however—Cooper trying to think things through the way Gibson might—that the maid's search, had she lived long enough to conduct it, might only have been sufficient to convince herself that her boss hadn't fucked her over.

He checked behind the engine block, beneath the seats, under the rug in the cargo hold, below the toilet seat in the lavatory apparently built for passengers the size of chimpanzees. He was forced to wipe the blood and exhaust grime from his swollen eyelids three or four times a minute just to see what he was doing, but in due course he found an access panel on the plane's tail. In order to remove it, he had to retrieve a wrapped package of tools he'd discovered under the pilot's seat; during the time it took him to get back and forth between the two sections of the plane, another missile rose into the sky from the hill.

Behind the panel he found a hydraulic assembly which he assumed controlled the plane's rudder. He stabbed his head through the opening, peered through his eye slits, and discovered within—held against the plane's interior skin with a series of suction cups and a stripe of Velcro—something that appeared to be a porcelain brick. Noting a barometric pressure gauge and a series of wires affixed to one edge, Cooper immediately knew what he was looking at, and it certainly wasn't a porcelain brick.

Judging from its color, he figured the chunky cube for either PENO or Semtex plastic explosive compound.

Cooper also figured the barometric pressure gauge affixed to the bomb was designed to accomplish for Gibson—and his late, doomed maid—precisely what Cooper sought to accomplish via the harebrained scheme percolating in his bruised mind.

He unfastened the explosive brick from the interior of the float plane's tail, tucked it under his good arm, and headed back up the beach. As he sped across the poolside marble and turned the corner past the Greathouse behind the wheel of the cart, another missile rocketed from its home and knifed into the sky.

63

Because of its proximity and the weapons it had on board, the destroyer USS *Scavenger* did not need to endure a sixteen-minute trajectory to apply its firepower against Mango Cay. Firing the *Scavenger*'s inventory of deadly weaponry, though, wasn't as simple a task as it might have seemed. Martinique, for instance, was part of France, and since the launching of cruise missiles against a NATO ally wasn't included on the crew's list of preauthorized actions, a recommendation had to be submitted, and approval granted from the Pentagon, before counterattack even became a possibility.

Further, the missiles rocketing from Mango Cay were not automatically understood to be a threat to the United States. Accordingly, it wasn't until twenty-two minutes following the first Trident's clearing of the hill—eleven missiles in—that the *Scavenger*'s initial salvo came.

To kick things off, the *Scavenger*'s captain targeted a pair of Tomahawk cruise missiles at the island's main heat source and sent four SN-3 "missile killers" after the two most recently launched ICBMs. At a distance of twelve miles from the launch point, the SN-3s had the deck stacked against them and went 0-for-4 in the first wave, narrowly missing missiles 8 and 9 as they climbed out of range. The Tomahawks reached their intended target, but without "bunker-busting" capabilities, merely succeeded in shearing eight feet of soil and surface rock from the crown of the island's hill.

Jerking and crumbling, the missile cavern survived the first wave of Tomahawk missiles, and Operation Blunt Fist continued forth.

Cooper crashed into the wall of the transport tunnel. Once he cleared the debris that had fallen in his path he was able to get going again, but as he approached the missile cavern, the tunnel was becoming so thick with diesel smoke and rocket exhaust that if he weren't able to cover his nose and mouth with some sort of filter, he was sure he'd suffocate, or simply die from the concentrated intake of too many toxins. He resorted to tearing off a piece of the pants he wore, which he tied over his face, a task made near impossible by the bullet lodged in his left shoulder blade.

He kept banging the cart into the walls of the tunnel, his course impossible to control as he steered through the field of rock shards dislodged by the Tomahawk strikes. Soon the toxic haze brightened a fraction, and in another twenty feet he was able to make out the shape of the doorway leading to the main cavern. Using the illuminated doorway as a target, he floored it, keeping the cart off the tunnel walls as best he could, and in another five seconds he shot from the tunnel and found himself immediately assaulted by a wall of heat.

The temperature in the missile cavern was pushing the mercury to a minimum of 165 degrees. In his condition Cooper knew he'd probably last about five minutes in this kind of heat, and with each successive launch—he'd heard three more while crashing his way down the tunnel—he felt sure the cavern would get another ten or fifteen degrees hotter.

He pulled Gibson's altitude-triggered brick of plastic explosive and the bag of warhead-extraction tools from the cart. He had to hold the heavy block in his right hand with the tool bag folded under the same arm—Cooper the one-armed man, he thought, here to save the fucking day.

He would have to pick the right missile. If he chose the next missile in the launch sequence, he'd be killed as it blasted off; if he worked on the forty-second, forty-one Tridents would make it out. He limped from one row to the next until he found a suitable number, settling on 16. He could see through the toxic haze that missiles 1 through 12, all in the same row, were gone, their silos burned to pieces. Paint and excess fuel and whatever else had been at the base of 12 burned in pockets of flame.

Cooper opened the cage door of the silo elevator, stepped in, and flipped the lever. The cavern shook with another impact from a heavy blast and another, less resounding explosion, both originating somewhere above the cavern. With no idea as to the source or nature of these external detonations, Cooper understood only that these blasts were having zero effect on the launch sequence and pelting him with clumps of lava rock in the process. With the elevator rising, he could see he was about to slip into the dankest portion of the haze cloud; he sucked in a maxed-out breath of midlevel air and held it. When he reached the access panel he got to work prying it off. He could already feel his body losing its battle against the heat.

He got the panel off and it tumbled to the ground, banging back and forth between the missile and silo on its journey down. The cavern shook beneath him, the silo trembling, then weaving, and suddenly a wave of intense heat and deafening noise blasted him from all sides as the missile in silo 13 underwent primary ignition. Cooper had to stop working and cover his ears. The noise chattered his skull as the missile rose within the cavern, the blast of wind from its launch temporarily clearing the cavern of the poisonous haze; then the silo door in the roof of the cavern folded downward, revealing the sky above, and the missile shot upward, slow at first, but accelerating exponentially. As the base of the missile passed through the ceiling of the cavern, the intense heat, shrieking wind, and jet-fuel-scented exhaust filled the cavern completely.

Then the missile was gone.

Cooper's hair was singed, his eyebrows burned completely off. Putting his free-diving lung capacity to use, he continued to hold the breath he'd taken on the way up, and ducked into the warhead bay. He secured Gibson's bomb as best he could to the skin of what he figured for the nearest warhead, picking a spot where the warhead, if that's what it was, appeared exposed. Then—lungs exploding, his skin on fire—Cooper jumped aboard the lift, pulled the lever, and waited with the increasing panic of a drowning man for the elevator to make its way down.

Alternating between passing out, vomiting, and crashing into the walls of the transport tunnel, he came awake for successive brief instants of the return trip, enough to recall where he was and mash his foot against the cart's accelerator before passing out again until the next crash into the wall. With each burst in this circuit of his own private demolition derby, he got the cart another fifteen or twenty yards along the muddy uphill slope of the tunnel; as he got farther he was able to breathe cleanly again, pulling in massive heaves of air and smoke alike while he sucked down enough oxygen to keep him momentarily conscious.

Negotiating the last turn past the Greathouse, Cooper the zombie began to lose consciousness, his head dangling forward and banging against the steering wheel while the cart, lacking any human hand to pilot its wheel, careened downhill, building speed, wobbling, then roving up for an instant on two wheels, utterly out of control.

About forty feet from the pool, the cart's velocity approached fifty miles an hour as, with no idea where or who he was or what was going on, Cooper whacked his head against the aluminum dashboard and slumped, unconscious, the world around him going black as his brain tuned out and shut down.

64

Once his equipment detected the signal from Cooper's homing beacon, Popeye's first action had been to contact Captain Sampson. Communicating with Sampson over his radio headset, he explained that the source of the beacon's signal was most likely the civilians the *Hampton* had retrieved earlier that morning. He told Sampson why the civilians had asked to be deposited on the island to begin with—that they had been onto whatever was going down on the island well before any of the shit had hit the fan. Popeye then said he thought it was worth Sampson's consideration to grant him permission to retrieve the civilians and bring them back aboard the sub, and to wait for him while he did it.

Sampson, who knew a lot more than Popeye about the situation above water, remained silent for somewhere around ten seconds before telling Popeye he would give him only twenty minutes—no discussion, no extension, and no guarantee he'd even wait that long.

"If additional shit hits the fan, SEAL," Sampson said, "we will not be here when you get back. It's your risk to take."

Popeye accepted the terms and, piloting the MSLC at top speed, reached the shore of the resort's lagoon in seven minutes. Two minutes later, he was in the process of slinging Laramie over his shoulder when the screeching tires of the careening golf cart sounded out on the poolside tile. Popeye turned just in time to witness the cart skid onto its side, slam directly into the poolside bar, then spin, catch, and roll end over end in a headlong whirl that concluded in the changing room of the nearest poolside cabana. The cart's long-since-unconscious occupant had been ejected from his seat during the second-to-last roll across the poolside tile, and, following a bounce, splash-landed in the pool.

Popeye mobilized, and from the time he pulled Cooper from the pool, it took him ten minutes and forty-seven seconds to get across the lagoon, out into the depths, and back into the clutches of the SEAL Hole, his passengers intact, latch closed, and Captain Zeke Sampson notified of his arrival thirteen seconds shy of the deadline Sampson had fully intended to enforce.

With Cooper out cold, Neither Sampson nor Popeye could have known how fortunate they had been that Popeye sealed the hatch between the SEAL Hole and the sea at the very moment he did.

Missile 16 launched much the way the preceding fifteen had before it. Flooding the cavern with flames, heat, and spent rocket fuel, it pushed partially up through the silo hole at the peak of the missile cavern, its blunt nose beginning to emerge from the hill above. Then, as the missile crossed the designated height of seventy-eight feet above sea level, the magnetic bubble within the air pressure-based altitude trigger of Spike Gibson's conventional bomb snapped into place, causing the strip of metal that housed the magnetic bubble to strike an electronic contact. A current then initiated the detonation of the Semtex compound.

The yield of the conventional explosion that followed was easily sufficient to vaporize the float plane Lana had planned on using to flee the island but would not, ordinarily, have been of adequate yield to penetrate or otherwise impact the skin of a W-76 warhead. The second round of SN-3s fired from the *Scavenger,* for instance, had taken down the fourteenth missile in a ball of flame, but no further detonations had resulted.

Missile 16, however, was one of the original Tridents Deng had salvaged from the USS *Chameleon*. Sustaining water pressure of some thirty-eight times that found at sea level, the warhead had incurred substantial weakening of its infrastructure and developed a subsurface longitudinal fracture that went undetected by Deng's scientists. Over time, the internal fracture had broken the warhead's skin, a minuscule crack reaching from nose to fantail.

Detonation of a W-76 thermonuclear warhead occurred when the bomb's conventional explosive charge, called HE for high explosive, was triggered by an armed altitude trigger functioning in the reverse capacity of the device in Gibson's bomb. Once triggered, the conventional HE explosion directed one subcritical U-235 mass against a larger, supercritical mass—110-plus pounds of fully enriched uranium. The splitting of the U-235 atom resulted in an uncontrolled chain reaction that took place in its entirety in under a millionth of a second.

To reduce size and weight, the HE substance chosen by the engineers was impervious only to heat of temperatures up to fifteen hundred degrees Fahrenheit. W-76 production had therefore been ordered by the Pentagon inclusive of this single known risk: that an accidental ignition of a substance that burned at exceedingly high temperature could cause the detonation of the HE compound, and therefore trigger the nuke blast, were the skin of the warhead somehow breached.

At the eighty-foot mark, the explosion of the Semtex compound ignited the fuel in missile 16's booster rocket. The dual explosions breached the skin of the flawed warhead, and the eighteen-hundred-degree heat of the explosions ignited the HE.

It was in this manner that a thermonuclear explosion occurred atop what had previously been a lush Caribbean island called Mango Cay.

The breach in the warhead's skin permitted a significant percentage of the energy released by the HE blast to escape. In the end, this meant that Cooper had managed to deliver only a low-efficiency nuclear explosion amounting to a yield of under one-half of one percent of the potential of a technically sound W-76 warhead. The blast nonetheless laid its wrath upon the world immediately surrounding its flash point.

The detonation vaporized the hill and decimated every item within the missile cavern, including the ignition and trigger mechanisms for Deng's secret, forty-third missile. A rim of water extending two hundred feet from shore immediately boiled, while an eight-foot tidal wave spread at great speed in an expanding circle from the explosion's epicenter. Instantaneously generated winds of nearly 250 miles per hour churned the atmosphere and the ocean's surface across a five-mile radius from ground zero.

Nearby, the USS *Scavenger* incurred debilitating structural damage and was nearly capsized by the one-two punch of the initial blast concussion and subsequent tidal wave. Beneath the surface of the ocean, the force behind the initial concussive blast was reduced by nearly fifty percent per quarter mile, so that the initial sledgehammer strike of the blast wave had less impact on the *Hampton* than on the *Scavenger*—but still, the *Hampton*'s crew, along with its limited civilian guest roster, got tossed around the sub like confetti in a windstorm.

Some repair work necessitated a delay in the provision of medical attention to the civilians in the *Hampton*'s SEAL Hole, but once Captain Sampson regained control of the vessel and conditions returned to normal, the civilians were taken to the sick bay and treated by the submarine's excellent medical staff.

Cooper and Laramie snoozed through the whole ordeal.

65

Of the fourteen Tridents that were able to clear the Mango Cay vicinity, only missiles 3 and 13 penetrated the NORAD-guided strategic defense weaponry to reach their targets within the borders of the United States. Missile 13 was a replica created by Deng's team of scientists and turned out to be a dud; failing to release its MIRVs, it crashed uselessly into the tarmac on the longest runway of one of its four intended targets, Ohio's Wright-Patterson Air Force Base.

Missile 3, an original, delivered fifty percent of its payload. Due to advancing age, poor maintenance, and the physical abuse wrought upon them by the sinking of the USS *Chameleon,* two of the missile's MIRVs nose-dived past the altitude-trigger height assigned their warheads and disintegrated on impact well off target near Mount Shasta, in northern California; MIRVs 3 and 4 delivered their warheads between ten and fifteen miles off course, at an elevation of approximately two thousand feet above, though well east, of the additional California-based targets of Edwards Air Force Base and Camp Pendleton.

With this limited list of strikes, Operation Blunt Fist failed to deliver the punishing blow Deng had sought. The planned invasions by the member nations of the so-called revolutionary brotherhood, already on hold following the demise of its leaders, were hastily aborted. The dual thermonuclear explosions nonetheless caused the deaths of 4,784 American citizens, in addition to 673 foreign visitors, within twenty seconds of their detonations. Authorities estimated another three to four thousand casualties would result from extreme radiation exposure outside of the core blast zone.

Once certain intelligence came to light—including photographs retrieved from a severely damaged digital camera strapped to the back of a Caribbean-based CIA operative—the United States implemented a series of military actions referred to by the president as "global peace-keeping efforts." Amassing significant naval power in the South China Sea to deter China from responding, the American military effected an occupation of Taiwan to ensure the republic's independence; peace-keeping or defensive occupations followed in Yemen, South Korea, and eight other nations around the globe.

The president used the catastrophe to his advantage in two additional ways: first, in a series of diplomatic summits with China's newly appointed premier, he gained sweeping free-trade concessions hugely favorable to American corporations; second, his stratospheric popularity ratings discouraged Senator Alan Kircher from seeking the Republican presidential nomination, virtually assuring the president's re-election.

66

Laramie was trying to get oriented. She found she was coming awake in a hospital bed someplace where the sun shone through her window. Palm trees swayed and flipped in an easy breeze. An anesthesiologist, and then a surgeon, visited her, each examining her before informing her she was doing just fine. She asked the surgeon where she was, and he told her she'd been brought here to South Miami Hospital by the U.S. Navy. When she asked why they'd brought her to Miami, he told her it was because of his expertise—that the navy relied on him for such things. When she asked what his area of expertise happened to be, he told her he was pretty good at repairing internal damage from bullet wounds, but that she didn't need to worry, since the bullet they'd been concerned with had failed to exact any long-term toll on its path through her lower back and upper hip.

She asked him whether there had been anyone else the navy had sent to him for treatment, and he told her there hadn't been, at least not recently. Laramie thanked the surgeon and he left.

She fell asleep the moment he was gone.

The sun was still out, though more orange than yellow, when she woke up again to see a nurse standing in the doorway of her room. The nurse apologized for the intrusion, but informed her there was a visitor who had been waiting in the lobby for some time, and was quite insistent on seeing her. When Laramie asked who it was, the nurse told her that the man had identified himself as Jacob Bartleby.

Laramie tried to shrug but found this to be unexpectedly challenging and discovered they'd put a splint on her right arm. It kept the arm pinned against her body.

"I don't know anyone by that name," she said, "but I suppose you can send him in."

A moment later, a short man wearing a navy blue business suit entered through the doorway, smiled curtly, and said, "Thank you for seeing me. I understand you're recovering from surgery, and so, will be brief."

"Thank you." Laramie felt vaguely woozy.

The man set a briefcase on the table beside the bed, opened it, withdrew a manila folder, and shut the briefcase.

"Please allow me to introduce myself—as the song goes," he said and smiled at his own joke. Laramie nodded dutifully.

"I represent a real estate investment firm incorporated in the Cayman Islands," he said. "From time to time my clients make strategic investments in exotic resort properties and related recreational assets."

"Recreational assets?"

"Deep-sea charter vessels, SCUBA training schools, tropical—"

"How can I help you? Excuse me, but I'm very tired."

"Of course." He withdrew a notarized sheet of paper from the manila folder and turned it around so Laramie could see it.

"As I understand it," Bartleby said, "this is the deed to your condominium property in Falls Church, Virginia. I'll leave this on the table for you, or would be happy to arrange storage in a safe-deposit box at the bank of your choosing."

"Deed—what day is it?" Laramie attempted to sit up and look around for a wall calendar but found she could neither sit up nor find a calendar, so she gave up and said, "The payment couldn't be that late, could it?"

"You're not late at all. Allow me to explain: my clients have paid off your mortgage."

"Excuse me?"

"My clients understand you to have been suspended without pay by your employer. And while my clients believe it unlikely the suspension will hold once the independent counsel submits its report on the matter to which your suspension relates, they have nonetheless arranged for your utilities, auto loan, health insurance, and gym membership to be paid in full for a two-year period beginning on the date of your discharge from the hospital. The U.S. Navy is apparently somewhat more appreciative of your recent activities than your employer, as they are footing the bill of your current hospital stay."

Bartleby withdrew a second sheet of paper to which a small blue rectangular slip had been stapled. Laramie watched, wondering whether the odd words coming from this man's lips meant that she was still asleep.

"My clients are periodically in need of research consultants—a scout, I believe they call the role—and a source has identified you as a candidate for one of these positions." He turned the sheet of paper around, and Laramie could see that the smaller slip of paper was a check. "This is an independent consulting agreement which you would need to sign, or can execute by deposit of the attached cashier's check. The mortgage payoff and utilities advances are in no way contingent upon execution of this agreement. Incidentally, the check is made out in the sum of one hundred thirty-one thousand dollars."

Laramie blinked and said, "Two years of my salary."

"I believe that is how the figure was calculated."

Bartleby stacked the contract, check, and deed on the bedside table, withdrew a pen from the breast pocket of his jacket, set the pen on the contract, then removed another item from the folder: a thin, colorful paperback book.

"You would be required to travel extensively but would receive a per diem and be entitled to first-class travel and accommodations. All such arrangements would be subject to your approval, and paid by my clients on a direct-billing basis." He held up the book, which Laramie saw was called *Caribbean Hideaways*. "Your assigned scouting duties would include the list of resorts described in this publication. You would be required to submit a report on each resort at the conclusion of your stay. My clients will provide you a notebook computer with wireless Internet access for this purpose."

He set the book on the table.

"If the terms of my clients' offer are acceptable to you, sign the consulting agreement at your leisure and fax the executed agreement to the number provided. And I apologize," he said, "but I nearly forgot to mention that you would of course not be expected to travel alone, and may bring a guest. My clients would pay the travel expenses of your guest as well."

Laramie narrowed her eyes, deciding it must have been the anesthesia that had made her a little slow on the uptake. "Mr. Bartleby," she said. "One question on the guest that you mention. Are you saying I can bring anybody of my choosing?"

"Anybody? Yes. Oh. Well, anybody but one, apparently."

"And that would be—?"

Bartleby nodded noncommittally. "I was told that an individual by the name of 'Professor Eddie Rothgeb' is not permitted as a guest on your assignments."

"Ah," Laramie said.

"But anyone else is fine."

"Of course."

Bartleby offered his curt but pleasant smile one last time. "Thank you again for your time, Miss Laramie," he said. "Speedy recovery."

Then he left.

Laramie got about halfway through the complicated series of actions required to crane her neck and get a look at the book and short stack of papers; then she stopped in mid-crane and slumped back into her mattress.

Considering there was a good chance that the odd visit from the little man in the blue suit had occurred only as part of a postsurgery dream, the only thing she figured it made sense to do was to go back to sleep. Yes, she thought, that's what I will do: sleep. And when I wake up again, I'll take another look at the papers on the bedside table.

If, after I've slept, the papers remain stacked where the man in the blue suit left them, I will consider the possibility that the man, and his papers, and his pen might have been something more than a figment of my imagination.

Decision made, Julie Laramie closed her eyes, tilted her head into the pillow, and fell back to sleep.

ACKNOWLEDGMENTS

I owe a deep debt of gratitude to my parents, Bill and Gail, for encouraging me to pursue my dreams no matter how ludicrous each new dream sounded—and still sounds. Same goes for Bart, my brother, for being my partner in crime in both art and life. And it goes without saying, for anyone who knows me—and yet still I will say it—I would never have finished this or any other novel without the inspiration found in my home every minute of every day. I mine this inspiration from my impossibly flawless wife, Nadine, and the bundles of thrill-seeking ambition she's given me so far, Sophie and Brick.

All that said, once the first draft of *Painkiller* had completed itself, I was lucky enough to count as a friend one Gregg Hurwitz, whose generosity confounds me to this day. Through Gregg came my introduction to the keepers of the real-life Force: Marc H. Glick and Stephen F. Breimer—men with no equals. Heroes, in fact. And to the most brilliant of mad scientists, Jess Taylor. And to warriors (and literary agents) Matthew Guma and Richard Pine. In the end, this greatest of teams took a supreme leap of faith on Cooper, Laramie, and, partially, me, delivering me to some of the smartest men alive: Michael Morrison and Rob McMahon. The razor-sharp judgment found in Michael and Rob led them to conduct the brash act of actually purchasing the publishing rights to this book—and then to instruct me on how to make it better.

To each of you, a salute: *Live slow, mon.*

If you enjoyed PAINKILLER,
you're going to love to see what happens to
Cooper and Laramie in
PUBLIC ENEMY,
Will Staeger's new thriller,
coming soon from William Morrow,
an imprint of HarperCollins Publishers.
For a sneak peek, turn the page!

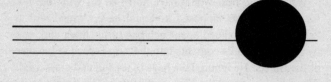

He pressed the button and the cacophony began.
The big door descended, wheels running noisily along the
twin metal tracks, and then it was over, and he stood in silence, and darkness. He thought of releasing his grip on the
handle of the coffee mug he held; he knew the ceramic mug
would shatter, the lukewarm coffee pooling on the concrete
floor, never to be swept clean. But he didn't drop the mug.
Instead, he made his way in the semi-darkness to the light
switch, and in a few seconds the ceiling-mounted rack of
fluorescent bulbs bathed the garage in a diffused moon-lime
glow.

A black Chevy Blazer occupied one side of the garage.
Along the opposite wall were rows of fertilizer bags, stacked
nearly to the ceiling. Beside the fertilizer stood bags of grass
seed and topsoil; two dozen red five-gallon fuel canisters
were pushed against the bags.

The man approached the workbench at the back of the
garage. He used pliers, a Phillips-head screwdriver, and a
soldering gun to secure a series of contents within seven

crimped lengths of narrow brass pipe. This took him about twenty minutes. When he finished, he set the seven devices in their own row on the bench.

What he did next would have horrified his wife, but not for the reason he supposed it should have. Armed with a fishing knife, he sliced open each bag of fertilizer and, one by one, emptied its contents into the cargo space in the rear of the Blazer. He ignored the bags of topsoil and grass seed. When he had filled the back end of the SUV nearly to its ceiling, he removed a step-ladder from its hook on the wall, stood it beside the Blazer's passenger-side door, and proceeded to pour the remaining complement of fertilizer through the sunroof, burying in three feet of ammonium nitrate pellets the leather seats his wife had demanded they include as an option.

He closed the rear doors and made sure each of the side doors was sealed. Then, mimicking his transfer of the fertilizer bags, he carried each of the five-gallon canisters of fuel from its place against the wall, up the step-ladder and, obscenely, poured each container's fuel in through the Blazer's sunroof. The garage soon reeked of diesel fumes.

He took the lengths of crimped brass pipe, reached in through the sunroof, and dispersed the devices evenly throughout the vehicle. From his perch on the step-ladder, he reached into his pocket and depressed the appropriate button on the Blazer's car-alarm remote; the sunroof closed and the parking lights flashed once, the doors locking noisily.

He came into his kitchen, where he noticed a plastic fire engine parked beneath the kitchen table. He took the toy from under the table and returned it to the playroom.

The kitchen stairwell took him into the basement. Once there, he opened the top door of the aging refrigerator-freezer reserved for soft drinks and beer. From his pocket came the trusty Phillips-head screwdriver, which he used to remove ten screws at the base of the freezer. When he had the screws out, he reached beneath the edge of the panel he had just unfastened and removed a metal storage container the size of a shoebox. He used a combination to open the container's lock and opened its lid to reveal fourteen glass vials, each plugged with a wax-sealed cork.

He pocketed a pair of the vials, resealed the container, and returned it to its hidden compartment.

In the kitchen, he ran warm water over the vials in the sink until the cold fluid became less viscous. Then, vials repocketed, he returned to the garage. At the work bench, he broke the seal of the first of the vials and removed its cork, revealing the gelatinous, deeply blue contents within. He stood, nearly motionless, observing the reflection made by the fluorescent lighting on the surface of the fluid. He had thought through this part upwards of ten thousand times, inevitably drawing the same conclusion he drew again now.

He had no choice.

Seizing the vial in his right hand, he lifted the tiny container to his lips, threw his head back, and consumed the flavorless fluid in a single swallow. He set the vial back on the work bench and stood still for nearly five minutes while his stomach grumbled noisily, objecting to the offensive drink it was forced to digest. He left the second vial in his pocket.

From an open cardboard box on the work bench he removed the last of the day's devices: a tiny black box with a green flip-switch. While approximately the same size as the car-alarm remote, it was nonetheless simpler in both design and purpose.

Using the step-ladder, he climbed onto the Blazer's roof and stretched out, face-down, on the cool surface of the vehicle's skin. In his right hand was the black-box remote. He looked at it, then readied his thumb beside the flip-switch.

Electing not to engage in further doubt or debate, he pushed the switch against its housing and closed his eyes.

He thought to himself in the instant before his death that he would be the first martyr of his kind. Perhaps nobody would know it; perhaps nobody would open, or understand, his message-in-a-bottle; perhaps when the truth emerged, if it ever did, his wife and son would come to understand; perhaps not. No matter. He knew he was acting piously, and that his actions were just, and necessary.

At that point his thoughts ended abruptly as, along with the Blazer and the majority of the house enveloping it, the man's body was dispersed in a sudden, crude, foul-smelling eruption of flame, black soot, and enflamed fragments which, in their violent fury, flattened nearly two square blocks of the suburban housing development in which the man and his family had once owned their home.

Powell Keeler III, Po to his friends, was following the sloping curvature of the Lesser Antilles in the 150-foot Trinity Seahawk motor yacht that was not his own. Po had taken his time since setting out from the Caracas Yacht Club four days prior; he'd been clear enough with his client, an old high school acquaintance and owner of three beachfront mansions and a multinational corporation along with the Trinity. He'd come to an agreement with him, taking the gig on one condition:

There wasn't any rush.

Po's client wanted the Trinity returned to Naples, a return leg on which the client did not care to use the boat following his six-week cruise south and east of Cuba. Having caught wind of this predicament, Po, bonded yacht transporter as he happened to be, offered up his services as a favor—such favor being predicated upon his old buddy's fronting him fuel money, a token fee, and sufficient cash to cover one month's premium on the bond Po held as a condition of his transport license.

Once his old pal acquiesced, Po headed down to Venezuela post-haste.

Standing now at the helm, Po eased the yacht along its northwesterly course, positioned some ten miles due east of Virgin Gorda. It was early, with the first orange crescent of sun an angry harelip on the black horizon. Seas were calm.

Po had elected to navigate around the British Virgins, looking to avoid its endless supply of reefs and shallows on his way to the evening rendezvous he hoped to share with the bikini-clad babes known to cluster at the main swimming pool of the Atlantis resort on Paradise Island in the Bahamas.

The Trinity was loaded with dual Furuno FR2115/6 radar units, which Po had taught himself how to use a few jobs back. This meant, among other things, that Po understood perfectly well what the instruments were telling him now.

Four vessels, one of them significantly bigger than the Trinity, loomed directly in his path. The fleet was camped out five miles to the north, with the two smallest boats on his screen closer than the others. The yacht's radar had also detected an airborne object that wasn't flying particularly fast, located halfway between the Trinity and the fleet.

A helicopter.

It had been five minutes since Po had spied a high-altitude speck in the brightening sky. The speck had passed almost directly above him, flying nearly as high as a commercial airliner. Based on what he'd been able to see of the speck, Po had a pretty good idea what kind of plane it was—and this, in turn, gave him a pretty good idea what the fleet of boats and their helicopter escort were all about.

The "speck" was a P-3 Orion surveillance aircraft. Having detected his early morning departure from Anguilla, the plane's occupants had tracked his subsequent route and, extrapolating, assumed the worst—as might, Po considered, be expected, considering their assigned duty: to intercept, impound, or destroy the seemingly endless supply of "go-fast" racing boats bound for Florida or alternate points north. The usual targets of the Coast Guard anti-drug task force fleets, go-fasts were super-high-speed racing machines with their cargo bays retrofitted to haul upwards of two tons of coke per run. Some three boats per day took their shot at the continental United States from the general vicinity of the Greater and Lesser Antilles.

On average, the Coast Guard was going two-for-three, season-to-date.

Po was well versed on how to deal with such drug-interdiction efforts, misguided though they were in coming after him. The problem—over and above the secret cargo he had agreed to cart up to Naples in the hold of the Trinity—was if you let the Coast Guard snatch you in international waters, you were pretty much doomed, since the Department of Homeland Security claimed to possess the right to impound and destroy any "suspicious" boat in such waters, whether or not such boat was shown to be holding contraband. The preference, upon seizure, was to immediately destroy the boat. By taking out vessels, the task force reduced the pool of drug-running ships it had to battle; plus, scuttling ships relieved the task force of the time it took to cart the impounded vessels to San Juan or Miami, where seized boats were broken into their base parts and prepped for federal auction.

Po toggled the radar display and the zoomed-in perspective on the monitor revealed that one of the smaller boats had kicked into gear and was now approaching the Trinity at speed.

He saw that the helicopter too had set its sights on him.

Gunning the yacht's throttle, Po gave the wheel a quarter-turn to port, making a steep turn out of the open waters of the Atlantic into the territorial reign of the British Virgin Islands. As Po was well aware, drug-interdiction etiquette dictated that in NATO-ally territorial waters—the BVIs, Martinique, Montserrat, as examples in the Caribbean—Coast Guard officers could board and inspect a vessel only with its captain's permission. Even then it was mostly a waste of time, since the Coast Guard held no official power of arrest in the sovereign territory of another nation—and Homeland Security had no interest in jurisdictional conflagrations with the UK, France, or any other friendlies.

In such instances, even when a couple tons of uncut coke was found in the cargo hold of a drug-runner's boat, it took a drawn-out extradition process to bring the offending party to justice. As such, in NATO-ally territorial waters, the task force preferred to pin down the offending vessel and summon the local authorities for arrest and impound.

Sporting the benefit of a two-mile cushion between the Trinity and the chase boat, Po zipped down the middle of the Sir Francis Drake Channel, steaming past Virgin Gorda to starboard before steering to port, where he headed for the friendly confines of Road Harbor—the bay abutting Road Town, Tortola, capital city of the British Virgins.

It seemed to Po that the early-to-rise local populace and overwhelming presence of tourists on the most populous island in the BVIs would at least lessen the likelihood that the Coast Guard task force would fuck with him.

When the first of a pair of 22-foot Coast Guard "OTH" chase boats, accompanied by the aerial support of its teammate, an MH-68A "Stingray" helicopter, met up with Po Keeler and his client's yacht, it happened just inside the rocky spit that shielded Road Harbor from the rolling swells of the channel. The encounter that followed might have proceeded in a perfectly civil manner were it not for the condition Po's secondary client had imposed upon him as part of the shipment of the eight large cargo crates stacked in the hold of the Trinity.

The cargo was to be accompanied for the journey from Caracas to Naples by two men, whom Po's secondary client referred to as "security personnel." The security personnel possessed, according to the secondary client, all required documentation and approvals—in other words, while they were Venezuelan, and spoke no English, their passports were ostensibly stamped with a U.S. Department of State authorization number that would, Po was told, "have significant meaning" to inquiring American customs officials. The client assured Po the "security personnel" would stay out of his way on the trip, and in fact were instructed to leave him entirely alone. They brought their own provisions, promised to remain in the vicinity of their cabins, and agreed never to leave the boat.

Po frequently accepted money in exchange for hauling illicit shipments during his licensed transport gigs, and in so doing stood by a strict set of rules: no drugs, no guns, no explosives. And while he had never before agreed to cart "security personnel" along for the ride, the Venezuelan who became his secondary client was paying big money, and his cargo, whatever it was, otherwise complied with Po's rules.

Thus, despite his misgivings, and largely influenced by the hefty cash advance, Po agreed to the deal, and watched as a group of locals loaded the eight crates into the hold. Load-up complete, the two accompanying "security personnel" and their luggage boarded the Trinity from the pier at the Caracas Yacht Club, skulking aboard without so much as looking at him. The two men hadn't made so much as a peep during the first week of Po's journey.

A squat, rubber-hulled speedboat featuring a deck-mounted turret gun and little else, the "OTH," named for how fast it could get itself "over the horizon," had four sol-diers aboard for its approach on the Trinity. One manned the deck gun, aiming it in the general direction of Po Keeler; two stood on the yacht's side of the OTH, hands held near their firearms like a pair of cowboys set for a Wild West draw. The fourth spoke into a hand-held microphone that broadcast his voice over a set of loudspeakers Po observed to be mounted on bow and stern.

"This is the U.S. Coast Guard District 7 task force!" the agent said. The sharp treble tone of the loudspeakers al-lowed his voice to be sharply audible despite the roar made by the Stingray helicopter hovering behind the yacht. "Re-quest permission to board your vessel!"

The Stingray eased lower, banking slightly against a gust of wind.

Po descended the steps that led from the cabin to the deck of the yacht. Keeping his arms stretched away from his body, he brought his right hand to his forehead in a salute, made a two-fisted thumbs-up gesture, and waved the task force agents aboard.

As two of the soldiers on the OTH prepared to board the Trinity, Po turned slightly to the side. This allowed him to see, from his position on the deck, something the soldiers could not. When he saw it, an ulcerous burn that had been coagulating in the vicinity of Po's heart—establishing itself the minute the "security personnel" had skulked aboard his boat—sank suddenly into his gut and exploded.

What happened next played out for Po in the manner of a slow-motion scene from a Hollywood film.

With only their jet-black hair visible to begin with, the heads of first one, then both of the Venezuelan skulkers emerged from the hatch Po knew to access the engine room. As the men rose from their hiding places, Po observed each to be armed with weapons appearing both bulky and slim— bulky enough to be of military grade, slim enough to have been stowed in the suitcases the fucks had toted aboard the boat.

Po made the instantaneous decision to abandon ship.

In two leaping bounds, he reached the polished chrome railing at the bow of the Trinity, planted a foot on its gleaming edge, and propelled himself outward and down. And while he intended it only as a survival measure, Po's dash-and-splash maneuver served, unfortunately, to distract both the soldier manning the OTH's deck gun and the man at the controls of the helicopter's machine gun in a way that gave the Venezuelan gunmen an extra instant-and-a-half— precisely what they would need to accomplish their intentions.

With the Uzis they'd stowed in disassembled form in their suitcases, the men took aim at the deck of the OTH and threw down, strafing much of the chase boat's rubber hull with their poor aim but nonetheless managing to dispatch all four of its crew before a single bullet was fired upon them in return.

The pointless nature of this proactive salvo was illustrated in abrupt fashion as the machine-gunner aboard the Stingray helicopter, only momentarily distracted by Po's dive, let loose on the Venezuelans with his .50-caliber sniper gun. In a guilt-ridden overcompensation for his failure to properly defend the agents aboard the OTH, the machine-gunner continued to pummel the bodies of his targets with round upon round of shells long after both men had died, riddling the rear, then the midsection, then the whole length of the Trinity while shouting obscenities at the offending gunmen he'd already killed. The machine-gunner sought satisfaction and revenge through sheer destruction and, seconds later, got it, as, first, sparks flew, then smoke spewed, and finally the entire stern of the Trinity erupted in a blast-wave of orange flames. Roiling black clouds followed the explosion into the Caribbean sky as flames licked skyward, reaching twenty or thirty yards above the deck of the yacht.

It wasn't until this pyrotechnics display had been all but consummated that the machine-gunner remembered and refocused on the man who'd dived overboard.

By then, however, the pilot of the helicopter had begun screaming at the machine-gunner through his radio headset to cease fire. When the gunner did not comply with his order, the pilot pulled the Stingray up and back—out of the fray.

As the machine-gunner finally relented, both he and the pilot could plainly see Po Keeler's outstretched arms—raised skyward in hapless surrender. He was treading water almost directly beneath the helicopter, head mostly submerged, Po sputtering and gasping as he sought to reach his hands as high in the air as possible to indicate his innocence in matters.

Po, seemingly unable to swim, determined he wasn't going to get shot and began a frantic dog-paddle for the hull of the OTH chase boat. He held one arm aloft as he pulled himself aboard with the other, maintaining his one-armed ges-ture of surrender throughout. At length he managed to turn himself around and plant his rear end on the gunwale of the chase boat, where he proceeded to raise his other arm and drop his head in relief and disgust.

Following an update from the helicopter pilot, the task force commander followed the protocol he'd been instructed to heed in cases of armed conflict within foreign territorial waters. Working the radio, he hooked himself into a satellite phone line and dialed the man he knew to be the head of law enforcement operations for Road Town.

The Coast Guard's designated liaison for any such drug-interdiction activities inside the borders of the British Virgin Islands, the man the task force commander called was the longtime head of the Royal Virgin Islands Police Force and newly elected Chief Minister of the entire BVIs. He was a man who, despite his elevated status as Chief Minister, still went by the nickname he'd bestowed upon himself during a time when he'd held a more junior position on the force.

The name of the task force's designated BVI liaison was Roy Emerson Gillespie, but those who'd met him—and even a few who hadn't—knew to call the man by his pre-ferred, self-appointed nickname of Cap'n Roy.